Wedding Bells for
Nurse Connie

Wedding Bells for Nurse Connie

JEAN FULLERTON

First published in Great Britain in 2016
by Orion Books,
an imprint of The Orion Publishing Group Ltd
Carmelite House, 50 Victoria Embankment,
London EC4Y 0DZ

An Hachette UK company

1 3 5 7 9 10 8 6 4 2

Falkirk Council	
Askews & Holts	2016
AF	£19.99

ISBN (Hardback) 978 1 4091 5114 2
ISBN (Ebook) 978 1 4091 5116 6

Typeset by Input Data Services Ltd, Bridgwater, Somerset

Printed and bound by CPI Group (UK) Ltd, Croydon, CR0 4YY

www.orionbooks.co.uk

To my wonderful agent,
Laura Longrigg of MBA Literary Script Agents,
for all her help, support and guidance over the last ten years

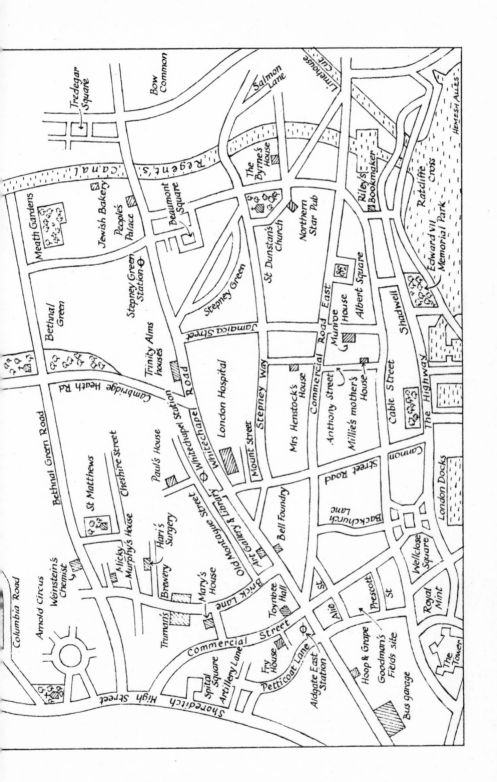

Chapter One

As the early morning July sunlight crept around the edges of the faded curtains, Sister Connie Byrne, the senior nurse for the Spitalfields and Shoreditch Nursing Association, flicked her head in an attempt to dislodge the lock of her golden-red hair from her temple, without success.

But then, wasn't it always the same? As soon as you tied your mask and put on your sterile gloves, your nose started to itch or a stray hair tickled your forehead.

Ignoring it, she wriggled her fingers in her rubber gloves. 'Right, Mrs Sinclair, one more push and I should be able to see baby's head.'

Margaret Sinclair, a slightly built young woman with fluffy blonde curls, rolled her grey eyes. 'I bloody 'ope so.'

Margaret and Don Sinclair and their four – soon to be five – children lived on the third floor of Fallow House in Brushfield Street, just a stone's throw from Petticoat Lane. The three-room dwellings must have seemed like palaces to the artisans who first moved into them a hundred years before but now they were one of the dozens of damp, overcrowded Victorian tenements waiting demolition under the LCC's post-war slum clearance programme.

'Right, Margaret,' she said, placing the labouring woman's left foot against her own hip. 'With the next pain I want you to tuck your chin in and push down into your bottom.'

Margaret nodded then, taking a deep breath as another contraction built, she lowered her head and strained.

Cupping her hand around the woman's bulging vulva, Connie waited for the baby's head to appear. It did almost immediately, showing Miss or Master Sinclair to have a full head of sticky black hair.

'Slowly now,' Connie said in an even tone as she supported the stretching flesh.

Mrs Sinclair's perineum went white and, just as Connie feared it would tear, the head popped clear.

'Rest now,' said Connie, gently easing the baby's head out.

Connie's patient gasped and flopped back as the baby instinctively turned. There was a moment of calm and then Margaret caught her breath again.

'That's it,' said Connie. 'One more push should see him born.'

Margaret tensed again and, cradling the baby's head with one hand and holding a shoulder with the other, Connie lifted the baby out.

'Hello, young man,' Connie said, smiling at the baby's screwed-up and mucus-smeared face.

Margaret collapsed back against the headboard. 'Is he all right, sister?'

Her son answered for himself by letting out a wail.

'Ten fingers, ten toes, a full head of hair and a good pair of lungs, so I'd say he's just fine,' laughed Connie.

Like every midwife, Connie had delivered her share of stillborn babies so, no matter how straightforward the labour or delivery, she was always thankful to hear her small patients' first cry.

Laying the newborn on his mother's stomach, Connie clamped the cord and automatically thanked the Virgin, then glanced down at her watch.

Seven-fifteen. With a bit of luck, she would be back at the Fry House in time for breakfast.

Margaret grunted and delivered the afterbirth, which Connie checked then rolled in newspaper to burn on the fire later.

'What are you going to name him?' she asked, taking the infant back from his mother and wrapping him in the towel.

'Stewart. After Stewart Granger,' said Margaret, reaching for her tobacco tin on the bedside table and taking out a roll-up. 'I loved him in *Fanny by Gaslight*.'

Taking the sling and fishermen's scales from her bag, Connie removed the towel from around the child and gently laid him in the middle of the netting. Looping the corners of the sling onto the hook, she raised the scales.

'Seven nine,' she said, when the marker settled.

Margaret blew out a puff of smoke. 'And didn't I know it.'

After putting him in a nappy, Connie dressed the newborn in the well-washed vest and leggings that had been placed ready on the dressing table, then she wrapped him in a crochet shawl. He yawned and started rooting around.

Mrs Sinclair pinched out her cigarette and put the stub behind her ear. 'Give 'im here,' she said, her rounded face forming itself into a sentimental expression.

Connie handed baby Stewart over.

Margaret tucked him in the crook of her arm and kissed his damp forehead.

'Do you want me to help get him on the breast?'

Margaret grinned. 'Ta, luv, but I can manage. And leave all that stuff,' she said, indicating the pail of blood-stained linen that Connie was just about to take hold of. 'My sister Vi will be here after she's seen her kids to school and she'll sort that out in the laundry downstairs.'

'Are you sure she won't mind?'

Margaret shook her head. 'Course not. You get on.' She winked. 'It's a big day for you lot down at Fry House, isn't it?'

'Too true,' said Connie, remembering that the good and the great from far and wide were due to descend on Fry House later that morning to drink tea, scoff cake and make interminable speeches. For today, Monday 5 July, 1948, was the start of the much-talked-about new National Health Service. From today onwards, doctors, nurses, hospitals, medicine, spectacles, visits to the dentist, everything in fact, would be free.

'I heard there was royalty coming,' said Mrs Sinclair.

'No, just the mayor,' Connie replied. 'Do you want me to fetch your husband?'

'You better had or he'll be late for work,' Margaret replied.

Connie wrapped her dirty instruments in a cloth before placing them inside her bag, then she went to the door and called for Mr Sinclair.

There was a thump along the small hall and Don, dressed in the paint-splattered overalls of his trade, appeared.

'Another chip off the old block,' said Margaret, turning the child so her husband could see his latest offspring.

Don grinned and went over to the bed.

''Allo, son,' he said, running a calloused finger over the baby's soft cheek.

'Coooeee,' called a woman's voice from outside the room.

'In here, Vi,' called Margaret. 'But you've missed all the action.'

A blonde-haired woman, dressed in an overall with a printed scarf tied in a turban on her head, hurried into the room. As Margaret and Vi marvelled at the baby's small hands and ran through the family members he resembled, Connie packed the last few bits of her equipment away and wrote up her notes.

Don gave his wife a swift kiss on the head. 'I'll have the foreman after me if I don't get on.'

Husband and wife exchanged a private look, then Mr Sinclair turned to Connie. 'Here you go, sister.' He rummaged in the pocket of his worn trousers and offered her a ten-shilling note. 'Worth every penny.'

Connie held up her hand. 'Bevan's already paid me.'

Don looked blank for a moment. 'Course, I forgot.' He shoved the money back in his pocket. 'I'll raise a glass to the old Welshman later in the Three Feathers when I wet the baby's head.'

He gave his wife another peck on the cheek, then tramped out of the bedroom. The front door banged and Vi rubbed her hands together. 'Right, then, who wants a cuppa?'

'Not for me, thank you,' Connie replied, snapping her case shut. 'I've still got a half a dozen visits before the bun fight starts at eleven.'

With her summer blazer fastened and her felt hat firmly on her head, Connie closed the Sinclairs' faded front door. Standing back to let the children from the flat next door hurry past to school, Connie walked to the stairs then made her way down to the street below, carefully avoiding the puddle of urine by the bottom step.

Although the early July sun was now fully over the horizon, it hadn't yet managed to breach the red-brick tenements that lined both sides of the street.

As Fry House, the five-storey Georgian townhouse that served as both a clinic and a nurses' home, was only a short distance from the Sinclairs', Connie had opted to walk when she'd taken the call asking her to attend Mrs Sinclair earlier that morning.

4

As she stepped out into the road, two girls, dressed in the distinctive navy uniform of Sir John Cass school, dashed out of the adjoining stairwell and almost collided with Connie.

'Sorry, miss,' said the taller one of the two. 'We didn't see you.'

'I'm not surprised.' Connie laughed. 'Where are you off to so early? The running track?'

The other schoolgirl gave her a toothy grin and shook her head. 'Nah. Netball practice. We're up against Morpeth in the area semi-finals,' she called behind her as the two of them scooted off towards the main road.

Connie turned the corner into Commercial Street. It was the start of a working day and the thoroughfare was already busy with people and traffic as buses and trams trundled towards the dock to the south and the City to the west.

Waiting until a wagon with Plashet Fruit and Veg painted on the side had passed, Connie crossed the road and headed northwards.

As she drew level with the tall iron gates of Christ Church, she attracted the attention of a gang of market porters hogging the pavement outside the Ten Bells with pints of beer in their hands after a long night's work.

'Oi, oi, sweetheart,' called one beefy individual with a red handkerchief tied at his throat. 'Why don't you give us a bed bath?'

Those around him sniggered and nudged each other.

'Ignore him, luv,' called another, a younger chap in a worn leather waistcoat. 'Why don't you come and sit on me lap and see what pops up?'

There were cat calls and wolf whistles, but keeping her expression cool and her eyes ahead, Connie walked on until she at last turned into Duval Street, where Fry House was situated.

Well, the street sign riveted to the wall at the entrance of the narrow passageway said Duval Street but everyone called it by its original name of Dorset Street. The last of Jack the Ripper's victims was found butchered in Miller's Court, a passageway opposite the clinic. In those days Fry House had been Moody's doss house as the faded paint on the brickwork on the side of the house testified.

Stepping over a swirl of dog dirt on the pavement, Connie

5

tripped up the three steps and pushed open the front door. The smell of porridge and fresh bread filled her nose, setting her stomach rumbling again. Above her head the sound of water running in bathrooms and the soft sound of someone singing along to the wireless drifted down as the nurses who lodged in the rooms above got ready for the day.

Shrugging off her jacket, Connie hooked it on a spare peg on the coat stand. The postman had already delivered the early post but, as she caught sight of the pile of manila envelopes with Ministry of Health stamped across the top, Connie's heart sunk.

Leaving the unwelcome correspondence where it was, Connie headed for the narrow stone stairs at the far end of the passageway and made her way down to the basement where the refectory was.

Although only a few of the twenty-five or so nurses who lodged at Fry House were down for breakfast, there were hardly any places left at the half a dozen tables.

Having been built some century and a half ago and originally intended as a place of business, Fry House was cramped, there was no other word for it. The high-ceilinged, airy room with a large window at the front of the house, which they now used as a treatment room, had once been the main trading area of the weaver's shop beneath the family living quarters, while the square room overlooking the yard served as the nurses' office.

The superintendent didn't fare much better as she had to work in what was little more than an understairs cupboard off the ground-floor passageway. Someone had put a triangular-shaped window in there to let in light, probably at the same time as they'd piped in running water at the turn of the last century.

Connie looked round the room and spotted Rose Williams, the sister who covered the Club Row end of Bethnal Green Road. She was wedged at the table beneath the metal grill which let in light from the street above. Rose, seeing that Connie was looking for a seat, indicated that the chair next to her was free.

Connie smiled gratefully. Collecting two slices of toast and a cup of tea, she squeezed between the chattering nurses to join her.

'Who were you called out to?' asked Rose as Connie pulled her chair in.

'Mrs Sinclair, just after five.' Connie yawned. 'It was straightforward enough but she'll need a follow-up visit in a couple of hours.'

'I'll add her to my list for later,' said Rose, taking out her notebook. 'I'm over that way to see one of my deliveries this morning so it's not a problem.'

'Thanks. With everything that's going on here I'll be lucky to get out of the place at all today.' Connie yawned again. 'Still, at least I'm a half-day tomorrow. I tell you, after a week of being on call I'm all but done in.'

Rose pulled a face. 'Well, I'm sorry to give you the bad news but you've been written up for the baby clinic tomorrow afternoon.'

'Have I?'

''Fraid so.'

'What about Fran?'

'She's on her day off and she's gone to see her sick sister so she isn't even around,' Rose said.

'Moira?'

'Dr Marshall phoned yesterday and requested a nurse to assist him in the surgery all day,' Rose informed her.

Connie looked aghast. 'Didn't the super tell him we couldn't spare her?'

Actually, given Miss O'Dwyer's hair-trigger temper, Connie was surprised she'd not heard the superintendent bellowing her response from her third-floor bedroom above the super's office.

'She wanted to but the chairwoman, Mrs Howard, told her that as Old Goddamnit Marshall has paid for a nurse to help at the surgery, we have to honour it, so she couldn't say no,' said Rose.

Up until today the Spitalfields and Shoreditch Nursing Association, like every other District Nursing Association in the land, was responsible for raising its own funds.

Some of their money came from the council in order to provide statutory antenatal and childcare services plus nursing for those with tuberculosis or a notifiable disease. It also covered the care of those in receipt of National Assistance and the like, but the bulk of their money came from charging their patients: one and six for a straightforward dressing, half a crown for something more involved or ongoing and one pound ten shillings to deliver a baby. However, as the association covered one of the poorest areas in London, it had a constant struggle to raise money. Knowing this, doctors like Dr Marshall sometimes hired the association nurses to do the less savoury work of ear syringing, ulcer dressings and to nurse their private patients at home.

'Well, at least after today we can tell him to whistle for it,' said Connie, sprinkling a spoonful of sugar in her tea. 'And I'll tell him so when I see him later.'

'Don't be too swift to rock the apple cart, Connie,' said Rose, scooping up the last of the porridge in her bowl. 'According to my friend at the Health Board, some of the local doctors are unhappy with the National Service for Health and might not play ball, perhaps we should keep him sweet. Jane has been allocated to help in the clinic but you know a trainee Queen's Nurse can't be in charge.'

Connie forced a plucky smile. 'Well, it could be worse.'

'How?'

'Marshall could have purloined Jane too.'

Connie took the cover off the butter. Thankfully there was a knob of creamy Anchor, enough for her two slices, nestling beneath. Although butter had come off rationing a few months back, it was still scare and Mrs Rogerson, Fry House's motherly housekeeper, often could offer them only marge for their bread.

'You want to come to the Empire with me and Florry later?' asked Rose, cradling her cup in her hand. 'They've got a new dance band that's supposed to be top notch.'

'I'd love to but I'm seeing Malcolm tonight,' Connie replied.

Rose looked puzzled. 'I thought he was at his Scout troop on Monday.'

'Usually,' Connie replied. 'But the Memorial Hall is being decorated so they've cancelled the meeting.'

Rose grinned. 'So are you going out somewhere nice?'

Before Connie could reply, the refectory door banged open and Miss O'Dwyer, the Spitalfields and Shoreditch Superintendent, marched into the room with a grubby-looking toddler balanced on her ample hip.

Bridget O'Dwyer was a hair's-breadth over four feet ten inches with a broad, scrubbed face. Her navy uniform was in the old pre-war style and had mutton-chop sleeves with a full skirt which stopped mid-calf. Her starched collar, cuffs and the frilly cap on her steely grey hair were pristine and you could have seen your face in the polished toes of her laced-up nurse's shoes.

With a physique like an Irish hurling full forward, the association's senior nurse was not someone you'd want to tangle with. That is unless you were a patient and then she'd carry you on her back to Jerusalem if it would help you back to health.

Clutching a wodge of letters in her free hand, she now filled the doorway and the room fell silent.

With a look of thunder on her face, Miss O'Dwyer scoured the room until she spotted Connie. Shaking the screwed-up paperwork above her head, her voice boomed across the space.

'You'll never guess what those bloody ijats at the Ministry—'

There was a scrape of wood as the nurses in the room stood up from their breakfast. 'Good morning, superintendent,' they chorused.

'And a bright morning to you all, too, me darlings,' Miss O'Dwyer replied, flapping her hand up and down.

The nurses resumed their seats as the superintendent waddled over to Connie and flopped down on the spare chair between the two nurses. The child, now perched on Miss O'Dwyer's knee, lunged at Connie's tea which she moved swiftly out of harm's way. She broke off a crust of toast and handed it to the child who grasped it with chubby fingers.

'Ministry of Health,' the enraged superintendent muttered. 'Ministry of Numbskulls, more like.'

'What do they want now?' said Connie, indicating the crumpled correspondence in the superintendent's hand.

'Figures.' The superintendent flourished the mangled manila envelopes again. 'More blasted figures. And today of all days! Sure to Heaven don't they know I've half of Bethnal Green and Spitalfields descending on me in less than three hours? What time will I have to look at figures?'

'But didn't you send them all our records two months ago?' asked Connie, as she buttered another piece of toast.

'To be sure,' grumbled Miss O'Dwyer. 'But they aren't satisfied with making me go boss-eyed with all the numbers once, now they're are asking that I "kindly go through them again".'

She laid the letters on the table and the baby plonked a butter-smeared hand on them.

'They say "they can't balance them against the ones the association's secretary sent". Well, I tell you, it's no problem of mine if they can't do their job, now is it?' Miss O'Dwyer rolled her eyes. 'And if the one who turned up here last time is anything to go by, most of them so-called ministry officials are only just off their mother's teat.'

'Well, he was a bit on the young side, I grant you, but he seemed to know his stuff about nursing associations,' said Connie, taking the Ministry of Health's letter from the baby to prevent him cramming it into his mouth. 'Whose child is this?'

'Brenda Riley's little Johnny,' said Miss O'Dwyer, looking dotingly at the baby. 'Darling little man, so he is.'

'I'm sure he is,' said Connie as a ribbon of dribble left the child's mouth and descended towards the superintendent's starched cuff. 'But why is he here?'

'His brother kicked an empty milk bottle over and then proceeded to tread on it,' Miss O'Dwyer replied. 'Went right through the sole of his plimsoll, poor lad. I said I'd mind him until Mrs Riley comes back from Casualty.'

'But what about getting ready for Fry House's handover ceremony?' asked Connie.

'Well, I thought you being the darling girl you are, Connie, you could scoot around the place to make sure all is as it should be.'

'Connie's only just got in from a delivery, superintendent,' Rose said.

A sentimental smile lifted the superintendent's fleshy face. 'And who's the happy mother?'

'Mrs Sinclair,' Connie said. 'A boy.'

'She'll be needing a check visit later.'

'I said I'll pop in after lunch,' said Rose.

'Well, now,' said Miss O'Dwyer. 'The Sinclairs live no more than a hop, skip and a jump away so perhaps I'll get out of your hair, Connie, and take a stroll round there when Brenda picks up Johnny in a while.' Miss O'Dwyer sighed and, closing her eyes, she drew in a deep breath. 'Don't you just love the sweet smell of a newborn?'

She stood up, holding Johnny in her beefy arms, and headed for the door.

'Haven't you forgotten something, superintendent?' asked Connie, holding up the letters from the Ministry.

'Leave them on my desk,' said Miss O'Dwyer over her shoulder as she continued on her way.

As Connie watched the superintendent's broad hips squeeze between the tables, she couldn't help wondering, with the world and his wife descending on the place in less than three hours, if sniffing Master Sinclair should really be Miss O'Dwyer's number-one priority this morning.

As the grandfather clock in the hall showed eleven o'clock, Mr Granger, the chair of the Regional Health Board, stepped forward and grasped the red ribbon that Connie and Miss O'Dwyer had pinned across the treatment room door the night before.

'On behalf of the Minister of Health, it gives me great pleasure to declare Fry House officially part of the National Health Service,' he said, snipping through the ribbon.

The nurses and patients who had packed into the corridor and up the stairs cheered and then spontaneous applause broke out as everyone, including Connie, clapped enthusiastically. Miss O'Dwyer, who was telling anyone who'd listen that she'd not had a wink of sleep for the past month with the worry of it all, crossed herself twice. Fortunately, Brenda Riley had collected her son just after handover at eight-thirty which allowed Miss O'Dwyer time to dash to the Sinclairs' to welcome Stewart and be back at Fry House by nine-thirty, just as the baker arrived with the sandwiches.

Mr Granger stepped through into the treatment room, where the refreshments were being served, and a surge of people followed.

Connie stood back until the gathering thinned and then strolled into the treatment room, stifling another yawn as she remembered her early start.

Mrs Rogerson's spread was already being devoured by local dignitaries including a handful of councillors with plates piled high with sandwiches. The various religious communities were well represented, too. Reverend Michaelson, the vicar of Christ

Church, wearing a baggy suit, grey shirt and dog-collar, was chatting pleasantly with Rabbi Abrahams from Quaker Street synagogue and the skeletal Father Flaherty from St Anne's, the Catholic church. In contrast with the everyday garb of his colleagues, Father Flaherty was dressed in a black cassock with a stiff upright collar encircling his neck while a wide-fringed belt was tied tightly around his sinewy middle. He had a heavy gold chain and crucifix slung around his neck and the grey hair on his skull-like head was clipped so close that, from a distance, he looked completely bald. His hooded eyes surveyed his fellow clerics with mild interest while the corners of his mouth lifted just a fraction, being as near to a smile as the priest could ever manage.

The housekeeper had arranged for Kossof the baker to supply kosher tit-bits for the Jewish members attending the opening, so the rabbi too was balancing a full plate of food as he talked. Mr Dawkins from the Shoreditch Chamber of Commerce had no such restriction on his diet and was therefore cramming a sausage roll in his mouth while talking to the mayor, who in full regalia was sweating profusely in the overcrowded room.

Collecting a plate from the pile at the end of the table, Connie helped herself to a couple of corned beef sandwiches and a fairy cake.

'So that's it, is it?' said Rose, as she and Fran ambled over to join her. 'We're all working for the government now.'

'Not according to the front page of the *Sketch*,' said Fran, taking a pilchard sandwich from the pile. 'They say we're all working for the people.'

'Well, whoever we're working for, I for one am very grateful that from today I can throw my collection book into the bin and just concentrate on my job,' said Connie.

'You're right,' said Rose. 'I don't suppose there's a nurse in the land who will miss taking money from their patients, myself included.'

'Hear, hear,' said Fran, raising her teacup.

Connie and Rose chinked theirs against it by way of a toast to the new Health Service.

'Three pretty nurses. Just what our readers like to see,' said the photographer from the local newspaper, pointing his camera at them. 'Can you do that again, girls?'

Connie and her two friends raised their cups.

'Cheese!'

'Cheese,' they repeated.

The flash popped and Connie blinked to clear her vision of the white stars caused by the bright light.

The photographer moved on to another group of well-wishers.

'Of course, not everyone is happy about things being free,' said Rose.

'You mean that lot over there?' said Connie as she looked across at the handful of well-heeled local GPs, including Dr Marshall, who stood puffing cigars.

Despite the momentous occasion, the doctor in charge of the Christ Church surgery, who had at least a thousand souls depending on him for their medical needs, was wearing an old grey suit, which by the look of it hadn't been pressed since the day war broke out, over a dingy shirt with frayed cuffs, his necktie was stained and threadbare.

'My Harold said they blooming well held the country to ransom until the government coughed up,' continued Rose, cutting into Connie's thoughts.

Dr Marshall pulled a silver hip flask from his pocket and, after offering it around, took a swig.

As if sensing he was being watched, Dr Marshall looked over. He regarded the nurses for a second or two then, shoving the flask back in his pocket, he started towards them.

'We'll see you later, Con,' said Rose.

'Cowards,' Connie hissed as her friends slipped away.

Dr Marshall stopped in front of her.

'Sister Byrne,' he said, giving her a toadying smile. 'How nice to see you.' His eyes slid over her. 'And looking as lovely as ever.'

Connie smiled politely.

'So here we are,' he said, casting his condescending gaze over the throng surrounding them. 'Bevan's utopian world, although what a grubby Welsh miner's son knows about medicine is beyond me.'

'I'm sure he has good people to advise him,' said Connie.

Dr Marshall grunted by way of an answer. He took out his flask and uncorked it.

'There is tea if you'd like it,' said Connie.

Dr Marshall took a swig and shook his head. 'I need something stronger than tea to get through this circus.' He put the bottle to his lips again and swallowed. 'Still,' he said, smacking his lips, 'at least we're all in it together, aren't we, sister?'

'I'm sure the National Health will be a great relief to our patients.'

'Oh, of course. We mustn't forget the patients, our new master, must we?' Spite flashed across his fleshy features. 'Queuing up outside the surgery since first light demanding—' A tic flickered above his right eye. 'Do you hear? *Demanding* I see them. Goddamn them.'

'Any news on getting another GP for the practice?'

'Now you mention it, there is,' he replied, taking a new cigar from his pocket and biting off the end. 'I'm advertising for an associate again.'

Connie looked amazed. 'Really?'

'Yes.' Pulling a lighter from his pockets, he lit his cigar. 'Now the goddamn Ministry have put their hands in their pockets at last I can afford to.'

Connie gave him an artless smile. 'Well, I hope you appoint someone soon because now we're employed by the NHS you won't be able to borrow Fry House's nurses to cover your surgeries any more.'

A purple flush stained Dr Marshall's jowls. 'You do know that even in this goddamn NHS nurses are still under the direction of doctors?'

'We do and I'm sure I can speak for all the nurses in Fry House when I say we look forward to working with your colleague when he arrives.' Connie smiled sweetly. 'Now, if you'll excuse me, I have to get on with my visits. Doctors aren't the only people with patients queuing down the street today.'

Humming along to Dinah Shore singing 'Buttons and Bows' playing on the radio, Connie dragged her brush through her unruly curls. It was now a few minutes short of seven-thirty and she still hadn't put on her face. Malcolm, who was always punctual, would be here any moment and, as always, she was late.

It was hardly surprising. Even though she'd intended to start on her rounds immediately after her exchange with Dr Marshall, when she'd stepped into the hallway she'd seen Miss O'Dwyer cornered next to the linen closet by Mr Edwards, the local MP.

As he had just asked the superintendent what she thought about the Ministry of Health's handling of the changeover, Connie had felt obliged to join them in case Miss O'Dwyer took the opportunity to tell Mr Edwards exactly what she thought of the whole affair.

This meant she'd left the clinic over an hour later than she'd intended to. In anticipation of the disruption the inaugural day of the NHS would inevitably bring, Connie had moved three of that day's visits to later in the week. Therefore, with just a couple of quick calls to make, she'd cycled out of the back gates with a high expectation of making it back for Mrs Rogerson's Monday beef hotpot at one o'clock as usual. Of course, she hadn't reckoned on being called upon to look at a whole selection of ailments.

So far she had inspected a three-day-old bruise on a woman who'd walked into a footstool, directed a man with curly long toenails to the nearest chiropodist and then spent half an hour explaining to a chap missing his front teeth that, yes, dentures were free now but they had to be fitted and supplied by a dentist not a district nurse. By lunchtime she was so far behind on her visits she didn't have time to return to Fry House so she'd snatched a quick Spam sandwich and a mug of tea in The Railway cafe before setting out on her afternoon calls. Mercifully, they all went without a hitch.

After finally arriving back at Fry House at six, she'd thrown her supper down her throat in fifteen minutes flat. Thankfully there was a free bathroom so after a quick freshen up she was now back in her bedroom.

As a senior nurse she had been allocated one of the better rooms in the house. It was situated on the third floor and had a blue and white tiled fireplace in which sat, somewhat incongruously, a modern three-bar electric fire. There was a washbasin in the corner of the room and the association also provided a bed, wardrobe and dressing table. Although it was a little cramped, Connie had squeezed a bookcase under the window.

The room had been freshly emulsioned when the old house had been refurbished three years ago, but with the end of household rationing wallpaper and paint were now more freely available and so Connie had got her eldest brother Jimmy to paper the room in a bright flowery pattern which, along with the new curtains she'd bought in the January sales and the various knick-knacks and family photos dotted around the place, gave the room a very homely feel.

Having put on her brassière, knickers, stockings and suspenders, Connie went over to the washbasin and delved into her make-up bag resting on the shelf above.

After lightly applying Max Factor Pan-Cake over the freckles on her nose, Connie grabbed the oblong box of mascara. Flipping the top open, she took out the brush and spat on the block within. After rubbing the brush back and forth a couple of times she leant towards her reflection and applied the brown goo to her top and bottom lashes twice then, satisfied with the result, popped the brush back and snapped the case shut.

There was a knock on the door.

'It's open,' Connie called.

Jenny, the nurse responsible for the Boundary Estate at the north end of the patch, poked her head around the corner.

'Your Malcolm's here,' she said.

'Tell him I'll be two minutes,' Connie replied, rummaging around for her lipstick.

'Will do.' Jenny winked. 'Although if he's anything like my Richard I'm sure he'd be happy with you as you are.'

Connie rolled her eyes. Jenny left, closing the door behind her.

Connie twisted the case and applied a liberal coating of Tropical Sunset. Pressing her lips together to distribute the colour evenly, she took the dress which was hanging on the front of the wardrobe and slipped it over her head.

Hopping onto the dressing table chair so she could see her legs in the mirror, Connie checked her stocking seams were straight then jumped down and slipped on her shoes. She grabbed her handbag then hurried out the room, banging the door behind her.

With her hand resting lightly on the polished wooden banister and wondering if perhaps she should have worn a skirt and jumper rather than a dress, Connie ran down the stairs. As she turned the last corner on the first floor, she saw Malcolm.

Dressed in his usual tweed jacket, fawn-coloured flannel trousers and brogues, Malcolm was sitting on a bench next to the treatment room with his fedora resting on his knee and his pipe jutting from the right side of his mouth.

It struck Connie – not for the first time – that her boyfriend was really quite a good-looking chap. Not in the flashy Italian-style suits and slicked-back hair way that was increasingly popular, but in a more traditional English gentleman way.

As she started down the last flight of stairs, he looked up and smiled. Connie smiled back and hurried down the last few steps.

'Sorry I'm late,' she said, crossing the black and white tiled floor to greet him. 'I didn't finish until gone six.'

'That's all right, you're worth the wait,' he replied, giving her a hug.

Connie inhaled his warmth and aftershave with just a hint of damp wool. She reached up to kiss him but he moved his head and pressed his lips onto her cheek.

Connie gave him a questioning look.

'There're people around,' he explained, indicating the two trainee Queenies chatting at the other end of the hall.

Connie dropped her arm and Malcolm went over to the coat rack. He unhooked her royal-blue jacket and held it out for her.

Ignoring the crushed feeling in her chest, Connie turned and slipped her arms into the sleeves.

'I'd still be in the treatment room now if Margery hadn't volunteered to load the steriliser for me so I could get ready,' she said.

'Margery's one of the student nurses, isn't she?' said Malcolm.

Connie took her hat from the top shelf. 'No, she's the nurse who runs the Bethnal Green Road patch who you've meet at least three times.'

'I can't say I—'

'The blonde nurse who's about my height, comes from Bristol and has a West County accent?' said Connie, looking at him in the reflection of the hall mirror.

He looked blank.

'Short, curly hair to here.' Connie indicated her ear lobe. 'I introduced you two at the association's Easter fundraising tea.'

Still not a flicker of recollection from Malcolm.

'Her fiancé served on HMS *Anson* during the war. In the Mediterranean,' said Connie, jabbing a long pin through her everyday brown felt hat to secure it.

'Oh,' said Malcolm, as several pennies dropped. 'The jolly girl marrying the naval chap.'

Connie turned back to face him.

'Good of you to remember, Malcolm,' she said. 'Especially as we're guests at their wedding in April.'

He put on his whipped spaniel expression. 'Sorry. You know I'm rubbish with names.'

'No, I'm sorry, Malcolm,' Connie replied, guilt clutching at her chest. 'Sorry for being a bit testy.'

He smiled. 'I forgive you.'

They exchanged a fond look, then Connie picked up her handbag.

'All right,' she said, hooking it over her arm. 'What are we going to see?'

'Well, actually, Connie —'

'I fancy *Letter from an Unknown Woman*,' continued Connie. 'But if you prefer a crime film, I've heard *Calling Paul Temple* is good.'

'I'm sorry, Connie,' said Malcolm, the whipped spaniel look returning. 'But Mum's not very well.'

'Oh,' said Connie flatly.

'She said she's not been feeling good for a day or two . . . but didn't want to make a fuss,' continued Malcolm. 'She said it was nothing and we should go out and enjoy ourselves but I said we'd sit in with her tonight in case she had one of her turns. You don't mind, do you, Connie?'

Mind? Why would she mind? After all, who wouldn't want to swap an evening canoodling in the dark for tedious hours of having to sit an arm's width apart under Malcolm's mother's caustic gaze?

Connie forced a smile.

'Of course not, Malcolm,' she said, trying very, very hard to sound as if she meant it.

Chapter Two

Forcing his right foot not to jig, Dr Hari MacLauchlan waited as Doctor Marshall scanned his application on the desk yet again.

'I see you were a senior houseman in St James's in Leeds.'

'Yes, in '39,' Hari replied pleasantly.

Dr Herbert Marshall, who was somewhere in his mid-fifties, was squeezed into a scruffy navy suit at least a size too small. Under this was a washed-out shirt with frayed cuffs and missing buttons. The dishevelled scarecrow look was completed by a badly knotted tie and scuffed brogues.

'Pity,' said Dr Marshall, as he took a battered pack of Benson & Hedges from his inside pocket. 'I'm looking for someone with experience of practising in the capital.'

'I think I'm right in saying, Dr Marshall, that the advertisement in *The Lancet* specified "city hospital" experience,' replied the young man sitting next to him.

He was Mr Merriweather and had introduced himself as the junior minister overseeing the implementation of the National Health Service in the north-east London area.

In contrast to Dr Marshall's well-fed physique, the man from the Ministry was in serious danger of being blown away by a strong wind. With flaxen hair and pale eyes, he had the look of a pubescent grammar school boy wearing his big brother's clothes rather than one of the Minister of Health's right-hand men. He'd informed Hari by way of introduction that, due to the special demands of the area, both organisational and health-wise, he was taking a very close interest in the new arrangements, which is presumably why he was interviewing with the GP who was looking for an associate.

'And the last time I looked,' continued Mr Merriweather in his rounded, public school tone, 'St James's hospital was smack bang in the centre of Leeds.'

Dr Marshall lit his cigarette and didn't reply.

It was somewhere near to half past two and Hari was sitting in the upstairs committee room of Toynbee Hall, and had been for the past twenty minutes. The dark oak panels and maroon curtains were lightened by the early August sunlight streaming through the sash windows overlooking Commercial Street. The interview panel sat in high-backed chairs at the far end of the oval conference table while he sat at the other.

While the urbane young man and the dishevelled doctor shuffled papers and scrutinised his application yet again, Hari gazed out of the window and schooled himself to stay calm.

It wasn't easy.

This was his seventh interview for a GP post in London in almost as many weeks and with a sky-high rent to pay for what was little more than a glorified attic in Clerkenwell and dwindling funds in the Westminster Bank, he was getting desperate.

Little did he imagine when he'd stepped off the boat train at Waterloo on the first day of May with a dozen letters inviting him for interviews in his briefcase, that he'd still be without a position three months later. However, it would seem that despite a chronic shortage of doctors in London and his first-class credentials, being the son of a Scottish father and an Indian mother meant he hadn't been quite the right man for the job.

Crossing one long leg over the other and resisting the urge to drum his fingers on his black flannel trousers, Hari maintained his pleasant expression.

'So, to summarise,' said Mr Merriweather. 'You got a first at Cambridge. Were junior houseman at Bart's and senior at St James's and had just been offered medical registrar at Guy's when war broke out.'

Hari nodded. 'And I signed up to the army's medical corps immediately and went with the British Expeditionary Force to France.'

Pulling the cut-glass ashtray nearer, Dr Marshall flicked a pile of ash into it. 'I see you also served in the Far East.'

'I did. After the evacuation from Dunkirk, my field hospital was reassigned to the India Fourth Army,' Hari explained. 'I was with them throughout the Burma campaign.'

Dr Marshall tapped the application form with a tobacco-stained finger. 'And you were captured by the Japanese at Singapore, so I see.'

'Yes, in '42,' said Hari. 'I was the medical director of Changi Hospital in Singapore when the Japanese swept in. I stayed with the wounded while the rest of the company retreated.'

'Very heroic, I'm sure,' said Dr Marshall. 'But it did mean you missed all the action thereafter.'

Images of starved and beaten men in the Japanese prisoner-of-war camp flashed through Hari's mind.

'Oh, I wouldn't say that.' He regarded the elderly doctor coolly. 'I was in a little place called Kanchanaburi Camp. You may have heard of it. It's where the British and Allied soldiers working on the Burma railway were held.'

A mottled patchwork of purple spread up Dr Marshall's neck and he stubbed out his cigarette.

Mr Merriweather gave Hari a sympathetic look. 'You must have had a pretty rough time of it all round.'

'Indeed,' Hari replied flatly. 'I served with Colonel Dunlop. You may have read the article in the *BMJ*.'

Dr Marshall stubbed out his cigarette. 'Can't say I recall it.'

Hari smiled. 'Pity.'

'But I see since you were demobbed you've returned to general medicine,' said Mr Merriweather.

'I was visiting my mother in Delhi when an old friend from the camp told me there was a new hospital being opened in Bombay. The clinical director was looking for someone with an expertise in tropical and domiciliary medicine to set up a number of clinics to serve the general population,' Hari explained. 'I applied and got the registrar post.'

'Very impressive, I'm sure,' said Dr Marshall, sounding anything but and lighting up again. 'Although dealing with the population of some colonial cottage hospital can hardly compare with what is required of a general practitioner in London.'

'I'd hardly call the Prince Aly Khan Hospital a cottage hospital,' Hari replied.

Dr Marshall blew a stream of smoke from the side of his mouth but didn't comment.

'So tell me, Dr MacLauchlan,' asked Mr Merriweather. 'Why

have you now decided to move into general practice and why in London and not India?'

'My experience working with the area clinic in Bombay has led me to a greater appreciation of general practice and I feel I would like to continue in that area of work. I was approached by a couple of surgeries in the suburbs of Bombay but once the partition of India started, with an English father and Indian mother, I had no choice but to come home. Anglo-Indians are looked upon with suspicion and mistrust by both sides of the conflict.'

Dr Marshall gave him an innocent look. 'You're an Anglo-Indian, are you?'

'Surely you can see that,' Hari continued.

'I can't say I noticed,' lied Dr Marshall. 'I just thought you were a bit tanned from being in the tropics.'

'I'd be a bit tanned if I'd been in the Arctic,' Hari told him. 'But as I went to Westminster Prep, then Repton and Cambridge, I'd say I'm as English as anyone. Wouldn't you?'

There was a loaded pause then, holding his half-smoked cigarette between his teeth, Dr Marshall shoved Hari's application back into the manila envelope.

'Well, thank you for your time, Dr MacLauchlan,' he said, a professional smile spread across his fleshy features. 'I'm sure you'll understand that we will have to delib—'

'Tush.' Mr Merriweather waved his words aside. 'I think we can cut through the red tape on this occasion, don't you, Dr Marshall?'

Marshall's jowls quivered. 'I am sure the minister would take a dim view on handing out prime appointments without considering other candidates.'

Mr Merriweather raised an almost invisible eyebrow. 'I wasn't aware there *were* any other candidates.'

Marshall shuffled in his chair. 'Not as such, but—'

'Well, in that case . . .' Mr Merriweather took the paperwork from the doctor. 'If I were you, I'd be more worried about what the minister would say if he found out we weren't using the funds he has provided to ensure we have sufficient doctors.'

Dr Marshall's mouth pulled into an angry line as he ground his spent cigarette in the ashtray.

Mr Merriweather smiled at Hari.

'The salary is five hundred and eighty-four pounds seventeen shillings annually plus accommodation, which is a two-bedroom flat situated above the surgery. It has recently been refurbished with all the modern conveniences, isn't that right, Dr Marshall?'

'Uh . . . Well . . .' Marshall replied, taking a cigarette from his case and lighting it.

'The contract is initially for three years but can be extended beyond that,' Mr Merriweather continued.

'Or terminated by either party giving two months' notice,' Dr Marshall chipped in.

'Either party being yourself, Dr MacLauchlan, or the Area Health Board who are funding the post,' clarified Mr Merri-weather. 'Are those terms acceptable?'

Almost six hundred a year and accommodation!

Holding back the large grin that was threatening to take over his face, Hari nodded.

'Very,' he replied soberly, thinking of his depleted bank account.

Mr Merriweather smiled. 'Then I have great pleasure in offer-ing you the post of assistant GP in the Christ Church surgery.'

Hari smiled back. 'And I have great pleasure in accepting.' He got up and strode to the other end of the table.

Merriweather rose to his feet as Hari approached.

'Thank you, sir,' said Hari, offering his hand as he towered over him.

The diminutive minister shook his hand firmly. 'Glad to have you on board, MacLauchlan. There is a great deal of work to be done regarding patients' records and . . .' He glanced briefly towards the man sitting beside him. 'The introduction of up-to-date clinical procedures.'

Hari relinquished the other man's hand. 'I understand the Ministry plans to introduce a programme for all children to be inoculated against diphtheria.'

Mr Merriweather nodded. 'And for polio and whooping cough within the next few years. Because of the poor standard of hous-ing in Spitalfields and Shoreditch, the Ministry has designated it as one of the very first areas to have mobile X-ray screening.'

Hari looked impressed. 'Well, I certainly look forward to being involved in that.'

Leaving Merriweather to tidy away his paperwork, Hari turned to Dr Marshall.

'Thank you, sir,' he said, thrusting out his hand.

Marshall regarded it sourly for a second, then lumbered to his feet and accepted the proffered hand.

'Yes, well.' He shook Hari's hand just the once before pulling his nicotine-stained fingers back.

Hari maintained his cool smile. 'I look forward to working with you, sir,' he said, trying to sound sincere.

After untangling the wheels of the pushchair from a woman's coat draped over the back of a chair, Connie pulled out the nearest seat.

'Here you go, Mum,' she said as her mother waddled through the crowd of shoppers.

It was the first Saturday in August and a full month since the start of the NHS. As usual Connie, her mother and her eldest sister, Mo, plus Mo's two-year-old daughter, Audrey, were in Stratford shopping.

Connie was one of three girls: Mo the eldest of them all, then her brother Jimmy followed by Bernie and herself in the middle and lastly Bobby the baby, who was having a whale of a time doing his National Service in Germany. Their parents had had three others Connie never knew, all of whom were now lying with Nanny and Grandad Byrne in the City of London cemetery.

Even at a modest five feet three and a half inches, Connie topped her mother's height by six inches but what Maud Byrne lacked in height she made up for in girth. However, despite her age and size, she was still quick enough to fetch a lad a clip around the ear for cheeking her. She ruled Maroon Street, where she was the longest-standing resident, with a rod of iron, feeling it was her duty to personally vet all newcomers. If they managed to pass her exacting standards of respectability, they might be let into the select band of doorstep gossips.

'Praise be to Mary,' puffed Connie's sixty-year-old mother as she flopped her forty-four-inch-plus hips onto the seat. 'Me blooming plates are murdering me, I can tell you.'

She and Mo had met their mother just before eight that morning and, after catching the number 25 bus over the old Victorian

Bow Bridge, had alighted on the Broadway half an hour later just in time for their mother to get the best of the bargains in the fruit and veg market. Having loaded the shopping bags on the pram, they'd then spent the rest of the morning mooching around the clothes stall before moving onto the high street. Having bought almost all they came for, they were now in the restaurant in Boardman's department store opposite the tram garage.

Connie took the menu from between the condiment rack and offered it to her mother. 'What do you fancy, then?'

'What I always have, pie and mash,' Maud replied without glancing at the neatly typed cream-coloured cardboard. 'But it seems that some of us are too posh to be seen in Cooks' these days.'

'You saw yourself the queue stretching back to Woolworths,' said Connie.

'We could have waited.'

'We could have if it hadn't been for the fact you've been going on about your aching feet for the past hour.' Connie placed the menu on the table in front of her. 'Now stop complaining and decide what you want.'

Plonking her sizeable handbag on the table, Maude ferreted around for her glasses while Connie read the specials chalked up on a blackboard behind the counter.

'It was like blooming Chipperfield's circus in the ladies,' said Mo, who had nipped off to spend a penny when they'd arrived.

As the oldest girl of the family, Mo had taken on the traditional role of mother's helper sometime during her seventh year and had never relinquished it. She'd left school at thirteen and gone straight into a clothing factory in Commercial Road where she'd worked a nine-hour day on the heavy industrial sewing machines.

Like their mother she was tough and resourceful, which women had to be or the family starved, and woe betide any stallholder who sold her rotten fruit from the back of the display. There were a few wisps of grey around her temples and four children had spread her figure, but to Connie, Mo was still just her big sis who'd given Ivy White a pasting when she'd pushed Connie over in the playground and had dried her tears when Peter McMahon broke her heart when she was eleven.

'What are we having?' Mo asked.

'I'll have egg and chips,' said Connie.

'That sounds all right to me,' said Mo. 'Audrey can have a few of my chips but can you see if they'll do us a boiled egg, too? What about you, Mum?'

'I'm not sure I fancy anything,' Maud replied with a sniff.

Connie and her sister exchanged an exasperated look.

'They've got liver and onion,' said Mo encouragingly.

Their mother pulled a face.

'Well, what about shepherd's pie?' Mo asked. 'Or even gammon and pease pudding? You like that.'

Maud gave the menu another scathing glance. 'I suppose I might take a chance on their sausage and mash.'

Connie's shoulders relaxed. 'And tea all round.'

Her mother nodded. 'And I'll have a custard tart for me afters if they have one.'

Connie unclipped her handbag to retrieve her purse but Mo put her hand over Connie's.

'I'll get it, Con,' said Mo. 'I won five pounds on the housey-housey at St Pat's this week so it's my treat.'

'Are you sure?'

Mo squeezed her hand. 'Course.'

She went to join the queue.

Connie made a funny face at Audrey and the toddler held out her arms.

Connie leant forward and lifted her out of the pushchair.

'You'll spoil her,' said Maud.

'Course I won't,' said Connie, settling her niece on her knee and kissing the child's soft curls, then combing her fingers gently through them. 'I love the way it curls,' she said as the ash-brown strands twisted themselves into a cascade of ringlets. 'She's such a darling.'

A sentimental expression crept into Maud's watery blue eyes. 'Eleven grandchildren,' she said softly. 'Who'd have thought it? Of course, if Jimmy's Sheila hadn't lost one last year it would have been twelve.'

'I'm afraid that happens sometimes,' said Connie.

Maud's lips pulled tight. 'I told her not to carry the laundry to the washhouse but . . . you know Sheila. Won't take a blind bit of notice of me.'

'I don't think Sheila doing the washing had anything to do with it,' Connie said.

'So you've said.' Maud folded her arms across her substantial bosom. 'But I know what I know.' She cast an appraising eye over Connie. 'You know, it suits you holding a little 'un, Connie.'

'Not again, Mum, please,' said Connie wearily.

'Not again, what?' asked Mo, sliding a tray laden with plates, cups and cutlery onto the table.

'What do you think?' said Connie, adjusting Audrey on her lap to stop her grabbing the hot teapot.

'Can you just give it a rest about Connie getting married just for once, Ma?' Mo said, setting her mother's lunch in front of her.

Connie gave her sister a grateful look as she filled half the baby's beaker with milk.

Setting the tea strainer on the open top of the beaker, Mo topped up the milk with hot tea then, screwing the top on, she handed it to her daughter.

'Aren't you going to put a bit of sugar in it?' asked Maud.

'Connie was telling me that doctors think it's bad for children to have too much sugar,' said Mo.

Maud rolled her eyes, indicating her views on the matter.

Connie gave Audrey a fat chip from her plate as her sister set out the table.

'I'll feed her,' said Connie as Mo put the boiled egg in the eggcup.

'Are you sure? She might get butter and egg all over you.'

'That's all right,' said Connie, tucking a paper serviette around Audrey's neck. 'You eat your lunch.'

Mo poured their tea and Connie gave them a quick run-down on how the new National Health Service had made her week even busier than usual.

In turn, Connie asked after her sister's husband and two older children. Mo told them that Eddy had tried to get a week in Butlin's at Skegness but he'd been too late this year as the holiday company was already full, so he'd booked them for the first week in August next year and Bernie, their other sister, her husband Cliff and four children might be joining them.

'That'll be nice for your three to have their cousins to play with,' said Connie, skilfully managing to get a spoonful of boiled egg into Audrey's mouth without the toddler grabbing the spoon.

'And for me and Bernie.' Mo looked heavenwards. 'A week of no cooking. Bliss!'

Connie laughed and handed Audrey a crust. 'Well, I hope you have good weather.'

'Me too,' said Mo. 'But even if it rains every day it'll be nice for Eddy. He's been doing so much overtime recently to scrape enough together for a deposit on that house in East Ham, he could do with a break.'

Connie wiped a stray blob of butter from Audrey's cheek with her handkerchief, then kissed the spot. 'You've got a good dad, Audrey.'

Mo carefully put her knife and fork together on the plate.

'I hope you don't mind me saying, Connie,' her mother said, regarding her youngest daughter thoughtfully. 'But as far as starting a family goes, you're not getting any younger.'

'Thanks for pointing that out, Mum,' snapped Connie. 'But in case you've forgotten, I'm twenty-six, not thirty-six.'

Her mother adjusted her bosom with her forearms. 'I'd had our little Artie, God rest his innocent soul, Mo and Jim at your age.'

'Well, there've been two world wars since then and things are different now. Besides which, Malcolm and I have only been courting properly for just over two years. And you know what they say: "Marry in haste, repent at leisure."'

Her mother tutted. 'Me and your father were wed within the year.'

'Well, it just goes to show Connie's right then, don't it,' said Mo, smiling broadly at her mother. 'Because poor old dad's regretted it ever since.'

Maud shot her eldest a furious look.

'Look, Mum,' Mo continued before her mother could find her voice. 'Our Connie's got a good job, all her money's her own and lots of people look up to her. There's more to life than getting married and having kids, ain't that right, Connie?'

Audrey threw the remnant of her bread on the table then, putting her thumb in her mouth, snuggled into Connie. A warm glow of happiness started behind Connie's breastbone.

28

'Yes, of course there is, Mo,' said Connie, but pressing her lips onto the toddler's brow she couldn't think of anything better just at that moment.

Although it was only just 9.30 on a Monday morning, Connie was already feeling the heat as she walked along Grey Eagle Street.

As usual, after a wet start to the school summer holiday four weeks ago, just as families were sewing labels on uniforms and buying new shoes ready for the next school year, the sun came out and now, at the very end of August, they were experiencing an Indian summer.

The light through Connie's curtains had woken her just before seven, saving her alarm clock a job. After wolfing down her porridge and toast and checking the Overnight Book in the hall for any messages, Connie set out, just as the rest of the nurses were filing in for report.

Connie and Miss O'Dwyer had written up the allocations and discussed today's patients after supper the night before so the superintendent had told her she didn't have to attend this morning's meeting, but she'd made Connie swear by everything holy and otherwise that she would be back by one-thirty at the very latest to act as her 'blessed shield and sword'.

A little dramatic perhaps even for Miss O'Dwyer, but after she'd sent in the second set of clinic figures to the Ministry, a letter with an official stamp had arrived saying two officials would be calling round to discuss a few issues. And today was the day. Connie decided she should pop into Christ Church surgery first as requested rather than risk Dr Marshall bellowing down the phone at them all when the men from the Ministry were on the premises.

Like most of the roads in the Brick Lane area, Grey Eagle Street was lined on both sides by dilapidated three-storey houses built some two hundred years ago when Spitalfields was a prosperous and desirable area to live and work in. The once-large family homes belonging to wealthy weavers had all been converted into multiple dwellings and there was now a family or two living on every floor. The one exception was the house on the corner – Dr Marshall's practice, Christ Church surgery, where Connie was heading.

Chaining her bicycle to the railing outside the surgery, Connie took her bag from the front basket. As usual there was a line of battered prams outside, the babies sleeping peacefully while their mothers waited their turn to see Dr Marshall. The shabby Georgian door with just a few remnants of blue paint was open so Connie trotted up the three worn stone steps and into the hallway. The interior of the house was as dilapidated as the outside with floorboards pitted and splintered by decades of boots tramping over them.

The waiting room was in a similar state of disrepair as the hallway and the addition of a few faded pre-war health posters and half a dozen rickety chairs did little to improve its appearance. Patients wisely avoided sitting on the chairs for fear they would collapse, although some did avail themselves of the rough bench that ran along the back wall.

'Morning,' Connie said chirpily, as she popped her head around the door.

Most of the people waiting knew her and muttered a greeting.

'Do you mind if I pop in before the next patient?' she asked.

'You mean the first patient, luv,' said one man with a tatty bandage around his ear. 'The quack ain't even started yet.'

'Didn't even arrive until ten minutes ago,' said a woman in a headscarf nursing a fretful baby on her lap. 'Most of us have been standing outside since eight.'

'It's a bloody disgrace, that's what it is,' said a beefy-looking chap wearing a leather jerkin and cap. 'I thought things were going to be different under this new system,' he said, flicking his cigarette butt into the empty fireplace. 'I've got a good mind to ring Bevan himself and tell him a few things about this bloody surgery and its bone-idle doctor.'

'Yeah,' said a middle-aged woman with a black eye. 'After all, it was us ordinary people won the ruddy war and it's about time those up top did right by us.'

There were mutters of agreement.

'Well then, I'd better pop in and tell Dr Marshall there're patients in the waiting room.'

'You do that, duck,' said an old woman, wearing a pair of men's boots and sitting in the bay window. 'And tell him if 'e don't get a poxy move on we'll report him to his doctors' council wotsit.'

Leaving Dr Marshall's patients putting the world to rights, Connie made her way to the back of the house where the consulting room was situated.

Knocking on the bare wooden door, she waited for a moment then knocked again.

'District nurse!' she called through the woodwormy panels.

'Come!'

Connie turned the unpolished handle and walked in.

The consulting room was in the same appalling condition as the rest of the house, with faded striped wallpaper and crusted windows. The room was dominated by a very old and very scuffed roll-top desk littered with prescription pads, dog-eared leaflets and unanswered correspondence. On top of this disorder sat a stethoscope that should have been in a museum and a patella hammer with a broken handle. Through a half-glazed door which led through the sluice, which still had its original pipes and taps, Connie could see a variety of instruments and bowls. The only concessions to modern medical practice was the hot water Ascot fixed above the sink and the small steam steriliser on the bench.

Dressed in his usual dishevelled manner, Dr Marshall sat in his battered leather chair puffing a cigarette, his feet up on the desk, perusing a copy of *The Times*.

He looked over his paper.

'Ah,' he said, as ash fluttered down onto his lapels. 'It's little Nurse Byrne.'

Connie's lips lifted just a fraction. 'You asked me to call.'

'Oh yes, a couple of old biddies to go on your morning wash and dress list and some stupid bugger who sliced the top of his finger off in a meat-processing factory needs daily dressing. I've written them down.' He indicated a foolscap sheet with a circular tea stain on it lying at the far end of the desk.

Connie picked it up, folded it in four and then slipped it into her pocket. 'Anything else?'

'Not that I can think of,' he replied. 'Except, can you make a note at the clinic that the new doctor is starting in two weeks?'

'You've actually got someone!'

'Yes, a Dr MacLauchlan. Not my choice but that's this new goddamn world Atlee and his socialist underlings at the Ministry are foisting on us. Still, at least when he arrives I won't be rushed off my feet all day.' He smiled munificently. 'Thank you, nurse. You can run along now.'

Connie went towards the door but, before she opened it, she turned back.

Clamping his cigarette tightly between his lips, Dr Marshall turned the page of his newspaper.

'You do know you've got a dozen patients in the waiting room, don't you, doctor?' Connie said.

'Of course.' He blew a stream of smoke towards the nicotine-stained ceiling. 'And I'll get to them presently,' he said, turning the page of his newspaper.

Connie walked out of the office and was greeted by a chorus of chesty coughs, brought on no doubt by the recent damp weather, from the waiting room, which echoed around the dank hallway. Holding her breath against the aroma from the drains, she hurried down the passageway and into the bright sunlight.

Putting her bag in her bicycle basket, she unlocked the chain and rolled her bike onto the road but, as she rested her foot on the pedal, Connie paused and looked up at the dilapidated building.

Well, whoever this Dr MacLauchlan is, God help him.

Later that afternoon, the second hand on the superintendent's wall clock ticked away yet another silent minute while Mr Ogilvy and Miss Tubshaw, the civil servants from the Ministry of Health, scanned the columns of numbers in front of them.

Connie was perched on the chair in Miss O'Dwyer's office while the superintendent, in a newly laundered uniform and starched cap, sat behind her large desk wearing a worried frown. She clearly understood the seriousness of the ministerial visit as, for once, she didn't have an infant or toddler sitting on her lap.

The officials had arrived on the dot of one-thirty and had spent over an hour reading through the clinic's records.

Mr Ogilvy, the regional official in charge of National Health funding for district clinics, was a slightly built man in his early thirties. He was dressed in a suit you could buy off the peg in Moss Bros or Hepworth's for a couple of guineas and, judging by the thickness of the lenses in his glasses, he was extremely short-sighted.

In contrast to the youthfulness of her colleague, Miss Tubshaw, with stout arms and several chins, was easily in her sixth decade. Wearing a hairy tweed suit, crew-neck jumper and a trilby with a rabbit's foot brooch pinned to one side, the regional nurse overseeing nursing standards looked as if she should have been striding through the heather with a broken shotgun hooked over one arm in search of game, not working her way through the minutiae of the Fry House paperwork.

Miss O'Dwyer, who was chewing the inside of her mouth, caught Connie's eye. Connie tried to give her a reassuring smile but couldn't.

Mercifully, as the second hand started yet another circumnavigation of the dial, Mr Ogilvy raised his head and looked expectantly at his colleague.

She scribbled something at the bottom of her notepad and then laid it open on the surface in front of her.

'Well, Superintendent O'Dwyer, Sister Byrne,' Mr Ogilvy said, smiling professionally at them both, 'thank you again for your time and patience, but you understand with the changes coming into effect recently we want to ensure every clinic is functioning efficient—'

'To be sure,' Miss O'Dwyer interrupted.

'So first we'd like to ask you about the clinic accounts,' said Mr Ogilvy.

Miss O'Dwyer's face drained of colour. 'What about them?'

'Well, Miss O'Dwyer,' said Miss Tubshaw drily as she adjusted her gold-rim glasses. 'I can see all the money is accounted for, but the figures are somewhat unusual in the way they are set out.' She glanced at the account book on the desk, its open page covered with Miss O'Dwyer's spidery squiggles. 'Most people enter the incomings and outgoing in columns down the page but you seem to enter them across the page.'

'Doesn't everyone do them sideways?' Miss O'Dwyer said, her plentiful eyebrows rising in astonishment.

Miss Tubshaw's nostils flared. 'No, they don't, which is why it took the regional Health Board's accountant almost a week to make sense of them.'

Miss O'Dwyer sighed heavily and threw her hands up. 'Ah, well now, when the hens are home to roost I'm a nurse not a bookkeeper.'

She grinned, inviting the two inspectors to join in.

They didn't.

'Well, be that as it may,' continued Miss Tubshaw drily, 'now the Ministry is picking up the bill for Fry House, they are going to want to see proper monthly accounts, especially as all the materials you use will be paid for directly by the Area Health Board. You will be required to submit an itemised account of any supplies you order from local pharmacists so they can be checked against the invoices sent.'

'I can assure you that we will have Fry House clinic's monthly accounts in order by next return,' Connie replied, giving the stern-faced officials on the other side of the desk her warmest smile.

Miss Tubshaw's glacial expression thawed a little. 'I'm sure the area board would be obliged if you could, Sister Byrne. Now, perhaps we can turn to the matter of the nurses.'

A fearsome expression screwed up Miss O'Dwyer's rounded face. 'I give you fair warning I'll not take kindly to the good Lord himself saying a harsh word about my girls.'

'And we're not,' said Mr Ogilvy hastily. 'In fact, they are to be commended for carrying out their duties so well in such a deprived and difficult area.'

'Never a truer word has been spoken,' Miss O'Dwyer replied. 'My girls see sights that would make the saints above turn to drink but they just roll up their sleeves. Angels they are, I tell you, blessed angels.'

Mr Ogilvy's cheeks flushed a little. 'I'm certain they are but unfortunately there just aren't enough of them.'

'According to the Queen's Institute Association Regulations you should have one Queen's Nurse for every 6,000 to 7,000 patients,' Miss Tubshaw continued. 'The '39 National Registration showed there are almost 200,000 people in this area but you've only got twenty-three nurses. In my books that makes a ratio of 8,000 people to every nurse, which means you are at least eight nurses short so I'm afraid you'll have to start recruiting immediately.'

'Eight nurses!' spluttered the superintendent. 'In the name of all mercies, how am I going to afford eight more nurses, I ask you?'

Mr Ogilvy smiled urbanely. 'My dear Miss O'Dwyer, Ministry Area has already allocated the funds.'

The superintendent looked astonished. 'Has it?'

'Indeed it has,' said Mr Ogilvy.

Miss Tubshaw frowned. 'Surely you got the information pack from the QNI's head office explaining how nursing associations were to be incorporated into the new Health Service.'

'Of course I did,' Miss O'Dwyer replied, half-heartedly shifting a couple of papers on her desk. 'I have it somewhere.'

The nurse inspector glanced at the in-tray on the corner of the desk. It was piled high with unopened letters, including a fat one near the bottom with the Queen's Institute of District Nursing insignia across the top.

'Well, no matter as it's no longer your concern, Miss O'Dwyer.' A munificent smile spread across Mr Ogilvy's thin face. 'All you have to worry about is finding more nurses.'

'Eight nurses, you say?'

'Indeed,' said Miss Tubshaw briskly. 'And I'd expect to see at least half that number in place by the end of the year.'

The superintendent's mouth pulled into a determined line. 'Consider it done.'

Connie wasn't quite so optimistic.

Fry House's four QN students sat their exams in a little over a month but one was getting married and moving to Oxford and another had already signed her papers to be a Ten-pound Pom. That left Kate and Yvonne but, even if they stayed, they would have to find at least two others by January. Every hospital and district association was recruiting and, according to the newspapers, there were three jobs for every registered nurse and most of them in more salubrious places than Spitalfields and Shoreditch.

Connie forced her most self-assured smile. 'We'll get the advertisement drafted and in to *Nursing Mirror* by the end of the week. Won't we, superintendent?'

'Indeed we will,' the superintendent replied.

'Splendid,' said Mr Ogilvy, who tapped his papers into a neat pile before stowing them in the briefcase on the floor besides him.

He and Miss Tubshaw stood up and so did Connie and the superintendent.

'Thank you for your time, Miss O'Dwyer,' Mr Ogilvy said, offering the superintendent his hand.

She took it briefly and then let go.

He smiled. 'Perhaps I might use your facilities before I . . .'

'Of course you can.' Miss O'Dwyer side-stepped out from behind the desk. 'I'll show you.' She headed for the door.

'This building must be over two hundred years old,' said Mr Ogilvy, casting his gaze around the high windows and lofty ceilings.

'I should say,' agreed Miss O'Dwyer, as she opened the door. 'If you have a mind to look you can just about make out Moody's Lodging House painted in red above the door.' She chuckled. 'Of course, if you ask me, I reckon in those days lodging house really meant knocking shop.'

Mr Ogilvy laughed. 'How fascinating.'

They left the room.

Miss Tubshaw regarded Connie thoughtfully for a few moments, then picked up her handbag and hooked it over her arm. 'It's been a pleasure to meet you, Sister Byrne.'

'You too,' Connie replied.

'And I wish you the best of luck with your recruiting efforts and getting Fry House's accounts in order.' She glanced down at the jumbled account book and sighed. 'From what I've seen, you are certainly going to need it.'

Connie looked coolly at the older woman. 'I'll tell you straight, Miss Tubshaw, if someone you loved was sick or dying you'd want Miss O'Dwyer to be caring for them because I've never met a better nurse.'

'Your loyalty is very commendable, Sister Byrne, and I do not doubt for one moment the truth of your statement but' – a hard glint flickered in Miss Tubshaw's grey eyes – 'I'm afraid being a caring nurse isn't enough in the modern National Health Service.'

Chapter Three

On the second Monday in September and careful to avoid the collection of rotting vegetables clogging the drain, Hari stopped in front of the last house in Grey Eagle Street. He stared at the ramshackle building for a moment, then pulled the letter from the pocket of his suit jacket and checked the address.

There were a couple of women outside the house, loitering in the early afternoon sunshine that lit the narrow passageway. They eyed him suspiciously as he climbed the worn steps to the front door. Pushing the grubby brass plate with his index finger, it creaked open and Hari walked in.

Although the hallway and the room to his left, which seemed to be full of damaged chairs, were as silent as a morgue, the sounds of an orchestra drifted out from the back of the house.

'Good afternoon!' Hari called.

There was no reply.

Closing the door behind him, Hari advanced along the corridor.

He stopped outside the room from where the classical music was emanating and knocked.

'Surgery's closed.'

Hari opened the door.

Dr Marshall, dressed in the same dishevelled apparel as the last time Hari had seen him, sat in a leather-bound office chair with his feet up on an open roll-top desk. Beneath his heels were letters, pamphlets and a pink dog-eared copy of the *Financial Times*. On the desk there was also a horse hoof fashioned into an ashtray which was overflowing with cigarette and cigar butts. Dr Marshall's eyes were closed and, using a stainless steel tongue depressor, he was conducting the melodious sounds coming from the Bakelite radio on the window sill.

'Goddamnit! Are you deaf?' he barked without opening his eyes. 'The surgery is closed.'

'Good afternoon, doctor,' said Hari pleasantly.

Dr Marshall looked around. 'Dr MacLauchlan.'

'The same,' Hari replied, with just a fractional lift of his right eyebrow. 'You are expecting me, aren't you?'

'I am, but your letter said two,' Dr Marshall replied, swinging his size tens off the desktop.

'Yes, I'm sorry I'm a bit early but as it's such a fine day I decided to walk from Liverpool Street,' Hari replied.

Dr Marshall beamed at him. 'Splendid. Gives you more time to get yourself acquainted with the place.' He glanced at the small attaché case in Hari's left hand. 'Is that all you've brought?'

'No, this is just my stethoscope, sphyg and the like,' Hari replied, resting it on the wooden chair opposite the desk. 'The rest of my luggage is being delivered at six.'

Dr Marshall beamed at him. 'Capital. Did you have a good trip?'

'Not bad,' Hari replied, somewhat taken aback by his colleague's affable manner after their last encounter. 'Bit of a hold-up outside Farringdon but nothing to speak of.' He glanced at the kettle and cups sitting on the dresser. 'I wouldn't say no to a coffee though.'

'I'm sure,' Dr Marshall agreed. 'But why don't I give you the grand tour first, then you can settle in.' He rummaged around on the desk in front of him and pulled out a packet of Benson & Hedges. Taking a gold lighter from his pocket, he lit up and then stood.

'You passed the waiting area as you came in and this' – he swung his arm around – 'as a bright chap like you has no doubt already deduced, is the consulting room and these are the patient records.'

Flicking his hand, Dr Marshall scattered ash over the antique set of cabinets leaning against the wall. He strode across the room and after a couple of attempts shoved open a half-glazed door at the back of the room.

'This is the sluice.'

Hari peered into what had once been a Georgian scullery where the cook would have gutted poultry.

A strip of carpet worn thin over the decades barely covered the unpolished terracotta tiles and a chipped brown-stained sink that wouldn't have looked out of place in a nineteenth-century workhouse was piled high with enamel bowls waiting to be washed. The iron tank which sat above it had accumulated moss around its welded seams.

'The dustbins are in the backyard.' Marshall nodded at the door at the far end of the narrow room. 'They are collected every Tuesday.'

Hari stepped back from the room.

'The lotions and potions are there,' Marshall continued, jabbing a chubby finger at a white enamel cupboard. 'The key's in the top drawer. This—' He thumped the cracked leather surface of the examination couch sending up a little puff of dust. 'Is a bit temperamental and the screen has a couple of wobbly wheels. I keep all the spare equipment and the old patient notes in the room alongside this. You can access it through the door to your left in the hall,' said Dr Marshall. 'Anything you can't find in the treatment room will probably be in there. I'm sure you'll work it out.'

'I'm sure I will,' Hari replied.

Dr Marshall smiled affably. 'I bet an eager young chap can't wait to get stuck in, can you?'

'Indeed,' Hari replied, thinking perhaps he'd misjudged his new colleague, who was being much more helpful than he expected.

'Good.' Dr Marshall marched out into the hall and opened the understair cupboard. He pulled out a set of golf clubs. 'I'll leave you to look around the accommodation, it's upstairs,' he said, heaving the bag onto his shoulder. He glanced at his watch. 'Good thing you arrived early. You've got best part of the afternoon before surgery starts at four-thirty.'

Dr Marshall turned and headed for the door. 'Oh, feel free to make coffee but you'll have pop to the shop at the end of the road to get some milk.'

He strode out, banging the door behind him.

Hari stared around for a couple of seconds then, leaving his briefcase on the chair, left the surgery. Turning the lock in the door leading to his accommodation, he climbed the creaky stairs to the floor above.

If Christ Church surgery downstairs was Edwardian, the upstairs was positively Dickensian and a few short paces brought him into what was the lounge. The room on this level had apparently once been the family bedroom and was of a reasonable size, but the putty-coloured walls were completely bare, as was the sash window with a cracked pane overlooking the backyard. Under the dusty cast-iron mantel shelf was an equally dusty fire grate with a screwed-up copy of the *Daily Sketch* proclaiming Labour's landslide victory three years before.

In addition to a couple of upright wooden chairs, one of which had the spoke missing from the back, there was a saggy green pre-war sofa with a suspicious stain on one cushion, a circular rug that made you itch just looking at it and an oblong coffee table with an upturned red brick instead of a leg.

Leaving the room where he was supposed to relax after a long day's work, he strolled into the kitchen. The window here was also bare but intact, although stuck as he discovered when he tried to open it to release the overwhelming smell of stagnant water. This was due to the shallow puddle of brown water in the sink caused by a blockage in the drain which was of endless fascination to the handful of blue bottles circling around it. There was an old skeletal-style gas cooker that would probably blow the house to kingdom come if he were ever foolish enough to light it. There was a kitchen dresser with most of its blue paint flaked off and an awkwardly wedged drawer and some mismatched crockery resting on it. As far as he could see, the only item in the room that had been manufactured since the end of the war was the electric kettle sitting on the scrubbed draining board.

With his heart sinking ever lower, Hari mounted the narrower servants' stairs to the third floor and found two further rooms, one of which had been converted, around the time of the Boer War if the plumbing was anything to go by, into a bathroom. In here was the only evidence of the 'refurbished with all the modern conveniences'; a new toilet basin and washbowl. However, it was the bedroom that took the 'utterly appalling' prize above every other room in the house as the furnishings consisted of one upright chair, one cast-iron bed with a discoloured and stained mattress standing on a square rug with more hessian backing showing through than actual weave. There was no linen, curtains, hanging rail or mirror, and a solitary lightbulb hanging from the central rose.

Hari stared at it for a moment, then marched downstairs past the lounge and back into the main surgery. Shrugging off his coat, he hooked it over the back of the chair then, continuing through to the sluice, found a bucket and scrubbing brush. He rolled up his sleeves as the water from the tap spluttered into the bucket. After a bit of rummaging about downstairs, he found some Lysol in the lotions cupboard and tipped it in too. Grasping the bucket in one hand and the scrubbing brush in the other, Hari made his way back upstairs to his new home.

As the door closed on the last patient, Hari screwed the top on his pen and threw it on the desk. Putting his hands around the back of his neck he stretched in the chair.

It was very fortunate he had arrived earlier than planned because since his so-called colleague's abrupt departure, Hari had taken up both rugs from the flat above and banished them, along with the mattress, to the backyard ready for the dustmen to collect. He'd then stripped off his shirt and set about scrubbing the whole place from top to bottom including the floors before turning his attention to the kitchen and bathroom. With a bit of jiggery-pokery and a quantity of boiling water, he'd managed to unblock the kitchen sink and then poured some of the surgery's industrial-strength bleach down it. On closer inspection, the encrusted bath was beyond redemption and so Hari just left it.

Having satisfied himself that the upstairs was at least vermin-and-mould-free, Hari turned his attention to straightening the mess in the consulting room; cleaning equipment and searching out dressings.

After a bit of trial and error, he'd managed to get the steriliser working and as long as it didn't explode he'd have sterilised instruments in case he was called upon to lance any boils. Only then did he put on the kettle for his long overdue hot drink.

Dr Marshall wasn't lying when he'd said there was no milk but what he'd omitted to mention was that there wasn't any coffee either.

Hari hadn't expected to find a selection of the finest ground coffee in the local corner shop, but he had hoped for a tin of Nescafé or Maxwell House. Sadly, the only thing remotely resembling coffee, amongst the firelighters, boiled sweets and broken biscuits, was Camp Coffee.

He bought it and two blocks of carbolic soap, which the surgery seemed to be out of. Mr Winkleman had offered him everything from razor blades through to aniseed balls. He'd declined them all tactfully but was now beginning to regret not taking up Mrs Winkleman's offer of a salt beef sandwich to take with him.

Hari glanced at his watch. Six forty-five. A glow of satisfaction spread through him.

Despite Dr Marshall's incomprehensible filing system, Hari had written up all his patients' notes and was finished for the day, and only fifteen minutes after the surgery officially closed. Of course, if half a dozen people hadn't walked in, taken one look at him and walked straight back out again muttering, 'bloody darkie', he would probably still be seeing patients. And if he had a pound for every time someone asked him where he came from, he'd have earned his weekly salary by now.

His belongings had arrived on the dot of six, just as he was painting a child's throat with antiseptic tincture to ease the soreness, and he still had to unpack, but that could definitely wait until after supper.

Grabbing his mug, Hari swallowed the last mouthful of coffee, stood up and then shrugged on his jacket.

One of his patients had told him there was an eating house around the corner that did a reasonable meal. After tidying the stack of notes and closing the roll-top desk, Hari took the surgery keys from the top drawer and his hat from the stand and headed out.

Picking up an *Evening News* from the newspaper seller outside Aldgate East Station, Hari made his way towards Commercial Street, pushing through the throng of people heading home at the end of their day's work. Within a few moments he found himself outside Alfredo and Marie's restaurant and cafeteria which, according to the sign, offered homemade breakfasts, snacks and dinners at a reasonable price.

After a quick glance at the menu displayed in the steamy

window, Hari pushed on the chrome diagonal handle and opened the door.

As he'd expected, the restaurant was self-service and had a large counter running along the back of the room with square tables seating four set out in neat rows in front.

The owners had clearly refurbished the premises since the war as there was a very modern feel to the black, yellow and chrome decor. This bright theme was continued with the Formica-topped tables and chrome chairs. In contrast to the coolness of the early September evening outside, inside was a warm fug of fried food, boiled milk and cigarette smoke. The room was packed and the chatter and good-humoured laughter of the patrons added to the upbeat atmosphere.

As Hari let the door close behind him, the bell above it rang and dozens of pairs of eyes turned in his direction. The room fell silent. A couple of the customers nudged each other.

Putting his hands in his pockets and an affable expression on his face, Hari strolled between the tables' gawping customers to the counter.

Behind the stainless-steel worktop stood a portly man dressed in a striped blue and white apron with his sleeves rolled up. Beside him stood a woman who was about the same age and with a similarly hearty physique.

'Good evening,' Hari said in his best Oxbridge accent, smiling warmly at them.

'Evening,' mumbled the man.

Hari raised his eyes to the blackboard over their heads and studied the menu.

'I think I'll have chicken pie, mash and peas, followed by spotty dick and custard,' he said, as they and the rest of the shop studied him, 'and a cup of strong coffee, if I may?'

Without taking her eyes from him, the woman shouted the order through the hatch behind her then went to the espresso machine at the end of the counter.

The man removed the tea towel hooked in his apron and wiped the top of the counter. 'I can't recall seeing you around here before.'

'You wouldn't have,' Hari replied. 'I only arrived this afternoon.'

Then came the inevitable question.

'Where from?'

'Clerkenwell.'

'No, I mean originally?'

'Scotland.'

The man scoffed. 'You don't look Scottish.'

'I decided to leave my kilt at home,' Hari replied lightly.

'I mean—'

'I know what you mean,' Hari replied, fixing him with a piercing glare.

The restaurateur lowered his gaze and wiped the counter again. The woman came back and placed a frothy coffee in front of him.

'That'll be half a crown,' she said, thrusting her hand out. 'I mean two shilling and six pence.'

Hari dragged the change out of his pocket. 'There you are. Two bob and a tanner,' he said, smiling as he handed her the coins.

A heavily made-up young woman with red lips, bouffant hair and wearing a frilly apron came out from the kitchen carrying a tray loaded with Hari's supper. She spotted him and her face lit up. She wiggled over.

'There you go, mister,' she said batting her mascaraed lashes at him. 'Chicken, spud and peas and pud and custard.'

She added a knife and fork wrapped up in a cheap paper napkin and the coffee to his tray, then slid it along the counter towards him.

'Thank you.' Hari smiled at her. 'And it's doctor, not mister.'

He looked around for a free chair and headed towards it, causing the couple already occupying the table to hastily finish their drinks and leave.

Sitting down at the table, he laid the newspaper open beside him and, ignoring the curious stares directed at him from all, casually opened it.

The people around him resumed their supper and soon the cafe was again filled with chatter and laughter. He'd just swallowed the last square of chicken pie when the bell over the door tinkled again.

Hari looked up as a shapely young woman with a cracking

pair of legs strolled in, the circular skirt of her blue and red summer dress swirling around her as she swayed.

The cafe owner's dour face lifted into a jolly smile. 'Watchya, miss.'

'Evening, Alf,' she called, her wavy hair the colour of a newly minted penny bouncing pleasantly as she advanced towards the counter. 'Sorry I'm late with this.'

She dropped a couple of coins into his hand and his chubby fingers closed around them.

'You shouldn't have gone out of your way,' he said, ringing open the till. 'Could have dropped it by tomorrow. After all, it ain't as if I don't know where you live.'

She laughed, a low full-bodied laugh that caught Hari in the pit of his stomach.

She turned, revealing animated blue eyes and a smiling face that were as pleasing to look at as her figure.

'See you tomorrow,' she called over her shoulder as she strode towards the door.

She whisked past Hari's table without glancing across but he caught just a hint of gardenia in her wake. Hari watched her walk out and wished he was seeing the copper-haired beauty tomorrow, too.

Chapter Four

Picking up the last square of gauze impregnated with petroleum jelly, Connie laid it on the raw burn on Linda Harrison's left forearm.

Linda, who was sitting on her mother's lap, flinched but didn't murmur. Her mother had rushed the screaming three-year-old in a week ago after the child had grabbed the kettle from the stove and tipped the boiling water over herself.

Mercifully, Connie had got the limb under cooled water quickly enough to stop any further damage before packing them off on the bus to Casualty at the London a mile away.

'That's the last one,' said Connie, giving the little girl a happy smile. 'All I have to do is bandage it in place and you're done.'

Picking up a fresh bandage from the dressing trolley beside her, Connie secured it loosely around her patient's thumb and wrist, then wound the crêpe up her little arm in a herringbone pattern.

It was just about three-thirty on a warm Wednesday afternoon and, as usual, Connie was in charge of Fry House's dressing clinic.

The walls of the treatment room had been emulsioned in a dull mushroom colour before the war and were long overdue a refurbishment. However, Miss O'Dwyer did her best to offset the drab decor by displaying lots of colourful health posters. She favoured ones with children. The poster reminding mothers Don't Forget the Cod Liver Oil, which showed a cherubic baby being guarded by a chirpy robin, was given pride of place behind the nurses' desk while one of evil-looking flies crawling towards a pork chop on a plate instructing you to Keep it Covered had been tucked out of sight behind the door.

Two stainless-steel floor-to-ceiling cupboards stood against the far wall. One was a locked lotions, potions and liquids store and the other was where the instruments such as scalpels, stitch-cutter, arterial forceps and a brass ear syringe were stored along with invalid feeding cups, inhalers and sputum bowls.

Squashed in with all of this were a desk and stool for nurses, an examination couch, and a pair of threadbare screens which were supposed to give the patient being treated a little privacy. How effective they were in such a confined space was another issue, which, along with inadequate supplies and faulty equipment, Connie was still waiting for the new Health Service to replace.

'There you are,' said Connie, gently slipping her finger under the bandage and fastening it with a safety pin. 'Try not to get it wet but if you do or it comes loose, just pop back.'

'Thank you ever so much,' said Linda's mother, a thin woman with dark smudges under her eyes. 'I only turned my back for a second.'

'I'm afraid that's all it takes and in future make sure you put the kettle and pots on the back of the stove,' said Connie.

Linda hopped off her mother's knee and headed to the upright scale where she started sliding the weights back and forth until her mother pulled her away and dragged her out.

Gathering up her dirty equipment, Connie was just about to take it through to the sluice when Frances, the Cambridge Heath Road sister, came in followed by her Queen's Nurse student Pam.

'Are there many more outside?' asked Connie.

Frances nodded. 'Aren't there always? Any news on when we're getting reinforcements?'

Connie gave her a regretful look. 'I'm afraid we didn't have much luck with the first advert. We only got three applicants and none of them were suitable.'

'I suppose we're not the only clinic in London looking for nurses,' said Pam.

'I'm sure we're not,' said Frances. 'But we can't go on like this.'

'We won't,' said Connie. 'I spoke to Miss Tubshaw, who has managed to get Area to agree for us to advertise for part-time nurses in the local newspaper.'

'Do you think we'll get any?' asked Frances.

Connie nodded. 'I'm sure there are dozens of nurses stuck at home who'd jump at the chance of doing a few hours while their children are at school. They also agreed that we could take on nursing assistants, like during the war, to help with the daily washes and weekly baths. We're advertising again with a half-page spread in the *Nursing Mirror and Times*, plus the Friends of Fry House have generously offered to pay the relocation expenses of any QN sisters who take up a post with us, so we're optimistic we'll get some more takers this time around.'

'Let's hope, or we'll soon need nursing ourselves,' said Frances. 'Oh, and by the way you've got a message in the book to call on a Dr MacLauchlan?'

'Doctor . . . ? Oh I know, the new GP at Christ Church surgery,' said Connie. 'Did he say it's urgent?'

Frances shook her head. 'Just to call in.'

'You could leave it until the morning,' suggested Pam.

'I could but it might be urgent,' said Connie. 'It would be tonight as my sister's expecting me for supper so I was hoping I might be able to get away a bit early.'

'We've done all our afternoon visits so we could finish off here for you, Con, couldn't we?' said Pam.

'Yes, of course,' said Frances, already pushing Connie's dirty dressing trolley towards the sluice, 'but only on the condition you give a detailed report about Dr MacLauchlan later.'

'It's a deal, chalk me up, will you?' said Connie, indicating the blackboard hooked on the back of the door where the nurses listed their visits.

'And don't forget to find out if he's married,' added Pam, as she marked 'GP' next to Connie's name.

Connie laughed. 'I wouldn't get too excited, Pam. With a name like MacLauchlan he's probably a crusty Scotsman with a ginger beard, bad breath and dinner down his tie.'

It was just over a week since he'd arrived at Christ Church surgery and Hari had worked solidly from morning to night. And even when the surgery was closed on Saturday afternoon and Sunday, he'd spent a good deal of his free time completing the forms and inventories which seemed to arrive daily from the Ministry of Health. Of course, in reality, as Dr Marshall owned the practice, it wasn't Hari's role to complete the paperwork required by the Ministry but as Marshall seemed to divide his time between the golf course and his other practice in Chingford, someone had to do it. After all, if the Ministry didn't reimburse Christ Church surgery for its services, it wouldn't be Marshall and his practice in the leafy suburbs who would suffer, it would be the poor souls hereabouts.

Marshall had popped in a couple of times, ostensibly to take surgery but as he usually left within an hour of arriving, Hari knew he was just keeping an eye on him.

As patients were already waiting outside when he got back from his home visits at three-fifty, Hari had started surgery half an hour early at four. He'd half-hoped it might mean he wouldn't still be writing prescriptions at seven-thirty as he had been yesterday and the day before. So far that looked a forlorn hope.

'Next!' he bellowed.

The handle rattled and a woman with curlers in her hair and wearing a grubby fawn mac limped in.

She looked around. 'Where's the doctor?'

'I'm the doctor,' said Hari for the umpteenth time.

'But you're a, you know . . . a Lascar.'

'Half-Lascar, half-Scottish and a whole doctor,' Hari replied.

'But where's Dr Marshall?'

'On the nineteenth hole by now, I should expect,' Hari replied wearily, as the rotary fan on the window sill blasted a gust of warm air over him. 'I'm Dr MacLauchlan. How may I help you?'

She looked Hari over again. 'When is Dr Marshall back?'

'Tomorrow. Is it your foot that's the problem?'

'How do you know?'

'Just a shot in the dark,' Hari replied.

Her eyes flew open and she grabbed the crucifix hanging around her neck.

'For goodness sake, woman, you're limping,' snapped Hari. 'Now, I've haven't eaten for six hours so I can either look at it or I'll call the next patient in and be a step closer to my supper.'

She studied him for a few moments, then perched on the edge of the chair.

'Now, what's the problem?'

'It's me foot,' she said.

'What about your foot?'

She looked puzzled. 'Well it hurts.'

'I know that, but why?'

'You're the doctor, don't you know?'

'I am a doctor but I'm not a mind-reader,' said Hari, just about keeping a grip on his temper. 'So tell me why it is hurting. Have you knocked it, cut it or twisted it at all?'

She shook her head. 'Nuffink like that, when I saw Dr Marshall two weeks ago 'e said it were a bunion and that was that but it's so sodding painful I can hardly walk on it. And it's leaking into me shoe.'

Hari frowned. 'Perhaps I ought to take a look.' He stood up and, walking around the desk, pulled the threadbare screen in front of the couch. 'If you could take your stocking off and pop yourself up on the treatment couch,' he said, returning to his side of the desk. 'And who are you?'

'Ada Nunn. Mrs,' she replied, as she limped behind the screen.

While his patient got ready, Hari went to the antique filing cabinet and found her file.

Scanning over the notes, he saw the usual set of complaints he was now beginning to expect from the people registered with the surgery; notably bronchitis, stomach upsets and runny eyes. He also noted that Dr Marshall had scribbled bunion on the last line and prescribed his patient something called Vitality Tonic.

Tonics of one sort or the other were standard fare for most doctors and were often of the practitioner's own devising. They usually contained extract of yeast, which had a range of B vitamins, and ferrous sulphate and calcium, listed as iron, and a bone-strengthener. These were mixed with some sort of fruit cordial, along with liquorice and sugar, and patients were instructed to take a spoonful once a day. They were a hangover from the previous century when doctors frequently concocted such things at their kitchen sink. These days it was more often than not a local pharmacist who dispensed it on the doctor's instruction. They were often prescribed so the patient felt they had something to show for their half a crown consultation fee. Hopefully, now the NHS was picking up the bill, these dubious pick-me-ups would soon be consigned to history in the same way treating syphilis with mercury and prescribing sulphur for stomach ulcers had been. At best they had no effect whatsoever, at worst they could kill you.

There was a cough.

'Are you ready, Mrs Nunn?' Hari asked.

'As I'll ever be,' came the reply.

Hari went over and pulled the screen aside.

Instead of sitting on the sheet draped over the couch, Mrs Nun had it wrapped around her in the manner of a long skirt, presumably to stop the sight of her bloated white leg firing his savage passion. Her right foot poked out from the bottom of the sheet.

Hari pulled over the chair she'd just vacated and sat down. Lifting her chubby foot he studied the knuckle joint of her big toe. Running his index finger over the surface of the red, raw flesh he felt something sharp.

Mrs Nunn flinched.

Ignoring the fetid odour drifting up, Hari leant forward and, looking closer, saw a faint brown line beneath the surface.

'Have you been in a pub recently, Mrs Nunn? Or a brewery?' he asked, straightening up.

'I clean in the Bear and Staff twice a week, as it happens,' she replied. 'But I don't see what that's got to do with my bun—'

'I suspect it's a sliver of glass causing you trouble not your bunion,' Hari replied. 'Now, if you give me a minute I'll get my instruments and I'll have it out.'

Leaving Mrs Nunn on the couch, Hari went into the sluice. After rolling up his sleeves and washing his hands, he returned a few moments later with an enamel tray laid up with the biggest hypodermic needle he could find in the steriliser, sanitised rubber gloves, a galley pot of iodine, gauze and a bandage.

Setting his equipment on the bench beside his patient, Hari sat back in the chair.

'Now, this is going to sting but if you hold it still it will be over in a second,' he said as he swabbed the inflamed area with gauze soaked in iodine. 'It's just like getting a splinter out.'

Hari took a firm of hold of Mrs Nunn's heel and she gritted her teeth. He prodded it a couple of times, then picked up the scalpel and, with a quick flick, the angry-looking patch burst. Using a gauze square Hari pressed hard, and pus along with a small slither of brown glass came out. Hari wiped the cut with a fresh gauze square and pressed a clean dressing on it to staunch the blood. He balanced the brown shard on the tip of his finger.

'There you go, Mrs Nunn,' he said, twisting it so she could see.

'Well I never,' she said, going cross-eyed as she looked at it. ''Ow on earth did that get there?'

'I don't know but it's certainly what's given you all the pain.' Hari threw the scalpel in the tray and bandaged the dressing in place, then stood up. 'I'll leave you to straighten yourself up.'

Taking his equipment back into the sluice, Hari stripped off the rubber gloves and draped them over the edge of the sink to sterilise later. When he came back into the room, Mrs Nunn was already sitting at the desk with her handbag on her knees.

'Fancy such a little thing giving me so much trouble.'

'Indeed, although I'm surprised Dr Marshall didn't see it himself when he examined you last week,' said Hari.

Mrs Nunn looked astonished. 'Oh no, he didn't look at me foot,' she explained. 'I told him it hurt and he said it was me bunion playing me up again.'

Hari lips pulled into a hard line. 'I want you to go to the clinic in Fry House in three days' time so the district nurse can have a look at it,' he said, resuming his seat behind the desk and taking his pen from his top pocket. 'I've asked one of them to call in at the surgery later so I'll tell them to expect you. If they are happy with it then you can carry on, but if not you'll have to come back to see me.'

'Thank you, doctor,' said Mrs Nunn in a respectful tone.

'And I'd advise you to wear stouter shoes when you're cleaning in future,' Hari replied.

'I will. And thank you, doctor,' she said.

'Good day to you, Mrs Nunn,' he said wearily. 'Now, would you mind telling the next patient to come in as you leave?'

Picking up his pen, Hari started documenting Mrs Nunn's treatment as she hobbled out of the room.

Sliding his patient's notes into the back of the oblong box on his desk, ready to file later, Hari loosened his tie before reaching for his prescription pad.

You'd think after years in the tropics he'd be able to handle a British summer. Of course, it was easier to keep cool holding a

G&T on a veranda than dealing with the ailing population of Spitalfields in an airless back room.

There was a knock on the door.

'Come!' he called without looking up.

The door opened and closed.

Hari scribbled his signature on the docket. 'Now, if you could just take a—' He looked up to see the copper-haired beauty who'd walked into the cafe, and frequently into his thoughts, standing in the doorway.

Of course this time she wasn't wearing a bright summer dress that swirled around her but a navy-blue district nurse's uniform.

A smile spread slowly across Hari's face. 'Good afternoon, sister. How very nice to see you.'

Dr MacLauchlan clearly was not so much a crusty Scotsman with a ginger beard; more a maharaja in a Savile Row suit.

Well, in truth, he was in his shirtsleeves with his collar button undone and the knot of his Royal Medical Corps tie loosened, but his well-cut single-breasted navy jacket hung over the back of the chair. He had strong, angular cheekbones and the welcoming smile on his well-formed lips softened the bluntness of his square jaw. Unlike most men, Dr MacLauchlan's ebony hair wasn't plastered in place with Brylcreem and it was cut just a little longer than current fashions dictated.

Gathering her wits together, Connie smiled. 'Good afternoon, I'm Sister Byrne from Fry House. You must be Dr MacLauchlan.'

'I am indeed.' His smile widened. 'It's a pleasure to meet you.'

'And you,' said Connie.

'You might not say that when you see the list I've got for you.' He stood up. 'Do you mind if I scrub a couple of bits while we talk?'

'Of course not.'

He strolled to the sluice.

Depositing her bag on the chair and extracting her notebook, Connie followed.

Although the old scullery was large enough to accommodate two people, Connie stopped at the door. She couldn't help but notice it seemed to have been cleaned thoroughly and restocked since she'd last seen it.

Dr MacLauchlan, who had to be six two if he was an inch, turned on the tap and threw in a handful of shredded carbolic soap. He swirled it around under the running water, plastering the covering of dark hair to his forearm in the process.

'Firstly there is Mrs . . .'

Dr MacLauchlan ran through half a dozen patients who required a visit and Connie jotted down his instructions precisely.

'And lastly,' he said, shaking the water from his hands, 'there's the woman you saw hobbling out a few moments ago, Mrs Nunn. She had a bit of glass in her foot. It didn't look infected but I'd like you to give it the once-over just to make sure. I've told her to pop in to see you three days from now, so could you look out for her?'

'Of course, doctor,' replied Connie. 'Is there anything else?'

'Well, you can tell me what chemist Fry House uses for their supplies,' he asked, grabbing the towel

'Weinstein's in Bethnal Green Road but I think Dr Marshall uses Crowther & Sons in Middlesex Street.'

Dr MacLauchlan gave her a wry smile

'I know. That's why I'm going somewhere else,' he replied, rolling down his cuffs and rebuttoning them.

Connie stepped back so he could return to his desk.

A faint mix of aftershave and carbolic drifted up as he walked past. His arm brushed against her notebook and knocked it to the floor.

Connie bent to rescue it but Dr MacLauchlan got there first and picked it up.

'I'm sorry,' he said, offering it to her. 'I didn't mean to barge past you like that.'

'You didn't,' Connie replied, noticing the shadow of his end-of-day stubble. 'It was an accident.'

As she took the pad from him, Connie's finger brushed against his, sending an odd flutter through her.

Feeling ridiculous at her silly reaction, Connie returned to the chair on the far side of the desk.

'Will that be all, doctor?' Connie asked, slipping her notebook into her bag and picking it up.

'Yes, thank you,' he replied. 'Except, do you think your superintendent would be happy for me to visit Fry House every now and again?'

'I'm sure Miss O'Dwyer would be delighted to see you. We have afternoon tea at three so if you drop by then you could get yourself a cuppa and a slice of cake too,' said Connie. 'Although I have to say none of the other doctors do.'

'Well, that's their loss, I'd say, especially with cake on offer, and I think you'll find, sister, I'm different.' He smiled and a flutter ran through Connie again. 'Thank you for popping in, but now, if you don't mind, could you send the next patient in?'

'Of course, doctor.'

As she emerged into the corridor, she met Mrs Kepple, one of their long-term patients, shuffling towards the consulting room, her nicotine-stained fingers grasping her stick tightly.

'Oi, sister,' wheezed the old woman as she drew closer. 'I've heard we've got a new quack. What's 'e like?'

'Different, Mrs Kepple,' Connie told her. 'Very different.'

Stifling a yawn, Connie slipped the pearl stitch off and then slid the knitting needle through and looped the double-knit wool around the end ready for the last stitch on her needles. Turning the plastic row counter to nine she wound the wool around her fingers and peered at the pattern of the colourful winter cardigan balanced on her knees.

It was just after three-thirty on the Sunday following her encounter with Christ Church surgery's new GP.

Malcolm's mother, Hilda Henstock, was reclining in one of the two fireside chairs with her feet on a pouffe, while Jean Metcalf joined families across the airwaves in *Two-Way Family Favourites*.

Mrs Henstock was a thin woman in her mid-fifties who dressed as if she was in her mid-seventies. Instead of the clean-cut tailored suits and gowns favoured by most of her contemporaries, Mrs Henstock stuck stubbornly to the draped layers of washed-out lavenders and mute greys edged with lace that were last fashionable in the pre-war years. She completed the Miss Havisham look with several long strings of pearls and wore her hair swept up into an Edwardian top-knot held in place with tortoiseshell combs.

'It looks like a very complicated design,' said Mrs Henstock.

'Not really, Mrs Henstock,' she replied, pulling a length of wool from the ball ready to start the next row.

Malcom's mother regarded Connie over her half-rimmed metal spectacles. 'I hope you don't mind me saying, but do you not think that shade's a bit too bright for your colouring?'

'No, I don't, Mrs Henstock,' said Connie lightly, refusing to rise to the bait. 'I bought it to match my new winter skirt.' She smoothed the apple-green fabric against her leg. 'I thought I might wear it when we go to my Cousin Margery's wedding next month.'

'Another wedding!' Mrs Henstock looked heavenwards. 'What with your family and those girls you work with, all you seem to do is go to weddings.'

'Well, that's because lots of people I know are getting married, and it's nice to celebrate with them,' Connie replied.

Mrs Henstock opened her mouth to speak but just then the door opened and Malcolm walked in carrying a tray.

He'd removed his jacket while helping her with the dishes. He had his shirtsleeves rolled up and his tie loosened which, for the briefest second, reminded Connie of Dr MacLauchlan.

Putting their afternoon tea on the occasional table, he stirred the pot and then poured them all a cup.

He placed the first one on the hearth in front of the tiled fireplace next to his mother. 'There you go, Mum, nice and sweet.'

An oddly girlish expression crinkled Mrs Henstock's sallow face. 'Just like you.'

He gave her an awkward smile, then picked up the remaining cups and carried them over to where Connie was sitting, placing them on the small side table at her elbow.

He pulled his trouser crease up a little and went to sit.

'Malcolm, please,' said his mother in a hurt tone.

'Sorry, Mum,' he sighed.

Unrolling his sleeves, he trudged back into the kitchen, and emerged a few moments later shrugging on his jacket. After re-buttoning his collar, he straightened his tie.

'That's better,' his mother said, smiling approvingly as he sat beside Connie on the sofa. 'Call me old-fashioned but I like to keep up a certain standard.'

Connie picked her tea and took a sip. 'Lovely.'

'It's not too milky, is it?' he asked.

It was but she shook her head. He smiled and shuffled a little closer.

Mrs Henstock's eyes narrowed. 'You don't have to squeeze yourself onto the sofa alongside Connie's knitting, Malcolm, when the other chair's free.'

She indicated the chair on the other side of the fire from her.

'There's plenty of room, Mum,' he replied.

'But you might catch a draught from the window,' she persisted, her narrow forehead gathering in a worried frown. 'And you know how a cold always goes straight to your chest.'

Malcolm smiled indulgently at his mother. 'I'm fine.'

'I was just telling your mum how nice it was to celebrate when friends married,' said Connie, moving so their thighs touched.

He smiled and pressed his leg against hers.

The older woman's lips pulled into a tight bud. 'Well, if you ask me people get married far too quickly these days. They meet someone one week and marry them the next. Love at first sight they call it but I'd call it something altogether less complimentary if I wasn't so well brought up.'

'Well, my cousin and her fiancé have known each other for almost five years so I hardly think you can accuse them of rushing things,' said Connie. 'In fact, if you ask me, Brian should have proposed to Fran three years ago.'

'Huf!' snorted Malcolm's mother. 'I was courting Malcolm's father for eight years before he proposed and then we waited another four before we walked down the aisle. He wasn't in a rush like young men are nowadays.'

'But that was before the war,' said Connie. 'For instance, there was a survey in *Woman's Weekly* last week that said that most men propose after eighteen months.'

'Well, most men are idiots.' Her gaze shifted to her son. 'You wouldn't catch my Malcolm being that stupid.'

Malcolm swallowed hard. 'Well, I'm hoping to get married some day, Mum,' he said, a slight flush creeping up his cheeks.

Mrs Henstock smiled benevolently. 'And I want to see you happily settled before I go to join your father, what mother wouldn't, but I know you're too sensible to rush into anything until you're sure you've found the right girl.'

Under the cover of the knitting, Malcolm's hand found Connie's and gave it a little squeeze. 'I won't, Mum.'

Mrs Henstock's eyes darted between them and her mouth pulled into an ugly line.

'With A Song in My Heart' drifted out of the radio signalling the end of the family request show. There was a pause, then the announcer informed them that that afternoon's Round Britain Quiz would be coming from Hull in the East Riding of Yorkshire and Kendal in Westmoreland and the band featured in *Variety Bandbox* was the Household Calvary band who had just returned from their duties in Germany.

'But now,' he said in his plummy tones, 'Have a Go with your popular host, Wilfred Pickles . . .'

'Not with me he's not,' cut in Mrs Henstock. 'Whatever possessed the BBC to put some northerner who can't speak proper on a Sunday afternoon is beyond me.' She gave Malcolm a sweet smile. 'Would you mind turning over to the Home Service for the gardening programme, Malcolm?'

Malcolm sighed and released Connie's hand. 'Of course, Mum,' he said, rising to his feet.

Watching him twiddle with the knobs, Connie finished her tea. The wireless wowed and whistled a bit until Malcolm found the right wavelength but, as he turned, his mother grabbed her cup and thrust it at him.

'Would you be a treasure, and get me another?' she asked.

Malcolm took his mother's cup and saucer.

'I'm sorry to be a fussy old woman,' she said as he put the strainer on the cup. 'But you know how I hate stewed tea so would you mind making a fresh pot, dear?'

Malcolm smiled wanly. 'Of course not, Mum.'

He sighed again and tramped back into the kitchen, his adoring mother's gaze following him until he left the room.

As the door closed, Mrs Henstock turned her attention back to Connie.

'Such a good boy,' she said as if describing a five-year-old who'd eaten all his dinner. She glanced at the clock and smiled sweetly again. 'Not that I want you to go, Connie dear, but what time did you say you had to be back at Fry House?'

58

Chapter Five

Connie signalled right, turned out of Cambridge Heath Road and joined the late-morning traffic crawling west along Old Bethnal Green Road. Crawling because, like her, the drivers could barely see a hand in front of their face.

It was the middle of October and the mild autumn weather they'd been enjoying for the past few weeks had vanished overnight. According to the *Home Programme*'s morning weather forecaster, it seemed that a combination of an anticyclone over the south of England and people keeping their fires alight all day to keep out the autumn damp had created a choking pea-souper on both sides of the river.

It had first settled over the area last Monday and showed no signs of shifting. Those poor souls with bronchial trouble had had to shove screwed-up newspaper around window frames to keep the noxious atmosphere out.

The yellow headlights of a Number 8 loomed out of the choking gloom and trundled past her. PC Woolmer, the local beat officer, marched between the studs of the pedestrian crossing blowing his whistle; he held up a large white-gloved hand to stop the oncoming traffic. The traffic ground to a halt as the pedestrians, holding handkerchiefs and newspapers over their mouths and noses, shuffled across the road.

As usual, she'd been dashing from one patient to the other since eight-thirty and still had an enema to give to Mrs Freeman in Valance Road. However, as Weinstein's, the chemist, was en route Connie thought she'd kill two birds with one stone and drop Fry House's weekly order in while she was passing.

As she walked by the bombed-out shell of St Jude's on her right, Connie slowed to a halt outside her destination.

Weinstein & Son was sandwiched between a cardboard box factory on one side and a trimmings wholesaler on the other.

Isaac Weinstein, whose name was painted in bold gilt letters across the shop doorway, had opened the dispensary in 1897, the same year that Queen Victoria celebrated her diamond jubilee. He had emigrated from Poland, along with thousands of his faith escaping Russian oppression, and had set up his chemist shop. His son Michael now ran the shop. Sadly, despite being married for almost fifteen years, Michael and his wife Esther had never heard the patter of tiny feet.

The narrow-fronted window was jam-packed with artistically arranged boxes of Radox salts, Pond's face creams, with their pastel-coloured lids, and Twink perm lotion, next to a neat line of shaving brushes with a stick of shaving soap between each.

Securing her bike to the Weinstein's awning bracket and taking her bag from the front basket, Connie headed for the shop door but, as she went to push it, the door opened.

A young mother came out holding a child of about four or five by the hand while two others, who were older, followed behind.

Letting the family pass, Connie stepped into the narrow shop and the smell of soap, camphor and embrocation oil hit her.

The counter ran across the width of the shop with a cast-iron till at one end and a set of baby weighing scales at the other, between them sat a rubber mat saying Exlax for a Regular Life. There were also two charity collection boxes, for Barnardo's and the Jewish Children's Fund, on prominent display in front of the till. Behind the main counter was a screen with stripes of reflective glass, which hid the dispensary from general view but allowed Michael Weinstein to keep an eye on the shop while he was counting out pills. There was a glass display counter on one side which contained cards of hair grips and children's slides, along with packs of razor blades. Above them, in a purpose-built cardboard Max Factor display, were lipsticks and a selection of Pan-Cake foundation with an immaculately made-up Judy Garland endorsing both. The less glamorous items, such as senna pods, haemorrhoid cream and Izal antiseptic toilet paper, were kept on shelves behind the counter, as was the rat poison, bedbug powder and fly paper.

There were a couple of customers in the compact shop waiting for their prescriptions and, as usual, Esther Weinstein was at the end of the counter offering a little lad standing with his mother a lollipop from the constantly refilled jar beside the enamel scales.

The bell above Connie's head tinkled again and Esther looked up and smiled.

Esther was in her late thirties, comfortably built with just the odd grey strand streaking through her dark brown hair. As always, she was wearing bright red lipstick and a spotless three-quarter-length white overall over her dress.

'Off you go now,' she said, ruffling the child's hair. 'And you be a good boy for your mother. You hear me?'

The child nodded solemnly.

Connie stepped aside as his mother led him from the shop, then walked over.

'You'll have Mr Freeman after you again,' she laughed.

'Dentist, Smentist.' Esther threw up her hands. 'A mouthful of sugar, what's the harm?'

Connie smiled back. 'I'm sorry it's late but I have Fry House's order.'

'Come, Connie, come.' Esther beckoned her through to the back of the shop.

Connie slipped behind the counter and into the dispensing area.

Giving Michael, who was mixing up something that looked like Thames mud, a quick wave, Connie followed Esther through to the back.

Like most shopkeepers in the area, Michael and Esther lived above their shop so the minute scullery on the ground floor doubled as an overspill store for items that would spoil if left in the lock-up in the yard. So along with two old armchairs there were boxes of Dr White sanitary towels, bath salts and baby milk stacked around the room.

Esther was already filling up the kettle by the time Connie got into the room.

'I can't stay long,' said Connie, knowing it was a hopeless plea.

'Tush, there is too much rushing here, rushing there,' said Esther, spooning tea into the pot. 'Now, sit, sit.'

Knowing it was fruitless to argue, Connie moved aside a box of Dylon dyes from one of the chairs and sat down, tucking her bag beneath. Esther made the tea and cut her a generous slice of cake.

'Thanks,' said Connie. She yawned.

Esther tutted.

'Look at you,' she said, shaking her head. 'You're wearing yourself to the bone. You girls at Fry House work too hard. It's not right.'

'It can't be helped,' said Connie.

'I thought you were getting more nurses,' said Esther.

'We are,' said Connie. 'In fact, we're interviewing a handful of local nurses next week and we've had a better response from our national advertisement this time around but even if they're suitable we'll have to soldier on for a few more months as they won't start until the new year. Hopefully after that things will get much easier.'

'Well, from your lips to God's ears,' said Esther. 'Have you got the weekly order?'

'Yes,' said Connie, taking the list from her bag and handing it to Esther. 'It's the usual, give or take, but we do need some extra iodine this week.'

'That's fine. Michael's ringing the wholesaler later,' Esther replied, placing the plate in front of Connie. 'So what do you think of our new doctor, then?' Esther asked.

'Do you mean Dr MacLauchlan?' asked Connie, oddly enjoying saying his name.

'Such a lovely boy,' said Esther, pouring the tea. 'So pleasant. So polite, not like that *mishegas* Marshall.'

'Yes, Dr MacLauchlan does seem to be cut from a different cloth,' said Connie.

'And handsome!' continued Esther, carrying the cups over and sitting in the chair opposite Connie. 'Puts me in mind of Tyrone Power, he does. It's a pity he's not Jewish. I have two nieces, lovely girls both, who would be perfect for him but . . .' She gave an exaggerated shrug. 'No doubt one of you nurses will catch his eye.'

'He might already be involved with someone,' said Connie.

'He's not,' Esther replied. 'He did have someone but while he was away fighting she married someone else.' She rolled her eyes. 'Oy vey what could she be thinking? Anyhow, his father was an engineer with North India Railway Company and his mother's related to a Maharajah. He went to Repton School, where he was in the first eleven hockey team and studied at Cambridge and Barts but joined the Royal Medical Corps as a captain when the war started.'

'Goodness,' said Connie, trying not to imagine Dr MacLauchlan in an officer's uniform. 'Did he say where he served?'

Esther shook her head. 'I didn't like to pry. So, Connie, my dear.' She winked. 'He's free.'

'But I'm not, am I?' said Connie.

'Oh, yes, I forgot. Malcolm,' said Esther. 'How is he?'

'He's got a bit of a cold at the moment,' Connie replied. 'Nothing serious although the way his mother's going on you'd think he's got double pneumonia. She keeps carping on about his weak chest.'

'Has he got a weak chest?' asked Esther.

'Not as far as I can tell,' Connie replied. 'But she insists he rub in some disgusting embrocation she gets him at her chemist. When I get home, some nights I smell like I've been out with a mothball.'

A mischievous glint appeared in Esther's eye. 'Do you think Dr MacLauchlan ever needs embrocation rubbing on his chest, Connie?'

'Stop it, Esther!' Connie laughed.

Esther gave her a wide-eyed innocent look. 'I'm just saying.'

Connie laughed again. 'And I'm just going.' She drained the last of her tea. 'Or I'll never be back in time for lunch.'

Pulling her bag out from under the chair, Connie stood up.

'I'll make sure the clinic supplies are delivered as soon as they arrive,' said Esther, rising to her feet too.

'Thanks,' said Connie, as she headed back towards the front of the shop.

'And when you see Dr MacLauchlan give him my regards,' Esther called after her.

Wrapping her scarf back around her mouth, Connie unchained her bicycle and, battling to ignore the images of rubbing embrocation into Dr MacLauchlan's chest, she set off back to the clinic.

Listening to the one o'clock news on the Home Service, Hari sat with his legs folded and a half-filled cup of coffee in his hand as he girded himself for his afternoon visits.

This was his fourth Monday at Christ Church surgery. The first surgery of the week was always busy, however, with the choking fog that had descended over the area the week before, his patient list comprised of both young and old coughing and wheezing with clogged bronchi. All morning he'd been listening to lung crackles and hacking coughs and prescribed so much coal tar for steam inhalation that he wondered if the chemists would soon run out of stock.

Draining the last of his drink, Hari put down the mug. His lounge now bore no relationship to the room he'd walked into on the first day. On a patient's advice he'd taken a stroll down Hackney Road where numerous cabinetmakers plied their trade. As a result he'd been able to replace the woodwormed Victorian sideboard with a new beech one that had sleek modern lines, and a matching low-level coffee table. The suspicious-smelling moth-eaten sofa had been carted away by the rag and bone man and been replaced by a two-seater sofa with moss-green upholstery and two matching fireside chairs. Being just a street or two from Petticoat Lane, Hari was able to buy all the sheets, blankets, towels and curtains he needed at a vastly reduced price, along with a full set of crockery and cutlery from a flamboyant stallholder who threw a complete set in the air to prove its durability.

The Victorian monstrosity that was the cast-iron bed went out the day after he arrived. Having slept on a bare board in the Japanese prison for three years, it was no hardship for Hari to do so again until the new divan from Wickham's had arrived.

As the plummy BBC radio announcer gave the introduction to the next programme, the surgery's front door banged shut.

Rising from the chair Hari picked up his bag and unhooked his coat, scarf and hat from the back door, put them on, then made his way downstairs.

Stepping into the corridor, Hari locked the door to his accommodation. He walked the short distance into the treatment room where Dr Marshall was already sitting behind the desk with a cigarette dangling from his mouth and a newspaper spread out in front of him. He looked up as Hari entered.

'Good afternoon,' said Hari pleasantly.

'Afternoon,' mumbled his colleague. 'I thought you'd be out on your round by now.'

'I'm just going,' Hari replied. 'But before I do, can I raise something with you?'

'Is it going to take long?' asked Dr Marshall, glancing at his watch.

'A minute or two,' replied Hari.

'Very well,' replied Dr Marshall. 'But make it quick.'

'I was told at interview,' he said. 'that the accommodation I was being offered was furnished and had been modernised.'

His colleague's piggy eyes narrowed. 'What of it?'

'Well, for a start it isn't,' Hari replied. 'Even though, according to Mr Merriweather, you've already received a £270 grant from the Ministry for the work. I can't tell you how surprised he was when I queried the matter with him a few days after I arrived. Actually, surprised isn't the right word for his reaction. Downright livid would more accurately describe his state of mind when I informed him that, other than a new toilet bowl and sink, the flat above the surgery looked like Fagin's hideout.'

Dr Marshall chewed the inside of his mouth. 'I grant you the bathroom needs finishing off, but—'

'He was all for sending the auditors down to examine your accounts but I told him you probably intended to complete the work but that you've been caught up with other things,' said Hari.

'It's true. I have been very busy,' said Dr Marshall. 'And the plumber let me down so I—'

'Well you don't have to worry now because I have the matter in hand.' Hari dipped into his top pocket and took out a sheet of headed paper. 'This is the bill from Hanson & Mills, the builders.'

As Dr Marshall scanned down, the purple hues returned to his jowls. 'Free-standing kitchen cabinets, cooker, refrigerator, gas fire in all rooms,' he blustered. 'A bath with a shower and new *boiler*!' He glared at Hari. 'Goddamnit. Have you gone mad?'

'I imagine you have such things in your house,' Hari replied.

'That has nothing to do with the matter,' Dr Marshall bellowed. 'Where do you think I'm going to get the money for all this?'

'From whichever account you deposited the account with £270 from the Ministry in,' Hari replied. 'But you don't have to concern yourself with replacing the scraps of wood and upholstery you laughingly described as furniture, because I've got my own including a new bed. I've put whatever was upstairs in the old stable block at the back and you can take it whenever it suits you. Although I have to confess I had the council take the mattress away for disposal as it was so disgusting even I gagged as I carried it down to the backyard. I have a duplicate copy of the bill but they are expecting payment within the next two weeks. If there is a problem I'll be very happy to speak to Mr Merriweather again.' He touched the peak of his hat. 'I'll be back at four if anyone wants me.'

Leaving Dr Marshall to chew over what he'd said, Hari walked out of the surgery and, with his university scarf covering his mouth, walked into the smog.

Half an hour later, and with a rapidly rising temper, Hari strode to the end of the street and peered up at the street name plate above his head, then down at the A–Z in his hand.

Damn. If this was King Edward Street then Hopetown Passage was in the other direction. Shoving the book in his pocket, Hari retraced his steps as other pedestrians loomed out of the miasma as they approached. He'd been out for three hours and had visited five patients so far and still had three awaiting visits. It was now almost three and the temperature had dropped away allowing the damp to seep into his bones.

Although after four weeks he was becoming familiar with the chief roads dissecting the patch, once he turned off the main thoroughfare it was much more difficult. The area behind Whitechapel High Street was a maze of Victorian alleyways, which twisted and turned north to south and east to west. The confusion was further exacerbated by the fact that many of the street names, removed when the German invasion was thought to be imminent, hadn't been put back. Navigating this labyrinth was difficult enough with normal visibility but in the fog one wrong turn and you easily became completely disorientated amongst the pathways, cut-throughs and courtyards. This was the position Hari now found himself in: cold and damp and hopelessly lost. He knew Quaker House was around here somewhere but feared he was nowhere nearer to locating it than when he turned into Old Montague Street twenty minutes ago.

Trudging back along the road, Hari turned right and by some miracle recognised the baker's shop on the corner. Heading

66

towards it, Hari turned left and could have shouted with joy when he saw the four-storey nineteen thirties block of flats looming out of the grey murk.

Thankful that at last he'd found his next patient, Hari picked his way up to the third floor, carefully stepping between discarded cigarette packets and broken beer bottles on the stairs to number 37. Skirting around a child's tricycle, Hari stopped in front of a dirty-looking door and knocked.

A dog launched itself at the door making it rattle with the impact, appearing every now and again in the frosted glass panel as it jumped up. After a few moments there was a scuffling behind the door and a man shouting and then the door opened.

Standing in the doorway and holding what looked like a bull dog crossed with a Doberman by its leather collar stood a stout man in his mid-twenties with a shaved head. He was wearing shabby trousers held up by a length of washing line and a stained shirt over a grey vest unbuttoned to reveal curly chest hair. A roll-up dangled from his lips, dropping ash as he struggled to hold the dog in check.

'What you want?' he asked, giving Hari a belligerent look.

'I'm looking for Mrs Poe,' Hari replied.

'What for?'

'I'm Dr MacLauchlan and I believe she asked for a doctor to call,' said Hari as the dog snapped and snarled.

'Who is it, Len?' screamed a woman's voice from inside the house.

'Some cheeky darkie saying he's a doctor, Ma,' Len shouted back, not taking his eyes from Hari.

A door slammed and heavy footsteps approached, then an old woman with thinning grey hair and wearing a washed-out overall thrust herself in front of her son. She was no more than four foot ten with a face like a pickled walnut.

She looked Hari up and down. 'Who are you?'

'Dr MacLauchlan,' Hari replied.

'Yeah, and I'm the fucking Queen of China,' she spat back.

'Look, Mrs Poe,' said Hari in as even a voice as he could. 'Someone called the Christ Church surgery this morning to say you were unwell and asked for a doctor to call. I am that doctor.'

'Well you can sling your hook,' snapped Mrs Poe. 'Cause I

ain't having no bloody coon doctor giving me the once-over, so clear off.'

Len dragged the dog in and the old woman slammed the door in Hari's face.

'I'll get the district nurse to call on you in three days, Mrs Finkelstein, but don't take the dressing off until then,' shouted Hari.

Mrs Finkelstein cupped her ear. 'Eh?'

'I said, the nurse will be here in three' – Hari raised the appropriate number of fingers – 'days so don't take the bandage off until then.'

Ledah Finkelstein, who was eighty if she was a day, was dressed in a drab grey dress which hovered around her ankles, thick woollen stockings, scuffed shoes and a threadbare shawl over her jet-black sheitel. Her neighbour had called the surgery when they'd seen the old woman loaded down with shopping and climbing the stairs with blood pouring down her right leg. Thankfully, it was just a bad graze so after giving her a quick check-over and finding nothing amiss, Hari had applied a dressing.

She was Hari's last home visit for the afternoon although it would need a great deal of imagination to see the cramped attic room at the top of a Victorian hovel as a home.

'Don't take the dressing off,' the old woman repeated.

'Not until the nurse gets here,' bellowed Hari.

Mrs Finkelstein's wrinkled face lifted in a toothless smile and she nodded.

She grabbed his arm. 'You're a good boy. How much do I owe you?'

'Nothing,' Hari yelled. 'It's free.'

Mrs Finkelstein looked baffled. 'Free?'

'Yes, under the NHS,' hollered Hari, feeling his vocal chords protest. 'In fact, if you like, I'll refer you for a hearing aid that's free too.'

'Don't trouble yourself, young man.' Reaching into her pocket she pulled out a metal box, a plastic shell and a jumble of wires. 'I've got one but it doesn't work.'

Ten minutes later, after carefully negotiating his way down the creaking stairs, Hari was once again in Fournier Street. It was somewhere close to three-thirty and the atmosphere in the street was now even murkier. The clocks had gone back the weekend before and so now the little sun there had been was rapidly disappearing and the damp chill was creeping in.

Turning up his collar, Hari walked to the end of the street to get his bearings. Thankfully he recognised the dress factory, Gay Paree Mode, on the other side of the road so he knew he was in Commercial Street. Passing the locked-up fruit market on his right, Hari started back to the surgery. However, as he reached the parish church, a district nurse who he didn't recognise whizzed by him on a bicycle and shot around the corner in front of him.

Glancing up at the name plaque, Hari smiled. Then he turned into the same street.

The familiar smell of surgical spirit and iodine drifted up to his nose as he strode into the main hallway.

It was a stock early Georgian house with numerous doorways leading off the main tiled floor hallway and a sweeping wooden staircase leading up to the nurses' quarters above.

Unbuttoning his coat, Hari looked around and spotted the hotel bell on the hall table, went over and bounced his hand off it twice.

A door to his right opened and a stocky middle-aged woman, in an old-fashioned nurse's uniform, a massive white cap reminiscent of a nun's wimple and a sticky-looking infant balanced on her hip, stepped out.

'Good afternoon, matron,' he said.

'It's superintendent,' she said, looking him over suspiciously. 'And as you look both hale and hearty, what can I be helping you with?'

'I thought I might drop by and introduce myself while I'm in the area.' He offered her his hand.

'Introduce yourself, is it?' Her eyes narrowed. 'Well, I hope you're not one of those blasted numbskulls from the Ministry?'

'No, I'm not,' Hari replied. 'I'm Dr MacLauchlan from Christ Church surgery.'

'Are you now?'

'I am.' He offered her his hand. She looked him over again and then, shifting the infant a little, took it.

'Well then, I'm Miss O'Dwyer,' she said, her sandpaper-like grip squeezing his fingers.

'And who's this little chap?' asked Hari, tickling the child she was holding under the chin.

Her wary expression softened a little. 'This is Jimmy Dooley,' she said, twisting the child towards him.

'Hello, Jimmy,' Hari said, giving the child a friendly smile.

Jimmy buried his face in Miss O'Dwyer's shoulder.

'He's a bit shy. His mother has her hands full, so she has, with a new baby so I said I'd mind him so she can have some peace.' She shifted Jimmy onto her other hip and her guarded expression returned. 'Is there anything in particular you're interested in seeing, doctor?'

'Well now you ask, superintendent, having got myself lost twice already this afternoon and being frozen to the marrow, this doctor would be very interested to see if you've a cup of tea left in the pot,' Hari replied, giving her his best smile.

Miss O'Dwyer's round face lifted in a maternal smile. 'I'm sure we can squeeze you one.'

With Jimmy bouncing on her hip as she walked, she led Hari down the corridor and into the modestly furnished staff room. The nurses who were lounging in the chairs and sofa rose to their feet as they walked in.

'Good afternoon, nurses,' Miss O'Dwyer said.

'Afternoon, superintendent,' they replied, as half a dozen pairs of eyes fixed onto Hari.

'This is Dr MacLauchlan,' the superintendent said. 'He's just popped in to say hello.'

'Hello,' he said, as they regarded him with interest.

'So will you fetch the man a cup of tea and make him feel welcomed.'

Three nurses lunged at the tea trolley and between them managed to pour him a cup of tea, a tall blonde nurse handing it to him.

'Thank you, Nurse . . . ' he said, taking it from her.

'Nurse Mason,' said the blonde, a little breathlessly.

Hari smiled. 'Nice to meet you and I hope I'm not disturbing your afternoon tea.'

'Of course not,' said a curvy brunette nurse. 'Cake?'

'Thank you,' Hari replied, taking a plate with a huge rock bun on it.

A nurse with short brown hair exchanged a look with her red-headed friend. 'You can drop by any time, doctor.'

Hari smiled politely, then turned his attention to his refreshments which were delicious.

'So, Dr MacLauchlan,' said a curly-haired nurse perched on the arm of the sofa. 'What brings you to Shoreditch?'

Hari looked up and for a fleeting moment regretted Sister Byrne wasn't amongst the bevy of young women gathered around him, but then his smile broadened. 'Well, ladies, where do I start?'

The mouth-watering smell of lamb stew filled Connie's nose as she walked through the back door of the clinic at four-thirty.

Holding her nurse's bag in one hand, Connie headed for the treatment room to offload her dirty instruments and restock ready for tomorrow when a fit of giggles and high-pitched chatter started in the staff room to her right. Wondering what was going on, Connie opened the door.

The small room at the back had a battered three-seater sofa that was probably made around the time Mafeking was relieved. There was also an odd assortment of easy chairs of a similar vintage. Usually at this time of day there would be one or two nurses lounging around waiting for the dinner gong to sound but today there were a handful of them, including Jane, Beryl and Fran, all chatting excitedly.

'Oh, Connie, there you are,' Fran said, spotting Connie in the doorway. 'You've missed all the excitement.'

'Excitement?'

'Dr MacLauchlan,' laughed Jane as she and Beryl hurried over. 'He was here. Just now. In fact, he's only just walked out of the front door. I'm surprised you didn't bash right into him.'

'I came around the back,' said Connie flatly.

The door opened again and Miss O'Dwyer strolled in wearing what could only be described as a coquettish smile.

'Well, what a lovely man,' she said.

'Wasn't he?' said Fran.

'A real charmer, I'd call him,' agreed Moira Brett, the Hackney Road QN.

She was at least a dozen years older than Connie and had two school-age children, but her eyes shone like a young girl's behind the lenses of her glasses.

'That he is,' Miss O'Dwyer continued. 'Naturally I was on me guard when he walked in as I wouldn't put it past the slippery devils from the Ministry to send some doctor to snoop on us so I says, "Is there anything in particular you're interested in seeing, doctor?" Well, says he, "I would be very interested to see if you've a cup of tea left in the pot," so says I, "I'm sure we can squeeze a cup."'

Moira tapped her cigarette ash into the ashtray. 'And we did, too.'

'Me and Beryl were just finishing afternoon clinic in the treatment room when he arrived,' said Fran.

'He asked lots of questions,' continued Beryl. 'And he wished me luck with my exam.'

'He seems very up to date with things,' said Fran.

'Was he here long?' asked Connie.

'About half an hour,' said Jane.

'He was so pleasant, wasn't he?' said Beryl.

Jane nodded. 'And gentlemanly, too.'

'I thought he was remarkably friendly, for a doctor,' said Fran.

'Said he was just passing so thought he'd pop in,' said Moira.

'Is his mother an Indian princess?' asked another.

'I wonder if he's married,' someone else giggled.

'Or courting?' asked one.

Fran nudged her playfully in the ribs. 'Why didn't you tell us he was so handsome, Connie.'

'I didn't notice,' said Connie, picking a bit of fluff from her jumper.

'Not notice!' Jane rolled her eyes. 'How could you not notice?'

'She's only got eyes for Malcolm,' said someone at the back.

There was a titter of laughter and then the dinner gong sounded.

An image of Dr MacLauchlan surrounded by a cluster of giggling colleagues suddenly formed in Connie's mind.

'To answer your questions; yes, no and I don't know or care if he has all his own teeth,' said Connie, suddenly irritated by their silly interrogation. 'Now, I don't know about you but I'm starving so I'm going down to have my supper.'

Chapter Six

Connie scribbled notes against the last question on her sheet and then looked up at the young woman siting on the other side of the desk.

'Thank you, Miss Copeland,' she said, smiling at the young woman with the bright blonde bob and open face. 'That's all my questions.'

It was the last Wednesday in October and a little over two weeks since Dr MacLauchlan's unexpected visit. Unusually for Connie she wasn't up to her ears weighing babies, explaining how to correctly make up formula milk and advising how to treat nappy rash at the mid-week baby clinic. Instead she was sitting alongside Miss O'Dwyer, who was dressed in her best uniform, frilliest starched cap, and inevitably had a toddler dressed in a blue romper suit playing on the floor at her feet.

Finally, their half-page advert in both the *Nursing Mirror* and *Nursing Times* back in September had paid off and this afternoon she and Miss O'Dwyer were interviewing the handful of experienced applicants who looked most suitable.

'And that's all from me, too,' said Miss Dwyer, tapping the papers together. 'Is there a question you'd like to ask yourself, me darlin'?'

Elizabeth Copeland shook her head. 'No, you've made it all very clear.'

'Well then, thank you for coming, Miss Copeland, and you'll be hearing from us in the next couple of days,' said Connie.

Picking her handbag up from beside her chair, Elizabeth stood up. 'Thank you very much for your time.'

She left, closing the door behind her.

'Well,' said the superintendent, turning towards Connie. 'What a lovely girl and she will fit into Fry House like she was born here.'

'Yes, I'm sure she will,' agreed Connie.

'Well, we're not doing bad then,' said the superintendent.

'No, considering everyone's screaming out for nurses,' said Connie.

'It's a crying shame that other one withdrew her application,' said Miss O'Dwyer, looking at the fourth name on Connie's list which now had a red line through it.

'I can't say I blame her as she lives in East Ham and Church Road clinic in Manor Park is nearer,' said Connie. 'Still, at least we have two definites, Miss Jessop and the one who's just left. I certainly don't think we should offer the second one a post as she couldn't tell the correct proportions of water to salt and starch for an ulcer bandage.'

Miss O'Dwyer's thin lips pulled together. 'You have the right of it there, Connie, and her skirt was a little too short for my liking.' Having untied the superintendent's shoelace, the little boy beside her started to grizzle. Reaching down, Miss O'Dwyer lifted him onto her knee. 'And we still have another to see.'

'Yes, a Miss Grace Huxtable,' said Connie, picking up the last application. 'She has got quite an impressive nursing background.'

Miss O'Dwyer rubbed her roughened hands together. 'Then for the love of Mary, Connie, will you show the woman in?'

Connie laughed.

Standing up, she walked around the desk and opened the door.

Sitting on the end chair alongside the collection of battered prams sat a young woman with glossy black hair, almond-shaped brown eyes and perfectly proportioned cheekbones. She raised her head as Connie stepped out.

Dressed in an elegant and somewhat expensive-looking tailored suit, Grace Huxtable sat with one well-shaped leg crossed over the other.

Her arched eyebrows were carefully pencilled on and her cheeks lightly powdered. 'Miss Huxtable,' said Connie in her most professional voice.

The young woman's Cherry Crush lips lifted into a smile as she stood up.

'Yes.'

Connie offered her hand. 'I'm Sister Byrne, deputy superintendent. Did you find us all right?'

74

'Yes thank you, your instructions were very clear,' Miss Huxtable replied, taking Connie's hand in a firm grip.

Connie showed her into the office.

'This is Miss O'Dwyer,' said Connie.

The superintendent beamed at the young woman standing beside Connie. 'And pleased we are to meet you, Miss Huxtable.' She looked at the baby on her lap. 'Aren't we, Terry?'

The child on her lap blew a dribbling bubble by way of reply.

Miss Huxtable forced a smile. 'You have a little friend, I see.'

'This is Terrence Watson.' Miss O'Dwyer tickled him under the chin making him squirm. 'His mother's had to see the headmaster about his brother so I said I'd mind him.'

'Please take a seat,' said Connie, indicating the empty chair.

As her prospective colleague made herself comfortable, Connie sat back down.

'Well now, me dear,' said Miss O'Dwyer, breaking off a piece of the iced bun that was sitting on a plate at her elbow and offering it to Terry. 'Why don't you tell us a wee bit about yourself?'

Miss Huxtable briefly ran through her childhood in St Albans and her life as the eldest of three vicarage children before moving onto her nursing career.

'I joined the September '36 set of probationary nurses at Barts and qualified a week before war was declared. I joined the QA immediately. I did a stint in the military hospital in Roehampton then, after Dunkirk, I was assigned to Hastings Memorial Hospital. I worked my way up to ward sister and then matron, and in '41 I was reassigned to the 8th Army. I was shipped out to North Africa and then on to Italy where I ran a rehabilitation wing of the main army hospital until the end of the war. When I was demobbed in September '45, I applied to the Epping and District Nursing Association to train as a Queen's Nurse. I started my training in January '46 and qualified last January. I have been sister in charge of the Theydon and Ivy Chimney's area ever since.'

Miss O'Dwyer's eyes flashed up like a pair of lightbulbs. 'Well, you sound like just the sort of nurse we're after, don't you think, Sister Byrne?'

She looked at Connie.

'Indeed.' Connie looked over the young nurse's application

form again. 'You have outstanding references from the superintendent and Mrs Whitworth, the area officer. She even mentions that you would be in the running for the deputy superintendent's post at the Harlow Clinic.'

Miss Huxtable smiled. 'That's kind of her to say.'

Connie referred back to the application form again. 'I also notice that you were off sick from February to May this year—'

'Yes,' said Miss Huxtable. 'I had a nasty chest infection and spent a few months in the country convalescing.'

'And are you back to your old self now, pet?' asked Miss O'Dwyer, her face full of concern.

'I am, thank you,' Miss Huxtable replied. 'Mrs Whitworth was kind enough to keep my post open until I returned to work at the beginning of June.'

'I'm glad to hear as much,' said Miss O'Dwyer as Terry's chubby hand reached up and grabbed her scissor chain. 'I'm a martyr to the bronchioles myself so know it can be the devil's own job to shift them.'

Miss Huxtable smiled politely.

'That was kind of your superintendent,' said Connie.

'Yes it was,' Miss Huxtable replied. 'She was very supportive while I recuperated.'

Connie folded her hands across the paperwork on the desk in front of her. 'In view of that, I wonder why you've applied to come to us.'

Miss Huxtable's serene expression faltered a little and she re-crossed her legs.

Her eyes flickered over the child on the superintendent's lap. 'I felt in need of a change.'

'Well glad we are you do.' Miss O'Dwyer fed Terry another morsel of bun. 'Are you after quizzing us about anything, Miss Huxtable?'

'I don't think so,' the nurse replied. 'It was all explained very well in your initial letter.'

'Grand,' said Miss O'Dwyer, taking her glasses from the end of her nose and slipping them in her top pocket.

Connie smiled. 'Well then, it just leaves me to thank you for coming, Miss Huxtable, and you'll be hearing from us in the next couple of days.'

'That you will,' added Miss O'Dwyer. 'But I think I can be forgiven for saying on this occasion that I look forward to meeting you again.' She tapped the side of her nose and winked. 'Now, if you'd excuse me, I want to pop into the baby clinic before it ends so I'll leave Sister Byrne to see you out.'

She stood up and, heaving Terry onto her hip, hurried out, leaving Connie with Miss Huxtable.

Connie rose to her feet.

'Well, Miss Huxtable,' she said, offering the nurse her hand again. 'It seems we'll be seeing each other again.'

'I look forward to it, Sister Byrne,' Miss Huxtable replied as she took Connie's outstretched hand. 'And, as I said, I'm in need of a change.'

A wry smile lifted the corner of Connie's mouth. 'Well, believe me, after leafy Epping, Spitalfields will certainly be that.'

Connie listened to the pitter-patter sound she could hear through her foetal stethoscope and counted the number of repetitions as the second hand of her watch went from 12 to 6, then she stood up.

'Well, Mrs Atkinson, everything seems to be as it should be.' She placed her instrument on the stainless-steel trolley beside her. 'You can straighten your clothes.'

It was Thursday afternoon, the day after interviewing Grace Huxtable and the other nurses and, as usual, the antenatal clinic had been packed with pregnant women and toddlers since Connie had opened the doors at 1.45 p.m., two and a half hours ago.

Irene Atkinson was a petite red-haired woman with pale eyes framed by almost invisible lashes. She looked like someone whom a strong wind could carry away, not a mother of three, soon to be four, children. She was one of Connie's regulars and each year she produced a small but perfectly formed replica of her husband, Bill Atkinson.

Connie picked up her patient's notes. 'According to your due date, you've a little over a month to go so have you got everything ready?'

'More or less,' Irene replied, wriggling her dress over her

bump. 'Although 'ow I'm going to squeeze another kid into the back room is anyone's guess.'

'I thought you said the council offered you something,' said Connie.

'Yeah, in Dagenham, right out in the bleeding country,' Irene replied.

'I've heard it's very nice,' said Connie. 'The houses have three bedrooms, a bathroom and an inside lavatory so you won't have to share like you do now.'

'It don't sound bad, I grant you, sister,' Irene replied, 'but 'ow am I supposed to get back to go shopping with me muvver down the Roman on Saturday?' She eased herself off the examination couch and stepped into her scuffed, down-at-heel shoes. 'No, we're staying put until the council finds us something in Bethnal Green.'

Connie rolled the screen surrounding them aside and Irene waddled over to the battered pram parked next to the door. Mary, last year's baby, was propped up at one end while Donald, the one from the year before, was sitting up at the other. Taking a pack of ten Senior Service from her pocket, Irene stuck one in her mouth and lit it.

Grabbing the handle of the pram, she kicked off the brake. 'Come on then, youse two,' she said, cigarette smoke escaping from her mouth as she spoke. 'We'd better get 'ome and get your dad's tea on the table or there'll be hell to pay when he gets in.'

She pushed the pram towards the door just as Harriet Henson and her student Queen's Nurse, Jane Paget, walked in.

Harriet, who oversaw the Cambridge Heath Road area, was curvy, with curly light brown hair and a contagious smile. Her student Jane, in contrast, was a slender blonde with blue eyes who wouldn't look out of place on the front of a *Vanity Fair* or *Vogue*.

'You've done well,' said Harriet.

'Yes, haven't we?' said Connie. 'It may have something to do with the good weather so I expect we'll be swamped next Thursday.'

Harriet pulled a face. 'Just my luck to be in charge then, but still it won't be long and hopefully we can put Jane on the rota too.'

78

'Of course, I forgot you've got your exam soon,' said Connie.

'Yes, I got the letter a couple of days ago,' said Jane, not looking too happy about it.

'Don't worry,' said Connie cheerfully. 'I'm sure you and the other two will pass with flying colours, Jane.'

Jane gave a wan smile.

The door opened and Beryl, a happy-go-lucky brunette and Jane's fellow student, walked in.

'You're finished early,' she said, dumping her bag on the nearest chair.

'Thanks goodness,' said Connie. 'Maybe for once I can get off duty on time.'

'You out with Malcolm then?' asked Harriet.

Yes,' said Connie. 'And it would be nice not to be late for once.'

The door opened again.

Miss O'Dwyer's head appeared around the edge of the door frame, causing Jane and Beryl to stand up straight.

'Ah, there you all are,' she said, casting an exasperated glance around the treatment room. 'Can none of you hear that there blasted telephone in the hall?'

'No, superintendent, did it ring?' said Connie.

'Of course it rang,' replied the superintendent. 'Why else would I have been picking it up?'

'I think there's a dodgy connection,' said Harriet. 'The hall one wasn't ringing yesterday evening. Perhaps we should get the Post Office in to check it.'

'I'll get onto them in the morning,' said Connie.

'And be sure to tell them it's urgent,' said Miss O'Dwyer. 'We can't be having people ringing and getting no answer.'

She went to leave.

'What was the phone call?' asked Connie.

'Phone call?'

'The one we didn't hear.'

'Heaven have mercy,' said Miss O'Dwyer, rolling her eyes. 'Haven't I got a head so full of holes today? It was from that darling man, Dr MacLauchlan—'

'Dr MacLauchlan,' said Connie and her three colleagues in unison.

The superintendent beamed. 'Says he's got a patient who needs an urgent visit in the morning but he wants to talk to a nurse about it before we go in so could someone go and see what he has to say.'

'Thank you, superintendent,' said Connie. 'I'll pop in when I've finished.'

'I'm obliged to you, Connie,' said Miss O'Dwyer.

She left.

'You've been up to your neck in it all afternoon, Connie,' said Beryl pleasantly. 'I'll go around to Dr MacLauchlan if you like.'

Connie smiled. 'That's all right. It's my surgery and it won't take a minute once I've cleared up.'

'Didn't you say you wanted to get away on time so you can meet Malcolm?' asked Harriet.

'Well, yes, I did but it—'

'I'll go,' cut in Jane.

'I wouldn't want to put you out,' said Connie.

'You're not,' Jane replied. 'I've got another call to make, so—'

'I haven't,' chipped in Beryl. 'I could be around there and back in the blink of an eye.'

'Beryl, that's so kind of you.' Jane gave her the sweetest smile. 'But my last call is in Hanbury Street so I actually walk past Christ Church surgery.' She heaved a sigh. 'Oh well, I'd better not keep Dr MacLauchlan waiting.'

Catching her bag as she passed, Jane shot out of the door.

Connie stared after her for a moment, then grabbed the sheet from the examination couch and ripped it off.

'Well, I suppose I'd better get tidied up,' she said.

'We'll see you later,' said Harriet.

She and Beryl left.

Guiding the trolley with her foot and carrying the used sheet, Connie headed for the sluice room.

Dropping the sheet in the linen skip, she collected her used instruments and dropped them in the butler sink. She turned on the Ascot and threw a handful of grated carbolic soap into the boiling water. As the acrid smell of the foaming water drifted up and tickled her nose, Connie wondered if there was any truth in the old saying that gentlemen preferred blondes.

*

'That's it done,' said Hari, throwing the probe onto the trolley beside him and dusting the gaping wound with antiseptic powder. 'Now, just place your hand over it while I bandage it into place.'

Hari's patient was Cyril Willis, a beefy-looking porter from Spitalfields market who somehow had been walking about for a week with an abscess the size of a tomato.

'Right you are, doc,' he said and clamped a grubby hand over the gauze behind his right ear.

Picking up a fresh bandage, Hari wound it round his patient's sandy-coloured hair, remembering doing much the same for dozens of malnourished men with jungle ulcers but then he'd had to make do with banana leaves as padding and threadbare strips of vests as a bandage.

Securing the dressing with a safety pin from the trolley, Hari stood back and studied his handiwork briefly before returning to his side of the desk.

'I've got all the muck out for now,' he said, pulling Cyril Willis's notes towards him and taking his pen from his top pocket. 'But you'll have to go to the Fry House clinic so they can clean and pack it each day. I'll let them know to expect you.'

'Ta, doc.' Cyril shoved his hand into his corduroy trouser pocket.

'It should heal up fine,' Hari informed him. 'But be sure to come back if it starts weeping—'

The door flew open and Dr Marshall, with the surgery account book in his hand and dressed as if he were about to spend an hour or two pottering around in the garden, stormed in.

Cyril jumped to his feet and backed away as Dr Marshall barged past him.

'I want a goddamn word with you, MacLauchlan,' he bellowed, jabbing a chubby index finger at Hari.

Hari regarded his colleague for a moment, then looked at Cyril.

'So, Mr Willis,' he said pleasantly. 'Present yourself to the nurses at Fry House tomorrow and keep the dressing dry in the meantime.'

Cyril cast a nervous look at Dr Marshall who stood red-faced and chewing his lip beside him. 'Yes, doctor. And thank you, doctor.'

Whipping his cap from his jacket pocket, Cyril fled.

Hari rested his elbows on the table and laced his fingers together in front of him. 'And a good afternoon to you too, Dr Marshall.'

Dr Marshall's florid colour darkened to an unhealthy purple. 'I don't need the likes of you telling me how to behave.'

Hari stood up. 'I thought perhaps we could at least attempt to be civilised, but no matter. So what is it that is so urgent you have to burst in on me while I'm seeing a patient?'

Dr Marshall held the ledger up. 'I've been going through the prescriptions and—'

'You don't mind if I carry on while we talk,' Hari said, calmly walking over to the trolley he'd been using.

He pushed it towards the sluice door which was behind his colleague. Marshall didn't move.

Hari's mouth pulled into a hard line as he held the other man's gaze. Marshall glared at him for a moment, then stepped aside.

Turning from his colleague, Hari unloaded his equipment into the sink. 'You were saying?'

'I think I made it abundantly clear when I appointed you that I am the senior doctor in this surgery,' said Marshall.

'You did,' Hari replied.

'Well then, I demand to know what right you have to challenge my diagnosis and why you have prescribed a completely different course of treatment?'

Hari turned on the tap. 'Which patient are you referring to?'

'That Jewish boy with the jug ears whose parents own the dry cleaner's around the corner.'

Hari regarded him coolly. 'I think you mean ten-year-old Maurice Klienman.'

'That's him,' said Marshall, pulling out his cigarette.

'Well that's simple.' Hari grabbed the towel. 'I changed the treatment because your diagnosis was completely wrong.'

Marshall's mouth opened and shut a couple of times, then he found his voice. 'Now you look here—'

'No, *you* look here,' cut in Hari. He dried his hands and returned the towel to the hook. 'Firstly, don't ever interrupt me while I'm dealing with a patient. Secondly, you didn't appoint me, the Health Board did and I answer to them not you. Lastly,

I changed Maurice Klienman's treatment because when Mrs Klienman brought her son to see you three days ago complaining of an upset stomach, you diagnosed worms and prescribed Diphenan and a salt enema every other day.'

Dr Marshall's eyes shifted around Hari's face. 'What of it?'

'Unfortunately for Master Klienman, he didn't have worms he had gastroenteritis,' Hari informed him. 'And by the time his mother brought him back yesterday, he had a raging fever and was so dehydrated his eyes had almost disappeared into his head.'

Marshall's eyes flickered. 'Nearly all the little snotty-nosed urchins I see have worms. I thought he was one of them.'

'Well, perhaps if you'd taken his temperature or felt his stomach, as I did, you might have realised his abdominal cramps were not the result of a worm infestation, but eating a dodgy pie in the market,' said Hari tightly. 'Under the circumstances I'd say you're lucky Mrs Klienman came back or the Klienman family might be sitting shiva for their son as we speak.'

Rolling down and rebuttoning his sleeves, Hari stepped past Dr Marshall and resumed his place behind the desk. Picking up his pen, Hari started write up Cyril Willis's notes.

'Now, if there's nothing else I have patients to see. Could I trouble you to tell the next patient to come in as you pass the waiting room, Dr Marshall?' Hari asked without looking up.

Out of the corner of his eye Hari saw Dr Marshall hover uncertainly for a second or two before marching towards the door.

As it clicked shut, Hari threw down his pen and raked his fingers through his hair. Leaning back he stared at the tobacco-stained ceiling.

There was a knock on the door.

Hari sat forward, knocking his pen onto the floor with his elbow.

'Come!' he shouted, reaching down to pick it up.

The door opened and closed.

Looking across the floor from under the desk he saw a pair of solid lace-up flat shoes, a pair of black-stockinged legs and the hem of a navy nurse's uniform.

A smile lifted the corners of Hari's mouth as he straightened up.

'Good afternoon, sister . . .'

'Good afternoon, Dr MacLauchlan,' said the willowy blonde standing in the middle of the room. 'And it's nurse. Nurse Ogilvy.'

'Thank you for calling, Nurse Ogilvy. If you'd like to take a seat I'll run through the patients I'm referring,' Hari said, hurriedly concealing his disappointment.

Perching on the chair on the other side of the desk Nurse Ogilvy gave him a lavish smile. 'It's Jane, actually, doctor.'

Suddenly realising he preferred warm copper curls to the cool ash-blonde variety, Hari returned the smile professionally. 'Well, Nurse Ogilvy, shall we begin?'

'It's been just the same here, Millie,' Connie said. 'We've had patients queuing halfway down Middlesex Street every day.'

It was somewhere near to five on the first Thursday in November and the curtains had been closed and the light on against the dark night since four in the afternoon. With the room snugly warmed by the three-bar electric fire in the old grate, Connie was sitting with her back against the footboard of her bed while Millie Smith, her long-standing friend, sat at the other end of the bed.

She and Millie, a lively brunette, had sat in this comfortable and informal way for some eight years or more.

Their friendship had been formed as student nurses in the London Hospital's 1937 intake into Tredegar House and had been forged in fire when, as third-years, they had volunteered to stay behind at the outbreak of war instead of being evacuated to Brentwood.

They went their separate ways to do both parts of their midwifery training but were reunited for the Queen's Nurse training at the St George and St Dunstan's Nursing Association, based just three miles down the road in Stepney. Millie still worked there as deputy superintendent but now lived in Leytonstone.

Millie had become Mrs Smith the previous December when she'd married the Right Honourable James Percival Woodville Smith. However, despite his aristocratic background, Millie's husband, who was desperate to be adopted as a local Labour

Party candidate, insisted on being called Jim Smith, to underpin his egalitarian credentials.

Handsome and charming, Jim Smith would set any woman's heart racing but Connie wouldn't trust him as far as she could throw him.

Millie laughed. 'I suppose I can't blame them. And I'm sure things will soon settle down.'

Connie didn't look convinced. 'You've been saying that for months and it's still no better but at least there's more of us now to deal with it all.'

'Lucky you,' said Millie. 'Miss Dutton won't hear of having part-time nurses. Says it's not "professional".'

'That's a great shame because now we have Penny and Eileen, both experienced district nurses, who work two days a week apiece while their children are at school. Polly covers the odd night on call with midwifery when needed, plus Lilly, Rose and Lucy to help with the bath and wash rotas. And there are three new QN sisters starting in January.' Connie gave her friend a satisfied smile. 'So now in Fry House we have nurses who live out, are married women, part-time nurses and ancillary nursing assistants.'

Millie gave a wry smile. 'Old Sister-Iron-Knickers-Bradshaw must be turning in her grave.'

Remembering their Queen's Nurse tutor who held it an unforgivable sin for a nurse to have a private life, Connie laughed.

They chatted on between cups of tea about Millie and Jim's decision to put off starting a family until he'd secured a seat and then onto the latest gossip at their respective nursing associations until the conversation got round to Connie's love life.

'How's Malcolm?' Millie asked.

'Oh, same as ever. Monday we sit in, Wednesday it's the pictures, Saturday at the Rose and Punch Bowl for a quiet drink, and then Sunday lunch at his mother's one week and mine the other,' Connie replied flatly.

'Oh, that's nice,' said Millie, her tone saying otherwise.

'Of course Malcolm goes to his model railway club on Tuesday and I go shopping with Mum on Saturday while he's train-spotting at Stratford,' Connie added, annoyed with herself for sounding defensive.

'What do you do on Thursday?'

'Wash my hair.'

Millie took another mouthful of tea.

Connie didn't blame her friend for thinking her and Malcolm's unvarying social life was dull because it was and saying it out loud only confirmed that.

'And how long have you been walking out?' asked Millie.

'Two years, three months next week, since the St Andrew's Hospital funding dance at Poplar Town Hall.'

Millie smiled. 'Has he mentioned anything about getting engaged yet?'

Connie expression slipped further. 'We've discussed it a couple of times but we don't want to rush things. And neither does his mother.'

'I can imagine,' said Millie. 'Every time I've met her she seems to make a point of telling me how she and her late husband were courting for twelve years before they got married.'

'Which goes some way to explain why she only had Malcolm, but I'm not bothered,' said Connie, trying to sound as if she meant it. 'With all the things going on at the moment, I'm quite pleased he's not rushing to settle down. Did I tell you that we're setting up a special health programme for the prostitutes in the area?'

'Goodness,' said Millie. 'It's about time, but I can't see any of the local GPs being very keen to take it on.'

'Neither did I but Super asked the new doctor appointed by Area if he'd be interested in the project and he suggested me as the lead nurse so, even if Malcolm proposed tomorrow, I haven't got time to sort out a wedding and set up a home. Now, have you got time for another?'

Millie glanced at her watch.

'Oh, all right,' she said. 'But I have to be on the train by five if I don't want Jim walking into an empty house.'

That wasn't likely because as far as Connie could tell, Jim, who worked for the Ministry of Labour, rarely got home on time and sometimes not at all.

Connie stood up. 'You put your feet up while I go and put the kettle on.'

Picking up the tray, Connie hurried down to the kitchen and made another pot of tea.

86

She returned to find Millie studying the picture of Malcolm propped up on Connie's bedside cabinet.

Connie handed her friend her replenished cup and put hers on the floor next to where she was sitting.

'I haven't seen this before, is this a recent one?' asked Millie, indicating the photo.

'Last year,' Connie replied, settling back on the bed. 'But I've only just prised a copy off his mother.'

She glanced at the familiar photo of Malcolm in his usual tweeds and knitwear with his pipe clenched between his teeth and holding a model steam train in one hand and a rosette in the other.

'He won first prize in the Great Eastern Railway oo-gauge pre-1939 Locomotive Class at the East of England Model Railway Enthusiasts' Club summer meeting at Stowmarket,' Connie continued.

'Were you with him?' asked Millie.

'Yes, we made a weekend of it,' she said, the tedium of three full days of debating gauge, engine class, and optimum track layout flashing across her mind.

Her friend winked. 'Separate rooms, I hope.'

'Millie Smith!' Connie said, struggling to suppress a smile. 'What are you suggesting?'

Millie laughed and Connie did too.

'So,' she said, taking a sip of her tea. 'Who's this new doctor?'

'Dr MacLauchlan,' Connie replied. 'He's working at Christ Church surgery.'

'Not with that dreadful Dr Marshall,' said Millie.

'I'm afraid so,' said Connie. 'Although, in truth, since Dr MacLauchlan arrived, I've hardly seen old Marshall as he seems to spend most of his time on the golf course.'

'Still, from the way you describe him this new doctor is better off without him,' said Millie.

'He is,' said Connie. 'Or he would be if Dr Marshall hadn't signed on dozens of new patients before the NHS started so he could collect the fees.'

'Typical.' Millie rolled her eyes. 'So what's he like, then, this new doctor?'

'He always seems very affable when I pop in and he hasn't

actually said anything but I get the impression he's had a bit of a rough time of it at first but over recent weeks people have been telling me how easy he is to talk to and always seems to know what's wrong and how to treat it,' said Connie.

'The opposite of Dr Marshall then,' said Millie.

'Totally,' Connie agreed. 'Of course there are still those who won't go to him because of his colour but they are becoming fewer and fewer. He's also very up to date, with all the new drugs and treatments too.'

'I'm sure he is.' Millie gave her a wry smile. 'But what I want to know is, is he handsome and single and have any of the nurses got their eye on him?'

'He is quite attractive,' Connie replied, in what she hoped was a neutral voice. 'And according to Esther Weinstein, he's single, went to Cambridge and is a Barts man but joined the Royal Medical Corps when war broke out.'

'And is he short and blond or tall and dark?' asked Millie.

'He's certainly tall,' said Connie. 'Six two, possibly an inch or so taller, and his mother is Indian so he's obviously dark.'

'He sounds gorgeous,' said Millie.

Connie's pulse quickened ever so slightly.

'I suppose he is,' she said, burying her nose in her mug to hide her warming cheeks from her friend.

'So, as you can see,' said Mr Rossiter, tapping the pointer in his right hand against the diagram suspended behind him. 'GPs who know their patients' health and circumstances better than anyone else are vital to the continuing success of the NHS.'

It was ten o'clock on a freezing November evening and Hari was sitting in the Redcoat Secondary school's main hall, surrounded by his colleagues.

Well, surrounded would be overstating it because sadly the vast majority of chairs in the room still had their information leaflets and sample forms untouched on their seats. In a hall that could comfortably accommodate eight classes of pupils, there were no more than a dozen local GPs.

Mr Rossiter, a beefy chap who looked as if he'd been poured into his suit, was the Ministry of Health's bureaucrat responsible for the area's GPs.

'May I point out that despite the minister agreeing to the set fees back in June we, the doctors without whom this ridiculous socialist fiasco couldn't function, still haven't received the reimbursement we are due,' barked Dr Marshall. 'So unless we see some positive movement in this regard, the General Medical Council has instructed us to follow the lead of every other Tom, Dick and Harry in this country and withdraw our labour.'

Hari had to confess he'd been surprised to see Dr Marshall already at the meeting when he'd arrived two hours ago. Marshall had acknowledged him with the barest of nods as Hari took his seat on the other side of the room. Ignoring the hostile glances from the knot of expensively dressed doctors gathered around his so-called partner, Hari settled down to listen to the man from the Ministry passionately extol Aneurin Bevan's vision of a universal health system before fending off a barrage of hostile questions.

'We're experienced doctors, not civil servants,' continued Marshall.

Mr Rossiter gripped the edge of the podium in front of him. 'As I have explained, the minister has conceded—'

'Minister!' sneered Marshall. 'Goddamn coal miner, you mean.'

The clique around him muttered their agreement.

'The minister has assured me that all outstanding fees and claims will be settled,' persisted Mr Rossiter. 'And perhaps we could remember there are ladies present.'

He indicated the lone female in the room, an elderly woman in tweed sitting a couple of rows in front of Hari.

'Your pardon, doctor,' said Dr Marshall, glancing at her.

She waved her hand. 'I've heard worse from better.'

There were a couple of chuckles and Dr Marshall's lips pulled into a hard line as he turned his attention back to the Ministry official.

'If you ask me, this welfare state is nothing more than Communism by the back door.' Marshall stood up. 'And I for one am in need of a drink.'

His cronies did the same and they headed for the door, scraping chairs and grumbling as they made their exit.

There was a pause and then Mr Riley, the chairman of the

local Labour Party, a chap in his mid-thirties with a pencil moustache, stepped forward.

'Well, I'm sure we would all like to thank Mr Rossiter for taking the time to come here tonight and explain some of the government's teething troubles. As promised, there are refreshments at the back and I'm sure Mr Rossiter will be happy to chat over a well-earned cuppa.'

Mr Riley led the applause and Hari joined in briefly before rising to his feet and heading for the table at the back of the hall.

Taking his tea and helping himself to a biscuit, Hari strolled back down the centre of the hall to study the chart propped up on an easel at the front of the stage.

It was a pictorial representation of the new Health Service structure. In the centre, there was a picture of a couple with a happy little girl beside them, this image was surrounded by a list of the services, such as blood transfusions, mental health care, domestic help and vaccinations, that the family would be able to access. His gaze came to rest on the image of a nurse, in the same uniform as Sister Byrne, who was bandaging a patient while they sat beside a roaring hearth.

'Well, how do you think it's working so far?' asked a woman's voice, cutting through Hari's musings.

He turned to see the lone woman in the hall standing beside him.

She was dressed in a tweed suit with a frilly blouse beneath and her crinkly grey hair was piled up and held secure by an assortment of combs, slung around her neck was a string of pearls and a chain with her metal-rimmed spectacles attached.

Although she must have been somewhere in her early sixties, her face was deeply wrinkled, her gaze penetrating as she scrutinised him.

'I'm Dr Gingold from the Cable Street surgery.' She offered her hand. 'You must be Dr MacLauchlan from Christ Church surgery.'

'How did you guess?'

'Shot in the dark,' she replied with a twinkle of amusement in her eye.

Hari smiled and shook her hand, surprised to find her grip matched his.

'You didn't sit with Dr Marshall,' said Dr Gingold, taking a sip of tea.

'We see more than enough of each other at the surgery,' Hari replied. 'And he didn't seem short of friends.'

A smile lifted the corners of Dr Gingold's pale lips. 'So have you settled in?'

'More or less,' Hari replied. 'Finding where I'm going for the home visits has been a bit of a problem but I think I'm finally getting the lie of the land. Although, I turned the wrong way two days ago and found myself in Brick Lane instead of Brushgate Street.'

Dr Gingold laughed. 'How are you getting on with the patients?'

'Once they get over the shock of seeing a darkie in a suit sitting behind a desk, they seem to be fine,' Hari replied. 'Although I am getting a little tired of being asked if I'm a real doctor.'

'Well, you have to admit you're a bit of a novelty.' Dr Gingold regarded him thoughtfully. 'It's not as obvious, but I'm an assortment myself. Russian and Austrian on my maternal side, Belgium on my paternal and Jewish on both. Thankfully, I was in Antwerp in May 1940 when the king surrendered to the Nazis so, along with thousands of others, I headed for the coast. I managed to clamber on a boat at Ostend and landed in Southampton with a small suitcase, my University of Vienna medical certificates and speaking not a word of English so, believe me, I know what it's like to be regarded as an oddity.' She took another sip of tea. 'Have you finally got a QN attached to Christ Church surgery?'

'Yes,' Hari replied. 'Sister Byrne. She seems very on the ball.'

Dr Gingold's face lit up. 'Pretty girl with the red hair?'

'Well, yes, she is quite good-looking but more burnished copper than a redhead,' said Hari. 'Do you know her?'

'Yes, Connie used to nurse with the St George's and St Dunstan's Association near me,' said Dr Gingold. 'Such a dear girl. Say hello to her from me, will you?'

'I will but I'm not sure when she's popping in next,' Hari replied.

'Oh well, you'll be able to catch her at the Friends of Fry

House Annual Dance next Saturday if not.' Dr Gingold gave him a questioning look. 'You are going, aren't you?'

'Well, it's the first I've heard of it,' Hari replied.

'Everyone goes,' Dr Gingold continued. 'The mayor, the local MP and even some of the consultants from the London. It will be good for you to put some names to faces. And Sister Byrne's bound to be there, too.'

Hari smiled. 'I won't promise but as I haven't got anything else on I might pop by. Where is it?'

'It's in the Shoreditch Town Hall, just a short walk away,' Dr Gingold replied. 'It starts at seven or thereabouts. Just ring the Friends of Fry House's secretary and she'll leave a ticket on the door for you.'

'Thanks.' Hari caught sight of the clock. 'I ought to go but can I see you safely home?'

Dr Gingold gave him a fond smile. 'God bless you for asking but I'm quite safe.'

Hari finished his tea. 'Well, it's been nice to meet you, Dr Gingold,' he said. 'I hope we run into each other again sometime.'

'I'm sure we will,' she replied. 'After all, we mongrels should stick together.'

Chapter Seven

'What do you think of this?' asked Connie, holding the blue polka-dot dress against her winter coat and swinging the full skirt back and forth.

'It's a bit dressy for the clinic's dinner and dance,' said Malcolm, his breath visible in the chilly December air.

It was the last Sunday in November and they were standing alongside Alma Ruben's clothing stall in the middle of Petticoat Lane market. As usual, the place was heaving. Although it was now almost midday and the stalls had been open for four hours, the market was still in full swing and would be for another two hours. A few of the nurses had already finished their shopping, their arms full of bargains, by the time Malcolm arrived an hour ago.

Predictably, once his mother had heard they were planning to meet at ten she decided to go to the nine-thirty service at St Philip's instead of her usual eight o'clock one.

'Well, I want to make a bit of a splash,' said Connie, studying herself in the mottled mirror tied to the metal rail. 'Do you like it?'

Malcolm, wearing his navy duffel coat, considered the question for a second or two, then nodded. 'It looks very nice.'

Connie swung it back and forth again and then grinned at him. 'Yes it does, doesn't it? In fact, I think it looks better than nice. It looks splendid.'

She turned to the stallholder hovering at the back of the stall where a couple of young women were trying on jackets.

'How much?' asked Connie, holding up the gown.

Leaving her undecided customers to their own devices, Alma hurried over.

Although she sold some of the most up-to-date dresses and suits on the market, Alma herself always wore a dark grey dress which skimmed her ankles with either a saggy cardigan in the summer or, as now, a man's khaki trench coat. Over the top of this outfit she wore a deep-pocketed apron tied securely around her waist. She was in her mid-forties and her grey hair was tucked away under a tightly tied scarf. She had a wily look in her soft grey eyes.

Alma studied Connie for a couple of seconds, then smiled. 'You're from Fry House, aren't you?' she said, flashing a gold tooth as she spoke.

'Yes.'

'I thought I recognised you.' Alma cast her eyes admiringly over the gown Connie was holding. 'It's very you.'

'How much?' Connie asked again.

Alma glanced over her shoulder and tapped the side of her nose. 'Straight from a factory supplying the top West End shops it is,' she whispered.

Connie suppressed a smile. 'So what are you asking for it?'

'Two pounds ten,' said Alma. 'And you'd pay four times or more in any shop.'

With a sigh and great reluctance, Connie put the dress back on the rail.

'I tell you what,' said Alma, rubbing her hands, 'and I'm robbing myself but give us two and a half quid and it's yours.'

'I'd love to, but . . .' Connie smiled regretfully and turned away.

'Your young man thinks you'll look beautiful in it, don't you?' she looked expectantly at Malcolm.

'Y . . . yes . . . y . . . you . . . will,' he agreed, blinking rapidly.

'All right, ducks.' Alma clapped her hands and then unhooked the gown, draping it over her arm. 'Call me a soft-hearted old fool if you like but bung me two guineas and that's as low as I can go.'

Connie considered for a couple of seconds, then smiled. 'I'll take it.'

'Course you will.' The stallholder winked. 'And you'll be glad you did when you see your young man's face when you wear it.'

While Alma folded her bargain into a crumpled paper bag with C&A stamped on the side, Connie counted out her money.

'There you go,' she said, handing over two pounds and a florin.

Alma's money-dirtied hand closed around it and she shoved it deep into the pocket of her apron. 'Come again and bring your friends,' she said over her shoulder as she returned to her other customers.

Malcolm glanced at his watch. 'It's almost one, we ought to get back.'

'Don't worry. We've got time to go back to the shoe stall for the patent pair I liked,' Connie said, slipping her arm through his. 'They'll go just right with the dress and Mrs Rogerson will keep us dinner if we're a bit late.'

Thankfully the shoes she'd spotted earlier were still there and after a bit of a toing and froing over price, Connie handed over five shillings, feeling well satisfied with her purchases.

Skirting around a blanket set out on the cobbles with clock-work toys swirling around on it, Connie and Malcolm headed home.

They turned into Commercial Street but, as they were about to cross the road by the Ten Bells public house, the door swung open.

A man with a shaven head and dressed in a navy Crombie stepped out. Holding the door open, his hooded eyes looked up and down the street, then he nodded.

Michael Patrick Murphy, wearing a camel-coloured top coat with a brown velvet collar, pinstriped trousers and polished leather shoes, stepped out.

Known as Micky the Knocker because of his unbeaten record in the boxing ring, he topped Connie by no more than a couple of inches. With cropped greying hair, a non-existent neck and shoulders so wide he would only just fit through a door, he resembled a corn-fed bull.

Although he insisted on being recorded as a gentleman of private means on the police charge sheets, Micky had a podgy finger in every business, legitimate or otherwise, in Spitalfields, Shoreditch, and much of the surrounding area. Rumour had it that, having strong-armed a doctor for a medical exemption from the call-up, Micky had set up MM suppliers in a railway arch in Bethnal Green but it was common knowledge, even to the police, that his most lucrative but stolen stock was secreted in dozens of anonymous sheds, cellars and lofts across much

95

of East London and Essex. That was almost ten years ago and although he still lived in the same workman's cottage in White's Row, Micky now had a Daimler, a gold ring on every finger and a race horse.

''Allo, Sister Byrne,' he said, a friendly smile lifting his heavy features. ''Ow is my favourite nurse?'

'I'm very well, Mr Murphy,' Connie replied politely.

Micky snapped his finger and his burly sidekick produced a gold case from his pocket and flipped it open.

Micky took one of the half-dozen Churchill-style cigars and bit off the end, his henchman held a Ronson lighter to the end of the cigar as Micky drew on it.

His gaze flickered over Malcolm. 'This your young man then?'

'Yes, this is Malcolm Henstock,' Connie replied. 'He works for the council in Roads and Highways.'

Micky's fleshy face took on a speculative look. 'You must know Bert Riley then.'

'Not very well,' admitted Malcolm. 'He's the head of the department and I'm just a junior.'

'But Mr Riley relies on Malcolm ever such a lot,' said Connie, remembering Malcolm's countless and tedious conversations about his boss.

Micky looked amazed. 'Does he?'

Malcolm nodded. 'Mainly when it comes to the sewers,' he said, beaming at the squat man puffing on a cigar. 'If there's a main drain that needs unblocking, I'm the first person Mr Riley calls for.'

Amusement rippled over Micky's face.

Connie hooked her arm through Malcolm's. 'We ought to go.'

'Me and Bert are always running into each other so perhaps I can put in a good word for you,' said Micky.

'That's very kind of you,' said Malcolm.

'Don't mention it.' Micky blew a stream of smoke skywards. 'And perhaps you can return the favour when my application for Brewer Street flats goes before the planning committee.'

'I'll try,' said Malcolm. 'Although I'm not sure Mr Riley will take much—'

'Nice to meet you, Mr Murphy,' said Connie, tugging on Malcolm's arm. 'But if we don't hurry we'll miss dinner.'

'Course,' said Micky affably. 'I wouldn't want to keep a man from his grub.'

Malcolm offered his hand. 'Nice to meet you, Mr Murphy.'

Micky grabbed it. 'And you. Henstock, did you say?'

'Yes, Malcolm Henstock,' he replied as Micky shook his arm from his socket.

Connie dragged him away.

'If he doesn't remember me tell him I'm the chap who sits at the desk by the back window,' Malcolm called over his shoulder as Connie hurried him across the road.

'He seemed nice,' said Malcolm, flexing the hand Micky had shaken. 'Do you think he will remember to mention me to Mr Riley?'

Connie cast a surreptitious look across the road at Micky Murphy moseying along with his chest out, smoking a cigar that probably cost more than most families spent on their daily food.

'I really hope not,' she said.

'I thought you might want to pace yourself a bit so I got you a plain tonic this time around,' said Malcolm, handing Connie her drink.

'For goodness sake, Malcolm,' said Connie. 'You make it sound as if I've knocked back a bottle of gin already.'

It was the first Friday in December and exactly three weeks to Christmas. She and Malcolm were standing under the ornately decorated Victorian arched celling of Shoreditch Town Hall at the Spitalfields and Shoreditch Association's annual dance.

Without the wealthy patrons and supporters that other nursing associations in more affluent areas enjoyed, the Spitalfields and Shoreditch had been strapped for cash since it was founded. To raise funds from some of the poorest people in the capital, the association's nurses were pulled in to play their part. During the Association Flag Day, the nurses could be seen on the main thoroughfare in the area rattling tins. Local shopkeepers were also asked to have a collection tin on their counters and many sold the association's monthly lucky draw tickets in an attempt to raise enough money to pay staff wages.

The annual dance was traditionally an important fundraising evening and at previous events Connie, along with every other nurse, had been obliged to dance with any man who had bought a ticket at the function. This was regardless of his personal hygiene, toe-crushing skills or level of halitosis. The tickets were always green, which reflected pretty much how the whole experience left the nurses around the gills.

However, this year the aim of the dance wasn't fundraising but fun, which meant Connie was free to dance with Malcolm all evening. That, of course, was if she could ever persuade him onto the floor.

Malcolm looked crestfallen. 'I was just thinking of you having to get up in the morning.'

'I know,' said Connie, placing her hand on his arm. 'But I don't think a couple of G&Ts will stop me hearing the alarm.'

She smiled and he smiled back and patted her hand.

'I'm a bit surprised you agreed to swap duty with your friend for tomorrow,' he said.

'I wouldn't have but Winnie's just got engaged and the two families are meeting up tomorrow while her fiancé's parents are in town,' Connie replied.

Malcolm's sandy-coloured eyebrows rose in astonishment. 'Another one of your friends getting engaged.'

'Yes,' said Connie, looking him in the eye. 'It's quite a common thing for a couple to do when they've been courting for a few years, Malcolm.'

He lowered his eyes and swallowed a mouthful of bitter shandy.

Connie turned to watch her friends and their partners glide around the room.

The hall was packed with revellers. The Swingerlier, the nine-piece band dressed in American-style wide-collared drape suits, was halfway through a stomping rendition of 'Sweet Georgia Brown'.

Now clothes rationing had ended, every woman in the room, including Connie in her blue polka-dot bargain, was wearing some variation of Dior's New Look. After years of being forced to wear close-fitting A-line skirts, the room was awash with colour, yards of fabric and swirling lace petticoats.

The lead trumpeter took the dancers seamlessly into 'Chatta-nooga Choo Choo' and the guests continued to dance.

'I love this one,' said Connie, her feet already tapping. She looked expectantly at Malcolm.

'It's a bit fast for me,' he said, taking another sup from his pint.

'Oh come on, Malcolm, just one dance,' coaxed Connie.

'When a slow one comes on, promise,' said Malcolm. 'And it's not as if you've not had a couple of turns around the floor.'

'Yes, with the chairwoman's husband and Mr Petroski the dentist, who could just about lift his feet as he's old enough to be my father,' said Connie, swaying with the rhythm. 'Honestly, Malcolm, what's the blooming point of coming to a dance if you don't want to enjoy yourself?'

'But I am,' he replied, looking a little wounded. 'I always enjoy being with you, Connie.'

Guilt-ridden, Connie slipped her arm through his. 'And I enjoy being with you, too,' she said, rallying a smile. 'It's just that—'

'Sorry, Connie,' Malcolm cut in. 'I've just spotted the chairman of the Ilford and West Essex Model Railway Club and I need to have a word with him about our East London Club boys joining them for their summer show. I promise I won't be more than two shakes of a lamb's tail.'

He downed the last of his pint and hurried off towards the far end of the hall.

Connie watched him for a second or two then, taking a sip of tonic water, she turned to watch the dancers again.

Her heart thumped painfully in her chest as her eyes fixed on the tall figure of Dr MacLauchlan.

The men, too, had taken advantage of the abolition of rationing and many in the hall wore the new square-shoulder-style jacket with sharp creases in their wide-kneed trousers, but compared with Dr MacLauchlan they looked as if they were dressed in potato sacks from the market.

Wearing a double-breasted navy suit that was clearly made to measure, he couldn't help but attract attention. As always, his hair was without brilliantine and swept back into gentle waves. The crisp whiteness of his shirt collar highlighted his tan skin and the Windsor knot of his Royal Army Corps tie completed his stylish appearance.

Holding a glass tumbler in his hand, Dr MacLauchlan

surveyed the scene with a relaxed smile, his toe tapping in time with the music. Connie also noticed that Jane and Beryl, who had been standing near the stage, were now just behind him.

The musicians played the last bars of the song and the dancers glided to a stop. Connie joined in the applause as the conductor bowed and turned to raise his baton again. As his arm lifted, signalling the start of the next song, the three violins sang out the opening bars of 'I Only Have Eyes for You'.

Dr MacLauchlan turned and looked at her. Connie held her breath as he stared across at her for a heartbeat then, putting his drink on the table, he strolled across the dance floor, stopping just in front of her.

'Good evening, Sister Byrne,' he said.

She smiled. 'Good evening, Dr MacLauchlan.'

If he thought Sister Byrne had looked pretty enough across the room, Hari was completely floored by how stunning she looked close up.

Under the soft light of the chandeliers overhead, the colour of her dress highlighted the blue of her eyes. Her hair, which had been rolled and tucked securely under her hat the last time they meet, now curled onto her shoulders and bounced as she moved.

'Are you enjoying the dance?' he asked.

'Yes, very,' she replied. 'But I didn't think I'd see you here.'

'You nearly didn't,' he replied. 'Would you like to dance?'

She looked a little taken aback. 'Er ... Of course, Dr MacLauchlan.'

Hari gave her his warmest smile. 'Sister Byrne, I'm not ordering you, I'm asking you.'

She smiled. 'Sorry, I'd love to.'

He held out his hand. She took it and he led her onto the dance floor.

If truth be told, Hari had thought Dr Gingold's suggestion that he should attend the Spitalfields and Shoreditch Nurses' Association dance was a jolly good idea as soon as she'd mentioned it.

He'd told himself it was because he'd be able to meet a number of the local health officials, fellow GPs and local councillors informally but, if he were honest, it was the prospect of a turn around the floor with Sister Byrne that had convinced him to attend.

The band was playing a quick step so, drawing her to him, Hari encircled her lightly with his right arm and she placed her hand on his upper arm. He held her for the beat and then they stepped off.

They danced to the end of the floor, the faint hint of gardenia drifting up as they moved.

He glanced around. 'There's a good turn-out.'

'Yes, isn't it?' Connie replied. 'The Christmas bash used to be our main fundraiser but after all we've been through I think people want to keep it going even if the government are paying for the Old Girl services now,' she replied politely. 'After all, the Spit and Ditch Christmas dance has been going for almost as long as the association itself and that's nearly seventy years.'

'Goodness,' he replied, guiding her into a back step.

'Yes, it was one of the first in the London,' she replied. 'When it was founded, Spitalfields was one of the worst rookeries in London.'

'Really?'

'Yes. In fact, Fry House used to be a doss house,' she continued. 'If you look up above the windows on the second floor you can just make out Moody's Lodging House.'

'I'll do just that when I pop in next time.'

Holding her close, Hari swirled her around to avoid another couple and her full skirt rustled against his leg.

'So how are you settling into the surgery?' she asked.

'Not too bad,' he replied. 'But I'll be a lot happier when the new bath gets plumbed in on Thursday.'

She looked shocked. 'You haven't got a bath?'

'Not one that you'd want to sit in.' Hari gave a wry smile. 'Thankfully I found the bathhouse in Goulston Street on my second day or you wouldn't have so readily said yes to a dance.' Hari did a half turn at the top corner and she followed the move perfectly. 'I've become a bit of a regular at the baths,' he continued. 'Although I get the impression that the washhouse attendant regards me turning up with a towel under my arm every other day as a bit eccentric.'

'I imagine he does, as most people around here make do with

a strip wash in the kitchen sink most days.' Amusement glinted in Sister Byrne's eyes for a second then she giggled. 'I'm sorry, Dr MacLauchlan, I've just got a vision of you marching down Middlesex Street with a towel under your arm.'

Hari joined in and then, realising how long it had been since he'd held a laughing girl in his arms, he swirled her around again.

'Didn't you complain about your accommodation?' she asked.

'I most certainly did,' replied Hari, 'which is why I've got a new bathroom suite being installed and the Gas Board fitting a new cooker on Friday. Once that's done, the place will be just like Buckingham Palace.'

Sister Byrne laughed again.

The last blast of the dance sounded out from the stage. The dancers slowed to a stop and Sister Byrne stepped out of his embrace.

'Thank you for the dance,' he said. 'I hope I didn't crush your toes too much.'

'Oh no, not at all,' she replied, looking up at him. 'You're a very good dancer, Dr MacLauchlan.'

The band started the next dance but neither of them moved.

'Can I buy you a drink?' said Hari.

'Miss Byrne is with me,' said a man's voice behind him.

Hari turned to find the tweedy fellow he'd spotted earlier standing behind him.

'Malcolm, this is Dr MacLauchlan. He's the new doctor at Christ Church surgery,' she said to Malcolm before turning back to Hari. 'This is my boyfriend, Malcolm Henstock.'

Hari and Malcolm eyed each other for a moment then Hari offered his hand. 'Nice to meet you.'

Malcolm hesitated briefly, then took it. 'And you.'

His grip was firm but Hari's was firmer.

'You local?' asked Malcolm, surreptitiously flexing his fingers against his leg.

'No, from a little place called Pitlochry on the edge of the Highlands,' Hari replied.

'Sounds nice,' Malcolm replied. 'But you'll find it a bit rougher in Spitalfields.'

'I'm sure Dr MacLauchlan met rougher when he was in the Royal Medical Corps,' said Connie.

Malcolm looked sharply at her then back at Hari. 'I suppose you served in some hospital away from the fighting?'

'I was chief medical officer in Changi Hospital in Singapore, actually,' Hari replied. 'Until the Japanese overran it and then I and the rest of the 187th medical station were shipped off to Kanchanaburi Hospital next to the Thailand–Burma railway.' He smiled politely. 'And yourself?'

Above his tight collar Malcolm's neck flushed.

'Malcolm was exempt on account of his asthma,' Connie said hastily. 'But he was in the medical auxiliary all through the Blitz.'

Hari's smile widened. 'Well, we all did our bit.'

Malcolm slipped a proprietary arm around Connie. 'Well, we mustn't keep you as there are so many young ladies looking for partners.'

Hari turned his attention back to Sister Byrne. 'Thank you for the dance, and I hope you enjoy the rest of your evening.'

'And you,' she replied as Malcolm hustled her across the dance floor.

'And I'll see you on Monday,' he called, noting with satisfaction the sudden stiffening of her scruffy beau's shoulders.

Connie flopped on the sofa beside Malcolm and kicked off her high heels. 'My feet are killing me.'

It was just before midnight and although usually by this time Fry House would have been locked up for the night, Miss O'Dwyer had extended the curfew until one in the morning to allow the nurses to get back from the Friends' dance.

She and Malcolm had arrived back about twenty minutes before and, as usual, they had ensconced themselves in the small lounge for their late-night cocoa. It was now cooling on the table in front of them.

'I'm not surprised,' he said, without looking at her. 'You haven't been off them all night.'

'I was enjoying myself,' Connie replied, putting her feet up on the pouffe and wriggling her aching toes. 'And even you would have to agree the band were very good.'

'They were better than that lot last year,' he conceded with a sniff. 'But that's not saying much.'

'Well, I thought they were brilliant,' said Connie. 'And so did everyone else I spoke to.'

'They played far too many American songs for my liking,' he replied.

'That's what people want to dance to,' said Connie. 'And anyway, I enjoyed it ten times as much as I did last year, it was so nice not having to dance with any Tom, Dick or Harry who had a green ticket.'

Malcolm turned to face her. 'It didn't stop you dancing with anyone who asked.'

Connie gave him a querying look. 'What am I supposed to do when you won't dance? And you've never said you minded before.'

'Well I never have before.' He turned to face her. 'But then I never thought you'd lower yourself to dance with the likes of that Dr Whatshisname.'

'You mean Dr MacLauchlan.'

'So you know who I mean,' snapped Malcolm.

'Well, as the only other doctor I danced with was Dr Driscoll, who belongs to your mother's church, I can't think who else you could be referring too,' said Connie.

'Doctor!' Malcolm laughed mirthlessly. 'I don't see how he can be a proper doctor when he's only just stepped off a banana boat. But what I'm really surprised about is that you haven't mentioned him before now.'

'I have, Malcolm,' said Connie. 'Several times, in fact.'

He looked sceptical. 'I think I would have remembered if you'd mentioned you were working with some foreign chap. And I'd take all that stuff about the Burma railway with a pinch of salt. He was just showing off, that's all.'

'Oh, Malcolm.' Connie laughed.

Malcolm's cheeks went from red to purple. 'You might think it's funny but I hope you made it clear to him you were spoken for?'

Connie gave him a cool look. 'Am I?'

'I thought we have an understanding,' he replied, looking somewhat taken aback.

'About what exactly?'

'Getting married,' said Malcolm.

104

'Do we?' asked Connie.

'That's what I thought you wanted,' said Malcolm.

'Perhaps,' Connie replied. 'But you've never asked me.'

Malcolm puffed out his chest. 'Well, I'm asking you now.' He slid off the sofa and down onto one knee. He took her hand. 'Connie Byrne. Will you marry me?'

Surprisingly, the word yes didn't spring to Connie's lips. In fact, considering she'd been waiting almost a year to hear Malcolm say those very words, Connie felt oddly unmoved by them.

'Well, will you?' Malcolm repeated, looking taken aback at her lack of response.

Shoving her inexplicable hesitancy aside, Connie flung herself into his arms.

'Yes. Yes I will, but you'll have to speak to my dad,' she said breathlessly. 'He'll be on the allotment tomorrow morning from 6.30 so you can pop by before you go for your Saturday morning trainspotter stint at Stratford and then we can tell your mum tomorrow when I arrive and my lot when you come to tea on Sunday.'

Malcolm shifted uncomfortably in her embrace.

'What's the matter?'

'I thought perhaps we'd wait until Christmas,' he said, forcing a smile. 'Make it a bit special, you know.'

'Don't be daft,' laughed Connie. 'I'm shopping with Millie next week and can't wait to see the look on her face when I tell her.' She threw her arms around his neck again. 'Oh, Malcolm, I'm so happy.'

'Me too.'

Connie hugged him again and then Malcolm scrambled back on the sofa.

He picked up his cocoa and took a sip.

'And we have to pick a date,' said Connie, shuffling up towards him. 'We can't have next March as Cousin Trisha's getting hitched then and—'

'One thing at a time,' Malcolm said, patting her thigh. 'Now, drink your cocoa before it gets cold.'

Connie picked up her mug and with thoughts of bridal fabric, bouquets and bridesmaids floating through her mind, she hooked her legs over Malcolm's.

He placed his hand on her knee and squeezed. Happiness swelled up in her but as she looked down she noticed that, compared with Dr MacLauchlan's square palms and long, sculpted fingers, Malcolm's pale, plump hands looked a tad limp.

The clock on the mantelshelf chimed quarter to four as Mo and Bernie rushed forward to embrace her. Swamped in a sea of sisterly hugs, lipstick kisses and ear-piercing squeals, Connie did her best to hug and kiss them back.

Looking over her sisters' heads she saw her brothers-in-law, Eddy and Cliff, slap Malcolm on his back and shake his hand.

They were in her mother's spotlessly clean and constantly polished front parlour having just announced their engagement.

The fifteen by twenty room, crammed with lumpy pre-war furniture, was used by the Byrne family only on Sundays and for special family events. Along with the drab low-seated three-piece suite there was a sideboard with a bowl of waxed fruit and a Murphy radio on it. A bow-fronted glass cabinet stood in the alcove next to the chimney breast displaying a bone-china tea set that was too delicate to use, novelty cruet sets, crystal sugar bowls, silver-lidded jam pots and jolly mementos from three decades of day trips to the seaside.

The drop-leaf mahogany table under the window was open and covered with a tablecloth on which the plates of pilchard sandwiches, pickled herrings, cockles and rock cakes were set out. The best cups, saucers and plates were stacked next to them, as was the butter dish and a pot of jam – ready for crumpets.

Her mother had wedged her rear into her usual chair beside the glowing hearth and facing the door, all the better to scrutinise anyone who ventured into her domain.

The children of the family had been summoned in from playing in the backyard, their scarfs, duffle coats and gloves discarded on the upright chair in the corner ready to be donned again once family duty was done. They'd left Bernie's toddler, Tony, napping on his grandmother's bed upstairs while Mo's daughter Audrey sat between her mother and aunt clutching her golliwog and looking bemused at all the excitement.

After enduring another round of cuddling and kissing from her sisters, Connie turned to her dad.

Arthur Byrne was just a little over five foot eight with a receding hairline and after forty years of Maud's cooking had a respectable girth. He'd passed his sixty-fifth birthday a year ago and having retired after fifty back-breaking years of humping goods on and off ships, now spent most of his time up at the allotment. He said it was to keep him fit and, of course, the fresh vegetables and the odd punnet of strawberries and raspberries in season helped her parents eke out their small pensions, but Connie guessed his preoccupation with the great outdoors might also be a way of keeping out of her mother's way. It was remarkable to think that whereas most fathers took their belt off on a regular basis to bring their children into line, the only time Connie could ever remember her father smacking her was when she unhooked the fireguard to retrieve a toy and singed her hair. He was a man of few words but when he spoke it was softly and often with an accompanying cuddle.

Connie embraced him, inhaling the faint but familiar aroma of brilliantine and tobacco.

'Well done, girl,' he said gruffly, holding her to him as he had for as long as she could remember.

Connie snuggled into him for a moment, then pulled away. 'Thanks, Dad, for saying yes.'

'I don't mind who you marry as long as you're happy,' he replied. 'And if Malcolm's the one who'll do that then it's all right by me.' He pulled her close again. 'Just don't let your mother take over,' he whispered.

Connie laughed and kissed his cheek.

Malcolm took her father's place beside her and put his arm around her waist.

'I'm so happy,' sniffed Maud, drawing a handkerchief from her sleeve and dabbing her eyes.

'You make a handsome couple,' said Bernie, looking a bit dewy-eyed.

Mo slipped her arm through her sister's. 'They certainly do.'

'So was your mother pleased when you told her, Malcolm?' asked Bernie.

Malcolm's body stiffened slightly, as did his smile. 'She was surprised.'

Dazed, shaken and hysterical would have been a better way

to describe Mrs Henstock's reaction, but Connie thought better not to elaborate.

'So when's the big day?' asked Bernie.

'We're no . . . not decided yet,' said Malcolm.

'But we did think possibly autumn 1950,' said Connie.

Mo looked baffled. 'But that's almost two years off.'

'I know,' said Malcolm. 'But there's no rush.'

'There is if you want to make sure you get the date you want at St Martha and St Mungo's,' said Maud. 'Father O'Connor tells me they're already taking wedding bookings for 1951.'

'Well, the thing is, Mrs Byrne,' said Malcolm, swallowing hard. 'My mother's a bit un . . . unsure about m . . . me getting married in a C . . . Catholic church.'

Her mother's eyes narrowed. 'Is she now?'

'Yes,' said Malcolm hesitantly. 'We haven't really discussed it—'

'There's nothing to discuss,' cut in Maud. 'Like her sisters, my Connie's getting married in St Martha and St Mungo's and that's an end to it.'

She fixed him with a challenging stare.

Mo and Bernie exchanged a glance while the men studied the wallpaper and carpet and the children stopped chattering instantly.

After what seemed like an eternity of silence, Malcolm cleared his throat. 'Of course, Mrs Byrne.'

A satisfied expression spread across Maud's face. 'Good, and now someone put the kettle on.'

Bernie went out to make the tea while Mo started removing the tea towels covering the food and the children went out to wash their hands.

The door opened and Bernie came back in carrying the large teapot. The menfolk headed for the sandwiches but Malcolm remained where he was.

'You'd better get stuck in before the children take all the cake,' Connie said jollily.

'My mum's not going to like it,' he said in a low voice, giving her a doleful look.

'But it's traditional for the wedding to take place in the bride's church,' said Connie.

Malcolm shifted from one foot to the other. 'I know but it's a Catholic church and—'

'Come on, Malcolm, get yourself some grub, man,' called Eddy through a mouthful of sandwich.

Malcolm sighed, then strolled over to join the menfolk at the table and started piling sandwiches on his plate.

'Oi! Connie!' called her mother, cutting across her daydream. She looked at her.

'Get yourself a plate of something and come over.' Maud patted the pouffe by her feet. 'We need to decide about bridesmaids.'

Chapter Eight

'I'm still not sure,' said Millie, pulling a paisley scarf from her shopping bag and regarding it critically.

'But it's so pretty,' Connie said, thinking she wished she had the money to buy something so costly.

Not that Millie flashed her new-found wealth about, quite the opposite; she still collected money-off coupons in magazines, but when you were married to a man with his own private income you didn't watch the pennies quite as much.

She and Millie were on their annual Christmas shopping trip to Oxford Street and after four hours scouring Selfridges, Peter Robinson's and countless other shops for gifts, they were now squashed in the corner of Bourne & Hollingsworth's fourth-floor restaurant with bags of Christmas shopping around their legs and a cream tea on the table.

'It is, but Jim's mother will hate it nonetheless,' Millie said, returning to the subject of her hostile mother-in-law. 'Because she hates me.'

'I'm sure that's not true,' Connie lied.

Millie contemplated her purchase glumly, then shoved the scarf back where it came from. 'I'm certain it is.'

'I take it you're not looking forward to Christmas at the manor house then,' said Connie before taking another bite of her scone.

'No, I'm not.' Millie sighed. 'It will be exactly the same as it is every time we visit. His mother will watch me with a face like she's been sucking lemons, Jim and his father will argue about politics over dinner until one of them storms off swearing. And if that weren't enough, I have to suffer his brother Lionel and his snide remarks about chirpy Cockneys. Even the servants look down their noses at me.'

Jim's father was the squire of some estate and village in Essex and, by all accounts, still lived in the grand manner of his forebears with house servants and estate workers. Connie had met the disdainful Lady Tolshunt only once, at Millie's wedding last year, and was in no hurry to do so again so she could understand her friend's reluctance at being holed up with her and Jim's other toffee-nosed relatives for the whole of Christmas.

'Poor you,' Connie said. 'Still, it's only for a couple of days.'

'Thank goodness,' Millie replied. 'And at least we'll see the new year in with my family. Where are you going?'

'My mum's for Christmas Day and Malcolm's on Boxing Day.' Connie's eyes lit up. 'I've had a bit of luck with Malcolm's present. Mum was in the market a couple of weeks back and one of the stalls was selling off skeins of wool, so she got me four and I've knitted a pullover for him.'

'What colour?'

'Grey,' Connie replied. 'The council's Highways Department frowns on its employees looking too flamboyant. What are you giving Jim?'

'I'm not sure yet.' Millie took a sip of tea. 'Changing the subject, did you hear that Annie is courting Patrick O'Toole?'

Annie was Millie's ex-Queen's Nurse student who still worked with her in Munroe Clinic and Patrick O'Toole, or Pat the Lad as he was known locally, was the incredibly handsome scrap metal dealer in Cannon Street Road.

'No,' said Connie. 'I can understand why. He's very easy on the eye.'

'He might be,' said Millie. 'But there's something about him that unsettles me.'

Connie laughed. 'I'm not surprised. Patrick's cast out of the same mould as Alex Nolan.'

Millie forced a laugh. 'Nonsense.'

'I grant you, he's not as broad and hasn't got the mass of wavy black hair.'

A bleak expression passed across Millie's face and Connie was mortified. How stupid of her to bring up Millie's ex-fiancé.

She reached over and covered her friend's hand with hers. 'I'm so sorry, Millie, I shouldn't have mentioned Alex.'

Millie gave her a dazzling smile. 'Don't be daft.' She glanced at her watch. 'I ought to be off. It's our anniversary and I'm making something special for Jim.'

'Goodness, I can't believe it's a year already, Millie,' said Connie, now feeling as if she was the worst friend in the world. 'What with Christmas and everything I forgot.'

'Don't worry. We're not making a big thing of it.'

Millie finished her tea and put her cup back in the saucer.

'Before you go, Millie, I've got something to tell you.' Connie took a deep breath. 'Malcolm proposed.'

'For goodness sake, Connie,' Millie said, looking incredulously at her. 'Why didn't you say something when I met you at Aldgate?'

Connie shrugged. 'I was waiting for the right moment.'

Millie rolled her eyes. 'Oh, Connie. You are the end!'

Connie poked out her tongue and Millie pulled a face.

'We're going up to Hatton Garden next Saturday. Isn't it wonderful?' said Connie, telling herself once she actually had the ring on her finger she would start to feel more excited.

'Yes,' replied Millie. 'I'm delighted for you, of course I am.'

'And you must, must, must be my matron of honour.'

'I'd never speak to you again if I wasn't,' replied Millie with a little of her old spark. 'I bet your mum's pleased.'

'She's beside herself,' said Connie. 'She's now referring to me as her engaged rather than her unmarried daughter, and my sisters are arguing as to who's doing what for the big day.'

'When is the wedding going to be?'

'October 1950, probably the seventh, although if Malcolm's mother has her way it will be October 1960,' Connie replied. 'But it will definitely be in St Martha and St Mungo's – whatever his mother says – and I thought perhaps pink for the bridesmaids and, as there'll be so many of us, a three-tiered cake. What do you think?'

'It all sounds lovely.'

'And now clothes rationing's over, I can have yards of fabric for my wedding dress,' said Connie, wondering if she'd ever be able to decide on a design. 'You'll come with me to choose it, won't you?'

'Of course I will. But . . .' Millie bit her lip.

'But what?'

'Are you sure Malcolm's the right man for you?' she asked.

'Oh, Millie, you are silly.' Connie laughed. 'Of course he is.

He's no Clark Gable, I grant you, and with his trainspotting and Scouts he can seem a bit dull. But I'm certain he'll be a wonderful husband. Just like Jim.'

A bleak expression flashed across Millie's face. 'I'm glad to hear it,' she said, giving Connie a too bright smile. 'I don't want you marrying the wrong man, now do I?'

Connie regarded her thoughtfully for a moment. 'What's wrong, Millie?'

Millie's eyes filled with tears. 'I'm pretty sure I'm pregnant.'

'Oh, Millie, that's wonderful,' said Connie. 'Aren't you pleased?'

'Of course I am, it's just . . .' Millie took a handkerchief from her handbag. 'It's Jim.'

'What about Jim?'

'He wanted us to wait a bit longer,' said Millie.

'Well these things happen,' Connie replied. 'And as you were planning to have a family anyway—'

'But what with running for the Leytonstone and Wanstead by-election in February and the trouble with the dockers, he's got such a lot on his mind that he just flies off the handle at the slightest thing and . . .' Millie blew her nose.

Connie covered her friend's hand with hers. 'I wouldn't worry, Millie. I'm sure once he's over the initial shock Jim will be as pleased as punch he's going to be a father.'

Millie rallied a plucky smile. 'Do you think so?'

'Of course,' said Connie.

They exchanged an affectionate look, then Connie let go of her friend.

'Right, I know you've got to get home but before you do—' Connie raised her hand and a waitress started to make her way across the tea room towards them. 'We're having another cuppa to drink to Baby Smith and discuss names.'

The group of children on the stage sang out the final note of 'Ding Dong Merrily on High' and Connie, along with the other adults in the hall, applauded.

Mrs Miller, the head dinner lady, sitting next to her, wiped her eye. ''Ow could anyone hurt 'em?'

Connie swallowed the sentimental lump in her throat and smiled.

She was sitting, in full nurse's uniform, in the front row of Blue Coat School's main hall for the Christmas concert on the last day of the autumn term.

Unlike most of the schools in the area, which had been built in the latter half of the last century when education was made compulsory, Blue Coat School, which sat halfway down Hanbury Street, had been founded by a philanthropic Non-Conformist one hundred and fifty years before, as the statues of a boy and girl in Georgian clothing above the front entrances testified.

The school-educated children, aged from three and a half to eleven, then moved on to one of the local secondary modern or grammar schools.

Alongside Connie sat other invited guests, including the new curate from Christ Church, Reverend Maddox, a handsome man in his early thirties with a full head of chestnut hair and a ready smile, and Mrs Burton the school secretary.

Making up the party was Father Flaherty, looking as always like a spindly disapproving crow in his black cassock, his mouth permanently set in a thin sour line under his beaked nose. Although the angels heralded God's eternal love for all mankind, if the expression on Father Flaherty's cadaverous face was anything to go by, he clearly thought the Almighty was far too generous with his affections.

Dressed in their traditional royal-blue blazers with the founders' crest and motto on the breast pocket, the Blue Coat choir had given them a lively rendition of 'The Holly and the Ivy' and were now finishing with the softer 'Silent Night'.

The applause faded away and Mr Routledge the headmaster stood up.

'Well, thank you, children,' he said in his well-modulated tone. His piercing gaze ran over the visitors. 'And thank you to our Blue Coat School friends who have come to celebrate our saviour Jesus Christ's birth with us.'

The children looked at the row of invited guests and clapped loudly.

Connie smiled.

Mr Routledge raised his hand and the applause ceased immediately. 'Now, hands up who thinks our guests should be rewarded with a cup of tea and a mince pie for giving up their time to be with us today?'

A forest of hands strained into the air.

Mr Routledge gave his charges a tolerant smile. 'Well then, I'd like you to remain seated while I take them to the staff room and when the dinner bell goes in a few moments you can stand up and lead out in an quiet, orderly fashion.'

'Yes, headmaster,' two hundred voices shouted as one.

Striding down the stage steps the headmaster led Connie and the rest of the guests between the rows of cross-legged pupils and out of the hall.

The refreshments were already set out in the staff room so Connie wended her way past the easy chairs to the coffee table. As Reverend Maddox was talking to the school secretary, and the headmaster and Father Flaherty were deep in conversation, Connie stirred two spoonfuls of sugar into her tea, selected a mince pie and then drifted over to the noticeboard.

She'd just finished munching her way through the pastry and dried fruit as she studied the list of pupils who'd received special commendations when Father Flaherty came over.

'Good morning, sister,' he said, looking down from eighteen inches above her. 'I hope you enjoyed the concert.'

'Good morning, Father,' said Connie. 'As always, especially the nursery children's rendition of "Away in a Manger". I don't imagine there was a dry eye in the place.'

'Indeed,' he replied ponderously. 'Although perhaps it would have been better if Betty Crowther had held the Holy Infant up the right way.'

Connie laughed. 'And I had to smile at the poor lad playing Joseph.'

The priest's thin lips pulled into a tight line. 'I hope the headmaster has a stiff word with Master Longshaw about his performance.'

'It wasn't his fault the tea towel slipped off,' said Connie.

'He was portraying St Joseph, the earthly father of our Blessed Lord, not some snotty costermonger.'

'He's only six,' said Connie.

'It's never too soon to instil proper reverence,' boomed Father Flaherty. 'Since the war I've noticed standards are slipping and

I have made it my mission to ensure my flock are turned away from these so-called modern ideas such as women in church without a head covering, irregular attendance at confession, trying to limit the blessing of children and' – his grey eyes fixed on hers with a penetrating stare – 'the alarming rise in mixed marriages.'

Connie held his unwavering stare. 'I don't know if you've heard, Father Flaherty, but I've just become engaged.'

'I had and to a good Catholic, I hope?' he replied.

Connie smiled. 'C of E, actually, but he's happy to be instructed by Father O'Connor at St Martha's and St Mungo's.'

The priest's shaggy eyebrows pulled together. 'That's all well and good, Sister Byrne, but in my experience being instructed is one thing, complying is quite another.'

'Don't worry, Father.' Connie smiled. 'Malcolm has every intention of keeping the Church's teaching in the same way I do.'

'Can you hear that blooming racket?' asked Maud, thumbing over her shoulder at the chorus of snores rattling out of the front room.

It was the afternoon of Christmas Day and for the past hour Connie's family – nine adults and eleven children – had worked their way through two chickens, ten pounds of roast potatoes, two heads of cabbage and a pile of parsnips, sprouts and carrots, not to mention a Christmas pudding the size of a bucket and a quart of custard.

The racket her mother was referring to was the noise of the Byrne menfolk – her father, elder brother Jim, and Mo and Bernie's husbands, Eddy and Clifford – slumbering in the easy chairs and sofa in the front room while the children played with their new toys in the back. Malcolm was with them but he was engrossed in the biography of Isambard Kingdom Brunel, his Christmas present from his Aunt Minnie.

The womenfolk, having spent weeks shopping, baking and preparing the feast, were now clearing it away. Connie's mother was sitting at the kitchen table, ostensibly waiting until the plates drained a bit before drying them but in truth supervising Connie, Mo and Bernie as they worked their way through the dirty crockery.

As it was a special day, her mother had foregone her usual wrap-around apron and was dolled up in her best navy dress, accessorised with a marcasite brooch pinned to the collar.

Her sisters too were wearing new dresses and their best jewellery. Mo had treated herself to a chestnut rinse at the hairdresser's so the wisps of grey at her temples were less pronounced, while Bernie's dark curls had been cut and permed making them bob every time she moved.

Not to be outdone, Connie was wearing a new dark blue eight-panelled skirt she'd found on Alma's 'One-off designs' rail and a cream-coloured jumper that she'd seen featured in the November Seasonal Knits supplement in *Woman's Own*.

'It's the same every year,' said Mo, extracting a plate from the soapy water. 'As soon as we start peeling the sprouts, they nip out down the Star "for a swift half".' Even Malcolm had joined the men of the family for a shandy to be sociable, although beer before lunch gave him indigestion.

'A swift half-gallon more like,' said Bernie, swirling the tea towel haphazardly around a pudding dish.

It was a bit rich of Bernie to complain as she and Mo had managed to polish off half a bottle of sherry to Connie's one G & T over the course of the family feast and now both sisters glowed like a pair of Christmas candles.

'It's only once a year,' said Connie, taking a wet plate from the pile. 'And you'd only moan about them getting under our feet while we're getting dinner prepared if they didn't.'

'I know but seeing them all around the dinner table brought it home to me,' said her mother, taking her handkerchief from her sleeve.

Connie exchanged a long-suffering look with her sisters.

'I wish my baby were here, home from the war,' continued Maud, dabbing her dry eyes.

Connie laughed. 'Really, Mum, Bobby's twenty-two so I don't think he'd take kindly to being called your baby and we're not at war any more.'

'He'll always be my baby,' said her mother, crossing her arms emphatically over her considerable bosom. 'The last one born is always special, you'll know that yourself one day.'

'Give Con a chance to have her first one, Mum, before you

start telling her about her last,' said Mo, washing the same plate for a third time.

Bernie winked. 'Don't worry, Mo, she'll soon hear the patter of tiny feet once she's wed.'

'That's if she marries Malcolm,' said Mo.

Maud looked sharply at them. 'What do you mean *if*? Why wouldn't Connie marry Malcolm?'

'Well, maybe someone else might catch her eye,' said Mo, casting a teasing glance at Connie.

Their mother frowned. 'Like who?'

'Yeah,' said Bernie swaying ever so slightly. 'Like who?'

'I don't know,' said Mo. 'Perhaps that doctor chap she keeps talking about. You know, Dr Whatshisname who's with that old crusty one.'

Mo clicked her fingers and pointed at Connie. 'That's him. Dr M'Crockman the Jock.'

The image of Dr MacLauchlan smiling at her as he wished her a Happy Christmas the day before flashed across her mind.

Connie forced a carefree laugh. 'His name's Dr MacLauchlan but what on earth put that daft idea in your head?'

'Well, you're always talking about him, for a start,' said Mo.

'No I'm not!'

'Yes you are.' Mo nudged Bernie. 'She is, isn't she?'

Her sister gave Connie a considered look. 'Now you mention it, Mo, Dr Magooglans name does keep cropping up.'

'It's Dr MacLauchlan,' said Connie firmly. 'And of course I talk about him, I work with him.' Connie went over to the dresser and put the dried plates on the shelf.

Bernie and Mo exchanged a mischievous look.

'Does he wear a kilt?' asked Bernie, picking a saucepan up from the drainer.

Connie gave them an exasperated look and, stacking the pudding bowls together, went back to the dresser.

'Because you know what Scotsmen wear under their kilt,' added Mo.

'I'm sure our Con's seen it all before in her line of work, Mo,' giggled Bernie.

Her sisters hooted and held onto each other.

'Oi, that's enough of that sort of talk, you two,' snapped

Maud, giving her eldest two daughters a sharp look. 'It's Christmas. And I don't think you should be talking about . . .' she glanced over her shoulder, 'men's wotsits,' she whispered. 'And on our lord's birthday of all days.'

Bernie and Mo stared at their mother for a moment, then fell about laughing again.

Maud folded her arms and tutted loudly.

'Take no notice of them, Mum. They've had too much sherry,' said Connie, dipping her fingers into the sink and flicking suds over her sisters.

Bernie squeaked and jumped out of the way.

Mo whipped the tea towel off the end of the sink and held it in front of her as she started singing the chorus of 'Will You Stop your Tickling Jock'.

Hooking arms with her sister, Bernie joined in.

'Stop you twittering tiky tiddy tiktin,' they warbled, flipping their tea towels up at the end of each line.

Connie laughed. 'For goodness sake, you two,' she told them, wiping a tear from her eye.

'Icky wicky wikling,' they continued, jogging up and down as they sang.

Connie held her ribs.

'Is he married?' asked Mo.

'No,' said Connie. 'But I'm sure he must be walking out with someone and I don't suppose a handsome chap like him will stay unattached very long.'

Her mother gave her a wary look. 'Looker, is he?'

'The nurses are mad about him,' laughed Connie. 'Practically fighting each other to pick up his messages.'

The door opened and Malcolm's head popped around the corner.

'Sorry, ladies, to interrupt your fun,' he said, looking around at them. 'Mr Byrne's after a cuppa so I said I'd put the kettle on.'

'You'll do no such thing, Malcolm,' said Maud indignantly. 'I'm not having your mother thinking we don't know how to treat guests. Connie! Make your dad and Malcolm a cup of tea and I'll have one too, while you're about it.'

Collecting the empty kettle from the stove, Connie went to the sink and filled it.

'You girls seem to be having a good time out here,' said Malcolm, lounging against the pantry door, 'if all the giggling is anything to go by.'

'It was just Mo and Bernie having a laugh at my expense,' said Connie as she held the kettle under the running water.

'What about?' said Malcom.

'Nothing at all,' said Maud, giving her elder two daughters a hard look.

'No, nothing,' giggled Bernie, flapping her tea towel again.

She glanced at Mo and they started giggling again.

Malcolm looked uncomfortable and a flush started to spread upwards from his shirt collar.

'They were just teasing me,' said Connie. 'That's all.'

'About what?' asked Malcolm.

'Her handsome Dr MacThingybob,' Mo replied with a massive wink.

The red splash of colour around Malcolm's throat spread a little higher and he gave Connie a hard look. 'What about him?'

'Just some nonsense about him wearing a kilt,' said Maud. 'That's all. Now where's that tea, Con?'

Malcolm looked confused. 'A kilt?'

'Because he's Scottish,' Connie replied, trying to keep the exasperation from her voice.

'Is he?' asked Malcolm.

'He told you that at the association's dance.'

Bernie regarded Malcolm with interest. 'You've met him?'

'Just the once.' Malcolm sniffed. 'I can't say I was particularly impressed.'

'Well according to Connie all the nurses are "mad about" him,' said Bernie.

'I can't see why,' said Malcolm. 'I thought him a bit of a show-off, if you must know. All that talk about being captured at Singapore.'

'Well, Connie says he's the main topic of conversation in Fry House these days,' added Bernie.

Malcolm's mouth pulled into a hard line.

He looked at Connie and she felt her cheeks grow warm.

'Not me, of course,' she said quickly as the image of Dr Mac-Lauchlan's tanned features and wry smile formed in her mind.

'So tell us, Malcolm,' said Mo. 'Is the heart throb of Fry House tall, dark and handsome?'

Malcolm gave a hard laugh. 'Well, he's certainly dark: he's Indian.'

'Indian,' said her sisters in unison and stopping mid-jog.

'Half,' said Connie.

'Where does the other half of him come from then?' asked her mother.

'Scotland, that's why he's Dr MacLauchlan,' said Connie. 'His mother's from India but his father was a railway engineer. He studied medicine at Cambridge and was a captain in the Royal Medical Corps and only came back to England six months ago because of the Partition business.'

'You know a lot about him,' said Bernie.

'It's only what I've heard here and there,' said Connie.

Malcolm gave her a sharp look. 'You didn't tell me.'

'I have to talk to lots of people every day, Malcolm.' Smiling, Connie walked over to him and slipped her arms around him. 'I don't tell you because there's nothing to tell.'

Malcolm frowned. 'But—'

Connie stretched up and kissed him.

There were sighs and ahhs behind them from the Byrne women.

'And whatever Dr MacLauchlan is or looks like, it doesn't matter because I have you, don't I?' she said, smiling up at him.

Despite his awkwardness at being embraced in full view of her family, Malcolm's unhappy expression lifted and he smiled.

'Yes you have,' he replied, tickling her. 'And make sure he knows you're engaged to me so he doesn't get any funny ideas.'

Connie laughed and so did her sisters.

'Don't you worry about that, Malcolm,' chuckled her mother. 'My Connie's not that sort of girl and especially not with some darkie.'

Dragging his weary feet, Hari climbed the last step and pushed open the door to his flat.

Dropping his jacket over the back of one of the two dining chairs tucked under the handkerchief-size scrubbed table, he loosened his tie.

Collecting the tin of Kenyan coffee from the top shelf of the kitchen dresser, he spooned in three hefty scoops into his old coffee jug and then added another. He wondered if even that amount of caffeine would be enough.

For goodness sake, it was Christmas Day, weren't people supposed to be relaxing not carving the back of their hand instead of the turkey or burning the skin off their forehead with blazing brandy? So far, since he'd been woken by the phone at 7.30, he'd dealt with numerous incidents such as these and sent one person to hospital with a suspected heart attack and another with a gastric bleed vomiting what looked like coffee grounds.

He glanced at his watch. Four-thirty already and not only was he exhausted but hungry too. At two o'clock, when he should have been sitting down to a full turkey dinner with all the trimmings in the Bishopsgate Hotel, he was in a telephone box outside a block of flats beside the Cambridge Heath railway arches trying to organise for the entire Prescott family to be admitted to Bancroft Road Hospital with food poisoning.

Placing the pot on the back of his new Cannon gas stove, Hari lit the gas under it and left it to boil, then flicked on the squat Pye radio in the middle of the table.

Feeling utterly drained, he flopped into the easy chair he'd dragged through from the lounge. As the valves of the wireless warmed, he studied the ceiling, an uncharacteristic pall of despondency pressing down on him.

It wasn't that he was big on religion. How could he be with a Sikh mother and a lapsed Presbyterian father? But Christmas had always been a jolly time with his mother's relatives joining in the fun. The thought of Connie's honey-coloured complexion as she stood in his surgery drifted through Hari's mind and he smiled.

The sounds of the Royal Philharmonic Orchestra's Christmas concert cut across his thoughts and he rose to his feet.

Taking a mug from the cupboard, he poured himself a coffee. He took the bottle of milk from the window sill outside and poured a splash into his drink.

Hari went to the larder and cast his eye over the contents: a half-full box of Quaker's oats, a couple of tins of baked beans, one each of tomato, celery and chicken soup, Daddy's sauce and a tin of Jacobs crackers. He'd just shut the larder door on his miserable supplies when there was a knock on the front door. Suppressing the urge to ignore it, Hari left the kitchen and trudged down the stairs.

Opening the door, the icy air and ribbons of fog rushed into the hallway. In the yellowing light from the street lamp stood a man in a donkey jacket, muffled to the ears with a knitted scarf.

He touched the peak of his cloth cap respectfully. 'Evening, doc.'

'Good evening,' said Hari. 'What can do for you, Mr . . . ?'

''All,' the man replied. 'Sid Hall, from 'raund the corner. You saw my wife on Monday gone.'

'Ah, yes, the lady who tripped up and gashed her head,' said Hari, briefly remembering the blood as he'd stitched it.

'That's her,' said Mr Hall.

'Is she all right?'

Mr Hall nodded. ''Cept from looking like Boris Karloff.'

'So how can I help you, Mr Hall?' asked Hari, wishing he'd put his jacket on before coming down.

'She said I should give you this.' Mr Hall thrust out the bag he was carrying. Hari took it and a wonderful aroma of meat drifted up.

'She fort you being by your lonesome, like, you could do wiv a bit of home cooking.'

Hari looked down at the cream enamel casserole dish in the bag.

'Thank you,' he said, swallowing the lump in his throat. 'That's very kind of her.'

'You know what women are like.' Mr Hall winked conspiratorially. 'Always after someone to muver. I hope it's all right, I mean she don't have a clue what you people have at Christmas, but . . .'

Hari smiled. 'Please tell your good lady from me that my stomach is very grateful.'

Mr Hall looked relieved. 'I will. There's a bit of plum pudding, too, tucked down the side and she says she'll pick the dish up when she's passing. Merry Christmas.'

'And to you and your wife, Mr Hall,' said Hari.

Mr Hall touched his cap again and shuffled away.

Hari closed the door and, making sure he held the bag level, hurried back up the stairs. Delving in, he carefully lifted out a dish covered with an old plate and set it on the table. He lifted the lid to reveal three slices of turkey, carrots, cabbage and roast potatoes and a clump of stuffing all covered with gravy.

The smell of roast meat filled the warm kitchen and Hari's stomach rumbled.

Memories of the two Christmases he'd spent at Nakhon Pathom flooded back to him, bringing another lump to his throat. Perhaps tending to the sick in Spitalfields and having Mrs Hall's dinner to tuck into wasn't such a bad way to spend the day.

As Malcolm, who was sitting next to her on the sofa, turned the page of his book, Connie looked across at the carriage clock on the mantelshelf.

'Not long now, dear,' his mother said from the chair next to the fire.

Connie forced a smile.

Mrs Henstock was right. In just under half an hour somewhere to the west of them, Big Ben would strike the first note of twelve and they would move into the last year of the decade, 1949.

Shifting her position, Connie picked up last week's copy of *Woman's Realm* and flicked through the pages as the classical music from the gramophone filled the silence.

She skimmed over an article about a missionary's wife in Rhodesia, tips to keep rayon underwear white but, as she got to the section on dishes to make with turnips, the music stopped.

'Could you change the record, dear?' said Mrs Henstock.

Malcolm put aside his book and stood up.

'Something from Gilbert and Sullivan might be jolly?' his mother suggested as he made his way to the teak record cabinet at the far end of the room. 'And perhaps we could have another cup of tea?'

She looked expectantly at Connie.

'I'll put the kettle on,' said Connie, setting the magazine aside. 'But I thought we might be having something a little stronger.'

'What shall we have,' asked Malcolm, flipping through the rack of records. '*The Gondoliers* or *The Mikado*?'

Ignoring her son's question, Mrs Henstock's narrow lips pulled together. 'You know my views on alcohol, Constance.'

'I do, Mrs Henstock,' Connie replied. 'But surely a little one to toast in the new year wouldn't do any harm?'

Mrs Henstock crossed her arms. 'So says every drunk in the gutter.'

'Or perhaps *HMS Pinafore*?' asked Malcolm, holding up a record with a picture of a sailor doing the hornpipe on it. 'You like that one, Mother, don't you?'

'You remembered,' said Mrs Henstock, smiling adoringly at her only offspring.

'Of course I did,' said Malcolm, puffing out his chest as if receiving a school prize.

Taking the record out of its sleeve, he turned his attention to the gramophone.

'Do you know, Constance,' his mother continued, looking back at her. '*HMS Pinafore* has been my favourite since Malcolm's father took me to see it when we were courting.'

'I believe you have mentioned it once or twice.' Connie stood up. 'I'll make the tea then, shall I?'

'Thank you, Constance,' Mrs Henstock replied with the sweetest of smiles.

Leaving her future mother-in-law recounting yet again her unforgettable evening at the D'Oyly Carte, Connie made her way down the chilly hall to the kitchen.

After filling the kettle she returned it to the old-fashioned stove and lit the gas beneath. As she waited for it to boil, she opened the door and stepped out into the backyard.

Somewhere a few streets over she could hear someone hammering 'Roll out the Barrel' on an old piano and a chorus of 'My Old Man' belted out from somewhere else.

Leaning back on the wall, Connie stared up at the twinkling stars as the icy air cooled her cheeks.

Well, this was a fun way to see in the new year, she thought, imagining the girls from Fry House having a knees-up in Trafalgar Square and her family crowded around the piano having a sing-song.

The pianist moved on to 'Doing the Lambeth Walk' without missing a beat and a shout of Oi! went up. She was just wondering how Dr MacLauchlan was saying goodbye to 1948 when the door opened and Malcolm stepped out.

'There you are,' he said, smiling at her. 'Didn't you hear the kettle whistling?'

She shook her head.

'Don't worry, I've made the tea and it's brewing,' he said.

'Sorry.'

'That's all right,' he replied. 'I was just afraid you'd been stolen away by the fairies.'

Connie gave a short laugh. 'I'd go willingly if there was a chance of getting a G&T in Fairyland.'

Malcolm looked hurt. 'You know Mother won't have drink in the house, Connie, so I don't know why you're so put out.'

'Well, I'll tell you, shall I?' snapped Connie. 'For once New Year's Eve is on a Friday so as neither of us has to work in the morning we could have made a night of it and gone up West.'

'But it's always so crowded with—'

'—people enjoying themselves.'

Malcolm frowned. 'And how on earth would we get home?'

'Walk. Like me and the girls did on VE day,' Connie replied. 'And even if you didn't fancy going all that way we could have joined the party in the Northern Star.'

Malcolm pursed his lips. 'We were at your mum's for Christmas dinner so it seems only fair we spend New Year with my mum.'

'But we did spend the whole of Boxing Day with her and her sister listening to the *Third Programme* at full blast to make up for it,' Connie replied.

'Auntie Minnie can't help being deaf,' said Malcolm.

'I know but my ears were ringing by the end of it,' Connie replied. 'And I thought the fact that I spent most of my day in the kitchen would have been enough to appease your mother but it seems not.'

'You know she would have helped you with the food if she hadn't had one of her wobbly heads,' said Malcolm.

'Or the pain in her knees that means she couldn't stand so I had to wait on her hand and foot all day,' said Connie in as even a tone as she could manage. 'But honestly, Malcolm, if I'd known I'd be seeing the new year in by drinking PG Tips and listening to Gilbert and Sullivan I'd have volunteered to work.'

Malcolm face took on his whipped-puppy expression.

'I'm sorry,' she said, guilt clutching at her chest. 'I didn't mean—'

'You can be very sharp sometimes, Connie.'

'Malcolm, I'm just saying—'

'For a nurse, I mean,' he continued. 'I'd expect someone in your profession to be more understanding, more compassionate to the pain in others.'

'And I am, but—'

'Not to my mother.'

'Of course to your mother,' Connie replied. 'All I'm saying is—'

'You'd rather be dancing around in Trafalgar Square with your friends than be here with me,' he said, cutting into her uncomfortable feelings.

Connie looked up at him for a moment and then burst into tears.

His face went from irritated to indulgent in a flash.

'Now, now,' he said, gathering her into his arms. 'What's all this?'

'I . . . I . . . do . . . don't kn . . . know,' sniffled Connie.

Pressing herself into the familiar comfort of her fiancé's tweed jacket, she wept uncontrollably.

Malcolm held her until she got her jumbled emotions in check and then he spoke again.

'I think you're getting yourself all upset about nothing, don't you?' he said.

Connie stood away from him and nodded.

'I'm sorry, Malcolm. I don't know what . . .' A sob rose up and threatened to engulf her but Connie held it off. 'I don't know what's got into me.'

Malcolm gave her a wry smile. 'Is it that time again?'

As she'd had a period only two weeks ago it shouldn't have been but perhaps if it was coming early it might explain her sudden irritation with Malcolm.

Connie nodded, then slipped her arm around him.

'I'm sorry,' she repeated. 'And you know I'd much rather be here with you than having fun with my friends.'

'Are you saying I'm not fun?' he joked.

Connie wiped the last tear away with the heel of her hand.

'Don't be silly,' she replied, forcing a light laugh. 'You're lots of fun. It's me being a bit overemotional, that's all.'

She smiled.

'That's better,' he said, smiling back. 'I know what'll cheer you up. Why don't we sort out booking the church and the hall for the wedding next week?'

Connie stared at him in amazement. 'I thought you told my mum it was too early when she suggested it the other day.'

'I did,' said Malcolm. 'But thinking about it, if we want to get the date and venue we want, perhaps it would be better to book now rather than later.'

'Oh, Malcolm.' She hugged him. 'I do love you.'

He grinned. 'I should hope so too.'

A hooter blasted, followed by a car horn and then the church bells started.

Connie snuggled back into his embrace. 'Happy New Year, Malcolm.'

'Happy New Year, Connie.'

He lowered his head.

Connie tilted her face towards him and closed her eyes. However, instead of the passionate kiss she was expecting, Malcolm's lips brushed her forehead briefly.

The jumble of unsettling emotions bubbled up again and even when he added, 'Here's to the future Mrs Henstock,' they refused to disappear.

Chapter Nine

'And last but not least, this is your room,' said Connie, opening the door for Grace Huxtable to enter. It was 10th January and the new year had been accompanied by an icy blast from the Arctic and the promise of a blizzard. The snow hadn't arrived yet but thankfully the latest recruits to Fry House had.

Grace Huxtable, wrapped in a box-checked coat, knitted beret and wearing galoshes over her laced-up shoes, had arrived just before 8.30 that morning, along with the other two nurses, Elizabeth Copeland and Jennifer Jessop, recruited by Connie and Miss O'Dwyer back in November.

They had been greeted enthusiastically by the superintendent, as well she might. The previous week, Dot Moore, one of the New Road team, had handed her notice in as her husband had just got a job in South Africa and Kay Williams, the sister in charge of the Hackney Road patch, had announced she was pregnant. This had thrown the clinic's bed bath and midwifery rota into chaos as Kay couldn't undertake any heavy lifting and Dot was one of their most experienced midwifes.

After shaking the hands of the new recruits and calling them 'darling girls', Miss O'Dwyer had toddled off to visit a set of twins born the night before leaving Connie to do the necessary with the new nurses.

Although the nurses had forwarded their measurements for their uniforms on to the Area Health Authority before Christmas, it had taken Connie at least four phone calls to actually get their uniforms delivered. They'd arrived last thing the Friday before in one huge laundry bag so it had taken the best part of an hour in the nurses' small lounge sorting out which dresses, overcoats and hats belonged to whom.

The nurses' bags were easier, as Connie had ordered them plus the necessary equipment direct from the suppliers, so they could be sorted out after lunch.

Of course, this was very different from when she'd taken up her first post as a Queen's Nurse in 1943. In those days, because you were employed by a nurse association, nurses had to buy all their own uniform and equipment, including their bag. This had meant handing over precious clothing coupons. At the risk of turning into her mother, Connie couldn't help but think new Queenies nowadays didn't know they were born.

Grace stepped into the bedroom and looked around the fifteen by twenty-two foot space.

It had a single bed against the far wall with one of the clinic's washed-out counterpanes covering it. There was a solid square sink with a mirror above and a hand towel tucked over the support bracket beneath. On the wall opposite the bed was a single wardrobe with a dressing table next to it. Although the clinic heating was on, Connie had been to each of the allocated rooms to turn on one bar of the electric fire and now the room was comfortably warm.

'It's not the Ritz,' said Connie. 'But once you add some personal touches and a few photos, it will be a great deal more homely.'

'It's fine,' said Miss Huxtable. 'And bigger than the room I had in St Maragret's.'

'I thought as you were the most experienced of our new nurses you'd appreciate having one of the larger rooms,' said Connie.

Putting her case down on the lino, Grace smiled. 'That's very thoughtful of you.'

'It's about the same size as mine next door and as we're at the back of the house we get the sun for most of the afternoon. Of course it also means it is best to keep your window shut when the brewery is steaming a batch of hops.' Connie gave her new colleague an apologetic smile.

Grace laughed. 'I'll bear it in mind, sister.'

'Connie, please,' Connie replied. 'We're a friendly bunch here, so as long as there are no patients around, it's just first names.'

'That's a relief,' said Grace. 'At my last place the superintendent insisted we address each other as sister or nurse even over meals.'

'I had a superintendent like that in my last clinic,' said Connie, pulling a face. 'You daren't leave a pair of stockings to dry on the radiator in case she did a room inspection and fined you for untidiness, but as you can see Miss O'Dwyer is a lot less formal.'

Grace laughed. 'Can I ask, does she always have a baby with her?'

'Pretty much,' Connie replied. 'And mothers often leave their little ones with her if they have a hospital appointment or something.'

Grace looked amazed. 'Doesn't Area object?'

'I'm not sure they know and even if they do, what can they say?' asked Connie. 'The superintendent's job is to ensure that mothers and babies are cared for and that's just what she's doing in her own inimitable fashion.'

In truth, some days Fry House was more like a day nursery than a NHS clinic, but no matter.

'Don't worry, I'm sure you'll get used to it.' Connie laughed. 'And if you feel a bit broody you can always have a sneaky little cuddle, like I do.'

A stark look flickered across Grace's face as the colour drained.

'Are you all right?' asked Connie.

Grace nodded. 'Just a little light-headed, that's all.' She smiled wanly. 'It's my fault. I had to catch the 6.30 shuttle from Ongar so I'm afraid I skipped breakfast this morning.'

Connie glanced down at the watch pinned to her apron.

'Well then, as it's almost ten forty-five and Mrs Rogerson will be wheeling the elevenses into the nurses' lounge any moment now, I'd say this is the perfect time for you to sample some of her excellent fruitcake.'

Hari scribbled his name followed by 18 Jan '49 on the bottom of the notes and shoved them in the back of the wooden box.

'Next!' he bellowed.

There was a pause then the door opened and a carthorse of a man stomped through the door, his hobnail boots dropping brick dust on the carpet.

'About bleeding time,' he said, glaring at Hari. 'I've been waiting for almost an hour.'

'Have you?' Hari replied, matching his patient's hostile stare.

'Yes, I bleeding well 'ave.' He took a drag from the roll-up curled in his palm.

'Well, I've been waiting for three hours for my lunch,' Hari snapped back. 'Now, if you want me to treat you, sit down. If not, I'll call in the next patient.'

Thanks to the damp conditions most of his patients lived in, a seasonal bout of flu had swept through the neighbourhood bringing bronchitis and pneumonia with it. As there was already a queue stretching down the street when he'd arrived back from his house calls at one-thirty, Hari had thought he'd clear some of the backlog first and then grab a sandwich when the crowd thinned. Unfortunately, the hacking coughs, sticky eyes and wheezy babies just kept coming. Mr Whoeverhewas, standing there in his grubby trousers and with three days' worth of stubble on his lantern jaw, was the twenty-third patient and Hari's temper and good humour had walked out somewhere around patient number ten.

All he was concerned with now was clearing the waiting room before eight and then putting on the extortionately expensive coffee percolator he'd bought himself in the January sales the week before and making himself an extra-strong pot of coffee to drink while he soaked in his new bath.

Hari drummed his fingers on the table.

The man chewed the inside of his lip for a moment, then plonked himself on the chair on the other side of the desk.

Hari fixed the labourer with an unwavering stare. 'And I don't allow smoking in my surgery.'

The man looked as if he were about to argue, but then thought better of it and pinched out the end of the roll-up and stuck it behind his ear.

Hari went to the antiquated filing cabinet. 'Name?'

'Donavan, Michael.'

Hari extracted a file. '17 Albert Mansions?'

''Sright.'

Hari sat down and smiled professionally. 'Now, Mr Donavan. What seems to be the problem?'

'Me chest,' said Mr Donavan.

'What about your chest?' asked Hari.

Mr Donavan punched his sternum. 'Feels a bit tight.'

'When did it start?'

'A couple of days ago and I've been coughing up phlegm,' Mr Donavan replied.

Picking up his stethoscope Hari rose to his feet again and went round to his patient.

He opened the sphygmomanometer on the edge of the desk. 'Will you roll up your sleeve?'

Mr Donavan gave him a suspicious look but rolled up his frayed cuff nonetheless.

Hari wrapped the fabric band around Mr Donavan's beefy bicep. He hooked his stethoscope in his ears and placed the other end on his patient's brachial artery. He pumped up the machine then slowly released the pressure, noting where the pulse stopped and resumed.

'Can you unbutton your shirt and sit forward,' said Hari.

Mr Donavan gave him a disgruntled look.

'I never had all this mucking about with Dr Marshall,' he muttered as he unfastened what buttons remained.

Hari didn't reply. Putting the earpieces back in position, he slipped the cup of the stethoscope between Mr Donavan's smelly shirt and grey singlet.

'Breathe normally,' said Hari.

After listening to the wheezing and rattling on the labourer's chest for a minute, Hari withdrew his hand.

'Well, Mr Donavan,' he said, returning to his side of the desk and sitting down again. 'You have the start of a very nice chest infection there.'

He reached for his prescription pad.

'I want you to dissolve two tablespoons of this,' he said, scribbling on the prescription pad and adding his signature to the bottom, 'in a basin of boiled water, then put a towel over your head and inhale the vapour. That should loosen things a bit but I want you to rest up and keep warm. Who do you work for?'

'The council,' said Mr Donavan.

'Well, see how you go for a couple of days but don't spit, cover your mouth if you cough, and make sure your wife boils your hankies. I've written you up for aspirin, in case you start a fever. The chemist will write on the dosage for you, but don't take more than it states.'

Hari offered him the prescription.

'What about some tonic?' asked Mr Donavan.

'Tonic?'

'Dr Marshall always writes me up for a tonic to give me a bit of a pick-up,' explained the labourer. 'Old Crowther in the chemist makes it up special, like. I know I have to have it private but—'

'Save your money and your breath, Mr Donavan,' said Hari. 'As I've told everyone, they'll have to see Dr Marshall as I'll not prescribe it. If you want to feel better an apple a day and two helpings of cabbage will do you just as much good.'

Mr Donavan stood up and reluctantly took the offered sheet of paper.

'You've got a nasty deep rattle when you breathe,' Hari continued as he snapped the top back on his pen. 'And if you want to steer clear of chest problems in the future, my advice is give up smoking.'

Mr Donavan snorted. 'Give up me fags? Why? Dr Marshall told me himself it helped clear the bronchioles.'

To illustrate the point, Mr Donavan took the cigarette from behind his ear and strolled out banging the door behind him.

Hari massaged his temples to keep the throbbing headache that was trying to take hold at bay then shouted, 'Next.'

Hari let his head fall back onto the chair as he waited.

There was a long pause, then the door opened.

He opened his eyes and raised his head. 'And now, M—'

He smiled.

'Sister Byrne,' he said as his gaze ran over her. 'How very nice to see you.'

He wondered if, like him, she was remembering their very pleasant turn around the dance floor. Was she recalling the way their bodies moved in time to the rhythm or the feel of his arm around her trim waist?

He was just starting to wonder if perhaps her dazed expression was a reflection of some kind of feeling towards him when she spoke.

'For goodness sake, Dr MacLauchlan, I don't think I've ever seen so many people in the waiting room.'

*

'That's the last patient, doctor,' Connie shouted along the corridor as she closed the surgery's front door.

'Thank goodness for that,' Dr MacLauchlan shouted back.

Amen to that, thought Connie.

After leaving the new nurses to settle in, Connie had started out on her afternoon round. As it was easy to go past Christ Church surgery on the way back to Fry House, she'd decided to drop in on Dr MacLauchlan and pick up any messages to save him the trouble of phoning them through.

She'd only expected to be a minute or two but instead she'd walked straight into utter mayhem.

She should have twigged something was up when she saw the line of battered prams against the railings outside. The waiting room itself was packed to the gunwales and Connie found herself fighting her way between at least a dozen people in the hall just to get to the consulting room door.

It was now just before seven. Turning the lock on the front door, Connie went into the waiting room.

Pushing the shabby half a dozen chairs back against the wall and switching off the electric fire, she tidied away the dog-eared magazines and then walked back down the hallway to the consulting room where Dr MacLauchlan was still writing up notes at his desk.

He looked up as she walked in.

A grateful smile spread across his face.

'Sister Byrne,' he said, throwing his pen down. 'How can I ever thank you enough?'

'You don't have to,' said Connie. 'And besides, I could hardly leave you battling on alone.'

'You could have,' he replied. 'But I am eternally grateful you didn't. Do you know how many we saw in total?'

'Thirty-one,' said Connie. 'It would have been over forty but I told a couple of patients with bumps and bruises to go to the Fry House dressing clinic in the morning.'

Dr MacLauchlan raised a well-formed eyebrow. 'Did you indeed?'

'I certainly did,' Connie replied. 'They don't need to waste your time with a scuffed knee when we can dab a bit of iodine on it at the clinic.'

She picked up the box of patients' notes from the desk.

'It's all right I'll do that later, sister,' he said wearily.

'It's no trouble,' said Connie.

'Are you sure?' he said. 'You've done enough already and I'm sure you should have been off duty an hour ago.'

It was an hour and a half actually, but Connie smiled.

'Honestly, I don't mind, doctor,' she said. 'And now I've worked out the system, I'll be done in a jiffy.'

Dr MacLauchlan rose from his chair and, coming around the desk, stood in front of her.

'Well then, in that case,' he said, smiling down, 'while you do that I'll do something to show how grateful I am.'

A couple of possibilities flashed through Connie's mind and her heart did a little double step. 'There's no—'

He raised his finger. 'I insist.'

He strode out, leaving the faint smell of aftershave and surgical spirit in his wake.

Connie stared after him for a second, then straightened the prescription and sick certificate pad. Next she picked up the discarded stethoscope. Her finger scraped against a raised marking and she looked at it. Most doctors and nurses now used the new type of stethoscope with a Bakelite percussion that lay flat on the patient, however, Dr MacLauchlan's was a much older design with a cone-shaped end and what looked like ivory earpieces. It also had Cpt JHCM 17th IA stamped on one of the arms.

She had just hooked it back when a rich, enticing smell reached her nose as Dr MacLauchlan walked back into the consulting room holding a tray with two mugs, a sugar bowl, milk jug and an American-style coffee pot.

He set it down on the table, then pulled out the chair on the patient's side of the desk.

'Sister Byrne.' He gave an exaggerated bow. 'If you'd care to take a seat?'

Connie laughed and, tucking her skirt under her, sat down. 'It smells delicious. Is it real coffee?'

'It most certainly is.' Dr MacLauchlan set out the mugs. 'And I'll tell you, in the last few days it's the only thing that's kept me upright.'

'I know what you mean,' said Connie with feeling. 'It's been the same at the clinic. I don't think there's been a day in the last week we haven't been bandaging legs and arms until six o'clock.'

'Well then, I'm even more grateful to you for staying to help.' He poured their coffee. 'Milk and sugar?'

'Yes and two, please.'

Dr MacLauchlan stirred in two heaped spoonfuls and offered her the mug.

'Thank you,' she said, feeling a little odd having a doctor wait on her rather than the other way around.

She took her drink and her fingers brushed his.

'My pleasure,' he replied, his eyes dark and warm as they ran over her face.

Connie gave him a shy smile and Dr MacLauchlan returned to his chair.

'Do you mind if I take off my jacket?' he asked.

'Of course not,' said Connie.

Dr MacLauchlan shrugged it off and hung it on the back of his chair. He turned back his cuffs a couple of times, revealing muscular forearms, then unbuttoned his collar and loosened his tie.

Connie's gaze flickered over the triangle of tanned skin with a sprinkling of dark hair between his throat and collar bone.

'That's better,' he said, wearily reaching for his coffee.

His chair creaked as he leant back and studied her for a moment.

Feeling suddenly warm under his gaze, Connie took a sip of coffee. 'Did you have a nice Christmas, Dr MacLauchlan?'

'Quiet.' He laughed. 'Although I couldn't say I was alone as I spent most of the day going from one sick patient to another, topped off by a visit to the Prescotts' because Mrs Prescott decided to have a chicken for dinner and gave her entire family food poisoning.'

'Oh dear,' said Connie.

'It wasn't so bad,' said Dr MacLauchlan. 'And I had my belated Christmas dinner at my Aunt Janet's in Essex a week later. What about you?'

'At my mum's with the rest of the family,' said Connie.

'Have you got a big family?'

'Massive if you count my aunts and uncles and cousins.' She laughed. 'But I've got two brothers and two sisters and except for me and my younger brother Bobby, all of them are married with eleven children between them.'

'Goodness, how do you all fit around the table?' he asked.

'We don't, the children have to eat first, then the adults,' Connie replied. 'But it's fun.'

'Sounds it.' Dr MacLauchlan laughed with a rich, throaty sound which set Connie's stomach fluttering. 'A bit different from me and my mother waiting for my father to carve the goose, not least because it was usually eighty degrees fahrenheit outside.'

'Sounds very exotic,' said Connie. 'But I can't imagine it being hot at Christmas.'

'And I must have been in my fourth year at Repton before I got used to going to midnight mass and singing carols with snow on the ground.'

Out of the corner of her eye, Connie caught sight of the clock on the wall.

'Goodness,' she said, bolting down the last of her drink. 'I'm supposed to be meeting someone in ten minutes.'

'The chap you were with at the dance?' asked Dr MacLauchlan.

'Yes.'

'Your boyfriend?'

'My fiancé,' Connie replied.

Something unreadable flashed across Dr MacLauchlan's face, but then he smiled broadly. 'Congratulations. When's the happy day?'

'October 1950.'

'That's a long way off.'

'Yes it is,' sighed Connie.

'I'd be worried if I were him,' Dr MacLauchlan said.

Connie looked puzzled. 'What about?'

Over the top of his mug Dr MacLauchlan's dark eyes ran slowly over her face. 'That someone might steal you away.'

Connie stared at him for a moment, then laughed. 'Someone steal me away? I don't think so.'

Dr MacLauchlan shrugged. 'Stranger things have happened.'

Connie laughed again, stood up and unhooked her coat from the peg.

Dr MacLauchlan rose from his seat and walked around the desk.

He took her coat from her. 'Allow me.'

Connie slipped her arms in and he settled the jacket on her shoulders.

She turned. Before she could stop herself, her gaze flickered down to the base of his throat before returning to his face.

He stared down at her for a moment, then picked her bag up from the floor. 'You'll be needing this.'

'Thank you,' she said, taking it from him. 'And for the coffee.'

'No, thank you, Sister Byrne,' he said in a rich tone. 'For your assistance.'

'I'll see you tomorrow,' she said, gazing up at him.

He smiled. 'I look forward to it.'

Giving him a shy glance, Connie left but as she strolled down the chilly corridor she chuckled. Who on earth would try to steal her away from Malcolm!

Chapter Ten

Two days later, with the weather being much the same, Connie waited patiently until the policeman on the school crossing patrol had stopped the traffic in Commercial Street.

It was nine-thirty in the morning and it had rained incessantly since dawn. Although she'd only been out and about for an hour she was already soaked through. Her first morning visit was to see Master Peter Daly who, according Fran's message in the overnight call-out book, was just a week old.

The Daly family had only moved into the area a few months ago and Mary, Peter's mother, had been an irregular visitor to the antenatal clinic during her pregnancy, but when she had attended there was nothing of note. With an uncomplicated pregnancy, Mary Daly had clearly passed through the system without causing a ruffle.

Connie turned into Thrawl Street and the temperature dropped by several degrees. The reason for this was, with the six-storey-high Rothschild Building on one side and the equally imposing Lolesworth Building on the other, that the sunlight rarely illuminated the narrow street.

Both tenements were funded and built in the 1880s by the wealthy Rothschild family and the other by the Four Per Cent Metropolitan Dwellings Company as the plaque above the main door proclaimed.

In their day the two-room apartments with their own scullery must have been nothing short of luxury, but now after years of crumbling neglect they were some of the most dilapidated homes Connie visited.

With her nurse's case gripped firmly in her hand, Connie walked into the second entrance and then turned into the dank stairwell.

The solitary light fitting above her head had broken glass where the bulb should have been and the smell of ammonia from the damp patch in the crook of the stairs and the smell of rotting vegetables from the communal rubbish bin was so overpowering that even Connie's cast-iron nurse's stomach rebelled.

Holding her breath and stepping over a discarded Durex, Connie headed up to the third floor.

Squeezing past a rickety pram and a rusty-looking mangle on the landing, Connie reached number thirty-five. As the door was on the latch, Connie pushed it open.

'Midwife,' she called, stepping in and closing the door behind her.

The hall she found herself in was bare of any furniture and, by the look of the faded wallpaper, hadn't been decorated for at least twenty years. The linoleum covering the floor was ancient and had worn through to the hessian backing in places. However, despite its original pattern being almost undistinguishable, the floor was swept clean and the Bakelite handguards on the doors were free from fingermarks.

Somewhere in the flat a heater was burning and Connie caught the unmistakable odour of a bucket full of soaking nappies.

She'd only taken a couple of steps when a toddler, bare from the waist down, shot out from the room at the far end, hotly pursued by a little girl of about eight or nine.

'Brian, will you come here?' she shouted to the child.

Brian grinned at his sister and continued running. Halfway down the hall he collided with Connie and promptly weed down her leg.

Connie smiled. 'Hello,' she said, trying to ignore her wet shin. 'Is your mum around?'

'She's in the front room,' the young girl replied, gawping up at her.

She grabbed her brother's arm to drag him away, but Brian threw himself on the floor and screamed.

Stepping over the tussling children, Connie went into the main room of the house.

A balsawood plane whizzed past her nose followed by a lad of about eight years old as he grabbed for the airborne toy. His brother, coming from the other direction, lunged at it too and both boys ended up in a tangle of legs and arms on the floor at Connie's feet.

The main room of the house was furnished with a few sticks of ancient furniture, all of which were draped with drying washing, as was the fireguard, where row upon row of off-white children's vests and knickers hung in front of the hearth. On the mantelshelf was a statue of Christ with a gilded bleeding heart and next to it was an ornate photo frame holding an image of the Virgin Mary with a rosary draped over it.

The drop-down table had a sheet draped over it to make an improvised house, inside which two little girls squabbled over a doll. By the door a small boy, with wild curly hair and a sticky face, sat in a highchair sucking a dummy.

Behind him, Mrs Daly shuffled out from the scullery holding a bottle of formula milk in her free hand.

She was probably no more than thirty or so but her brown hair was streaked with grey and there was barely an ounce of spare flesh on her bones. A faded blue dress covered with a wrap-around apron and shapeless slippers down-trodden at the heel made her look a great deal older than she was.

As expected, Mrs Daly looked heavy-eyed, but it wasn't just the natural tiredness of broken sleep but rather the bruised-eyed weariness of utter exhaustion. This wasn't surprising as so far Connie had counted eight children including the new baby. Despite this, although the children were dressed in what must have been third- if not fourth-hand clothing, all of it was clean and mended. In addition, the children were clearly well fed and had their hair neatly trimmed or brushed.

Connie smiled professionally and was just about to speak when the boys dashed back into the room firing imaginary guns at each other.

The taller of them let off a rapid round from his invisible machine gun at his brother, who dodged from the line of fire and knocked into the high chair.

The youngster sitting in it, who was clearly the twin of the nappyless boy, screamed, dropping his dummy onto the floor.

'For the love of Jesus,' shouted Mrs Daly, handing the crying child the bottle. 'Now will you give me a moment's peace and play in the bedroom.'

'Yes, Ma,' said the boys in unison as they skulked away.

'Those boys would have St Peter himself swearing like a

docker,' said Mrs Daly, retrieving the dummy from the floor.

'Mrs Daly?'

She nodded and after putting the dummy in her own mouth to clean it, she popped it back in the child's. 'Call me Mary, won't you?'

'I've come to give Peter his one-week check,' said Connie.

'He's in the room across the way,' said Mary.

The laughing toddler without a nappy ran through again with his sister still in hot pursuit, but Mary caught him as he dived past her.

'I'll just give this lot a bit of bread and scrap and I'll be with you.'

Leaving Mary to settle her children, Connie walked through to the room across the hallway.

The Dalys' bedroom was only really big enough to take the double bed and a single wardrobe which had clothes hanging around the outside. However, in addition to these two pieces of furniture, there was also a cot wedged at the foot of the bed and two mattresses, made up with sheets and blankets, on the floor. Again, although the counterpanes were old and the sheets had been turned edge to edge, they were clean.

In the middle of the bed, seven-day-old Peter lay in a large cardboard box which had a picture of an oast house and the words *From Britain's Own Garden* stamped on the side.

He was swaddled in a blue blanket and wore the serene, un-worried expression of total peace that's only seen on a newborn that is fed, warm and dry.

Resting her case on the end of the bed, Connie set out the mesh sling and fisherman's scales, then lifted the baby out of the improvised cot.

Peter stretched and raised his almost invisible eyebrows as he tried to open his eyes but, feeling himself in safe hands, he relaxed again as Connie laid him on the bedspread.

'I'm sorry, sweetheart,' said Connie, unbuttoning his white matinée jacket and taking it off. 'But you're not the only young man I've a date with this morning.'

She eased down his leggings and as the cooler air touched his skin, he opened his eyes.

Popping him quickly into the mesh net, Connie hooked it on

the scales and as the gauge settled on a number, Mary walked in.

'Six three,' said Connie, lowering Peter back on the bed. 'What was he when he was born?'

'Five ten,' said Mary. 'Bit of a tiddler compared to the others.'

'Well, I'm not surprised,' said Connie, as she checked the black stump of his umbilical cord, relieved to find it clean. 'I doubt you had much time to put your feet up while you were carrying him.'

'You've the right of it there, sister,' replied Mary. 'They're not bad kids just . . . you know . . .' She gave a weary sigh. 'And now the weather's turned, I can't even send the boys to play in the courtyard cos this damp will go straight to my Tom's chest. The weekends are murder with them all cooped up in here.'

'Couldn't you send the older ones along to Saturday morning pictures?' asked Connie. 'It would at least get them out of your hair for a few hours.'

'I would if I could afford it,' Mrs Daly replied.

'I'm sorry,' said Connie, annoyed with herself for being so insensitive. 'I didn't mean to—'

'You're all right, sister,' said Mrs Daly with the same tired smile.

Connie smiled. 'Haven't you got family nearby who could help?'

'I've got a sister in Southend, but her old man skipped off two years ago and she's got her hands full with five kids under eight,' Mrs Daly explained. 'My husband's family are in Ireland so we're pretty much on our tod.' Her expression softened. 'He's a good man and does all he can with the little 'uns but he's digging roads all week and then up at four of a weekend setting up market stalls in Wentworth Street, so by the time he gets back after a week on a building site and then getting up at the crack of dawn of a weekend he's done in.'

'I can believe that,' said Connie, popping the vest back over the baby's head and threading his little arms through. 'Still, the good news is young Peter here is putting on weight nicely now, although I'd like you to bring him to the Wednesday baby clinic at Fry House so we can keep an eye on him.'

Peter, turning his head towards his mother's voice, opened his mouth. Mary reached down and picked him up.

'How are you feeding him?'

'With nature's own,' she replied, settling herself against the headboard. 'It's free.'

Unbuttoning her blouse, she tucked him into her breast where he latched on immediately.

'I'm pleased to hear it,' said Connie. 'It's the best for him.'

'And meself, God willing, as it might stop me falling for another.' Mary ran her finger over her son's downy head. 'I love him so I do . . . but I don't know how I'd cope with . . .'

She hastily crossed herself.

'You don't have to, Mrs Daly.' Connie snapped open her nurse's bag at her feet and delved in. 'There are ways you can avoid getting pregnant.'

She handed Mary a leaflet with the words *Plan Your Family the Modern Way* in square bold print across the top.

'It's not only French letters nowadays,' said Connie, opening the paper. 'But gel pessaries and a cap too. The family planning clinic in Burdette Road will be able to advise you better and—'

'I'm sorry, sister,' said Mary, giving Connie the pamphlet back. 'I know you mean it kindly but I can't.'

'Why?'

'Father Flaherty says it's a mortal sin for any man or woman to interfere with the Almighty's plan so if I was to have any truck with the mothers' clinic or use any of the paraphernalia in your pamphlet there I'd have to confess and I know he'd refuse me communion.'

Mary changed Peter to the other breast.

Connie studied her patient's bowed head for a moment, then spoke.

'Look,' she said, placing her hand over Mary's. 'I'm a Catholic myself so I understand the problems with confession and communion and I know you've probably been given the Church's leaflet on the rhythm method by some older woman in the congregation but, believe me, there is only one way to stop yourself becoming pregnant again and that's by going to the family planning clinic.'

'Sure, sister, I know you mean well,' said Mrs Daly. 'But I'm afraid I'll have to do as I've done before and pray to the Lord and hope that this time he'll listen.'

*

Taking the chalk board from the hook behind the desk in the empty treatment room, Connie scrubbed her name off the weekend rota.

All in all, considering it was almost the end of January, the season of runny noses, chesty coughs and children red-throated with tonsillitis, it hadn't been a bad day for a Friday. It looked for once as if she might, just might, be dressed and ready for Malcolm when he arrived to collect her at seven-thirty.

Of course, as her mother was fond of saying, 'Mild weather at Christmas, full graveyard in January,' so the fact that it had been below zero since mid-December had probably helped kill off the usual new year germs.

All Connie had to do now was hand over to Miss O'Dwyer and then she'd be done.

Hooking the board back in its place, Connie glanced over at the stainless-steel dressing trolleys, concertinaed screens in the corner and clean examination couches and, finding them all in order, switched off the light and left the room.

Making her way down the hall to the superintendent's office, she knocked and, when she heard Miss O'Dwyer's reply, she opened the door.

As usual for a Friday afternoon, Miss O'Dwyer was sitting at her desk with the weekly rota and the nurses' timesheets in in front of her. However, they weren't the sole object of her attention because, as always, the superintendent had a young companion to keep her company.

Today it was a little girl of about nine months, dressed in a grubby pink matinée jacket and leggings. The superintendent was dandling the child on her knee as she filled in the nurses' wages sheet.

Miss O'Dwyer looked up and smiled. 'Hello, me dear. I expect you've come to tell me that everything is just as it should be, no more, no less?'

'I have,' said Connie, closing the door behind her. 'Is that Brenda McFee's Doreen?'

'It is indeed.' A doting expression lifted the superintendent's rounded face. 'And a little darling you are too, aren't you, me angel?' she said to the infant.

146

Doreen dribbled onto Miss O'Dwyer's beefy forearm by way of response.

'So where's her mum?' asked Connie.

'Calling in to see her sister in the East London Maternity Hospital,' Miss O'Dwyer replied.

Connie glanced at the clock on the wall above the superintendent's head.

'But visiting time finished almost three hours ago,' she said.

'I told her not to hurry,' said Miss O'Dwyer.

Connie sighed.

With such an invitation, Connie didn't think they would see neither hide nor hair of Brenda much before closing time, as no doubt she and the rest of the McFee clan would be in the Red Lion wetting the baby's head until then.

'The only change to the weekend rota is that as Lillian's mother is still poorly after her op I said she could stay over until Monday if I got cover,' said Connie. 'And so Margery has kindly agreed to do Lillian's stint on Sunday. I thought you wouldn't mind.'

'Nor do I,' said Miss O'Dwyer, as the baby in her arms made a grab for the fountain pen. 'Sure, wouldn't every daughter want to tend her mother?'

Doreen thrust out a sticky hand and grabbed one of the nurse's timesheets.

'How are you getting on with the weekly returns?' Connie asked, prising the paper from the child's chubby fingers.

'As always, the jumble of figures are scrambling me brain and flaying me temper.' Miss O'Dwyer looked heavenwards. 'St Matthew himself wouldn't have been able to make head nor tail of them, I can tell you.'

She looked imploringly at Connie.

'Would you like me to have a look at them over the weekend, superintendent?' asked Connie.

Miss O'Dwyer's face lit up like a lightbulb. 'Would you now?'

'Of course,' said Connie, mentally waving her Saturday morning lie-in goodbye.

'Isn't Aunty Connie a darling girl?' Miss O'Dwyer said, as she kissed the baby's untidy curls.

Doreen wriggled in her embrace and started chewing on her fist.

Holding the child firmly, the superintendent rose to her feet.

'I think someone wants her supper.' Settling the baby on her hip, Miss O'Dwyer waddled to the door. 'I'll be wishing you a grand weekend, Connie.'

Leaving Connie to tidy the papers strewn across her desk, the superintendent left.

The phone on the superintendent's desk rang, but as she was now officially off duty, Connie ignored it.

It rang a few more times until someone picked up the hall extension. Connie had just tapped the three dozen timesheets into order when there was a knock at the door.

'Come.'

The door opened and Moira's head poked around the corner.

'It's your friend Millie on the phone,' she said. 'She says it's urgent.'

Connie pushed open the door of the public house just opposite Aldgate Station. The wooden-fronted Georgian pub was squashed between an optician's and a denture repair business to its left and a photographer's studio on its right. As the front of the narrow public bar was crowded with market porters, City clerks and secretaries relaxing, the Hoop and Grapes was several steps up from a dockside alehouse but, even so, Connie still felt uncomfortable walking into a bar alone.

Peering through the whirls of smoke, she spotted Micky Murphy flanked by a couple of bruisers with busted noses; he was sitting in one of the booths at the back, puffing on a cigar. Wearing a flashy checked suit with a heavy gold watch chain slung across his ample middle, Micky was deep in conversation with a slightly built young man perched on the stool in front of him.

He raised his brimming glass as he noticed her.

Connie acknowledged him with a smile and a quick nod, then hurried over to the far corner of the bar where she'd seen her friend.

'Thanks for coming so quickly,' Millie said, standing up to embrace her.

Untying her rain hood, Connie shook out her hair. 'Don't be silly. Now, let me get a G&T and then you can tell me everything.'

She unclipped her handbag and pulled out her purse. 'What do you want?'

'I suppose another brandy won't hurt,' said Millie, looking forlornly into her glass.

'Another?' said Connie. 'How many have you had?'

'Two.'

Connie's fair eyebrows almost disappeared under her fringe, but she went to the bar and ordered their drinks.

'There you go,' said Connie after a few moments, putting a glass on the cork coaster in front of her.

'Thanks.' Millie took a large mouthful, pulling a face as it burnt the back of her throat.

'Where've you parked your scooter?' asked Connie, taking a small sip of her own drink.

'I left it at the clinic,' Millie replied. 'I thought it best.'

'I'm glad to hear it,' said Connie. 'I don't fancy your chances navigating around Stratford Broadway with three brandies inside you.'

Millie gave a sheepish grin and took another sip.

'Now,' said Connie, putting on her best matron expression. 'What's happened?'

'Alex phoned.'

'Alex?' Connie put her hand over her mouth. 'No!'

'Yes,' said Millie. 'An hour ago.'

'No wonder you're throwing back brandies,' said Connie. 'What did he say?'

'Nothing much,' Millie replied casually.

Her friend gave her a questioning look. 'You did tell him you were married?'

Millie looked down and swilled the drink in her hand. 'Not as such.'

'Millie!'

Her head snapped up. 'Well, it's not the sort of thing you can say easily over the phone. Is it?'

Connie looked aghast. 'You're not going to meet him?'

'Just for a quick cuppa, that's all. On Monday,' Millie cut in. 'What else could I say?'

'"I'm sorry, Alex, I'm married and so I can't meet you" might have done it,' said Connie.

'For goodness sake, Connie. We're having a mid-morning coffee in Kate's Cafe, not a weekend in Brighton.' Millie frowned. 'We were close once but a lot has happened since then.'

'Yes, like you being in the family way for a start,' said Connie, her gaze drifting down to Millie's still-flat middle. 'So you'll tell Jim, then?'

Millie looked up. 'Naturally. And I'm sure Alex will tell his wife.'

'Ah, yes. I forgot,' said Connie. 'He got married, didn't he?'

'He's probably got a baby, too, I shouldn't wonder,' Millie added. 'He always was mad keen to start a family.'

Connie scrutinised her friend's face for a couple of seconds, and then spoke again. 'Are you sure it's wise to open up old wounds?'

Millie forced a brittle laugh. 'Don't be silly, Connie. After all this time of course there aren't any wounds left to open. And I'm sure Alex is just as happily married as I am.'

She took another mouthful of her drink and so did Connie.

The pub door burst open and half a dozen beefy-looking men wearing off-the-peg suits and belligerent expressions burst into the bar. As those hoping for a quiet after-work drink edged away, the newcomers surveyed the scene for a moment until they spotted their quarry, then they stomped in.

'Murphy,' the one at the front bellowed.

There was a scrape of chairs as Micky's two henchman rose to their feet.

'DI Whitworth,' Micky replied through the cigar gripped firmly between his teeth. 'Fancy seeing you here.'

'Yer, fancy,' the CID officer replied. 'I want a word with you down at the nick.'

'About what?'

'The break-in at Robertson's warehouse the night before last,' the DI replied. 'Now, are you going to come quietly or are we going to have to persuade you?'

En masse the plain-clothed police officers surrounding him stepped forward.

The toughs either side of Micky did the same and one cracked his knuckles.

As the two groups of men squared up to each other, Micky threw down the last of his drink.

'It's all right, lads,' he said, rising to his feet. 'I'm 'appy enough to have a little chat with you, Mr Whitworth, down at your gaff but I can tell you here and now I don't know nuffink about nuffink.'

Puffing out his chest, Micky pulled down the lapels of his jacket and then bowled out, the officers surrounding the DI parted like the Red Sea to let him pass.

As the last officer departed, Connie let out a long breath. 'Goodness, I thought we were going to find ourselves in the middle of a pub fight for a moment there.'

'Yes,' said Millie in a thoughtful tone. 'I wonder if Alex has moved up into the CID as he hoped to.'

Squeezing the water from his hair, Hari stepped out from under the shower to let the next grubby player clean off. Grabbing his towel from the peg, he wrapped it around his waist, unhooked his wash bag and strolled out into the steaming changing room.

Around him in various stages of dress were his Old Bartonian team members and the players they had just beaten by two goals to one: the Imperial College Old Boy's hockey team. That not-withstanding, the good-natured horseplay and banter between the two sides showed the score wasn't as important as the satis-faction of a game well played.

Walking to his locker, Hari opened it and took out the hanger with his clothes on; he hooked them on a peg next to him. Un-winding his towel, he dried himself briskly before stepping into his underpants.

'I shouldn't talk to you after that last shot,' said a voice from behind him.

Hari swung around.

'George, you old bugger.' He laughed, grabbing his old friend's outstretched hand.

George Ewell was a year or so older than Hari and just above middling height. He was solidly built and his sandy hair was slicked back with Brylcreem; the spectacles sitting squarely on the bridge of his nose were a new addition. He and George had been undergraduates together at Cambridge where they'd played in the college's first eleven. They'd parted company when Hari took the post of a junior doctor in Barts and George went to

Imperial College. They'd meet up at conferences and the like but had seen little of each other until they'd found themselves at Aldershot for basic training. The last time Hari had seen George was on Waterloo Station in 1940 when he was shipping out to Malaysia and George had just been assigned to the 3rd Infantry Division field hospital.

Wearing casual slacks, a sports coat and Imperial College tie, George looked every inch the successful consultant.

Hari shook his hand vigorously.

'Where the devil did you come from? And why weren't you on the pitch playing?' Hari asked, putting his foot on the bench and running the towel over his leg.

'Because of this.' George rapped his knuckle on his right thigh and it made a tinny sound. 'A present from a German shell on Gold Beach.'

'Bad luck,' said Hari, taking his trousers from the hanger and shaking them out.

George shrugged. 'Could have been worse. I see you didn't come home unscathed.'

He indicated Hari's back and shoulders, strafed with scars.

'Courtesy of the Butcher of Nakhon Pathom,' Hari replied, stepping into his trousers. 'Loved his bamboo cane, did that man. Loved it so much that someone shoved it through his eye and out the back of his head the day after the camp was liberated.'

George blanched slightly. Hari didn't blame him. It wasn't a sight to imagine, let alone witness, as he had.

They stood quietly for a moment as memories of comrades who now lay in well-tended graveyards in foreign places flitted through both their minds, then Hari play-punched George in the upper arm.

'But we made it.'

His friend grinned. 'That we did.'

'And now,' said Hari, shrugging on his shirt, 'I feel there's a pint—'

'And a Scotch,' cut in George.

'If not two or three with our name on at the nearest hostelry and' – Hari buckled his belt – 'if I remember rightly I bought the last round on platform ten so it's your shout.'

One hour, two pints and umpteen pictures of George's wife

and children later, when they'd both run through their part in Hitler's downfall, Hari ordered them both a single malt at the bar.

They were sitting in the snug at the back of the Lamb pub just around the corner from Coram's Fields, where the hockey match had been held.

The old pub had survived the Blitz pretty well and most of its original etched-glass privacy screens and polished mahogany bar were still intact. Now a handful of locals, along with a couple of young doctors from the nearby Great Ormond Street Hospital, were enjoying a Saturday lunchtime drink.

'So what about you?' asked George as Hari set the glass in front of him.

'What about me?'

'Well, your family for a start?' said George.

'My father worked in the Home Office during the war, helping to keep the railways operating,' said Hari. 'He died two years ago.'

'I'm sorry,' said George.

'It was a blessing really,' said Hari. 'I'd just started working in the Prince Aly Khan Hospital as the senior registrar when my mother phoned. He'd been ill for some time, stomach cancer, and he'd been struggling on. Thank God I got back just in time.'

George looked sympathetic. 'I suppose your mother took it hard.'

Hari nodded. 'They'd spent most of their married life in India so, naturally, when she found herself a widow she went back. She lives at her brother's palace outside Lucknow.' A wry smile lifted the corner of Hari's mouth. 'In some luxury, I might add.'

'I'm surprised you're not out there too,' said George.

'I would be if it wasn't for politics,' Hari told him. 'Anyhow, I've landed on my feet so I'm not complaining.'

'I'm surprised you've not settled down yet,' said George. 'What happened to you and that lovely looking girl whose father worked in the Foreign Office?'

'You mean Edwina Mainwaring?'

'That's her,' said George.

'Married someone else,' said Hari.

George looked shocked. 'That's a bit of a rum deal.'

'I don't blame her,' Hari continued. 'She thought I was dead.'

'Didn't the Red Cross get a list of Japanese prisoners after the fall of Singapore?' said George.

'They did but it only had about half the names on it and mine wasn't one of them. To be honest, I think my pride was hurt more than my heart when I found out so it was probably for the best.'

'So are you involved with anyone at the moment?'

Hari looked down and took a sip of whisky. 'Not as such.'

George studied him closely for a couple of seconds.

'Now, tell me to mind my own business or just say "bugger off" if you like, Hari,' he blurted out, 'but do you remember my cousin Rosalind?'

Hari frowned. 'I'm not sure—'

'Slim girl with dark hair,' said George. 'She was training to be a teacher. She came up for the May Ball on our last year when Johnny Bodden fell in the river. You had a dance with her.'

'Oh yes, I remember her,' said Hari. 'Her family lived in Rye, didn't they?'

'That's her,' said George, looking encouraged. 'Well, she has had a bit of a bad run recently. She was planning to wed when the war finished, but her fiancé was killed in the Allied push across France so she went to live with her widowed mother on the south coast but lost her too, last year.'

'A bad run indeed,' said Hari.

'She's back in London now and working at a girls' school in Chelsea as head of English and . . . Well, she's not attached and neither are you, so . . .'

George gave Hari a sheepish look.

An image of George's slender cousin standing by the River Cam, her bouncy chestnut hair and floaty yellow dress blowing in the breeze, formed in Hari's mind.

He smiled.

'What a splendid idea,' he said, grinning at his friend.

George looked visibly relieved.

'Here's my telephone number,' he said, taking a pen from his inside breast pocket and scribbling it on a beer mat. 'Give me a couple of days to have a word with Rosalind and see if I can arrange a meeting.'

'Thanks, but I've got a better idea.' Hari fished out his business card and offered it to George. 'You find out if she's amenable to the suggestion and, if she is, then I'll ring her myself. Much more gallant, don't you think?'

'Very,' said George.

He picked up his drink. 'To who knows what.'

Hari raised his drink too. 'To who knows what,' he repeated, hoping that a pair of soft brown eyes and auburn tresses would be the antidote he needed for sparkling blue ones and copper curls.

Chapter Eleven

'So did she meet him?' asked Bernie.

Connie nodded and took a fairy cake from the plate her sister had offered her. 'She told him she was married and, according to Millie, he was very happy for her. They had a quick chat and parted as friends.'

It was just after four-thirty on the Thursday after her meeting with Millie, she'd just recounted the whole incident to her sister over a cup of tea.

She was sitting in Bernie's very comfortable front room. Although most of the furniture was in the pre-war style, her brother-in-law had recently redecorated the room with a geometric-patterned wallpaper which had odd angles and blobs of colour on it. The old opaque light shade held in place with chains had also gone and a chrome futuristic light fitting sprouting half a dozen individual bulbs had taken its place.

Coronation Street, where Bernie, her husband Cliff and her four children, Marlene, Gloria, Bette and four-month-old Anthony lived, was just off Plaistow Road.

Just a short walk from the district line station, the road her sister lived in was one of neatly painted doors and tidy front gardens. Unlike the area where Connie and her siblings had grown up, her sister's neighbours were bank clerks and Gas Board officials rather than dockers and market traders.

Bernie and Cliff had taken a gamble and bought the house for £155 at the height of the Blitz. Luckily it had survived the war and, much to Connie's mother's consternation, Bernie was already talking of moving further out and buying a bigger house in upmarket Hornchurch.

'And do you believe her?' asked Bernie.

'Not for one moment,' Connie replied. 'She had it bad for Alex and, if you ask me, she's still carrying a massive torch for him.' She took a bite of cake. 'It might have been all right them meeting up for old times' sake if he hadn't told her that he wasn't married after all. I've got a horrible feeling knowing that has opened up old wounds, especially the way Jim treats her.'

Bernie looked puzzled. 'I thought you said he was charm on legs.'

'He is,' agreed Connie. 'But I've got a horrible suspicion that all these late-night meetings aren't always for work.'

'You don't think her old man might be playing away from home, do you?' asked Bernie.

'I wouldn't be surprised,' said Connie. 'And I wouldn't want to be in Jim's shoes if Millie finds out.'

'Well, it just shows you how lucky you are with Malcolm,' said Bernie.

'What do you mean?' asked Connie.

'Well, your Malcolm wouldn't dream of throwing it all in and dashing off to some godforsaken place,' said Bernie. 'He's solid and dependable, that's what he is. You'll never have to worry about not getting his dinner on the table on time as I bet you'll be able to set your watch by him getting home each night.'

'I'm sure I will,' said Connie, feeling the years of unchanging married life pressing down on her.

'Are you all right, Con?' asked her sister.

'Yes, of course,' said Connie, shaking off the melancholy shadow. 'Why do you ask?'

'You look a bit gloomy,' said Bernie.

Connie forced a bright smile. 'I'm tired, that's all. With all this damp weather we've been inundated with people coughing and wheezing. I even had to step in and help Dr MacLauchlan out at evening surgery last week because he was snowed under.'

Bernie raised an eyebrow. 'Dr MacLauchlan, eh?'

Connie laughed. 'Now don't start all that again.'

'I'm just saying we seem to hear a lot about him,' said Bernie, her face a picture of innocence.

'No you don't.'

'Well, last time you told me how he realised the boy had an allergic reaction, not scarlet fever—'

'Well, yes . . .'

'And the time before it was about the new posters Dr

MacLauchlan has put up in the waiting room and how he got the council down to repair the drains in the surgery backyard.'

'I suppose I do mention him from time to time,' said Connie, feeling more than a little awkward. 'But it's only because after having to deal with old Marshall for so long, Dr MacLauchlan is a breath of fresh air, but it's purely professional, honest.'

Bernie reached over to squeeze her hand. 'I'm only teasing you.'

'All right,' said Connie. 'But promise you won't go on about him in front of Malcolm like you did at Christmas.'

Bernie held up her right hand with her little finger held down by her thumb. 'Girl Guide's honour.'

Connie laughed. 'You were kicked out.'

'Only because Gladys Lovejoy snitched on me,' her sister replied. She took a sip of tea. 'Talking about you and Malcolm,' said Bernie. 'Has Mum spoken to you about Aunt Peggy's Linda?'

'What about her?'

'Well, as she had chicken pox when Cousin May got married, she missed out on being a bridesmaid so Aunt Peggy wonders if she could be one of yours?' said Bernie.

'But I've already got your three, Jim's two and Mo's Audrey,' said Connie.

'I know,' said Bernie. 'But Mum thought as Malcolm's side hasn't got any girls, you might be able to squeeze Linda in.'

'But if I do won't I have to squeeze in Aunt Dolly's Janice and Patricia too?' said Connie.

'Mum didn't say,' said Bernie. 'But she's fallen out with Dolly.'

'This week,' said Connie. 'She'll be at odds with Peggy next week. You know what Mum and her sisters are like and, besides, I've got to pay for the dresses.'

'But if you have Linda you can have rainbow bridesmaids,' continued Bernie.

'Rainbow what?'

'Apparently it's becoming fashionable to have your bridesmaids in the seven colours of the rainbow,' explained Bernie.

'I suppose that's Mum's idea, too,' said Connie.

'She read it in last week's *Woman's Own*,' her sister replied. 'Did she?'

Bernie nodded. 'But of course it's your day so up to you.'

A vision of the shoebox on the sideboard in her mother's front room containing dozens upon dozens of clippings of bridal dresses, veils, headdresses and bouquets materialised in Connie's mind.

'I know,' she sighed. 'I just have to make sure Mum remembers that.'

Tapping the weight along half an inch, Connie watched as the arm of the scales steadied.

'Eleven pound three,' said Connie, lifting three-month-old Denis Lamb out of the scoop.

It was the second Wednesday in February and Connie was in charge of the afternoon baby clinic. Even though it wasn't yet three-thirty, she and Harriet had weighed at least two dozen infants, doled out dozens of bottles of concentrated orange juice and distributed almost the same number of tins of dried milk in exchange for a welfare chit.

Of course it should have been her and Grace in clinic that afternoon but, yet again, she'd swapped with another nurse.

It wasn't a problem exactly, and being dribbled and posseted on by an assortment of screaming infants, not to mention the overpowering smell of ripe nappies, wasn't everyone's cup of tea. However, having spent hours ensuring that the rotation of duties was fair, Connie was more than a little put out by Grace's actions.

Chewing over whether to raise the issue with Grace or not, Connie sat Denis Lamb on her lap facing her.

'You're getting a big boy, aren't you?' she said, making a happy face at the boy.

Smiling back, Mrs Lamb's firstborn son kicked his legs and blew a bubble in response.

'Just like his dad,' said Mrs Lamb, regarding her offspring with undiluted love.

Iris Lamb was a pretty brunette who'd married her childhood sweetheart, Fred, as soon as the army had finished with his services, and Denis was her honeymoon gift to him. They lived with Fred's parents in the back room of an old cottage just off Valance Road.

'How much is he taking on each feed?' asked Connie, moving

her finger back and forth and watching the baby's eyes follow the movement. Satisfied with his response, Connie handed him back, just in time, it would seem, judging by the small damp patch on her apron.

'Five ounces every four hours,' Iris replied.

'That sounds about right,' said Connie, taking out her pen and making a note. 'Any other problems?'

'Not that I can think of, sister.' Iris pressed her lips onto her son's fair curls. 'And once we get to the top of the list and get a little place in the country he can 'ave a little brother or sister.'

'Where have you applied for?' asked Connie.

'Our first choice is Dagenham because there's an underground station and second is Harold Hill,' Iris replied. 'But I don't mind really as long as I've got an inside bog and bath.'

Connie smiled and handed her Denis's weighing card. 'See you in two weeks' time.'

With her son balanced on one hip, Iris made her way out of the treatment room.

Connie wandered over to the table and tucked Denis's notes into the back of the box. She was just going to pick up the next set when the telephone on the desk jumped into life.

As Harriet was in the middle of showing a mum with two fractious children clinging to her legs how to paint egg white onto a baby's bottom to ease nappy rash, Connie picked up the receiver.

'Fry House, Sister Byrne speaking, how can I help you?'

'Hello, luv, it's Madge Gibbs here,' said a gruff voice down the phone. 'I live across from Doris Miggins. She says to tell you to come as 'er waters have gone and 'er pains are regular every two or three minutes and she's started to feel the urge to push so you'd better hurry.'

'Thank you, Mrs Gibbs,' said Connie. 'Can you stay with her for ten minutes until the nurse gets to her?'

'Course,' Madge replied. 'I'll boil your kettle and fetch you some towels too. See yer.'

Connie put the handset back in the cradle.

Moira, who was first midwife on call, had been called out before lunch and wasn't yet back, which was unfortunate as the second on call was Jane, who was off sick.

Squeezing her way past a group of toddlers playing on the floor, Connie hurried over to her colleague.

'I'm sorry,' she said as Rebecca repinned the nappy. 'I'm going to have to go out on a delivery so can you hold the fort until I find someone else to step in?'

'Of course I can,' said Harriet, wrapping the blood pressure cuff around a baby's chubby bicep. 'If you're lucky there might be someone back early for tea.'

Leaving Harriet in the treatment room, Connie hurried down the corridor to the nurses' lounge. As Mrs Rogerson would be wheeling the tea trolley through in fifteen minutes, Connie was hopeful she'd find someone to take over from her. However, her heart sank when she opened the door and found the room empty.

Frantically she searched in the small sitting room, the linen cupboard and the equipment store in the basement. She thought of trying to get Miss O'Dwyer to cover until she remembered the superintendent was attending an area meeting at St Andrew's Hospital in Bow.

With the minutes ticking away and an image of Mrs Miggins in labour stuck in the forefront of her mind, Connie dashed up to the rooms above, taking the stairs two at a time.

Having knocked and received no reply on three of the nurses' doors, Connie got to Grace's room.

She was just about to hammer on the door when it opened.

Elegant and perfectly groomed as always, Grace stood in the doorway wearing a slim-fitting Prince of Wales checked skirt and a ribbed jumper. She had a handbag hooked over one arm and a Liberty bag in the other with what looked like a box wrapped up in pink paper with a bow on top.

'I'm really sorry,' said Connie breathlessly. 'I'm going to have to ask you to cover the baby clinic as I've been called out on a delivery.'

Alarm flashed across Grace's face. 'But it's my day off.'

'I know, but—'

'And I'm meeting someone,' interrupted Grace.

'I'm sorry, but—'

'And I did it last week,' continued Grace, panic flitting across her usually calm face. 'My head was practically split in two with all those screaming babies. Surely there must be someone else—'

'I wouldn't be standing here if there was, would I?' Connie's mouth pulled into a flat line. 'Sister Huxtable, I have a clinic full of babies and a woman in advanced labour requiring my assistance, so I'm afraid whatever plans you have for this afternoon will have to be shelved as you're going to have to go down and help Harriet.'

Grace stared at her for a moment, then lowered her eyes. 'Yes, sister,' she said softly. 'Patients must come first.'

'They most certainly do,' Connie replied.

Grace nodded. 'I'll be down as soon as I've changed.'

'Thank you,' said Connie. 'And you can use the clinic telephone if you need to tell your friend you won't be able to make it this afternoon,' she called over her shoulder as she hurried back to the top of the stairs.

The sun was low in the sky by the time she left Mrs Miggins and her new daughter in the care of her neighbour. Madge hadn't been kidding when she said to hurry, Connie had only just managed to tie her mask in place and drag her rubber gloves on before the baby's head crowned. Seven pound two Lucy Miggins arrived in the world with surprising ease ten minutes later. Connie had washed, weighed and dressed the newest member of the family, then she'd changed the bed and given Doris a freshen-up before leaving mother and baby in the care of Madge.

Wrapping her scarf a little tighter around her ears to ward off the chill, Connie unchained her bicycle from the stairwell railings and wheeled it out into the street.

The heady aroma of lamb stew wafted over Connie as she opened the clinic door.

In contrast to earlier, the house was now buzzing with nurses who, at the end their shifts, were collecting uniforms from the laundry room, sorting their letters from the afternoon post and catching up on the day's events.

Unwinding her scarf and then taking off her coat and hooking it on the hall stand, Connie headed for the treatment room. There were no patients waiting, so Connie guessed Grace and Rebecca must be finishing up.

Connie opened the door to see Grace dealing with a smartly dressed woman with a young baby in her arms.

The young woman rose to her feet and after tucking her baby into a gleaming new Marmet pram by the door, she left.

Standing up, Grace stretched her arms wide and yawned.

'Busy afternoon?' asked Connie, scrubbing her scissors in the soapy water.

'We didn't stop,' Grace replied, gathering up the box of notes. 'Rebecca worked like a trojan all afternoon so I sent her off after she loaded the steriliser.' Putting the notes in the cupboard, Grace headed for the sluice. 'It should be done by now so I'll lay up for the morning clinic.'

'You've done enough,' said Connie, smiling warmly. 'The supper gong will be going soon so just get the instruments out so they can cool, then go and get changed. And I'll sort out the trolleys later.'

Grace nodded and went into the sluice at the end of the room. Connie had just rinsed off her forceps when there was a knock.

'Come!' she called, dropping them in the surgical spirit.

The door opened and Dr MacLauchlan stepped into the room.

His mac was unbuttoned to reveal his charcoal double-breasted suit and the now-familiar RMC tie at his throat. His hair was tousled and the evening chill had put a spark in his eyes.

Before she could stop it, Connie's heart did a double step.

He spotted her and smiled. 'The super said I might find you here.'

'Dr MacLauchlan,' she said, feeling a little breathless. 'Is there an emergency?'

'Thankfully not,' he said. 'I was just passing and—'

'That's the steriliser emptied,' said Grace, walking back into the room.

Shock flashed across Dr MacLauchlan's face. 'It can't—'

Grace stopped dead in her tracks.

'Dr MacLauchlan,' she said, her cheeks practically on fire. 'Grace . . . I . . .'

'Good evening, Dr MacLauchlan,' Grace said, visibly struggling to compose herself. She looked at Connie. 'If you don't need me for anything else, sister, I'll—'

'No, nothing, thank you,' Connie replied, feeling very awkward standing between them.

Grace gave her an uncertain smile and then her gaze flickered over Dr MacLauchlan. 'Good to see you again.'

'And you,' he managed to reply before the door banged shut behind her.

Dr MacLauchlan stared after her, then turned back to Connie.

'Sorry, Sister Byrne,' he said, giving her that boyish grin of his. 'I was just a bit taken aback to see Grace, that's all.'

Although something unpleasant seemed to have settled on her chest, Connie forced a jolly smile. 'That's all right, doctor. It's always nice to run into an old friend unexpectedly.'

Carrying a tray with two mugs of cocoa and a plate with half a dozen of Mrs Roberston's shortbread fingers on it, Connie reached the third floor of Fry House as the grandfather clock below sounded nine o'clock.

Making her way along the hallway, she stopped outside Grace's door. Shifting the weight so the tray balanced on one arm, she raised her hand and knocked.

'It's open,' Grace shouted from the other side of the door.

Grace was sitting on the bed in her dressing gown, her blonde hair was loose around her shoulders and her legs were crossed at the ankle.

Looking slightly alarmed when she saw Connie, she set aside the book she was reading and stood up.

'As you were,' said Connie, smiling at her. 'I've not come to tell you you're on call tonight or something equally awful. I've made you a cup of cocoa instead.'

Grace looked puzzled. 'That's very kind, but why?'

'To thank you for stepping into the breach this afternoon,' said Connie, setting the tray on the dressing table. 'And because I was a bit sharp earlier. Sugar?'

'One, please,' Grace replied. 'And you had every right to be sharp as I was forgetting a nurse's first duty.'

'To her patients,' said Connie.

'Exactly.'

'And how were they this afternoon?'

'Loud and complaining,' said Grace with a sigh. 'A toddler tipped over a pram by hanging on the handles while one of the babies projectile vomited all over the woman sitting next to its mother. I tell you, this afternoon's baby clinic made the chimps' tea party at London Zoo seem like lunchtime in a nunnery.'

Connie laughed. 'So just the usual then.'

Grace smiled. 'Indeed.'

Stirring in a heaped spoonful of sugar, Connie handed her colleague one of the mugs. 'Were you able to contact your friend in time?'

'Yes I did,' Grace replied. 'And thank you for letting me use the telephone.'

'It was the least I could do after ruining your afternoon,' Connie replied.

Tucking her dressing gown under her, Grace sat back on the bed and Connie took the armchair by the small fireplace.

'This is nice,' she said, sinking into the upholstery.

'I brought it from home,' said Grace, helping herself to a biscuit. 'Along with the bedspread and cushions.'

'Well you've certainly made it very cosy in here,' said Connie, glancing around.

The sterile room Grace had been allocated now had a very modern look about it. There were curtains with bold splashes of red, black and green at the window, a circular rug with geometric designs covered the lino floor and a lampshade like a Chinaman's hat hung from the ceiling.

'Very snug,' continued Connie, noting the Bush wireless and collection of novels on the bookshelf in the corner. 'And I like the nets.'

'I saw them in the linen shop just down from Wickhams when I was passing last week,' said Grace. 'Just one and nine a yard.'

'Bargain,' said Connie, looking impressed.

Grace took a sip of cocoa. Connie did the same, then spoke again.

'Fancy you and Dr MacLauchlan knowing each other like that,' she said.

'Yes, small world,' said Grace.

'I suppose you know him from Barts?' continued Connie.

Grace shifted her position on the bed. 'No, from the Hastings Memorial Hospital. His medical unit was evacuated there from Dunkirk and he was in charge of the medical ward where I was one of the nurses.'

'Well, you must have made an impression,' said Connie lightly. 'As he recognised you straight away and even remembered your name.'

Grace blew across the top of her cocoa. 'Yes, although I'm surprised he did. We only worked together for a couple of months, then I was reassigned to the 8th Army and his unit was sent to Malaysia. Until we bumped into each other by chance two years ago, I didn't even know Hari had survived the war.'

'Thankfully for the patients at Christ Church surgery, he did.'

When Grace didn't reply, Connie drained the last of her cocoa. 'Well, thank you again for this afternoon. Rose must be out of the bath by now so I'd better jump in before someone else does.'

'Yes, you had,' said Grace. 'And don't worry, I'll take the empties down before I turn in for the night.'

Connie stood up and as she did so, one of the pictures on the mantelshelf caught her eye.

'What a pretty baby,' she said, picking up the framed photograph.

'My sister's little girl,' Grace replied.

'What's her name?'

'Sarah.'

'How old is she?'

'She's three months there,' said Grace, taking the photo from her and staring fondly at it. 'But almost ten months now.'

'So gorgeous and all that lovely dark hair,' said Connie, tilting her head to see better. 'And I think she has your eyes.'

Grace looked startled. 'Really? I don't think you can tell at—'

'It's the same as my sister's little girl,' continued Connie. 'If you look at a picture of me at her age you could be forgiven for thinking it was Audrey.'

'I suppose there might be a family resemblance,' laughed Grace. She took Connie's mug. 'You'd better hurry or you'll lose your bath.'

Connie smiled and turned to go but when she reached the door she paused. 'I know we are informal amongst ourselves in Fry House,' Connie said in her best matron voice. 'But we refer to Dr MacLauchlan as Dr MacLauchlan in the clinic.'

Something flickered in Grace's eyes and she smiled. 'I'll remember that in future.'

Connie smiled. 'Have a good evening.'

Closing the door behind her, Connie headed back to her room. As she collected her nightclothes and towel, she caught sight of Malcolm's picture sitting on her bedside table. She picked it up, but instead of pondering her fiancé's image, Connie found herself wondering exactly how long Grace and Dr MacLauchlan had been calling each other by their first names.

Chapter Twelve

As the rush-hour stragglers hurried past him, intent on catching their trains to Surrey and beyond, Hari turned the page of his evening paper. It was the last Friday in February, just before seven, and he'd been standing under the clock at Charing Cross Station for ten minutes already but that was as he'd planned it. A gentleman always arrived early so a lady wouldn't be left waiting.

He was just halfway through a story about the proposal for another tube line to run from Victoria to Walthamstow when he sensed someone standing close by.

He raised his head and found himself staring into a pair of brown eyes within a heart-shaped face framed with bouncy chestnut curls. She was wearing a light-green dress and jacket with a brown hat.

'Rosalind,' he said, folding his paper away.

'Hello, Hari,' she said with a nervous smile. 'I thought it was you but . . .'

'I know it's been a long time,' he said.

'Yes, almost twelve years but you haven't changed,' she said, with a warm tone to her voice.

'Neither have you,' he replied.

She smiled. 'If only that were true, but it's kind of you to say.'

'Right,' said Hari, dumping his paper in a nearby wastepaper bin and rubbing his hands together. 'I hope you're hungry because I've booked a little place just around the corner.'

'I'm not hungry, Hari,' she laughed. 'I'm starving. I've come straight from a parents' evening and haven't eaten anything since lunchtime.'

Within a few moments of leaving the station, Hari guided Rosalind through the door of Mullins, a small family-run restaurant just off the Strand.

She chose a grapefruit cocktail to start, followed by braised beef with peas, carrots and dauphinoise potatoes, while Hari plumped for the minestrone soup, lamb's liver with spring cabbage, carrots and roast potatoes. He gave their order while she powdered her nose and their drinks arrived as she returned.

They did the polite chit-chat about family and mutual friends over their starters but as their main course arrived, their conversation moved on to their wartime experiences.

After accepting his condolences for the loss of her fiancé, Rosalind went on to tell him that she'd been evacuated with her school to just outside Tamworth, where she stayed until 1944 when the school returned to London.

By the sound of it she'd been very active while in deepest Wiltshire, with the WI programme of recycling clothing for Blitz victims, knitting socks for merchant seamen and was even the chairwoman of the village's fundraising committee to buy a Spitfire. After nursing her mother, Rosalind had taken the post as head of English at Brompton Road Girls' School and found lodgings in Pimlico. She brought her community spirit back with her and was now involved in amateur dramatics, the Townswomen's guild and fundraising for the Children's Country Holidays Fund as well as singing in her church choir.

'So, as you can see,' she concluded as the waiter took away their empty plates. 'What with work and everything else, I keep myself pretty busy. What about you, Hari? What have you been up to since we last met?'

Hari gave her a brief resumé of his pre-war medical career and a few amusing anecdotes about his basic training in the RAMC, a cleaned-up version of the Dunkirk evacuation and then his time on the south coast before being posted to the Far East. He spoke about his time in Bombay and some of his return after the partition of India.

'And that's how I ended up as a GP in the bombed-out East End,' he concluded, as his rhubarb crumble and custard and her baked apple arrived.

'But what about Singapore?' she asked, picking up her spoon. 'George said you were a POW on the Burma railway?'

'Yes, I was.'

Rosalind looked suitably shocked. 'It must have been awful.'

'You could say that,' Hari replied.

'When I saw those soldiers on the news reels marching out of the camps with those little towels around their waists and looking like skeletons, it made me want to weep,' she said. 'And you were one of those poor men who worked on that hellish railway.'

Hari forced a smile. 'Actually, I was one of the poor medics trying to keep them alive.'

'I understand, Hari.' She placed her hand over his. 'You prefer not to talk about it then—'

'It's not that, Rosalind,' cut in Hari, giving Rosalind his most charming smile. 'It's just when a gentleman is in the company of an attractive young lady, he wants to impress her with his stylish dress sense, sophisticated choice of restaurant, attentive manner but, above all, his scintillating conversation and I'm not sure my POW experiences with wood lice and snakes fall into that category.'

'Oh, Hari,' Rosalind giggled. 'You haven't changed.'

He grinned. 'How can you improve on perfection?'

She laughed again as the waiter brought their coffee.

Hari offered her sugar and she added two heaped spoonfuls to her drink.

'So,' she said, giving him a coy look as she stirred it in. 'As you're wining and dining me, I assume you're not involved with anyone.'

An image of Connie Byrne at the Christmas dance with her blue polka-dot dress swirling around her slim legs flashed through his mind.

'Regrettably not,' Hari replied.

'Regrettably?' asked Rosalind, giving him a curious look.

Hari smiled. 'Regrettably, because I haven't met anyone yet I want to become involved with but I live in hope.'

Rosalind picked up her glass of rosé. 'Well then, here's to hope.'

Hari raised his. 'To hope.'

They both took a sip.

'This has been very nice,' said Rosalind.

'Yes, it has,' Hari replied. 'We should do it again.'

A little flirtatious smile spread across Rosalind's lips.

'I'd like that, Hari,' she said. 'I'd like that very much.'

Connie tickled three-month-old Peter Daly's tummy as he lay on his mother's candlewick bedspread. Peter Daly, who was all smiles and dimples today, kicked his legs enthusiastically.

Mrs Daly's twin three-year olds were in the other bedroom having their afternoon nap so, except for the men drilling up the road below, for once the house was relatively quiet.

It was the middle of March and the warm early spring sunshine was streaming through the window. In contrast to her son's happy mood, his mother sat red-eyed on the bed opposite him.

'I'm so sorry,' said Connie. 'I came as soon as I got the message.'

'It's good of you to pop in at all,' Mrs Daly replied, forcing a smile through her tears. 'Considering how busy you are.'

'Losing a baby at any time is very distressing,' said Connie. 'So I thought I'd see how you are.'

Mary covered her face and sobbed quietly. Connie shuffled closer and put her arm around her patient's shaking shoulders.

'Now, now, Mary,' said Connie. 'These things happen.'

'You don't understand,' she said, raising her tear-stained face. 'I didn't want another baby and I prayed day and night that something would happen and . . . the truth of the matter is I'm so relieved.'

The front door banged and heavy footsteps tramped down the hall.

Mary grabbed Connie's hand.

'Don't tell my husband what I said,' Mary whispered.

'Of course not,' replied Connie under her breath.

Mary hastily wiped her face and blinked her reddened eyes.

The bedroom door opened and the head of the household stepped into the room.

Mr Daly was a wiry individual of somewhere around middling height with wavy hair that was on the verge of changing from carrot-red to pale russet. He was wearing a frayed shirt, worn cord trousers and a donkey jacket.

'Good day to you, sister,' he said as he spotted Connie.

'Hello, Mr Daly. Nice to meet you.'

'You're home early,' said Mary, forcing a bright expression.

'One of the gangs found an unexploded bomb where we were digging so we were all sent home,' Mr Daly replied.

'Did the council pay you the afternoon's work?' asked his wife.

'What do you think?' he replied flatly.

Mary looked anxious. 'But I've already put the last shilling in the gas an hour ago and if . . .'

'Don't you worry, none,' he said. 'I've got an hour or two's work later at the brewery loading up.'

'You're a good man so you . . .' She started sobbing again.

'Hush, hush now,' he said softly, bending to kiss his wife on the forehead. He looked at Connie. 'Mary's taken losing the little one hard.'

'It's understandable,' said Connie.

Bending down, he ran a calloused finger lightly along his son's cheek. 'Still, perhaps in God's good time we'll be blessed again, me darling.'

Mary blew her nose but didn't reply.

Her husband yawned and stretched. 'I'll be taking the older four to mass with me later, so if I don't want to fall asleep in the confession box I'd better catch forty winks before they get home.' He touched his forehead. 'Good day to you, sister.'

'Good day, Mr Daly,' Connie replied.

He tramped off back down the hallway and into the lounge.

'I'll pop in and see how you're getting on next week, Mrs Daly,' said Connie, reaching down and closing her bag.

'Thank you, sister,' said Mary, twisting her handkerchief around her fingers. 'But before you go, could you spare me one of those leaflets about the mothers' clinic?'

The midday factory hooters were just sounding as Connie closed Mary Daly's front door.

Ducking under the washing strung across the balcony and stepping around an old pram parked outside the end flat, Connie made her way back down the stairs to the street below. She was just pondering if she had time to pop in on Mrs Wilson before lunch when she turned into the street and was nearly knocked down by Father Flaherty.

'Good day to you, Sister Byrne,' he said, gazing munificently down at her.

'And to you, Father.'

'And as busy as ever, no doubt.'

'I certainly am,' Connie replied with feeling.

'And who is it that's had the benefit of your ministrations this fine day, I'm wondering?' he asked.

'One of your flock. Mrs Daly,' said Connie. 'You do know she lost a baby.'

'Indeed I did,' Father Flaherty sighed. 'The Lord giveth and the Lord taketh away. I'm just about to visit myself.'

'To pray with her?' asked Connie.

'No,' he replied. 'To enquire why the family hasn't been to mass for two weeks.'

'Well, I would have thought having suffered a miscarriage a week ago, plus caring for a small baby plus eight other children, I think Mrs Daly has enough to do getting them all washed, dressed and fed without worrying about anything else,' said Connie.

His bushy grey eyebrows pulled tightly. 'Our Blessed Lady never let motherhood stop her from fulfilling her religious duty and you'd do well to remember that, Sister Byrne.'

He raised his hand and, with the habit of a lifetime, Connie bowed her head.

'*Nomine patri spiritus sanctus*,' he boomed.

He swept past her and up the stairs but as she watched his cloak billow out behind him, Connie felt like a five-year-old who'd been caught using her rosary as a catapult.

Chapter Thirteen

'Did you and Malcolm have a nice time at your friend's wedding last week?' asked her sister Bernie.

They were standing at the temporary barriers set up along Central Avenue in Battersea Park, along with hundreds of other families out enjoying the mid-April sunshine.

The Easter Parade didn't start until 2 p.m., but Connie had met Bernie and the children at Aldgate just after nine so they could spend the day exploring the park. Thankfully, after a wet Good Friday, the rest of the weekend had been fine so the grass was bone dry when they'd spread out their picnic blanket within sight of the Guinness Clock at midday.

They were now holding the family's place in the crowd while Bernie's three girls played tag on the grass behind and Anthony had his afternoon sleep in the pushchair parked between them.

'We did. Gillian looked beautiful and her father had tears in his eyes as he gave her away,' said Connie. 'The village church was just perfect but packed. They had the reception at a local hotel.'

Bernie pulled a face. 'That's posh.'

'Well, she's the only girl so her parents splashed out a bit,' said Connie. 'The food was classy too. We had grapefruit to start, followed by lamb then trifle with real cream. The band later was very good, although as usual Malcolm wouldn't dance.'

'My Cliff's the same.' Her sister pulled a face. 'I think the last time we stepped on a dance floor together was twelve years ago when we got married. I suppose the next time will be a silver anniversary if I don't kill him before.'

Connie laughed. 'What's he done now?'

'Well, he blooming well forgot to book us on the Grey Green coach for our holiday,' Bernie replied, rocking the pushchair back and forth. 'Luckily there's so many people going to Butlin's, they've had to put on another coach to Skegness and we managed to squeeze on that.'

'Poor Cliff,' Connie laughed. 'I bet you gave him a right ear-bashing.'

'Too right I did. It would have been a right turn-up for the books if we'd booked a holiday with Mo and her lot only to find we couldn't get there because of old sieve-brain.' Her face softened. 'Still, I might let him off seeing how he's been working double shifts at Ford's for the past month to pay for it all.'

'Bet the girls are looking forward to the holiday camp,' said Connie.

'They've talked about nothing else since we told them, Marlene's even set up a chart in their room and is marking off the days,' said Bernie. 'Of course it's cost me a fortune in new clothes but I've packed them away so they've got them for when we go. It's only a week but it will be wonderful, especially having Mo and her four around. She tried to persuade Mum and Dad to go. Dad was keen but Ma pulled one of her faces. Mo said her and Arthur are going to enter into the ballroom dancing contest.'

'They should,' said Connie. 'After all, they were the Eastern Counties champions before they had the children. Where's your Cliff today?'

'Round his mate's helping him put a new water tank in the loft,' said Bernie. 'So it's as well your Malcolm is off looking at trains.'

Connie gave a tight smile. 'He didn't go.'

'What happened?'

'His mother's not well,' said Connie.

'Is she ever?' scoffed Bernie.

Connie raised an eyebrow. 'She's one of those people who enjoys bad health.'

'What's wrong with her this time?'

'Apparently, while he was cleaning his Thermos flask on Saturday, she came over all faint,' said Connie. 'So they're having a quiet day at home together.'

Bernie tutted and rolled her eyes. 'I'm glad she's not going to be my mother-in-law. How's Millie getting on? She's not got long now, has she?'

'Just two months,' said Connie. 'She seemed well enough

when I saw her a few weeks back although she can't see her feet any more.'

'Is her old man still out all hours?' asked Bernie.

'Yes he is,' said Connie. 'In fact, since he was elected as a MP he's hardly at home. She hasn't said anything but, reading between the lines, I don't think she's very happy at all and what makes it worse is she keeps running into her old flame Alex.'

'Poor Millie,' said Bernie with a sigh. 'But what else can she do? She'll have to suffer an unhappy marriage just like thousands of others.'

'You don't know Millie,' said Connie, with a hard laugh. 'If Jim oversteps the mark and pushes her too far, he'd better watch out.'

The crowd around them stirred; craning her neck, Bernie looked towards the gates.

'I think it's starting,' she said. 'I'd better call the girls.'

Leaving Connie with the pushchair, she squeezed her way through the people behind them to gather her children. The brass band at the front of the parade blasted out a chord and Anthony woke up.

'Hello, sweetheart,' Connie said to the bemused child.

Bending down she unbuckled his reins and lifted him out just as Bernie arrived back with her three daughters.

The three girls, all miniature versions of their mother, were eleven, eight and six. Marlene, who would be starting secondary modern school in September, was dressed in a rather grown-up dark blue dress with a Peter Pan collar and angora bolero while her other sisters wore identical lemon-coloured outfits with silhouetted poodles scampering around the skirt.

Stepping back to allow the girls into the prime slot against the barrier, Connie swung Anthony's legs over and sat him on the top so he could see.

Each year the Easter Parade had a theme and this year it was children's books and already Connie could see a collection of familiar characters marching along behind the band.

Slowly the lorries with the floats on the back rolled towards them with the storybook characters scampering alongside and shaking hands with their young audience.

'Look, girls!' shouted Bernie, pointing towards the front of the parade. 'Can you see Winnie the Pooh?'

Winnie, complete with an enormous pot of honey and Christopher Robin beside him, waved while Tigger, Eeyore and Piglet danced next to him. A few floats behind came Snow White surrounded by her dwarfs, and a very menacing-looking wicked queen was booed enthusiastically as she trundled past.

Connie's nieces squealed and waved as Heidi and Peter, dressed in traditional Swiss costume, skipped past, then they screamed in horror at Hansel and Gretel locked in their wicker cage.

'Look, Mum, it's Rapunzel,' shouted Marlene.

Connie turned to look at the float her niece was pointing at and saw a cut-out castle with a young girl sitting in the window.

The girl's false golden tresses flowed down to the bottom of her tower and the scenery had been skilfully painted to look as if Rapunzel's hair wound around the base. Walking next to the float was a young man in his mid-teens wearing blue tights and a silver satin doublet which was a tad large for his youthful frame. He was attempting to reach his one true love's golden tresses while the crone, who had imprisoned Rapunzel, thwarted him. As the wicked witch determinedly prevented the hero from whisking his princess away, Connie couldn't help but wonder why Malcolm's mother had never considered building a tower in her backyard.

Chaining her bike alongside the collection of prams outside Christ Church surgery, Connie lifted out her bag and trotted up the front steps.

It was just before lunchtime on the first Wednesday in May, two weeks after her day out with Bernie but as Connie had been up since five, she felt as if it were the middle of the afternoon. With two nurses on holiday, another off with a sprained back and Grace taking the half-day she was owed, Connie had hoped if she set out on rounds before eight she'd have a fighting chance of getting all her morning visits done for once. She might have made it too if she hadn't found Mr Snell flat on his back in his kitchen. Thankfully he'd only taken a tumble but he'd needed to go to hospital, so naturally she'd had to wait for the ambulance to arrive. Still, no matter, at least she wasn't doing the baby clinic this afternoon, it wasn't raining and if she was lucky Dr MacLauchlan would still have enough left in his percolator for her to have a quick cuppa while she picked up the messages.

Connie's pulse quickened as she stepped into the hallway but instead of the usual chorus of muttering and coughing coming from the waiting room, the house was unusually quiet.

When she knocked on the treatment room door and Dr Marshall's voice boomed 'Enter', she understood why.

Connie sighed and went in.

Dr Marshall was sitting behind the desk, he was dressed in his usual dishevelled manner with a half-smoked cigarette in one hand and *The Times* open in front of him.

He looked up as she entered and then leant back in his chair.

'Sister Byrne,' he said, the chair creaking under him. 'To what do I owe this pleasure?'

'Good morning, doctor,' Connie replied. 'There was a message from the surgery about a new patient.'

'I must say, you're looking very comely today, my dear.'

'Thank you, doctor,' Connie replied coolly, taking her notebook and pen from her pocket. 'Now, who is it you'd like me to visit?'

His piggy eyes roamed slowly over her for a moment, then he shifted forward.

'I have the details somewhere.' He rummaged around amongst the debris on his desk. 'Here it is. Mrs Gillespie in Weaver Street.' He held out a letter with the council emblem across the top. 'The public assistance officer from the council called in on her last week and thought she looked a bit poorly.'

'What's wrong with her?'

He shrugged. 'No idea.'

'Haven't you visited?' said Connie.

He stubbed out his cigarette and shook his head.

'No need. I know what the problem is,' he said, tossing the letter back on the pile. 'That son of hers.'

'What's wrong with him?'

'Feeble-minded.' Dr Marshall tapped his temple. 'On top of which he's a spastic. I've told her to put him in an institution at least a dozen times but she won't take my advice. I imagine it's all getting a bit much for her. Just pop in and see what you can do.'

'See what you can do' was doctor-speak for there's nothing further I can do.

In the case of elderly patients, it often entailed a twice-daily visit to get them out of bed and give them breakfast before returning to put them back to bed with a hot drink. Often nurses would arrange for a kindly neighbour to take in a midday meal.

However, in Dr Marshall's case, 'see what you can do' meant 'I don't care what you do as long as they don't bother me further'.

Connie regarded the corpulent GP coolly. 'Is there anyone else you'd like me to see?'

He shook his head, then took out another cigarette. 'Not that I can think of.'

'I thought Dr MacLauchlan was on duty today.'

'He should have been but he had to go somewhere,' Marshall replied. 'He had some meeting two weeks ago that was cancelled at the last minute so he took today instead and asked me to cover surgery.'

Connie gave him an artless smile. 'Was it something important?'

'I've no idea, but with a bit of luck, it's an interview for another post,' he replied, patting his pockets in an attempt to locate his lighter.

'Is he looking for another job?' said Connie, feeling oddly unsettled by the thought.

Dr Marshall shrugged. 'He could be flying to the moon for all I know because he barely passes a civil word with me.' Finally pulling the lighter from his top pocket, he lit his cigarette. 'It would suit me if he did push off as I'm sick of listening to his constant goddamn complaints. Keeps badgering me to buy some piece of equipment or other and tries to make out that we're snowed under, yet today I've had no more than half a dozen through the door and most of those were malingerers.'

'I ought to—'

'And while we're on the subject of MacLauchlan.' Dr Marshall inhaled deeply. 'How can I put this delicately? Is he being a bit too, let's call it, friendly?' He blew a column of smoke towards the ceiling. 'You know what I mean?'

'You mean does he pat our bottoms or squeeze us around the waist?' asked Connie.

'Yes, that's the sort of thing,' said Dr Marshall eagerly.

'Like you do?'

Dr Marshall scowled and flicked his ash into an empty teacup on the table.

'Really, Sister Byrne,' he snapped. 'Surely I don't have to spell out the difference between a bit of fun and what I'm talking about here, do I?'

Connie gave him a glacial look.

'I can assure you, Dr Marshall, that Dr MacLauchlan's behaviour towards me has been professional and without reproach on every occasion.'

'I'm relieved to hear it, Sister Byrne,' said Dr Marshall, looking quite the opposite. 'But if he does start to become too familiar or does something distasteful, I want you to come straight to me, do you understand?'

'I'll bear it in mind. Now, I really need to—'

'Because if he does I'll have his goddamn colonial head,' bellowed Dr Marshall, a purple flush spreading up from his collar. 'Do you hear?'

He glared belligerently at Connie but she held his hateful stare.

'Well, if that's all, doctor.' She snapped her notebook shut and shoved it in her pocket. 'I'll be on my way.'

Without waiting for his reply, Connie spun around and with her fists and jaw clenched tight she marched out of the treatment room, all but slamming the door behind her.

Ringing her bell as she turned left, Connie rolled into Weaver Street a little before four-thirty. The cobbled thoroughfare was one of a handful of pre-Victorian streets huddled around the back of St Clement's Church. Although Weaver Street had escaped the German bombers, the two-up two-down dwellings lining each side of the road were little more than inhabited rubble.

In truth, it would have been easier for Connie to walk but because it had taken her half an hour on the telephone to Bancroft Road to sort out a wrong delivery, Connie was now running late.

What with one thing and another, she'd be lucky if she got to Malcolm's and sat down for her own supper much before six-thirty.

Fortunately, Malcolm's mother, convinced she was teetering on the edge of death, had that very rare item in their house – a private telephone. Making a mental note to ring Mrs Henstock and tell her she might be late, Connie lifted her bag from the basket and walked up to the front door.

She was about to knock when a woman with her hair in curlers popped her head out of the front window of the house to her left.

'You visiting Mrs G?' she asked, the cigarette in her mouth jerking up and down as she spoke.

'I am,' Connie replied.

'Can you tell 'er that I'll fetch her shopping in once my old man's gone on shift and Stella'll pop by later to look after Paul?'

'Of course,' said Connie.

The woman went back inside.

Pulling the frayed string dangling out of the letterbox to re-lease the latch, Connie stepped into the house.

'District nurse!'

'In here,' came the reply from the kitchen.

Connie closed the door behind her and walked down the short hall to the scullery

Although the room was far from large, the lack of furniture made it feel spacious. There was a sink with a bleached draining board, a range that should have been in a museum and a cheap pine cupboard with a handful of mismatched china on it. There was also a battered zinc wash tub hanging up on the far wall and through the back window Connie could see turned and darned sheets flapping in the late-afternoon breeze.

Standing by the cooker stirring a pot was a woman in her late fifties. Her pale grey hair had been scraped back into a bun, a few loose strands showed a trace of its original golden blonde.

Wearing a dark blue dress and a knitted cardigan that hung loosely on her frail frame, Mrs Gillespie stood not more than five feet tall.

She looked around as Connie walked in and smiled, her lined features giving a hint of the young woman she'd once been.

'I won't be a moment, I'm just getting Paul's dinner ready,' she said, her soft blue eyes resting wearily on Connie.

'That's all right,' said Connie, casting her gaze over the shiny skin of the woman's swollen ankles. 'I'm Sister Byrne. Dr Marshall asked me to pop in to see if you and your son were all right.'

'That's kind of you, dear,' replied Mrs Gillespie.

Resting the wooden spoon on the side of the pot handle, she shuffled over to collect a bowl from the dresser.

'That smells nice,' said Connie.

'Tripe and onion,' Mrs Gillespie replied, as she returned to the stove. 'It's all there was at the butch—' She started coughing and her lips went blue. 'I'm sorry, I—'

Connie put her case on the floor and went over to Mrs Gillespie. 'Take a steady breath and don't try to talk.'

The woman waved her away. 'I'm all right.' She punched her narrow chest as a wet, deep rattling cough tore through her again.

'Let me finish that,' Connie said, taking the wooden spoon from her.

Mrs Gillespie didn't protest but leant back on the dresser as her chest rose and fell at an alarming rate.

Pretending to study the contents of the pot, Connie glanced down at the watch pinned to her chest. She observed Mrs Gillespie's breathing and counted a worrying twenty-four breaths per minute.

'There,' said Connie, giving the mixture a last brisk stir. 'I think that's ready.'

Taking the bowl, she poured the mixture in.

'I'm afraid it will need mashing, sister, or Paul won't manage it,' said Mrs Gillespie, having regained her breath.

Although tripe was the cheapest of the off-ration offal, the meal contained more onion and potato than meat so it didn't take Connie long to work the stew into a pulp.

She gave the bowl back to Mrs Gillespie and the old woman took it from her. 'Thank you, dear, would you like to meet Paul?'

'Yes, I would.'

'He's in the front.'

Mrs Gillespie walked out of the kitchen and Connie followed her through into the lounge.

No more than twelve by twelve, the main living room was decorated in faded striped wallpaper. The paintwork around the window frames, too, was yellow with age. There was an old threadbare sofa under the window with a multi-coloured crochet blanket slung over it and a pillow at one end. The furniture stood on bare boards and on the mantelshelf above the empty hearth were dozens of photos of Paul along with a statue of a china dog sitting on its haunches with Ramsgate written on its plinth.

There were two chairs on either side of the fireplace and on the one nearest to the window sat Paul.

Paul Gillespie had a mop of white-blonde hair, shaved around his head to just above his ears, and the shadow of his first beard was just visible. He would have been a long, gangly youth except for the contraction of his motor muscles which had twisted his bony frame.

His hands too were splayed and taut with the stretched tendons on the back standing out in relief. His long legs were contorted, bunching his worn grey trousers around his calves. Paul's face hadn't escaped the ravages of cerebral palsy and although his lips were loose, his jaw was off centre and tightly clamped.

In truth, he wasn't so much sitting in the chair as propped up in it as there was a selection of cushions wedged around and behind him to keep him upright. In front of him was a sturdy table on which there was an open book showing a map of South America. As he saw her walk in, his blue eyes, so like his mother's, locked with Connie's, daring her to pity him.

'Paul, this is Sister Byrne,' Mrs Gillespie explained as she set his dinner in front of him.

Paul's twisted mouth lifted in a smile and then he let out a hollow groan.

'Hello, Paul,' Connie said, stepping forward and taking his stiff right hand. 'Dr Marshall asked me to pop in to see if I can organise some help for your mum. I'm sorry if I'm interrupting your dinner.'

'That's all right,' said Mrs Gillespie. 'It's a bit hot yet.'

Connie tilted her head. 'Is that the Amazon river?'

Paul nodded and pointed a shaky finger at a picture of a panther.

'He's been reading all about the animals in the Amazon jungle, haven't you, Paul?' said his mother.

Paul nodded a wobbly yes.

'Have you ever seen any of the big cats?' Connie asked.

He nodded again.

'I used to take Paul to London Zoo every year until he got too big to go in the pushchair.'

183

'Goodness, that's a long way,' said Connie, wondering how the frail woman had managed the stairs on the Tube.

'Last month, I got him a book from the library about the Pacific Islands,' his mother continued.

Feeble-minded, indeed, thought Connie, watching Paul's intelligent eyes as they scanned the block of text.

'Paul is after something about rocket ships next month and the librarian said she'd order an encyclopaedia for him,' his mother said.

She took the towel that was lying over the arm of her son's chair and tied it around his neck.

Embarrassment flitted across Paul's face as his mother pulled a stool alongside him.

After checking the sofa for signs of bed bugs or fleas, Connie tucked her skirt under her and sat down. Putting her bag on the floor, she pulled out a fresh set of notes.

'The woman next door said to tell you that she'll bring your groceries in later and that Stella will be in to sit with Paul,' said Connie, as Paul's eyes remained fixed on her face. 'Do you get much help from the neighbours?'

Mrs Gillespie gave her son another mouthful of stew and smiled. 'I don't know what I'd do without Pearl next door. But she's not the only one, Stella from number seven is always popping by, as does Rita at twenty-two. She has four under five but she still comes over to sit with Paul while I go and get me bits in the market on Friday.'

'What about getting Paul upstairs to bed?' Connie asked.

A rivulet of gravy escaped from the corner of Paul's mouth.

'I used manage it myself but it's too much for me now and when he found out we weren't using the upstairs, the landlord let it to the Wilbers',' said Mrs Gillespie, wiping Paul's mouth with the tea towel. 'I don't mind really. After all, they have three young children and need the space more than me and Paul.'

'Where do you sleep, Paul?'

His eyes fixed on the sofa beneath her.

'Here?' asked Connie.

'It's a bit of a struggle in and out, but we manage somehow, don't we, Paul?' his mother said.

Paul gave a guttural rumble by way of reply.

'What about you?' Connie asked.

'I bed down there.' She nodded at the armchair on the other side of the fireplace. 'So I'm close at hand if he needs me.'

'Are you able to turn Paul?'

'I do, but it's got harder recently and now I'm so afraid he'll get bed sores,' said Mrs Gillespie, coughing again and punching her chest.

'And what about bathing?'

'I give Paul a strip wash at least once a week and a top and tail each day. I wish I could still get him in the bath, but . . .' Mrs Gillespie scraped the bowl clean.

'You're doing a marvellous job, Mrs Gillespie, but if Paul wants a bath I'm happy to organise one each week.' Connie looked to the young man who now had potato on his chin. 'How does that sound?'

He grinned and gave her a stiff thumbs-up.

Connie looked round the room, spotting the uncovered commode, a fat blue bottle circling over it. She also took note of the grubby pillowcase and the tidemark around Paul's neck. 'And I could put you down for a put-to-bed call and one in the morning, including a full wash, too,' she added.

'I don't want you to think I'm not grateful for you trying to help, sister,' said Mrs Gillespie. 'But I don't think I could afford more than perhaps a bath every other week.'

'But you don't have to, not now with the NHS.' Connie gave Mrs Gillespie a reassuring smile.

Mrs Gillespie's looked incredulous. 'I thought it was just medicine and the like.'

'No,' Connie replied. 'The government pays for everything. Hospitals, dentists, even children's and old people's homes.'

'Even homes for people like Paul?' asked Mrs Gillespie.

Connie nodded. 'Everything.'

Tears welled up in the older woman's eyes. 'Oh, if you could come it would be such a help.' She turned to her son. 'Won't that be nice, Paul, to have such lovely kind nurses coming to see you each day?'

Paul's bright blue eyes fixed on Connie and his lips pulled back in a crooked smile.

Chapter Fourteen

'I tell you, Millie, she is the very image of you,' Connie said. She was sitting beside Millie's bed in Whipps Cross Hospital in Leytonstone, admiring her soon-to-be god-daughter, who had been born ten days before on the 8th June, through the bars of the hospital's iron cot.

The old Victorian ward was bathed in the warm glow of June sunlight, which shone through the tall windows above the beds. Nearly everyone had a visitor sitting next to them, mostly anxious-looking young men trying to grapple with the correct way to hold their new offspring, but there was the occasional mother or friend keeping the new mum company before the enforced rest period between three and four o'clock.

'That's what my mum and Aunt Ruby say, but I don't know how you can tell at this age,' replied Millie.

'Of course you can,' said Connie. 'She's all you, from the shape of her face to her turned-up nose and she didn't get that mop of brown hair from Jim, did she?'

Millie smiled down at her daughter, who was now looking around peacefully after a feed and nappy change. 'I suppose not.'

'And you're looking more like your old self, too.' Connie ran her gaze over Millie. 'It won't be many weeks before you can fasten your skirt waistbands again.'

'I don't know about that,' said Millie. 'My stomach still feels like a half-set blancmange.'

'Pushing a pram to the shops each day will soon sort that out,' said Connie knowingly. Her gaze returned to Patricia, who had now drifted off to sleep. 'I can't believe she's almost two weeks old already.'

'No, neither can I,' said Millie softly.

'Is she still feeding all right?'

Millie nodded. 'She's put on four ounces already.'

Connie looked impressed. 'I don't suppose Jim's quite got used to the idea of being a father yet.'

Millie's happy expression vanished. 'Not quite.'

'And I bet your daddy rushes up here every day just to see his little girl,' Connie said to the sleeping baby. 'I tell you, Millie. If Malcolm is half as good as your Jim I—'

Tears welled up in her friend's eyes.

'What's wrong, Millie?' asked Connie.

'It's . . . it's . . . J–Jim,' Millie sobbed.

Risking the ward sister's wrath, Connie sat on the bed and put her arm around Millie. 'There, there. Don't upset yourself, this time tomorrow you'll be home.'

'You don't understand,' said Millie, reaching for her handkerchief. 'I don't want to go home. Everyone thinks Jim's such a wonderful husband. But . . .'

Connie listened sympathetically as her friend sobbed out the story of her husband's string of affairs, both before and after their marriage. The final blow had been when a woman answered the phone at two in the morning when Millie rang the hotel where Jim was staying during the Labour Party conference to tell him she was in labour.

To be honest, although she had no way of proving it Connie had suspected from the start that Jim Smith, who after a by-election was now a sitting MP, was a wrong 'un. Sadly for her friend, her instincts had been proved right.

'So you can see,' Millie concluded, blowing her nose, 'why I'm not relishing walking out of the hospital with Jim tomorrow.' She blew her nose. 'And if I never set eyes on the Honourable James Percival Woodville Smith again, it'll be too soon.'

'What do your mum and Aunt Ruby say?'

'I haven't told them. It would break their hearts.'

'Go round and punch him on the blooming nose, more like,' said Connie, feeling the urge to do the same.

Millie covered her face with her hands. 'I should never have married him,' she sobbed. 'But he seemed . . .'

'Everything Alex wasn't,' Connie said, knowing this was at the heart of her friend's unhappiness.

Millie looked up. 'What's Alex got to do with it?'

'It's no coincidence that you accepted Jim's proposal on the day you found out Alex was getting married, is it?' said Connie.

'Maybe you are right,' said Millie, plucking at the bedcover. 'Perhaps it's because I married Jim on the rebound that I was blind to what he was really like and I certainly had no idea how much he drank.'

Connie shrugged. 'Who knows, but what can you do?'

Millie's mouth pulled into a determined line. 'I haven't decided yet.'

'You're not thinking of leaving him, are you?' asked Connie, trying not to sound too shocked.

Although Connie encountered plenty of women who were locked in a miserable and often violent marriage, she knew friends and neighbours alike would point the finger of shame at any who didn't stand by their wedding vows.

'It's crossed my mind,' Millie replied.

'But what about Patricia?' asked Connie. 'Surely you don't want her to come from a broken home?'

'Of course I don't,' her friend replied as her gaze returned to her newborn daughter. 'But I don't want her to grow up with a drunken, womanising liar for a father, either.'

'Fascinating, isn't it?' said Malcolm, who was standing beside her.

Suppressing a heavy sigh, Connie looked up.

Only Malcolm could find a display of vegetable stems and seeds in glass boxes on a slowly moving conveyer belt fascinating.

It was the last Saturday afternoon in June and they, along with dozens of other couples, were in Oxford Street Hall to see an exhibition dedicated to the role of the colonies. Of course, to Connie, an afternoon up west meant Bourne & Hollingsworth, Marshall & Snelgrove or Selfridges, not shop mannequins stained brown and dressed in African tribal dress as they pretended to pound maize.

Having almost reached boiling point on the Central Line tube, Connie had hoped that the inside of the hall would offer some refuge from the sweltering June weather, but no such luck. In order to give the British public a greater understanding of life in the colonies, they'd had to pass through a papier-mâché tropical forest complete with humidity and jungle noises so now Connie felt as if she were on a quest to discover King Solomon's mine.

Still, she should be thankful for small mercies. Because of the number of people who wanted to see the exhibits, the crowd was ushered slowly past the displays, which meant that Malcolm couldn't linger over the model of the Malaysian northern railway extension.

'I mean,' Malcolm continued. 'It's hard to imagine that . . .' He pointed to strings of white unrefined rubber. 'Will become a car tyre or a pair of wellington boots or that . . .' He pointed to what looked like grubby cotton wool. 'Is what your dress is made of.'

'Yes, it makes you think,' said Connie, trying to muster some enthusiasm for raw Kenyan cotton.

'It makes you realise how lucky the coloured races are to be part of the empire,' said Malcolm, puffing out his chest as if he'd planted a Union flag or two himself.

She doubted the people in Malaya and Palestine would have agreed with him and who could blame them? She wouldn't have been happy either if the profits of her labour were shipped off to line someone else's pocket thousands of miles away, but as she didn't want to start an argument she held her peace.

The ushers moved them on and they shuffled towards the exhibit of locusts.

'They're a bit grisly,' said Malcolm, his nose just inches from the display glass.

Giving the insects munching on stalks of wheat a cursory glance, Connie slipped her hand into Malcolm's arm. 'Yes, Malcolm, now can we please have a cup of tea?'

Fifteen minutes of queuing later, Malcolm carried a tray with tea for two and a plate with two custard tarts on it to the table in the corner of the first-floor cafeteria.

'There we are,' he said, putting the afternoon refreshment down. 'Will you be mother?'

'I hope to be one day, Malcolm,' said Connie, winking.

A flush appeared on Malcolm throat. 'Really, Connie.'

Connie laughed. 'I'm only talking about having children.'

'I know but . . .'

'But what?'

'Someone might overhear,' he said in a lower tone.

189

'For goodness sake, Malcolm, it is 1949 not 1849! Talking of babies,' Connie said, picking up her cup, 'I thought while we were in Oxford Street we could get a christening present for Patricia.'

Malcolm's jaw dropped.

'You're not going surely, Connie?' he said, looking at her as if she'd announced she was going to dance naked on the table.

'Of course I'm going,' said Connie. 'Millie's my best friend and I'm Patricia's godmother.'

Malcolm scoffed. 'Well, I'm surprised she's got the gall to step into a church.'

Connie picked up one of the custard tarts. 'You mean because she's finally seen her pig of a husband for what he is and left.'

'I mean because she's broken her sacred marriage vows,' said Malcolm ponderously.

'As did Jim with that woman in Blackpool,' Connie replied, with a raised eyebrow.

'Yes, well.' Malcolm's gaze shifted a little. 'I'm not saying that's right but surely one little lapse isn't a reason for your friend to go running back to her mother.'

Sadly, Millie's return to the marital home after Patricia's birth hadn't gone smoothly and, within a month, she had loaded up all her worldly goods on Patricia's pram and had returned to her mother, taking her daughter with her. Millie hadn't gone into great detail about what had actually happened, but enough for Connie to know that despite his plummy voice and refined manner, the Right Honourable James Percival Woodville Smith was no more than a drunken wife-beater.

'There's more to it than that,' said Connie, licking her fingers. 'But if you ask me she's well out of it.'

'Well, I'm afraid I won't be going,' said Malcolm, noisily stirring his tea.

Connie looked at him in dismay. 'But, Malcolm, it's my best friend's baby's christening.'

'I'm sorry, Connie,' he said, drawing his lips tightly together. 'I discussed it with Mum and she agrees with me. If I went it would be as if I was condoning your friend's actions, so you'll have to make my excuses.'

Connie's mouth pulled into a tight, uncompromising line to match his as she gave him a cool look.

'Very well, Malcolm, I'll go by myself,' she said, realising unexpectedly that she was very happy to.

Scooping out a generous dollop of zinc and castor oil cream, Connie applied it liberally across Paul Gillespie's bony rear, pleased to see that after almost three months on the Association's books the bed sore that had been present on her first visit had all but disappeared. This wasn't the only change to the Gillespies' living arrangements since Connie had stepped in.

The day after her initial visits she, Jane and Beryl had spent the entire morning cleaning the Gillespies' two rooms from top to bottom and setting them in nursing order.

This entailed making sure there were sufficient bowls, buckets and towels for the nurses to use. They also left a list of items that they'd need, such as soap, talcum powder, lanolin cream and, if the patient was incontinent, old newspapers for use under the draw sheets to soak up moisture. A patient's family was expected to have all of this, plus freshly boiled water and an uncluttered room in which to work, ready for the nurse to use.

However, as it was clear Mrs Gillespie only just coped with getting herself and Paul fed and watered most days, the nurses put out the bowls and towels on the kitchen table ready for the next day's visit before they left.

Also, thanks to Connie's almost daily nagging, Mrs Gillespie was now in receipt of a small supplementary hardship grant from the Welfare Department. She'd also been given an old hospital bed through the Paupers' Aid Society charity which made nursing Paul a whole lot easier and saved the nurses' aching backs.

Wiping the excess ointment from her hand onto the dirty draw sheet under her patient, Connie took the towelling nappy, folded it longways in three, then tucked it between Paul's legs and pulled up his pants. Rolling him gently from side to side a couple of times, she replaced the used waterproof sheet and newspapers with fresh ones.

As she propped Paul up on the pillow, she looked across at his mother, who was on the other side of the bed.

'There you go,' she said, smoothing down Paul's shirt collar. 'All done and dusted.'

Paul's face contorted into a smile, the darkening down on his top lip showing more clearly as he did.

'Don't you look a handsome chap,' said his mother, looking lovingly at her son. 'Just like one of those Brylcreem boys.'

Mrs Gillespie tucked in the sheet on her side of the bed, then bent down to pick up the pail of dirty water.

'I'll carry that through,' said Connie, beating her to the handle. 'Why don't you take the sheets and towel?'

The older women scooped up the dirty linen but as she did she staggered sideways, her right hand clutched tight against her chest.

Somehow she managed to catch the back of the chair, her knuckles white as she strove to hold herself upright.

Putting the bucket down, Connie hurried over.

Casting an experienced eye over the older woman, she noticed the dark smudges under her sunken eyes were a little more pronounced today. In contrast, her lips were grey and sweat glistened on her forehead.

'Are you all right?' Connie said in a low voice.

Mrs Gillespie closed her eyes and didn't reply.

Placing a hand on the old woman's frail shoulders and her fingers lightly on her bony wrist, Connie glanced down at the watch pinned to her apron.

Watching the second hand move round the dial, Connie counted Mrs Gillespie's thready pulse before doing the same for her laboured respirations.

Paul let out a low moan.

'It's all right, dear,' Mrs Gillespie forced out, the veins in her throat distending with the effort.

'You'd better sit down,' said Connie, trying to guide her into the chair.

'In the kitchen,' whispered Mrs Gillespie.

'Are you sure you—'

'Please,' the older woman said, giving Connie a meaningful stare.

Connie turned and smiled.

'Don't worry, Paul, your mum just needs a bit of fresh air,' she said, putting a supportive arm around the old woman's shoulder.

Practically carrying Mrs Gillespie, Connie helped her through to the scullery where the older woman collapsed on the nearest chair.

Grey and gasping for breath, the old woman slumped in the chair with her eyes closed. Throwing open the back door to let in some air, Connie unbuttoned the front of Mrs Gillespie's blouse and loosened the collar. She took her pulse again and this time it was erratic with worryingly long spaces between beats.

Mrs Gillespie grimaced and clutched at her chest again.

'You need to go to hospital,' said Connie.

'I can't leave Paul,' rasped the older woman, gripping Connie's arm with surprising strength. She looked over at the kitchen dresser. 'Pills.'

Leaving her patient, Connie went and found a small bottle of double-strength glyceryl trinitrate on the top shelf. Turing back to Mrs Gillespie, Connie unscrewed the lid and tapped a tablet into the older woman's hand.

Popping it into her mouth, Paul's mother rested back and closed her eyes. Connie sat beside her for a moment and then took her pulse again. Mercifully it had slowed and settled back into a regular beat.

Connie stood up and walked over to the sink to refill the kettle.

'I'll make us a cuppa,' said Connie, putting it on the back of the antiquated stove and lighting the gas under it.

Mrs Gillespie opened her eyes and gave a weak smile.

Connie set out two mugs and Paul's invalid beaker with the elongated spout. 'You really should get Dr Marshall to refer you to the hospital.'

Mrs Gillespie shook her head. 'They'll only take me in and that old quack Marshall will send my Paul to Claybury or Warley lunatic asylum where he says he belongs.'

'Why don't I talk to Dr MacLauchlan?' said Connie. 'He's very understanding and I'm sure he'd be able to get Paul looked after on the convalescent ward in Bancroft Hospital while you're in.'

Mrs Gillespie shook her head emphatically. 'He sounds very nice by all accounts but I can't take the chance. Once Paul goes into one of those places I'm scared they'll say I'm not up to looking after him and he'll be in there for good.' She gave Connie a sad smile. 'Thank you for your concern, dear, but while I have breath in my body Paul's not going nowhere.'

Chapter Fifteen

Clutching his briefcase in his hand, Hari reached the top step of Westminster Station just as Big Ben opposite struck one-thirty, and joined the throng of pinstriped civil servants striding purposely back to their offices after lunch.

However, instead of crossing to the Palace of Westminster immediately he crossed Whitehall and walked around Parliament Square in the early July sunshine in an attempt to bring his racing heart back to its regular sixty-six beats per minute and clear his head. Although he'd got the letter from the Ministry of Foreign Affairs over a week ago, it was only in the last few nights that the invitation it contained had given him fitful and restless nights. After a slow amble down George Street past the statues of Palmerston, Disraeli and Robert Peel and along the length of St Margaret's Church, Hari felt he was suitably composed. Waiting for a pause in the stream of taxis and buses, he strolled over the road again, then marched up to the policeman guarding the Houses of Parliament's front entrance. As he approached, the officer stepped forward.

'Dr MacLauchlan, for the Paget Inquiry,' said Hari, offering him the letter with a portcullis embossed on the top.

'Very good, sir,' the officer said, handing it back. 'If you walk into the lobby, the porter will show you to the committee room.'

With the sun warm on his face, Hari crossed the courtyard to the Victorian version of medieval grandeur of the entrance hall where parliamentary officials in black tails and garter bustled back and forth across the tile floor. On producing his letter again at the porter's lodge, Hari was whisked down a long corridor lined with statues to three chairs placed outside a set of double doors at the end.

As he took his seat outside, Hari's escort slipped quietly into the committee room and returned within a few minutes.

After informing Hari he would be called very soon, he left.

Feeling his heart start to pound again, Hari closed his eyes and took a deep breath. The door opened and a clerk ushered him into a sizeable chamber with tall windows looking out over the Thames. There were shoulder-height oak panels on the other three walls with William Morris-style wall paper above. In front of the window was a long bench at which sat five men and three women. They were all dressed in the unassuming style and muted colours of those who walked the corridors of power.

The chairman, a grey-haired aristocratic-looking man in his early sixties wearing a frockcoat, stood up as Hari walked in.

'Dr MacLauchlan,' he said, offering Hari his hand. 'Sir Clive Paget. Good of you to come, especially as I suspect you've rushed here after morning surgery.'

'Not at all, sir,' said Hari as they shook. 'I'm only too pleased to be given the opportunity.'

'Please make yourself comfortable.' Sir Clive indicated the leather chair with a golden portcullis stamped on the back. 'Tea?'

'If I may,' Hari replied. 'Milk, no sugar.'

Sir Clive looked at one of the two young women stenographers at the end of the table and she got up.

'I'm sure you're a busy man, Dr MacLauchlan, so perhaps you won't mind if we make a start. '

Reaching across, Sir Clive pulled a box file with Hari's name on the side into the centre of the table.

'Did you get the transcript?' asked Sir Clive, his well-modulated tones cutting through Hari's frenzied emotions.

Hari pulled himself back to the here and now.

'Yes, thank you,' he said, unclipping his case and pulling out the hefty dossier that had arrived by special courier the previous Monday.

'As an ex-POW of the Japanese, I'm sure you have followed the newspaper reports of the inquiry progress,' said Sir Clive. 'But to explain the full remit for this inquiry to you and to put it into context, although the International Military Tribunal for the Far East has concluded, the British Government still has an ongoing investigation. This has two stated aims; firstly, to iden- tify and bring to justice any of the Japanese military who have slipped through the larger net and, secondly, it could be argued more importantly, locate and identify soldiers still missing so their families can at least lay them to rest in their minds if not, sadly, in fact.'

'Which is why I'm very pleased to have been invited,' said Hari, opening his file and pulling out the thick wedge of notes looped together by a treasury tag.

The members of the panel did the same from the pile of papers in front of them.

'I know we all have Dr MacLauchlan's notes to refer to,' said Sir Clive. 'But I think before we start examining Dr MacLauchlan's evidence in detail, it would be as well to actually see his patient records.'

Popping open the box file, he lifted out a collection of tatty, stained school exercise books, transparent sheets of disinfectant-impregnated toilet paper, squares of cardboard cut from food packaging and the odd sheet of curled foolscap paper.

Hari's gaze fixed on the patient records he'd diligently kept from his incarceration in Changi, on the suffocating journey north in a cattle truck, the long march to Kanchanaburi camp, the main work camp for the Burma—Thailand Railway and the four long years of brutality at the hands of the Japanese.

His heart thumped uncomfortably in his chest as the screams and cries of hundreds of men echoed around his head. At the corner of his mind ghostly images of the starved and beaten men darted in and out of his consciousness and in the hallowed calmness of a Westminster antechamber, the sickly sweet smell of his slaughtered comrades lying unburied in the outer perimeter of Alexandra Hospital in Singapore filled his nose.

Sir Clive spread out the collection of notes, now all carefully encased in cellophane so the rest of the committee could see.

There were mutters of amazement from the committee members, along with several approving glances.

'I propose that it should be recorded that the committee commends Dr MacLauchlan as an outstanding member of his profession for not only keeping such detailed patient notes in such appalling circumstance, but that he was able to preserve them as a record for posterity,' said Sir Clive.

There were nods of agreement.

'So,' said Sir Clive, smiling across at Hari. 'Shall we begin with one of your first entries, Private Stephen White?'

In his imagination the ghostly figure of the gunner Chalky White stood to attention as Hari turned to the first page of the transcript in his hand.

Taking another sip of whisky, Hari took out the first set of notes from the wooden box sitting on his desk and read Dr Marshall's brief and almost incomprehensible jottings.

His so-called colleague had created a mighty stink about covering the evening surgery but as Hari had been asked to give evidence to His Majesty's government, he couldn't very well refuse. That hadn't made him any less bloody-minded about it and he had disappeared as soon as Hari returned, leaving a dozen bewildered patients in the waiting room and without even the courtesy of wishing him a good night.

However, for once, Marshall's rude manner suited him. After three hours of answering the committee's questions and clarifying his notes to give them the full and terrible picture of the conditions in the POW's hospital, he wasn't in the mood for social niceties either.

That was an hour ago and now it was almost seven and although the patients he'd seen since arriving back had all been very straightforward, he really didn't want anyone else to walk through that door today. All he wanted to do now was collapse in his easy chair in time to catch the news and listen to *From Our Own Correspondent* on the wireless.

Satisfied that his colleague's prescribing of Epsom Salts for Mrs Kemp's constipation would do no harm, Hari was just about to tuck the record at the back when there was a knock at the door.

Damn!

'Come,' he called, cursing himself for not locking the surgery door after the last patient.

The door opened and Connie Byrne walked in. She should have been off duty over an hour ago but as she was still in her uniform and looked as weary as he felt, she must have been having a rough day, too.

'Good evening, Dr MacLauc—' Her eyes flew open in surprise.

He didn't blame her. He was without his jacket, with his sleeves rolled up and his tie off. He'd also unbuttoned his top three buttons so his shirt was gaping open. He had a drink in his hand and a bottle of Scotch at his elbow.

'Sister Byrne,' he said, putting the glass down and hastily trying to button his shirt. 'How lovely to see you.'

'Thank you, Dr MacLauchlan. I hope I'm not disturbing you,' she replied, her gaze sliding briefly over his bare arms.

'Not at all,' he replied. 'What can I do for you?'

'I was just going to ask if you could pop in on Mrs Gillespie as I think her ankles are getting puffy again,' said Sister Byrne.

Picking up his pen, Hari opened the surgery diary and scribbled himself a note. 'I'll drop by tomorrow. Anything else?'

She shifted her weight from one foot to the other uncertainly for a moment, then sat on the chair next to his desk. 'I hope you don't mind me asking, Dr MacLauchlan, but has something happened?'

'No, not really,' he said, running his hands over his face. 'I have just had a hell of an afternoon.'

'Have you crossed swords with Dr Marshall again?' she asked.

'I do that on a daily basis,' Hari replied with a rueful smile. 'But it's not him making me turn to drink. It's because I've been going through my POW medical records at the Paget Inquiry all afternoon.'

'That must have been hard,' she said, her expression full of sympathy.

'It was. Very,' he replied, remembering the pain of reading through his observations on dying soldiers for the committee's records.

Hari swallowed a large mouthful whisky.

'When I'm checking wheezy chests or looking at a child's inflamed tonsils, the faces of malnourished men shivering with malaria or dehydrated by dysentery are always hovering about in the back of my mind.' His eyes stung but he blinked the sensation away. 'And I thought that's where they'd stay, but today . . . Today, it . . .'

The murderous rage at the senseless brutality of life during his three years of captivity swept over Hari, robbing him of his words.

'Became real,' said Sister Byrne very softly.

He nodded, his eyes feeling tight again. 'When Sir Clive laid out those tatty scraps of paper that were my POW hospital patient records, it was as if all those men were in the room with me. I was back in that bug-infested ward with its bamboo roof that let in the rain. I remembered throwing scalding water on the operating theatre walls to kill the lice and bloodsucking parasites before we could operate. I remember orderlies having to hold men down because there was no anaesthetic while I and other medics amputated gangrenous limbs with improvised surgical knives and then sutured them up with boiled vegetable fibres.'

Sister Byrne frowned. 'I thought the Red Cross sent medical equipment into Japanese POW camps.'

'I'm sure they did, but we rarely got it and when we did the provisions had to be eked out. One of the biggest problems was beriberi caused by the lack of vitamin B_I, so Marmite was worth its weight in gold. If we got a parcel with a jar of that in it all the patients were given a tablespoonful.' He smiled ruefully. 'Like matron doling out the cod liver oil in the dorm, and it was just enough to stave off the disease. It was the same if we got a tin of sardines or any sort of meat, including anything we could trap. Food was always the problem and dominated every waking hour for all the men, myself included.'

'I saw the men from the camps on the news reels,' she said.

'Most of those shots were taken a month after the Japs capitulated and we'd had air drops of food,' said Hari. 'By the time the army got there we'd put on a few pounds. To give you some idea, I'm six foot two and weigh about thirteen stone, but when the camp was liberated I was seven stone two.'

She looked horrified. 'That's a stone less than me.'

'And I was one of the lucky ones. The men used to donate a spoonful of their rice rations to the medical team. We didn't want to take it, of course, but they insisted, saying if we got sick who was going to look after them? The rations were bad enough for healthy men, but a disaster for a man too sick to work; the bloody Japs cut him to half rations.' Hari's mouth pulled into a hard line. 'We traded everything for food; our clothes, equipment, watches, rings, everything. I even swapped this' – he picked up the old cone-ended stethoscope his father had presented him with as he shipped out to Singapore – 'for a chicken to go in the pot so the men on the malaria ward could have some protein.'

Sister Byrne gave him a querying look. 'So how have you still got it?'

Hari smiled. 'It was liberated from a Japanese general's trophy stash by an American GI who kindly tracked me down and returned it.'

He gazed at the old instrument and a soft expression crept into his eyes. 'Whenever I get angry or exasperated with a patient, this reminds me of the thousands of men rotting in unmarked graves along that bloody railway track and of the fragility and preciousness of life.'

The polished brass glinted in the soft evening light as he twisted the instrument in his hand and tears sprang into his eyes.

'I'm sorry,' he said, roughly brushing them away. 'I . . .'

She laid her hand on his forearm. 'Please don't apologise.'

Feeling her gentle touch on every part of him, Hari stared down at her pale, slender fingers resting on his light brown skin.

He raised his head and found himself gazing into her lovely face.

She smiled and, squeezing his arm, stood up. Going over to the lotions and potion cabinet, she pulled out a glass medicine beaker, then returned to the desk. Setting her improvised glass down next to his, she picked up the bottle and after replenishing his drink, poured herself three fluid ounces of Scotch.

She raised her glass. 'To fallen comrades.'

'To fallen comrades,' he repeated.

They chinked glasses and drank.

'To all our patients,' continued Sister Byrne. 'Be they stoic and uncomplaining . . .'

'Or quarrelsome and loud-mouthed,' added Hari, the spirit warm on his throat as he took another drink.

'To them one and all,' she said, their glasses touching again.

Connie took another swig of whisky, then Hari raised his glass again.

'Lastly. If I may, Sister Byrne, I'd like to raise a final toast: to life.'

'To life,' she echoed.

She touched her glass against his.

'May we live it to the full,' he said quietly.

'To the full,' she repeated, in the same soft tone.

Her blue eyes locked on his for a second, then she looked away.

'I ought to leave you to your supper,' she said, putting her drink down and standing up. She gave him a querying look. 'You have got supper, haven't you?'

'Yes I have,' he said.

'Good, I wouldn't like to think of you having just a liquid supper,' she said, pointedly looking at his single malt.

'And rest assured, sister, I do not make a habit of drowning my sorrows,' he said, pressing the cork back in the bottle. 'In fact, Mrs Cohen left me a pot of something to say thank you for treating her husband's carbuncle.'

'Really?' said Connie, looking very impressed.

'Yes, in fact, news must have got around about my terrible cooking,' he joked, 'because something seems to arrive at the end of most evening surgeries.'

A smile hovered across Connie's lips.

'What's funny?'

'Nothing really, except I doubt Dr Marshall ever had a pot of something left for him.' She picked up her bag. 'Have a good night.'

'You too.' He smiled self-consciously. 'And thank you again.'

'These things have a way of building up,' she said, smiling back at him. 'It's better sometimes to talk about them and I'm glad to have been of some help. I'll see you tomorrow.'

'I look forward to it,' Hari replied, never having meant those five little words so sincerely.

Holding the loaded tray of crockery steady, Connie nudged Doris Sullivan's kitchen door open with her foot and walked in.

'There we go,' she said as her friend looked around. 'I think this is the last lot.'

'Thank goodness,' said Millie who was up to her elbows in soapy water.

It was somewhere close to four o'clock on the first Sunday in August and, as if it knew it was Patricia's special day, the sun had shone unceasingly for her christening. Not that the special little lady was fussed about this because she was having her afternoon nap in her pram in the backyard while her mother, grandmother and godmother cleared away the remnants of the celebratory tea.

Millie's mother lived in one of the old cottages a few streets up from the Highway. It was a two-up, two-down affair with a handkerchief-sized backyard. Like Doris herself, the house was comfortable and homely. There was a kettle always simmering on the back burner ready to welcome any friend and neighbour in need of a cuppa and Millie's mum was always pleased to receive visitors. Since leaving Jim, Millie had moved into the minute second bedroom with Patricia, and now alongside Doris's neatly displayed china on the dresser were half a dozen feeding bottles. Tucked in the corner of the kitchen was a highchair ready for when Patricia was a little older, while under the sink was a zinc bucket for soaking nappies.

Connie put the tray down on the draining board to the left of her friend and picked up a tea towel.

'It was a lovely day,' said Connie, taking a tea plate from the pile draining in the rack.

'Yes, wasn't it?' said Millie with a tight smile.

Connie cast her gaze over the dark smudges under her friend's eyes. 'Do you want me to get you an aspirin?'

Millie gave her a wry smile. 'How did you know?'

'And why wouldn't you have a blinding headache given every-thing you've got on your plate at the moment?' Connie replied.

Tears welled in Millie eyes. 'Oh, Connie—'

The door opened and Millie's mother Doris walked in, car-rying two plates of leftover sandwiches. She was still wearing her straw clamper-style hat but now had an apron over her new rayon crêpe suit.

'I was just saying, Mrs Sullivan,' said Connie cheerfully, put-ting a dried plate on the kitchen table, 'we were lucky with the weather.'

'We were,' agreed Doris. 'In August you can never be sure. It was a pity that Malcolm couldn't come.'

'Yes, it was,' said Connie with an apologetic smile. 'But he's taking the troop away on summer camp next Saturday, so the leaders had to air the tents today.'

'Oh well, never mind but do send him my regards,' said Doris.

'Are you two all right carrying on with the washing-up while I pop these bits around to Trudy? Her husband's on short time and with all those mouths to feed I'm sure it won't go to waste.'

'That's all right, Mrs S,' said Connie. 'Me and Millie will probably be done by the time you return.'

'See you later, then,' said Doris. 'And I'll make us all a nice cuppa when I get back.'

She left to do her good deed but, as the front door banged shut, Millie rested her hands on the edge of the sink and hung her head.

Connie put her arm around her friend's shoulders and Millie turned into her embrace.

'It's all right,' said Connie, holding her friend as she sobbed uncontrollably for near on five minutes before getting a grip on her emotions.

'Did you see him?' she asked, as Connie let her go.

Connie nodded. She didn't have to ask who.

She had seen Millie's husband, Jim, dressed up like a Savile Row tailor's dummy and swanning about like he owned the place. She'd also seen him hidden behind the war memorial, oozing charm as he'd flirted with a giggly young woman.

Pulling out a chair from the kitchen table, Millie flopped onto it.

'Bloody hypocrite,' she continued, taking a handkerchief from her sleeve. 'Pretending he's a devoted husband and father and all the while knowing he's still not set up the maintenance payments. Slipped his mind apparently.'

'But he promised,' said Connie, picked up the tea towel again.

'He promised to be faithful, too,' replied Millie, blowing her nose. 'And that lasted as long as our honeymoon.'

'At least he had the decency not to come back to the house,' said Connie.

'I don't think even Jim would have had the gall to show up at my mother's house after what he's done,' said Millie sourly. 'But I'm not sure people believed my excuse that he had to catch a train.'

'Well, I'm afraid it's not the sort of secret you can keep for ever,' said Connie, stacking another dry plate on the pile in front of her friend.

Millie sighed. 'You're right, of course. It's bound to come out sooner or later. How could I have been so blind?'

'You were in love,' said Connie.

'I wanted to be, especially after Alex, but . . . well, never mind. It's all water under the bridge now.' She rallied a brave little smile. 'Thanks for pitching in to help, Con, with everything.'

'Don't be silly,' said Connie. 'That's what best friends are for. And don't forget I'm always up for babysitting if your mum can't.'

'That's good of you,' said Millie.

'Not really,' Connie replied. 'You'd be doing me a favour by giving me and Malcolm a chance to sit in without his mother or my family hovering around.'

Millie looked puzzled. 'I thought Miss O'Dwyer turned a blind eye to nurses having their fiancé in their rooms.'

'She does but you know Malcolm is never one to break a rule,' said Connie. 'Even one no one takes any notice of any more.'

Amusement lifted the corners of Millie's lips. 'Even for a chance of a bit of pre-nuptial canoodling?'

'We've decided to wait,' Connie replied.

Actually, if the truth were told, Malcolm had never shown the slightest inclination to extend his range past the odd squeeze of her knee.

Millie smiled. 'You know you're very lucky, Connie, because you'll never have to worry if Malcolm is seeing another woman.' Tears sprang into her eyes but she dashed them away. 'How could I have been such a stupid fool to believe all Jim's lies?'

Connie placed her hand over her friend's. 'You're better off without him.'

'I know, I know,' Millie said with a sigh. She jumped to her feet. 'I've had enough of talking about that loathsome husband of mine, let's talk about something else. Your handsome Dr MacLauchlan, for example?'

Connie's heart did a little double skip. 'What about him?'

'Have you found out what's between him and that new nurse yet?' asked Millie, resuming her place at the sink.

'No, only what I told you before, about them being stationed in Hastings together,' said Connie.

'Perhaps they had a wartime fling?' said Millie, shaking the suds from a platter.

Something painful gripped Connie's chest but she forced a light laugh. 'No, don't be silly.'

'Why not?' asked Millie. 'You know the sort of thing, thrown together in the danger of war and, unsure if they would see another dawn, their passions ignite.'

'They were in Hastings not Mandalay,' Connie replied, not at all happy contemplating Dr MacLauchlan's passions being ignited by Grace. 'And, besides, she's not his type.'

Millie regarded her thoughtfully. 'Isn't she?'

'No,' said Connie, picking up the next saucer. 'Grace has got a very sweet nature but is much too serious and I just can't see her and Dr MacLauchlan as a couple.'

Making a play of straightening the clean crockery on the table, Connie turned from her friend's curious gaze.

From outside the back door a little cry sounded.

'I think someone's awake,' said Connie.

Millie glanced at the clock. 'Right on time for the next feed.' She went to stand up.

'I'm on my feet,' said Connie, hooking the tea towel on the peg. 'I'll get her.'

Patricia had already kicked off the light blanket Millie had laid across her. Reaching into the pram, Connie lifted her up. She held her close, enjoying the feel of her god-daughter's little body and baby smell for a moment before kissing her lightly on her cheek and carrying her back.

'There we are, Mummy,' said Connie, handing the baby over to her friend. 'One hungry little angel.'

Millie took her and, opening her blouse, offered the infant her breast. Patricia rooted around for a moment then latched on, her tiny chin working up and down contentedly.

As Connie watched her friend nurse her baby, she tried to imagine herself in a few years' time doing the same. She tried to imagine what her and Malcolm's baby might look like but instead of her golden-red hair and Malcolm's hazel eyes, her mind added in a thick mass of ebony hair, very like Dr MacLauchlan's.

'I'll tell you one thing being married to Jim has taught me,' Millie said, cutting through Connie's disturbing but arousing thoughts. 'The importance of marrying the right man.'

Chapter Sixteen

'Right, Janice,' said Connie to the little girl standing in front of her. 'I just have to look in your ears and then we're done.'

Janice Lipman, a pale three-year-old who was sitting on her mother's lap, obligingly tilted her head.

It was the second Wednesday in August and three days after Patricia's christening, Connie, ably assisted by Wendy, one of this year's three Queen's Nurse trainees, was running the once-a-month child health clinic for the pre-school-age children.

This consisted of checking the child's weight and height against the Ministry of Health's chart and looking for signs of disease, such as nit and worm infestations or discharge from ears or eyes. There had been talk of the Public Health Department taking over the health check, but the council had not yet allocated funds to employ health visitors. So for now the task of child health checks remained with the district nurses.

As always, they were not only knee-deep in toddlers but their siblings. The chaos was compounded by the fact that while the weather outside was a balmy summer's day, inside the temperature was close to tropical. Connie fervently wished she'd put on her cotton petticoat under her uniform instead of the rayon one.

'There's nuffink wrong with her lug-holes, nurse, 'cept when I tell her to do something,' said Sadie Lipman, tickling her daughter.

Janice, dressed in a faded summer dress with a worn collar, was the youngest of the four Lipman girls and therefore all her clothing had been worn at least three times before an item reached her.

Ticking the box at the bottom of her checklist, Connie picked up the jar of jelly babies on the corner of the desk.

'You can have one for being such a good girl,' she said, holding it so the child could reach in.

Janice dived in and, fishing out a yellow one, popped it in her mouth.

Mrs Lipman slid her little girl off her knee and stood up.

Connie did the same.

'You'll get a letter calling Janice for her next check in a few months,' she said, pushing back the flimsy fabric screen.

Taking her daughter by the hand, Mrs Lipman walked out.

Connie put Janice's record card on the 'seen' pile, then stepped back out into the bedlam of the treatment room.

'Right,' she said, projecting her voice so it could be heard over the chattering women and whining children. 'Who's next?'

Freda Croft and Lena Potter, both holding a toddler by the hand and balancing a snotty baby on their hips, stood up.

'Oi, you,' said Freda, looking belligerently at Lena as she lumbered forward from the second row. 'It's my turn.'

'No, it ain't,' said Lena, dragging her offspring through a gaggle of small children playing on the floor. 'I was here first, weren't I, Vi?'

Vi Dunn, Lena's next-door neighbour, sitting two chairs away and feeding a jam doughnut to the child on her knee, nodded. 'You lost your place when you skipped out.'

'I had to change his bum,' said Freda, indicating the baby she was holding.

'Well, that's too bad,' said Lena, thrusting her son past the other woman.

'Don't you push me,' said Freda, bumping against Lena with her sizeable hips.

'Who do you think you're shoving?' snapped Lena, elbowing her back.

'Ladies, please!' said Connie, raising her voice further and stepping between them. 'I can't see both children at once, so Mrs Croft if you'd like to—'

'But she lost her place,' yelled Lena, her face just inches from Connie's.

'Please, Mrs Potter,' said Connie. 'If you'd just take a se—'

The door opened and, to Connie's utter surprise, Micky Murphy strutted in. The room fell instantly silent as everyone stared at him.

To be fair, they would have stared open-mouthed at any man

venturing into what was a strictly female preserve, but their chins were practically scraping the floor to see the area's guv'nor standing in the doorway holding his three-year-old daughter in his arms.

As usual, Micky was dressed as if attending a society function rather than strolling around the streets of Spitalfields. Today, from his extensive wardrobe, he'd selected a brown chalk-stripe double-breasted suit, oxblood-coloured brogues and an orange and lime-green tie secured with a colossal knot. There was a gold chain slung across his middle and a diamond twinkled from the signet ring on his right little finger.

Not to be outdone, his daughter Pamela wore a powder-blue taffeta dress with a full skirt and a navy sash that, unlike every other child in the room, fitted her perfectly. Her long white socks looked as if they were having their first outing and the light from the fluorescent strip above twinkled on her dainty patent shoes.

Standing beside father and daughter was Tina who, despite no actual wedding certificate, was called Mrs Murphy by all.

Tina was somewhere in her mid-twenties and ten years younger than Micky. She'd moved in with Micky three years ago when she was expecting Pamela. Her profession was listed as dancer on Fry House's records, but as she happily admitted herself, she was wearing nothing more than a smile and a couple of feathers when the Windmill Theatre's floodlight went up. She'd spotted Micky in the front row and it had been love at first sight.

It must have been because since carrying her case over the threshold at White Row, Micky hadn't been seen with another woman. Tina for her part had made him a flamboyant home with the help of Harrods, Heal's, Liberty and the odd Bond Street art dealer.

Today, the de facto Mrs Murphy was dressed in a stunning fern-green tailored linen suit ornamented by black leather gloves which matched impossibly high stilettoes and a handbag so small you'd struggle to get more than a lipstick, compact and handkerchief in. Her blonde hair was permed into the popular Rita Hayworth style and her lips were scarlet.

With his daughter perched on his brawny forearm, Micky surveyed the scene.

A mutter of 'Afternoon, Mr Murphy' and 'Nice to see you,

Mr Murphy' went around the room. Micky acknowledged the hushed greetings with a regal incline of his head, giving a knowing wink to those of closer acquaintance.

After a moment or two, the Murphy family advanced into the room as mothers gathered their children out of the way.

'All right, sister,' he said, stopping just in front of her.

'Mr and Mrs Murphy,' Connie said with a smile. 'Are you here for Pamela's three-year check?'

'We are,' he said, wafting expensive aftershave around her.

'Very well,' said Connie. 'If you just take a seat I'll—'

'He can have my turn,' said Freda, dragging her child back.

Connie looked puzzled. 'But you were just complaining—'

'I don't mind waiting,' said Freda pleasantly.

Connie looked questioningly at the woman Freda had been tussling with.

'Me neiver,' said Lena, giving the man looming over them an ingratiating smile. 'Mr Murphy's a busy man.'

Micky gave the women a boyish grin. 'I'm obliged to you, ladies, and, Freda . . .'

'Yes, Mr Murphy?'

'Tell your old man I might have a bit of work for 'im.'

'Thank you, Mr Murphy,' simpered Freda, almost curtsying as she backed away.

Micky's gaze returned to Connie.

'Very well,' she said.

Wendy gathered up a set of notes ready to book in their new patient, but Connie took them from her. 'It's all right. I'll deal with Pamela.'

Connie led them over to the height chart.

As Micky placed his daughter on the floor, Connie raised the measuring bracket.

'Could you stand nice and straight against the wall please, sweetheart?' she asked with a friendly smile.

Pamela did as she was asked and Connie lowered the arm until it rested on her golden curls.

'Three four two,' said Connie. 'Just above average.'

'Course it is,' said Micky, sweeping his daughter into his arms and planting a noisy kiss on her cheek. 'There's nothing average about my little princess.'

Pamela giggled and, hugging her father's bull-like neck, kissed him back. A soppy expression spread across Micky's hard-bitten face.

'Can you get Pamela to step onto the scales so I can weigh her?' Connie asked, stepping over to the scales.

Holding her as if she were bone china, Micky lowered his daughter onto the footplate.

'What a pretty dress,' said Connie, smiling at the child.

'Derry & Toms,' said Tina. 'From their exclusive children's wear range.'

Connie slid the weights along until the bar hovered in the fulcrum, then made a note of it on the card.

'If you'd like to follow me,' said Connie as Wendy came over to weigh the next child.

Connie led them into the cubicle, then closed the curtains.

Micky held the chair out for Tina, who sat down. She reached out to take Pamela onto her lap but Micky beat her to it and scooped his daughter into his arms as he sat on the end of the table.

'I'll hold her,' he said, settling her in a froth of petticoat and lace on his bulky thigh.

Resting the notes on the dressing trolley, Connie resumed her seat and took out her pen again.

Having established that Pamela was fully toilet trained, slept all night and didn't have head lice, worms or glue ear, Connie moved onto her diet.

'Has Pamela got a good appetite, Mrs Murphy?' she asked, smiling at the young woman perched on the bench.

'She has.' Micky patted his waistcoat, making the chain slung across it jiggle. 'Like her old man.'

'But she is a fussy eater,' added Tina.

'In what way?'

'Well, she don't like greens and she won't eat sausages from any of the butchers around here,' said Tina. 'So my Micky sends one of the boys up to fetch special ones from Smithfield.'

'Only the best for my little lady,' chipped in Micky, giving the child on his knee an affectionate squeeze.

'What about other vegetables?' asked Connie.

'Carrots and peas, yes,' said Tina. 'And I might manage to get a bit of cauliflower down her if it's smothered in gravy but she won't eat potatoes unless they're chips.' She gave Micky a sharp look. 'Of course, in my day, children had to eat what was put in front of them or—'

'Go hungry,' said Micky. 'But that was then and this is now and my baby's not going to have to eat nuffink she don't like.'

Pamela gave her father a loving smile and was rewarded with a kiss.

'What about fruit?' asked Connie.

'She likes bananas,' said Tina.

'Don't we all,' said Connie, trying to remember when she last saw one. 'Apples and oranges?'

'If you peel them and cut them,' said Tina. 'And she'll eat stewed plums or rhubarb if I can get the sugar to make it sweet enough.'

Connie leant forward and smiled at Pamela. 'So what do you like best – apples or oranges?'

'Them.' Pamela jabbed her finger at the jar of jelly babies in the middle of the table. 'I want some.'

'You'll spoil your tea,' said Tina.

Pamela's lower lip jutted out. 'Want one.'

Tina didn't reply.

With tears welling up in her big blue eyes, Pamela turned to face her father.

'They belong to the nice nurse,' he said, his resolution visibly crumbling under his daughter's beseeching stare.

A tear escaped and rolled down Pamela's soft cheek. 'Please, Daddy.'

Micky looked helplessly at his wife.

'Go on then,' said Tina, rolling her mascaraed eyes. 'If you must.'

With a palpable relief, Micky grabbed the jar and offered it to the child on his knee. 'Just one and I'll buy you a big cream cake from the shop on our way home.'

Pamela took a red one and popped it between her cherubic lips.

Tina smiled fondly at father and daughter, then she looked at Connie. 'She's got him wrapped around her little finger,' she said, somewhat unnecessarily.

'And so she should,' said Micky, hugging his daughter closer. 'My little girl can have whatever she wants.'

'Well, she's a very lucky little girl,' said Connie, patting the child's chubby knee. 'But not too many sweet things if you don't want too many trips to the dentist.' She glanced down at her notes. 'Now the only thing I need to mention is getting Pamela inoculated.'

'What's that when it's at home,' asked Tina.

'It's a way of making sure Pamela doesn't catch diphtheria or lock jaw,' Connie explained.

She took a leaflet from the rack on the wall beside her and handed it to Tina. 'It's just one little injection and then she's covered. Which surgery are you registered with?'

'Christ Church,' said Micky. 'Although I only see Old Marshall for his tonic. Perks me right up, it does. I take a dollop in me morning cuppa every day and now I'm fit as a fiddle, I am.' He flexed his right bicep. 'Feel that,' he said, thrusting his free arm towards her.

'Well, I—'

'Go on,' he urged.

Tentatively Connie closed her fingers around his upper arm and squeezed the firm muscle beneath the fabric.

'See, rock hard,' he said as she retracted her hand. 'Ain't I, Tina?' He winked at her and she giggled.

'Well, I'm afraid Dr Marshall hasn't signed up for the inoculation programme,' said Connie. 'But Dr MacLauchlan has so just pop her—'

'Are you talking about the blooming darkie doctor?' asked Micky.

Despite the fury flaring in her chest, Connie smiled professionally.

'He is Anglo-Indian, Mr Murphy,' she said coolly. 'And what Dr MacLauchlan looks like is neither here nor there. What is important is that he is extremely well qualified with a great deal of experience and an understanding of modern medicine, which, as far as the health of your family is concerned, is surely much more important.'

Micky's mouth pulled into an ugly line. 'I ain't having my precious baby be seen by no bloody punkah wallah half-caste.' He stood up. 'Come on, Tina, we're off.'

Tina hooked her handbag over her arm and rose to her feet.

'Mr Murphy, I would really urge you to get your daughter inoculated,' said Connie.

'Don't worry, sister, I will, even if I have to pay for a proper doctor to do it,' Micky replied.

'But Dr MacLauchlan is—'

'Because if you think I'm letting some wog quack stick needles into my baby then you need your bloody head examined.'

Cradling Pamela in his arms as if she were a Ming vase, Micky kicked the screen out of his way and strode out.

Connie turned to Tina. 'Mrs Murphy, could you speak—'

'Sorry, sister, I'm sure this doctor of yours is very good, but—'

'Tina!' bellowed Micky.

'Coming!' Tina called back and, giving Connie a regretful look, tottered after her husband.

Malcolm checked his watch and then peered up at the departure board situated above platform 11.

'I told you we'd be far too early,' said Connie, not bothering to hide her annoyance.

It was nine-thirty on the Saturday after Patricia's christening and they were standing on the concourse of Liverpool Street Station. It still served the same towns and villages, but since the 1 January of last year as the nationalised British Railways.

Today the building was full of people milling about, checking tickets and finding platforms. The trains waiting to depart puffed smoke and hissed steam into the already hot atmosphere. Now, as most of the factory workers had returned from their two-week break, it was the turn of salaried staff to escape to the coast. Unlike the workers who took coaches and a goodly supply of beer to the holiday camps along the East Anglian coast, the bank clerks, council employees and shop managers favoured the train to get them to their boarding houses in Clacton, Frinton and Southend.

Jostled by families hurrying to find their trains, Connie noticed a few people casting glances at Malcolm, who was diligently studying the running board overhead. She couldn't blame them their curious looks as he was dressed in a Scout uniform, complete with corduroy shorts, a neck scarf secured with a leather woggle and the wide-brimmed hat of a troop leader.

'Better to be early than late,' Malcolm replied.

'Yes, but not a blooming hour,' said Connie.

Malcolm looked hurt. 'You know my stomach plays up if I'm going to be late. I don't want to have to go searching around for a lavatory when I'm supposed to be in charge of my pack of overexcited Boy Scouts.'

Connie glanced at the station cafe next to the ticket office.

'Perhaps we could grab a cuppa while we wait,' she said, trying to make the best of the situation.

Malcolm shook his head. 'Some of the other leaders might be along soon. I don't want to chance it.'

'For goodness sake, Malcolm,' she snapped. 'The train isn't even up on the announcement board yet.'

'I know but . . .' He checked his watch again. 'Look, I'm a bit worried about the space in the baggage car we've been allocated so do you mind if I just pop over and check with the station controller?'

'No,' Connie sighed. 'Of course not.'

Giving her a boyish smile, Malcolm turned and strode across the concourse, his billy can and mug clanging together as his overloaded rucksack swayed from side to side.

Wondering why she'd insisted on coming to wave Malcolm and the 7th Stepney Green Troop off, Connie stepped aside to let a family with three children through.

'Sister Byrne?'

Connie turned and found herself staring up into Dr Mac-Lauchlan's liquid brown eyes.

'I thought it was you,' he said, a friendly smile lighting his face.

He was dressed in a chocolate-brown double-breasted suit with a matching fedora and his navy, cream and burgundy RAMC tie knotted in a double Windsor at his throat. The morning light highlighted his angular cheekbones and closely shaven chin.

'Dr MacLauchlan,' said Connie, feeling a little light-headed. 'What are you doing here?'

'I'm catching the ten past ten to Colchester,' he replied. 'What about you?'

'I'm seeing Malcolm off,' said Connie.

'Where's he going?'

'To Chingford,' Connie replied. 'His Scout troop is having this year's summer camp at Gilwell Park. He's one of the leaders,' she added.

A wry smile lifted the corner of Dr MacLauchlan's mouth. 'Well, I guessed he must be as he's a bit big to be a Scout.'

Connie laughed and Dr MacLauchlan joined in.

As if knowing he was the topic of conversation, Malcolm bounded back. His clipboard was tucked firmly under his arm and there was an infuriated expression on his face.

'Is everything all right?' asked Connie as he came to a halt.

'It is now,' Malcolm replied. 'As I suspected, the troop had been given a poky little shelf in the baggage car for their luggage.'

'Oh dear.'

'Don't worry. I've sorted it out.' Malcolm puffed out his chest. '"Have you ever tried to stow seven patrol tents, my good man?" I asked the greasy-looking wide-boy who called himself the baggage manager.'

'And had he?' asked Dr MacLauchlan pleasantly.

Malcolm shot him a questioning look.

'I'm sure you remember Dr MacLauchlan, Malcolm,' said Connie. 'You met him at the Christmas dance.'

Dr MacLauchlan offered his hand. 'Nice to see you again.'

Malcolm took it. 'You off for a weekend's fun in the country?'

'Actually,' he said, 'I'm off for a Nakhon Pathom POW reunion at Colchester Barracks.'

'I'm surprised you get together to commemorate being captured,' said Malcolm. 'I'd have thought you'd rather forget.'

'It's not so much a commemoration as a celebration of survival,' Dr MacLauchlan replied. 'And to remember those who didn't.'

Above his Scout leader's collar, Malcolm's neck flushed.

Dr MacLauchlan glanced up at the four-sided clock suspended from the central rafters of the station's ceiling. 'I ought to get my ticket. Have a good weekend.'

He raised his hat, smiled, and then walked briskly away.

As Connie watched his tall figure amble towards the ticket office, Malcolm turned to face her.

'What were you talking to him about?' he asked.

'Nothing really,' Connie replied. 'He asked me what I was doing here and I told him I was seeing you off to Scout camp, that's all.'

'Are you sure?'

'Of course,' Connie replied. 'He said hello a few minutes before you came back, what else would we be talking about?'

'I don't know.' Malcolm peered across the concourse. 'But I don't like the way he looks at you.'

'What are you talking about?' asked Connie.

'You know, all white teeth and smarmy.'

Connie laughed. 'Oh, Malcolm, you're not jealous, are you?'

He looked affronted. 'Should I be?'

The image of Dr MacLauchlan in his shirtsleeves smiling at her floated across Connie's mind, but she shoved it away and slipped her arm through Malcolm's.

'No,' she said, smiling up at him.

His stance relaxed but as she stretched up to kiss him, something behind her caught his attention and he broke away from her embrace.

'Over here!' he bellowed, setting his camp cutlery jingling again as he waved enthusiastically.

Stanley Unwin and Derrick Wood, Malcolm's two junior leaders, both weighed down with oversized rucksacks, hurried over.

'Morning, Akela,' they said giving him a sharp three-fingered salute.

Malcolm saluted back. 'Where's Baloo?'

'He's backing the truck into the goods entrance so we can unload,' Stanley replied.

Malcolm's second in command was Ernest Patermore, who owned a hardware shop in Roman Road and was the only person with a van big enough to transport the 7th Bethnal Green's array of camping equipment. Although rechristening the leaders as characters from the *Jungle Book* was more usual for those in charge of the younger Cubs, Malcolm extended the tradition through to his Scout troop.

'Good show.' Malcolm consulted his clipboard. 'I've got you, Unwin, down to check the primus stoves while I've allocated the sorting of the peg bags to you, Wood.'

The boys saluted again. 'Yes, Akela.'

Malcolm nodded his head sharply. 'Off you go, then.'

The two boys lumbered away.

Malcolm turned to Connie. 'There's a lot to organise and I ought to—'

'I understand,' she cut in. 'You've got a lot of responsibility.' She tilted her head back expectantly.

Malcolm glanced around, then gave her a quick peck on the cheek.

'For goodness sake, Malcolm!' she said. 'You are allowed to kiss your fiancée in a public place.'

'I know, but you know I find public displays of affection a bit—'

Connie kissed him on the lips. 'Have a good time and I'll see you in a week.'

He gave her an uncomfortable smile and then hurried off after his junior leaders.

Connie gazed after him for a second then, from the Tannoy above her head, the announcer's tinny voice called out, 'The ten past ten train to Colchester on platform nine, calling at all stations, is ready to depart.'

There was a whistle and steam hissed out of the wheels. This was followed by a screech of iron accompanied by a slow chug, chug as the train pulled away from the platform.

As Connie gazed through the barrier at the black smoke billowing behind the departing train, Connie couldn't help but wonder how Dr MacLauchlan viewed public displays of affection.

Collecting his change from the barman, Hari picked up his pint of bitter and moved away from the bar.

Sipping the froth off his beer, he moved further into the mess hall to join the two hundred other members of the Home Counties Far Eastern Prisoner of War Club.

The officers' dining room in Colchester Barracks had high ceilings with classical-style architraves, huge crystal chandeliers and a deep, plush carpet. Around the walls were portraits of redoubtable majors and generals standing to attention in full battle dress, their regimental flags draped behind them.

The room was full of men with campaign medals on their

chests. They all had the Overseas Operational medal, along with the General Service medal and the distinctive yellow, blue and red of the Burma Star. Like Hari, a few had other more specific medals – often unthinkingly won but proudly worn.

Skirting around a group of Royal Fusilier sappers reliving a precarious river crossing, Hari headed over to the open windows overlooking the formal garden. Standing in the cool breeze, Hari inhaled the smell of freshly mown grass which offset the cloying atmosphere of cigars and brandy in the room.

'Dr Mac?' a voice said behind him.

Hari turned around.

A slightly built man about his own age with russet-coloured hair and pale blue eyes stood behind him.

'I hoped I'd catch you at one of these shindigs sooner or later,' he said smiling nervously.

Hari scrutinised his face for a moment, then he smiled. 'Ken Tullock, isn't it?'

'I'm surprised you remembered me,' he said, looking inordinately pleased.

'Of course I do,' said Hari. 'From Hendon, weren't you?'

Ken nodded. 'That's me.'

'How are you?' asked Hari.

'I'm doing well,' said Ken. 'Me and my brother have opened a garage on the Great North Road near the Ace Cafe. And I've just got married.'

Hari's smile widened. 'Well done on both counts. What about the leg?'

Ken's jolly expression slipped a little. 'The doctors had to take it back to above the knee to get it to close up properly before they could fit the new leg.'

'I'm sorry to hear that, Ken,' said Hari. 'The important thing is for the stump to form correctly so the prosthesis doesn't rub.'

'That's what the doc at the Middlesex hospital said. But that's all over and done now and with this new lightweight one' – he rapped his knuckles against his right leg, producing a wooden sound – 'I'm almost as good as new.' He gave Hari an ironic smile. 'And at least this time I was unconscious when they operated.'

'We did our best,' said Hari.

'You did better than that, doc. Without you and the other medics, half of us wouldn't be here now, and the way you stood up to that Jap commandant that time in Nakhon Pathom, you deserve ten of them.' His eyes flickered to the Military Cross on Hari's chest, then he extended his hand. 'Thank you.'

Hari took it in a firm grip. 'My pleasure.'

Ken gave him a sharp salute then limped off to join a group of ex-service men standing at the end of the bar.

Taking another mouthful of beer, Hari gazed out of the window at the myriad bright reds, blues and yellows of the flowerbeds, interspersed with strips of lush grass. Something fluttered at the corner of his vision. Hari looked over and saw a young woman with a shopping basket walking through the low-lying clipped hedges holding a little boy of about six or seven by the hand. She was wearing a brimmed hat and a sky-blue dress with a full skirt, the same colour as the one Connie had been wearing at the station earlier.

Connie! The corners of Hari's mouth lifted a fraction. Sister Byrne to you.

'Well, strike me down wiv a feather, if it ain't old Mac,' rasped a gruff voice, cutting into his thoughts.

Hari turned.

Standing behind him were Chalky White, Ted French and Pete Arnold, the three ward orderlies from B ward. All of them had pints in their hands and all were at least six stone heavier than when he'd last seen them.

Hari rolled his eyes. 'I wondered if you ugly buggers would be here.'

'Course we are,' said Chalky, who in contrast to his name was a swarthy-looking individual. 'There's a mess bar, ain't there?'

Hari grinned. 'It's good to see you all.'

'You too,' said Ted. 'Although we'd hoped to see you at one of these bashes before now.'

Ted was a Nordic blond who had suffered more than most under the tropical sun.

'You would have but I only got back in May,' said Hari.

'I thought about you when I saw the bit on Pathé News about the trouble in India,' said Pete, a sympathetic look in his pale grey eyes. 'Was it bad?'

Hari's mouth pulled into a hard line. 'Very. Especially for the thousands caught in the fighting,' he said, thinking of the burnt buses, charred bodies and displaced people of his mother's country.

'You'd think after all the Indians went through with the Japs, they'd be a bit more live and let live,' said Ted.

The others nodded in agreement.

'I had that hope myself but it seems, for now at least, it's not meant to be.' Hari shrugged. 'However, the one thing the newly independent India and Pakistan agree on is that neither of them want us mongrels.'

Pete put a beefy arm around Hari's shoulder. 'Well then, I say India's loss is old England's gain.'

'I'd drink to that,' said Chalky. 'What you on, doc?'

'Bitter,' said Hari.

'Right, I'll get them in.' Ted downed the last of his pint. 'So it's double Scotches all round then.'

Hari laughed.

Leaving his pint glass on the window sill, Ted strolled towards the bar.

'So what are you up to?' asked Chalky.

Hari told them about his job with Dr Marshall.

'Bloody hell,' said Pete when he'd finished. 'I thought with all the letters you've got after your name you'd have found yourself a soft billet somewhere in the country, not somewhere that sounds like something straight out of *Oliver Twist*.'

'It's not that bad and there are compensations.'

'Oi, oi.' Chalky winked. 'Are we talking about a young lady?'

Hari laughed. 'No we're not.'

'I thought you were all but hitched to that diplomat's daughter in Bombay?' said Pete.

'I was,' said Hari. 'Until Singapore.'

'She married someone else?' asked Chalky.

'A tea merchant from northern Bengal,' said Hari.

'Here we go,' said Ted, holding a tray of what looked like four triple rather than double Scotches.

He handed them around and Hari took his.

'Now the doc's finally put in an appearance, *all* of B ward is at last reunited,' said Pete. 'I propose a toast. To those we knew who didn't come back.'

Hari raised his glass.

'Those who didn't come back,' he said in unison with the other three.

He took a mouthful of whisky.

Images of the flimsy bamboo walls of the operating theatre, dripping with humidity and crawling with flies, flickered through Hari's mind as the smooth spirit warmed his throat. He heard again the screams of those undergoing amputation with only diluted Eusol for antiseptic and fermented rice alcohol to deaden the pain. The sound of men sobbing for their wives, sweethearts and mothers. Instead of the peaty sharp aroma of the double malt in his hand, Hari smelt the sickly sweet stench of incinerated bodies.

Who didn't come back, he repeated in his mind as a lump clogged his windpipe.

'And now,' continued Pete, 'let's celebrate what they gave us: the future.'

Unbidden, the memory of Connie's soft blue eyes and dazzling smile jumped into Hari's mind.

His grim expression lifted.

'The future,' he echoed, raising his glass again.

Chapter Seventeen

Shaking out the threadbare grey vest, Connie stretched up and hung it over the wooden clothes dryer suspended above the cooker, then took a pair of Paul's trousers from the basket and did the same.

'You're very kind, nurse,' said Mrs Gillespie, who was sitting behind her at the kitchen table. 'But I could do that when you're gone.'

It was somewhere just before midday on the first Tuesday in September and as if the weather knew the children of the area were going back to school, the incessant rain of the last week had given way to warm autumn weather.

Although she'd already visited earlier that morning to get Paul up and ready for the weekly visit from Mrs Fergusson, his teacher, she'd decided to pop back as his mother had been very breathless. She was glad she had because when she'd arrived she'd found Paul's mother the colour of putty and struggling with a mangle. Under the pretence of being in need of a cup of tea, Connie had taken over while Mrs Gillespie filled the kettle.

Taking the next piece of washing from the basket, Connie cast a surreptitious look at the older woman.

Thankfully, the unhealthy grey around Mrs Gillespie's lips had gone and her breathing had more or less returned to normal. Well, normal for her, but it was still too fast for Connie's liking and the constantly swollen ankles were also worrying.

'That's all right, Mrs Gillespie,' said Connie, hooking a faded paisley blouse over the frame. 'I might as well do something while I'm waiting for Mrs Fergusson to finish.'

As if she knew she was being talked about, the door from the lounge opened and Mrs Fergusson's rosy face appeared.

'All done,' she said in a shrill sing-songy voice.

The council's home teacher was a woman somewhere in her mid to late forties with steely grey hair trimmed to just below her ears, a well-padded motherly figure and a permanently jolly expression. She also had a complete disregard for fashion, as was evident from the red skirt and orange blouse she was wearing today.

'That's well timed,' said Connie, shaking out one of Mrs Gillespie's nightdresses and hanging it over the bar. 'I've just finished and there's a cuppa brewing.'

Taking the rope dangling from the overhead pulley, she hoisted the washing towards the ceiling then secured the cord around the hook on the wall before following the two women back into the main room.

When she got there Mrs Gillespie was sitting in her usual place beside her son and holding the beaker to his lips.

As Mrs Fergusson had spread herself out on the two-seater sofa, Connie took her cup from the tray and sat on the straight-backed chair next to the sideboard.

'How did you get on today, Paul?' Mrs Gillespie asked, wiping a stray drip from her son's mouth.

Using a stiff finger Paul tapped out 'good' on the oblong wooden board painted with the letters of the alphabet that was propped up on the table in front of him.

'I think you're being modest, Paul,' his teacher said, looking at his mother over her metal-rimmed spectacles. 'You got full marks for arithmetic and eighteen out of twenty for spelling.'

A proud expression spread across Mrs Gillespie's face. 'I'm not surprised. You love your lessons, don't you?'

Paul nodded again and did a wobbly thumbs-up.

'But I think you'll have to give him more homework, Mrs Fergusson,' teased his mother. 'He's finished what you leave by Thursday.'

'Well, I'll have to put a stop to that.' Mrs Fergusson laughed. 'From next week, Paul, I'll be giving you double homework.'

Paul let out a stuttering laugh.

'I can't thank you enough, Mrs Fergusson, for coming each week,' said Mrs Gillespie.

'Well, I think you have to thank Sister Byrne for contacting the Education Department,' the teacher replied. 'Although I can't understand why Dr Marshall didn't contact us when Paul finished special school three years ago.'

'I'm sure he must have,' said Mrs Gillespie. 'But I expect they must have lost his letter, you know how thing were just after the war.'

She looked at Connie, who smiled but didn't comment.

Obviously Dr Marshall's letter to the Schools Department was lost, along with the one to the Welfare Department for a home help, the referral to the Physiotherapy Department at Bankcroft Hospital and the request to the Housing Department to get the Gillespies onto the priority list for rehousing, all of which Dr MacLauchlan did within a day of Connie asking.

He'd called too, to assess mother and son for himself. He had prescribed Paul a new drug which had eased his spasticity and referred his mother to the cardiac specialist at the London.

'And I don't know what I would have done these last few weeks without Sister Byrne,' continued Mrs Gillespie. 'Apart from all the equipment she's got us, every Friday she's fetched Paul's library books to save me carrying them and she's even looking out on her rounds for an old typewriter for Paul.'

Mrs Fergusson's generous eyebrows rose. 'What a splendid idea.'

'I just thought if Paul can tap on the letter board, perhaps he could do the same on the keys,' said Connie, feeling more than a little pleased with herself.

Mrs Fergusson drained her cup and stood up.

'Well, I must be off,' she said, gathering her copious leather bag from the floor. 'Don't forget, I'll be going over long multiplication next week, Paul, so make sure you practise your tables.'

Paul nodded again.

'And don't worry,' she said, as Mrs Gillespie struggled to her feet. 'I'll see myself out.'

Connie finished the last of her tea and put her cup next to Mrs Fergusson's on the tray. 'I ought to be off, too.'

'It's good of you to pop back,' said Mrs Gillespie, picking up the tray.

'I'll take that out for you,' said Connie.

She went to take it but the older woman got there first.

'It's all right, dear,' said Mrs Gillespie. 'I can manage.'

'I'll just get my bag,' said Connie, watching the vein in the older woman's neck knot as she reached forward.

Connie followed her back into the kitchen. As Mrs Gillespie put the tray on the draining board, she staggered. She caught hold of the sink, her knuckles white as she strove to hold herself upright.

Connie hurried over.

Mrs Gillespie's face was drained of colour and sweat glistened on her forehead.

'Sit down,' said Connie, guiding her to the nearest chair.

Mrs Gillespie didn't argue.

'Now take deep breaths,' said Connie, crouching next to her patient and taking her pulse.

It was strong enough but with a worrying number of missed beats.

Mrs Gillespie rested back and closed her eyes, after a moment or two her colour improved.

Putting her hand on her chest, Paul's mother opened her eyes.

'I'll call in at the surgery and get Dr MacLauchlan to drop in after surgery,' said Connie.

Mrs Gillespie shook her head. 'It's all right.'

'But—'

'I don't want to bother him and there's nothing he or anyone can do.' A contented expression lifted Mrs Gillespie's care-worn face. 'I know I ain't got long, sister, but at least now the Welfare State will look after Paul when I drop off me perch. I can die happy knowing when I look down from Heaven, Paul will be looked after in a nice big house in the country with lots of trees and flowers and kind nurses, like you, to put a smile on his face. He'll have his own room with somewhere to put his books and pictures and he'll be able to listen to the schools programmes on the wireless all the time.'

'So are you off for the weekend?' asked Esther.

'I am, thank goodness,' said Connie as she stirred a much-needed cup of tea. 'I feel like I've cycled to John O'Groats and back today.'

She was sitting in the back of Weinstein's with Esther, who had taken a break from stocktaking to brew a cuppa for them; Michael was holding the fort in the shop.

Having left Paul and his mother, Connie had decided to stop in. After finishing her last visit, Connie felt she'd earned a cuppa and five minutes to herself before going back to Fry House.

'It's been like a mad house here too,' said Esther, putting a plate with a generous slice of honey cake on the Cow & Gate box at Connie's elbow.

'Still at least you're a half-day.'

Connie grimaced.

She was supposed to be, but Miss O'Dwyer had mangled the clinic's supply invoices up again and, as they were due in on Friday, Connie would have to sort them out before she left so they could be picked up by the courier in the morning.

'Did you do anything with your young man over the weekend?' asked Esther.

'No I'm afraid he's not been well,' said Connie.

'Nothing serious, I hope,' said Esther.

'Just a summer cold,' Connie replied. 'He picked it up while he was away at Scout camp. He came back last Saturday with a bunged-up nose and no voice.'

'I'm sorry to hear that,' said Esther. 'Is he all right now?'

'Yes, he went back to work yesterday,' said Connie.

'How is your cake?'

Connie took a bite. 'Delicious.'

Esther looked smug. 'It's my new recipe.'

'It's utterly wonderful,' Connie continued, as apple and honey mingled in her mouth. 'Aren't you having any?'

Esther shook her head. 'I had some herring at my sister-in-law's a couple of days ago and it's still repeating. The woman can't pickle an egg, let alone a fish.' She patted her stomach. 'It's not been good this morning so I don't want to chance anything that might set it off.'

'Have you been to the doctor?'

Esther pulled a face. 'I wouldn't bother the doctor with a bit of indigestion. I'll get Michael to make me something up and I'll be as right as rain in no time.'

Connie glanced at the buttons straining to keep Esther's white coat together. 'Do you mind me asking, Esther, but when did you last have a period?'

She shrugged. 'They are so few and far between I can't rightly remember. That's been my trouble.' Pain flitted across her soft grey eyes. 'Nothing bubbling so nothing cooking. I went fifteen months once and now it must be be over six.' She rolled her eyes. 'I tell a lie. I had a quick one for a day a few months back, but I don't expect to see another. My mother went through her change early and this' – she placed her hands on her stomach – 'is too many matzo dumplings.'

'Was it before the children broke up for the summer?' persisted Connie.

Esther shrugged again. 'Yes, it was about a week after I took down the Father's Day display from the front window but it's nothing, I tell you, just the same as it's been nothing for eighteen years.' She stood up. 'Shall I top you up?'

Connie drained her cup and then set it on the empty plate. 'I'd love to but I must get on.'

She stood up.

'Ah well, these boxes won't count themselves so I ought to do the same.'

Esther rose from the chair but just as she straightened up she swayed.

'Are you all right?' asked Connie, putting her hand gently on the other woman's shoulder.

'Yes, yes. I stood up too quick, that's all,' said Esther, waving away her concern. 'Now, don't work too hard and I'll see you next week sometime.'

'Chance would be a fine thing.' Connie picked up her bag and looked over at Esther's pale countenance. 'And, Esther, if your stomach's not settled by next Tuesday; do me a favour. Pop along to the doctor.'

'And this is one of Cliff and Eddy taking part in the knobbly knees contest,' said Bernie, offering her another four-by-six photograph.

Connie took it from her sister, who was sitting beside her.

'Did they win?' she asked, smiling at the image of her brothers-in-law with their trousers rolled up.

'No,' said Mo. 'Some bloke from up north with knees like pickled walnuts got the most votes.'

Connie's mother, who was sitting on Bernie's other side, craned her short neck to take a look. 'Well, if you ask me they look a right pair of Charlies.'

It was the Friday after her visit to Paul and Esther and just before seven in the evening. Connie had finally arrived at her mother's house an hour and a half later than she'd intended. However, someone two streets away had lost their husband the day before and Maud had gone around to pay her respects and had only just arrived back herself.

So after catching up on all the family gossip over a late supper of vegetable soup, tongue sandwiches with gherkin relish followed by a slice of coconut cake, they'd got the deckchairs out of the shed and now the women of the Byrne family were sitting in the backyard in Maroon Street.

Although it was just after seven, the sun was still above the houses opposite allowing them to enjoy the warm evening without the glare of the sun.

'Oh, Mum,' laughed Connie. 'It's only a bit of fun.'

'That's right,' said Mo, sipping her soft drink. 'Everyone joined in.'

'I tell you, Mum,' said Bernie. 'It was the best holiday we've ever had. We were waited on at every meal—'

'And the kids made friends as soon as we arrived, so what with playing with the other children and the Red Coats' club, we hardly saw them,' added Mo.

'And the entertainment was wonderful,' continued Bernie. 'There was the comedian and the dance contests.'

'Not to mention the Mediterranean ballroom with an Eiffel tower in one corner and the Leaning Tower of somewhere or another in the other,' said Mo. 'I tell you, Mum, me and Eddy are already planning to book again next year.'

'So are we,' added Bernie. 'You and dad should come with us.'

Maud sniffed. 'I don't think I could enjoy myself with a bunch of strangers.'

'You wouldn't be with strangers, Mum,' said Bernie. 'You'd be with us.'

Maud didn't look convinced.

'I don't know why you want to spend all that money when we could go hopping for nothing,' Maud said. 'I remember how you used to jump off the coach and run straight into our hut waving your arms and shouting with joy.'

'Shouting to scare the mice away,' said Bernie.

'And waving our arms to get rid of the cobwebs,' added Mo.

Their mother's mouth pulled into a sulky line.

'They've got machines to get the hops off the vine now, Mum,' said Connie, pouring the last of her mother's stout into the glass she was holding.

Although she and her sister were enjoying some of Mo's freshly made lemonade, Connie had stopped off at the Northern Star on the corner to get her mother's bottle of Mackeson.

A maudlin expression crept into Maud's eyes. 'Such good times,' she said in a small voice.

Connie and her sister exchanged a long-suffering look.

'And here's a snap of the kids in the fancy dress,' Bernie said, passing Connie a picture of assorted nieces and nephews dressed as pirates, castaways and Hawaiian dancers.

'They look as if they're enjoying themselves, don't they, Mum,' said Connie, holding it so her mother could see.

Maud's took the photo from her. 'Such little sweethearts, all of them,' she said as her heavy features lifted into an indulgent smile.

The three sisters relaxed as their mother beamed at her grandchildren.

'Have you heard from Bobby?' asked Mo.

'Yes, I got a letter from him on Monday. Well, if you can call it a letter,' said Connie. 'It was just two sides and a lot of talk about the larks him and his friends had on a weekend pass in Munich.'

'Sounds as if he's having the time of his life,' said Mo.

'I'm sure he is,' said Bernie.

'But I'm glad he's coming for Christmas,' said Connie.

'So am I.' Maud sighed. 'After all, it could be my last.'

'I doubt it.' Connie raised an eyebrow. 'Not after the way you sprinted after that lad in the market last week.'

Mo and Bernie supressed a smile while their mother gave Connie a testy look.

'It's all well and good for you to joke,' she said, crossing her arms and adjusting her bosom. 'But who knows how long any of us have got, so it'll be nice to have Christmas Day with all my family around me.'

'Well, you might not have me,' said Connie.

'But you worked last year,' said Bernie.

'I know, but we had Christmas dinner with you last year,' said Connie. 'So I really ought to go to Malcolm's mother's this year.'

'Surely not with your brother home from fighting in Germany,' said Maud.

'The war's over, Mum,' said Mo.

'Then tell me, why have we still got thousands of our soldiers in Germany?' her mother asked.

Not wanting to hear Maud's views yet again on Hitler, the Nazis and the German population, none of her daughters replied.

'And anyway, until you and Malcolm are actually married your family comes first in such things,' said Maud emphatically.

Mo and Bernie gave Connie a sympathetic look.

'Malcolm's mother can't expect you to give her the consideration due to a mother-in-law until you've stood in front of Father O'Conner,' Maud continued. 'Talking about the wedding. Have you asked our Flo if she can do your flowers yet?'

'Considering we've got a year to go, don't you think it's a bit early?' said Connie.

Maud shook her head. 'It'll soon come around, and what about the menu for the lunch?'

'I haven't even thought about the food yet,' Connie replied. 'And it'll depend on what's still on ration.'

'You can get extra, you know,' said Mo.

'I know, but they will only issue them six months in advance so I was going to apply after Easter,' said Connie.

'You can still put together a draft menu,' persisted her mother. 'And I thought we could pool our sugar rations and have a four-tier cake.'

'Isn't that a bit excessive?' said Connie.

'Not with all our lot,' said Bernie.

'No,' added Mo. 'I think Mum's counted eighty-three already.'

Connie gasped. 'Eighty-three!'

'That's including all the cousins, their other halves and children,' added Mo.

'Surely we can cut the number down a bit,' said Connie, quickly multiplying two shillings and nine pence by eighty-three.

Her mother's mouth pulled into a hard line. 'I'm not having people say we skimped on your wedding.'

Connie raised an eyebrow. 'Who's paying for all this, Mum?'

'You know we would if we could, Connie,' Maud replied. 'But you know me and your dad have only got our pensions, and—'

'Then we'll trim the list,' said Connie firmly. 'And it's my wedding, Mum, and if you don't stop going on about it I might decide not to get married at all.'

Her mother's mouth dropped open.

'Call off the wedding?' asked her mother incredulously. 'You wouldn't do that, would you?'

'I might,' said Connie.

'But Malcolm's got a good job in an office, he's not a drinker or gambler and he likes children,' her mother replied. 'He's a bit under his mother's thumb, I grant you, but you'll be able to pull him in line once you're wed. And I'll tell you this, with Malcolm you'll never have to go through his pockets while he's asleep to get your housekeeping each week.'

'But surely there's more to choosing a husband than just picking one who's a good provider,' said Connie.

'Of course there is,' said her mother. 'And if he's handy around the house with a screwdriver or paintbrush then all the better, but—'

'I was actually referring to whether you loved him,' cut in Connie, pondering how she hadn't given Malcolm a second thought while he'd been away.

In fact, if she were to be totally truthful not only had she not missed him at all, she was secretly relieved that he'd returned with laryngitis so not only did she not have to listen to hours of tedious woodcraft talk but as he was confined him to bed and his mother wouldn't allow Connie into Malcolm's bedroom, she hadn't seen Mrs Henstock for almost three weeks.

'Oh, that,' said her mother, waving the notion away.

'Well, it's important, isn't it?' said Connie.

'It depends what you call love,' said her mother. 'But if you think marriage is all lovey-dovey like in the cinema you're going to be disappointed. And don't think that if things aren't all they should be you can do what that friend of yours Millie Smith has done. Blooming disgrace that's what it is and after he bought her that posh house in Wanstead.'

'I don't think that gave him the right to hit her—'

'Hit her,' scoffed her mother. 'She wants to ask Doreen Kelly around the corner about being hit. I've never yet seen that poor woman doing her Saturday grocery shop down the Waste without a shiner, but did she go running home to her mother? No she didn't, she stuck it out. That's what marriage is all about. Sticking it out to the end.'

'Don't take no notice of Mum, Connie,' said Bernie, shooting her mother an exasperated look. 'I'm not saying it's a bed of roses all the time but I wouldn't swap my Cliff for any man alive.'

'And even though he makes me so mad I could scream sometimes, I wouldn't be without Eddy either,' added Mo. 'And I'm sure you feel the same about Malcolm—'

'Of course she does,' cut in their mother. She swallowed the last of her stout. 'Now all this heat has dried me right out,' she announced, holding up her empty glass. 'So could you get one of the kids to pop along to the offy and get me another?'

'I'll go,' said Connie, rising to her feet.

'You sure?' said Mo, handing Connie the empty bottle so she could get the money back.

'Yes, won't be long,' said Connie over her shoulder. 'And the walk will do me good.'

Before her mother or sisters could reply, Connie hurried through the back gate.

Standing in the cool of the alleyway between the houses, Connie took a breath. Yes, she needed a walk, not least to try to dislodge the image of Dr MacLauchlan which seemed to have replaced the picture of Malcolm in her mind.

Having run through all Malcolm's good qualities by the time she'd reached her parents' local, the Northern Star, Connie had managed to regain her equilibrium, well almost.

Pushing open the off licence door, she walked in the narrow

passageway with a glass panel to divide her from the main part of the licensed premises. Leaning against the bar she was just about to call to Olive the landlady, who was chatting to a customer at the other end, when she spotted her dad in the corner of the snug listening to a boxing match on the wireless.

Retracing her steps, Connie left the side offy and went into the main part of the public house. Olive looked up as she walked in and held up a small bottle of tonic water. Connie smiled and the landlady popped off the metal cap and poured it into a glass. Leaving it on the edge of the bar, she returned to her conversation.

Connie collected it and her father looked up and smiled.

'Hello, luv,' he said as she slipped into the bench beside him. 'I thought you were soaking up the sun in the backyard with Mum.'

'I escaped.' Connie gave him a peck on the cheek. 'Actually, she wanted another stout and I volunteered.'

Her father chuckled. 'Well, she can wait for a bit, can't she?'

Connie smiled.

'I suppose she's been going on about the wedding again,' said her father, picking up his pint.

'As ever,' said Connie, with a sigh. 'You'd think it was next week rather than next year.'

'Well, that's your mother for you,' Arthur replied. 'Always organising everyone.' He took a slurp. 'You know, I pity the Almighty when she gets upstairs cos she'll have something to say about the way Heaven's run.'

Connie laughed. 'Yes, she'd soon be on at those angels for shedding feathers on the clouds.'

'And the saints for using too much Brasso on their halos,' her father added.

They laughed.

'But seriously, Dad,' said Connie. 'You think it was her getting married not me.'

Her father patted her knee. 'We shouldn't be too hard on her. You know with me getting shipped off to France she didn't have much of a bash when we got wed in '15. She was hoping to give Mo and Bernie something better but then, like everyone else, we didn't have two halfpennies to scrape together when Mo got hitched in '33 and then the war was on when Bernie walked down the aisle eight years later, so your poor mother's been cheated of a white wedding all her life.'

'But Jimmy had a big shindig,' said Connie.

Her father raised a bushy eyebrow.

'Oh yes, I forgot,' said Connie, remembering her sister-in-law Sheila's mother and her own having a stand-up row in the market about the bridesmaids' headgear.

The bell sounded for the next round and the ringside commentator started a blow-by-blow account of the action.

Connie sipped her drink as the round continued, then the bell sounded again.

'Dad.'

'Yes, luv?'

'What made you decide Mum was the one you should marry?'

Her father spluttered in his drink. 'Gawd, what a blooming question.'

'Well you must have some reason you asked her to marry you,' persisted Connie.

'Course I did,' said her father. 'I was going off to war and if I had to die I wanted to die a man.'

'Dad!'

'Well, it was a long time ago.'

'I know, but why Mum and not someone else?' persisted Connie.

'I don't know.' Her father gave an embarrassed laugh. 'Although I do remember she had a sort of way of laughing that made me smile and . . .' A tender expression crept into his eyes. 'Her hair, same colour as yours in those days, and she had this little curl just here.' He twiddled his earth-stained index finger next to his cheek. 'And . . .' He cleared his throat. 'Well, er . . . Anyway, why are you giving me the third degree, Con?'

Connie shrugged. 'I don't know really. I just wondered if, like Mum, you think Malcolm will make a good husband.'

Her father looked surprised. 'I suppose he will. He's a decent-enough chap, and your mum's quick enough to tell people your fiancé is high up in the council's Works Department and is paid monthly not weekly.'

'I know, but . . .'

'What?'

'I don't know,' she sighed. 'Will being practically teetotal, not knowing how to put money on a horse and able to knock a nail in a wall straight make Malcolm a good husband?'

'Perhaps, but the question you should ask is, whatever he can or can't do, is Malcolm the right husband for you?' said her father quietly. 'And only you can answer that, luv.'

Connie forced a smile. 'I know.'

The bell on the wireless dinged again, signifying the start of the next round, and Connie finished her drink.

'I ought to get Mum her stout,' she said.

Her dad slid his empty glass towards her. 'Tell Olive to put another half in that on your way out and ask her to put your drink on my slate.'

Connie smiled, picking up her father's glass as she stood up, but as she stepped away her father spoke, 'Connie.'

She looked around.

'You don't have to marry him, you know, luv,' he said softly, looking at her in the same way he had when he'd tucked her and her teddy into bed each night when she was younger.

'I know, Dad,' she replied, smiling affectionately down at him. 'I know.'

Chapter Eighteen

Connie rubbed her hands together briskly. 'It might feel a little uncomfortable, Mrs Longman, but I'm just going to check where the top of your womb is.'

Dora Longman, who was having her fourth child, was accompanied this afternoon by Tracy, her eighteen-month-old daughter, who was asleep in her pushchair outside.

It was the last Tuesday in October and although it was only just four-thirty, the clocks had gone back the previous weekend so the treatment room lights had been on since they'd started clinic at two.

Spreading her fingers as wide as she could, Connie tucked her right hand under Dora's swollen stomach and pressed firmly, she then rested her left hand just above her patient's navel. Gazing unseeingly at the faded fabric of the screen pulled around them, Connie concentrated as she palpated the top of the fundus.

'Absolutely fine,' Connie replied. 'Has baby been moving?'

'Doesn't stop.' Dora ran her hand gently over her bump. 'It's all front so my mum says it's another boy.'

'How is your mum?'

'Oh you know, nothing's right and everything's wrong, so the same as ever,' Dora replied. 'Mind you, her chest's been playing her up something rotten these last couple of days. Bringing up lumps of gob as big as your fist, but will she let me get the quack in? Will she buggery.'

'Do you want me to pop in on her?' asked Connie.

'If you could,' said Dora, giving Connie a grateful look.

Connie picked up the foetal stethoscope. 'I'm going to have a listen.'

Placing the broad end on Dora's stomach, Connie pressed her ear to the other end. She closed her eyes to concentrate and heard the gurgling sounds of Dora's lunch being digested plus the whoosh of blood pumping through the main arteries at a steady eighty beats per minute.

Connie shifted the cup to the side and heard the tell-tale rapid pitter-pattering of the baby tucked deep inside.

'That seems fine,' said Connie, putting the stethoscope on the trolley. 'You can get dressed now, Mrs Longman.'

Dora got off the couch. While her patient rearranged her clothing, Connie put away the equipment and replaced the draw sheet with a fresh one, she then quickly wrote up her notes.

'All done, and we'll see you in a month,' she said, pushing back the screen. 'Tell your mum I'll drop in tomorrow and don't forget to get your green ration book stamped by Nurse Small so you can get your extra milk.'

'Don't worry, luv, I won't,' said Dora, tucking the blanket in tightly around her still-sleeping daughter before she left.

Popping her pen back in her top pocket, Connie went over to the desk and was just about to tuck Dora's notes into the back of the box when the telephone sprang into life.

Connie picked it up. 'Fry House, Sister Byrne speaking. How can I help you?'

'It's Pearl Morris here, I live next door to Mrs Gillespie,' said the voice down the telephone. 'The police have just kicked the door down so I think perhaps you should come.'

Connie breathlessly screeched to a halt outside Mrs Gillespie's house where a small crowd of women stood, arms folded, by the front door. Also, ominously, there was a large black bicycle with a bull-eyed lamp fixed to the front and MP stamped in large gold letters on the crossbar.

Connie took her bag and hurried in. The Gillespies' door was hanging off its hinges and there were jagged splinters of wood where the lock used to be.

Paul was sitting in his usual chair but the books he'd been reading were scattered on the floor around him. Worryingly, he had a fresh bruise on his head that was fast growing into a sizeable egg, there was blood on his lips and cheeks and his hands were grazed.

He turned his head as Connie walked in, pain and grief etched onto his contorted face.

Connie hurried over. 'Oh my goodness, Paul, what's happened?'

Paul looked up and let out a long, shuddering groan. His eyes flicked to the scullery door as a well-fed policeman with florid cheeks and thinning hair walked out.

'Where's Mrs Gillespie?' Connie asked.

'In the kitchen,' he said, thumbing over his shoulder. 'But you won't need that,' he continued, jabbing his stubby pencil towards the case she was carrying. 'I'm Constable Standish, by the way.'

'Sister Byrne,' Connie replied.

She went into the kitchen and the officer followed.

Mrs Gillespie was lying on the floor with her arms splayed out and her eyes shut. Paul's china feeding cup lay broken by her right foot and spilt tea stained the flagstones.

Putting her bag on the chair, Connie went over and knelt beside the dead woman. Now the worries and cares of this world had left her, Mrs Gillespie looked younger and there was just a hint of the pretty woman she'd once been.

If Connie had a pound for every dead body she'd seen in the ten years of her nursing career, she would have had a nice little nest egg in her Midland Bank saving account by now. However, whether it was a mangled, broken body dug out from a bombed house or someone like Mrs Gillespie who had been left totally unmarked by the spirit's departure, Connie couldn't look on a deceased person without being moved. The day she did would be the day she gave up nursing.

'Has the doctor been?' she asked.

The officer nodded. 'The neighbour called the station at three and I arrived at twenty past and kicked the door in. The doctor from Christ Church surgery arrived just after.'

An image of Dr MacLauchlan with his sleeves rolled up flashed through Connie's mind.

'Which one?'

'Marshall,' replied Standish. 'Said we were lucky to catch him as he'd only called in for his golf clubs. I've phoned for the undertakers, too,' he added.

Reaching over, she lifted Mrs Gillespie's arms which were just beginning to stiffen and placed them across her chest. She got up and retrieved a triangular bandage from the side pocket of her nurse's bag, then knelt down again. Tucking Mrs Gillespie's top dentures firmly into place, she folded the cloth longways and wound it around the old woman's head and secured it firmly under the chin. She briefly placed her hand on Mrs Gillespie's cold ones, then stood up.

'Undertakers,' a man shouted from the other room. 'Anyone at home?'

'Just coming,' Constable Standish replied, strolling through to the main room.

Connie followed him and found two men dressed in dark suits standing in the middle of the room. The taller one had his arm around an upended stretcher while the other, half a head shorter than the first but double the width, carried a brown canvas sheet.

Paul was slumped in the chair with tears streaming down his face, but neither man seemed to have noticed. They acknowledged Connie with a quick up-and-down glance, then turned their attention back to Constable Standish.

'Bill Carp from Higgins & Son at your service, constable,' said the taller of the two. He produced a packet of Senior Service and offered the constable one. 'And this is me mate Dave.'

'PC Standish from Leman Street,' the constable replied, taking the box of matches from the mantelshelf and lighting his cigarette. 'You were quick.'

'We were just setting out for the Mildmay to pick up a couple of goners, so we thought we'd collect this one on the way,' said Bill.

Connie went over to Paul and put her arm around his shoulder. He opened his eyes and looked at her.

'I'm so sorry, Paul,' she said quietly, hugging his bony shoulders.

Paul let out another groan and heaved a howling, guttural sob. The three men stopped chatting and looked across.

'What's that?' asked Bill, blowing cigarette smoke upwards from the corner of his mouth.

'The old bird's kid.' Officer Standish flicked his cigarette into Mrs Gillespie's spotless grate. 'She's in there. Doc said it were her heart.' He chuckled. 'Said she was probably as dead as a dodo when she hit the floor.'

'For God's sake, can't you show a bit of feeling?' snapped

Connie, wiping a thread of spittle from Paul's lips with her handkerchief.

The three men looked baffled.

'This is Mrs Gillespie's son!' she continued, giving them her furious matron's glare. 'I don't know how you'd feel if it were your mother lying in the kitchen and you had people calling her an "old bird" and that she was as "dead as a dodo".'

Officer Standish looked offended. 'There's no need to get uppity, nurse. The doc said he wouldn't understand what's happened on account of him being wrong in the head.'

'The only person I know who is wrong in the head is ruddy Dr Marshall,' Connie snapped. 'And if you had half the brain you were born with, Constable Standish, you'd have seen that. And why has Paul got a bump on his head and scraped hands?' she asked, pointing at the youngster's swollen forehead.

'I found him halfway across the floor. Perhaps he fell out of his chair,' the officer replied. 'I put him back.'

Connie turned to Paul. 'Were you trying to get to your mum?'

The young lad gave another shuddering sob and nodded.

Connie gave the three men a withering look.

'And as for you.' Connie looked at the funeral directors. 'I doubt local families will be so keen to be dealt with by undertakers who call their nearest and dearest "goners".'

The two undertakers stood up a little straighter and exchanged a worried look.

'We didn't mean nothing by it, sister,' said Cyril. 'Just a bit of banter, that's all.'

'Yeah, we didn't know, did we? And we're a good family firm,' added Bill. 'I hope you'll be happy to tell all your patients that, sister.'

Connie let her expression soften a little. 'I might.'

Bill and Cyril exchanged another glance, then hurried into the kitchen.

Constable Standish stepped forward. 'If you're happy to stay with the lad until the ambulance—'

'Ambulance?'

The officer looked meaningfully at Paul and Connie nodded.

'I'm sorry about your mum, lad,' he said respectfully, then he left.

Paul's head wobbled and he closed his eyes. He kept them closed as, a few minutes later, Bill and Cyril carried his mother's body through the lounge.

The door banged behind them and there was silence.

As Paul sobbed quietly in her arms, Connie gazed around the room until her eye came to rest on the line of photos sitting proudly along the mantelshelf. There was a picture of Paul in his pram sucking a dummy with a very young Mrs Gillespie smiling into the camera, crouched down beside him. Next to it was a photo of Paul at about five sitting amongst daisies and butter-cups between his mother's legs and grinning despite the callipers on his legs. Further along, another photo showed them both at a funfair with Paul in a wheelchair and his mother, looking older and wearier, pushing. The last, which could have only been taken the year before, showed Paul sitting in his wheelchair in front of London Zoo's lion house.

As she studied them, Connie realised they not only charted Paul's formative years, but also revealed his mother's lifetime of selfless devotion.

As from an hour ago, Paul was now under the care of the Welfare State and Connie fervently hoped it would do as good a job of caring for him as his mother.

'Right, Mrs Willis,' said Connie, rocking back on her heels and surveying her neat bandaging of the old woman's stout legs. 'That should be fine until the day after tomorrow.'

She was in the tiny back room of Hammond's greengrocer's shop in Viaduct Street, which was run by Nora Willis's son-in-law, Vic. Vic and Nora's daughter, Eileen, had moved to a leafy square in Stratford a few years back but Nora, who was one of the clinic's daily patients, had lived above the shop for all her sixty-one years. Although Vic bought the veg from Spitalfields to fill the troughs nailed along the walls and took care of the weekly money side of things, Nora still pottered about the shop serving customers, many of whom she'd gone to school with.

Well, when she said 'shop', Connie really meant a converted house. Hammond's was one of those small family-run enter-prises you could have found in most streets before the war. In this case, some shrewd individual had turned the front room into a fruit and veg shop, but it could easily have been a pickle factory in the scullery, a sweatshop with three or four sewing machines in an upstairs room, or a boot-repair business in a ramshackle shed in the yard behind.

'Thank you, nurse,' the old woman replied.

'And don't stick a knitting needle down the side of the bandage to scratch your legs,' added Connie in her nurse-knows-best voice.

'All right, nurse, I'll try,' said Nora as Connie dropped the soiled bandages onto an old copy of the *East London Advertiser*.

'Oi, oi,' called a woman from the front room.

'Just coming, Mary,' Nora called back.

'I'll finish here if you want to serve your customer,' said Connie.

Nora's arthritic hands gripped the arms of her chair and she heaved herself to her feet then. 'Sling your rubbish in the grate and I'll burn it later,' she said as she hobbled out.

Connie packed her instruments in the tins ready for sterilisation at the clinic and screwed the top on the Dettol. Tucking her apron up into her waistband, she then put on her winter coat, collected her nurse's bag, and walked through into the shop. The customer had gone and Nora sat in her chair by an old wooden till.

'Sister Lovegrove will call tomorrow,' said Connie.

'Right you are, sister,' Mrs Willis said.

Connie walked to the door.

Twenty minutes after leaving Nora, Connie arrived back at Fry House. She shoved her cycle into the bike rack and grabbed her bag from the basket. She headed for the back door, looking forward to her afternoon cup of tea.

Judging by the sound of children screaming, the afternoon antenatal clinic was packed. Leaving her coat to dry on the coat rack in the hall, Connie decided to head for the kitchen but, before she had a chance, Wendy's flushed face appeared around the corner of the treatment room.

'Thank goodness you're back,' she said, stepping out with a sticky-looking infant clutching at her apron. 'You have to go and see Miss O'Dwyer straight away.'

'What about?'

'She didn't say,' Wendy replied. 'But she's been in and out of the clinic like a fiddler's elbow looking for you, so you'd better go and see right away.'

Connie sighed and, feeling her stomach grumble in protest, made her way to Miss O'Dwyer's office at the end of the hall.

Connie knocked.

'Come in, come in!' shouted Miss O'Dwyer.

'You're looking for me?'

She stopped.

Miss O'Dwyer was seated behind her desk looking as if the end of the world was nigh.

It probably was, although not because the Almighty had called time on creation but because Father Flaherty was sitting beside her.

Dressed in his full regalia he reclined in the guest chair with his long legs crossed and his skeletal fingers resting on the arms. Judging by the numerous empty teacups sitting on the tray in front of him, he'd been there some time. As his hooded grey eyes rested on Connie they hardened, as did his thin mouth.

'Oh, there you are, me dear,' said the superintendent, visibly relieved at the sight of her. 'I was just saying she'd more likely than not been held up by some emergency. Wasn't I, Father?'

'Indeed,' he replied, not taking his critical gaze from Connie.

'Good afternoon, Father, I'm sorry to keep you waiting,' said Connie, closing the door behind her. 'But I've only just finished my morning calls.'

Father Flaherty regarded her stonily so Connie turned her attention back to her senior nurse.

'You wanted to see me, superintendent?'

'That I do.' Miss O'Dwyer cast a nervous glance at the priest. 'See now, Connie, Father Flaherty—'

'If I may,' cut in the priest.

'Of course, Father,' said Miss O'Dwyer, tucking her hands on her lap and bowing her head.

Unfolding his long body, Father Flaherty rose to his feet.

'Sister Byrne,' he boomed. 'Are you a baptised and confirmed member of the Roman Catholic church?'

'I am,' Connie replied.

'And do you, under the penalty of damnation, uphold the rites and doctrines of Mother Church?' he asked.

'Of course,' she replied.

'Well then, why you are blaspheming against the Virgin Mary and tempting others into sinful ways?' he asked.

Connie was aghast. 'I'm . . . I'm . . . not . . .'

The superintendent forced a jolly laugh. 'There now, didn't I tell you the truth and nothing more. Connie's as good a Catholic as St Maragret, St Katherine and St Martha rolled together, and—'

Father Flaherty shot her an acid look and Miss O'Dwyer went back to studying her fingers.

The priest returned his unyielding glare to Connie.

'Did you,' he boomed, 'not only encourage Mary Daly to interfere with God's plan but instruct her by giving her this?'

Thrusting his hand in the pocket of his cassock, he dragged out the crumpled family planning leaflet she'd given Mary some weeks before.

Although her heart was beating wildly in her chest, Connie held the priest's stare. 'Yes, I did,' she said firmly. 'I understand the teaching of the church, Father, but I thought as Mary can barely cope with the children she has, and—'

'How dare you?' boomed the priest. 'Didn't the Blessed Virgin herself exemplify the model of motherhood all women should follow?'

'She did,' said Connie. 'But she only had the one.'

Colour splashed across Father Flaherty's sallow cheeks as Miss O'Dwyer crossed herself, her lips silently moving as she started reciting Hail Mary Mother of God.

'As a nurse and midwife, it's my job to help the mothers and families to be as healthy as possible,' Connie continued.

'Is it now?'

'Yes it is,' Connie replied, trying not to imagine her mother's face if she were to hear her back-chatting a priest. 'So I give advice to all new mothers and any married woman who wants to limit their family.'

'Well, let me tell you, Sister Byrne,' Father Flaherty bellowed, the veins on his head standing out in sharp relief. 'It's my job to save souls so I'll be condemning this filth' – he shook the tatty leaflet – 'from my pulpit and refusing absolution to any woman who has anything to do with this abomination.' He tossed the leaflet aside and it fluttered to the floor. 'And I suggest you, Sister Byrne, consider your own immortal soul.'

'I'm sure she will, Father,' said the superintendent. 'Thank you, Father.'

She bowed her head.

Father Flaherty's eyes contracted to two small pinpricks and he looked at Connie.

For a moment she resisted, but then she bowed her head, too.

Father Flaherty gave a swift benediction, then strode from the room.

Connie stared after him.

'Are you all right, me dear?' asked Miss O'Dwyer.

'As well as can be expected considering I've just been threatened with eternal damnation just for doing my job.'

'Now, Connie,' said Miss O'Dwyer. 'I know Father Flaherty can be a bit sharp—'

'Ferocious, don't you mean?'

Fear flashed across the superintendent's face and she crossed herself.

'I'm sorry,' said Connie. 'It's just I can't bear to see poor women like Mary Daly bowed down by life and not do something about it.'

Miss O'Dwyer reached across and patted her hand. 'Sure you are a good and kindly soul so you are, but for our sins we will have to accept his ruling on the matter as he is our Lord's representative on earth.'

'So the church says,' Connie replied. 'But if God's like Father Flaherty then there's no hope of Heaven for any of us.' She stood up. 'I ought to check the girls in the clinic are all right. I'll see you at supper.' With Father Flaherty's words bouncing around in her head, Connie left the superintendent's office and headed back down the corridor towards the mayhem and havoc that was the antenatal clinic.

Connie was about to enter the fray when Michael and Esther Weinstein walked out, both of them beaming from ear to ear.

'Hello,' said Connie. 'What are you two doing here?'

'Oh, Connie,' said Esther, hurrying over and excitedly grabbing Connie's hand. 'I'm so glad we've bumped into you.'

Are you?' asked Connie.

'Yes,' said Michael. 'So we can tell you . . .'

The Weinsteins exchanged a private smile, then looked at Connie and said in unison, 'We're having a baby.'

Tramping up from the eastbound platform in Aldgate East Station, Hari handed his ticket to the bored-looking collector and walked into the swirling fog.

He'd just returned from a meeting about the government's immunisation programme for diphtheria, whooping cough and tetanus at the Ministry of Health in Whitehall. It had been a long meeting full of diagrams and wall charts, but it had given Hari a chance to meet like-minded GPs from other parts of the country.

Reaching the exit next to Woolworths, Hari could just make out the clock face on Gardeners' Corner showing five past three, so, for once, he had plenty of time to brew a pot of coffee and get some warmth into his bones before starting evening surgery.

Thinking he might cut through Wentworth Street market and pick up something for his evening meal, Hari turned his collar up against the November drizzle and turned right. His mind still filled with the afternoon's discussion, he strolled into Old Castle Street.

Wrapped in her knee-length thick navy coat with her nurse's case clutched in her hand, Grace Huxtable stepped out from the tenement block stairwell and straight into Hari's path.

'Hello, Grace,' he said cheerily. 'Fancy meeting you here.'

She looked startled. 'Oh, Hari . . . I mean Dr MacLauchlan.'

'Hari's fine,' he laughed. 'After all, we know each other well enough by now, surely. How are you getting on?'

She tucked a stray lock of hair behind her ear and gave a nervous laugh. 'You know what it's like getting to grips with a new job and people.'

He smiled. 'I certainly do.' He glanced at the bag in her hand. 'New arrival?'

'Oh yes,' she replied, her eyes darting around like a cornered doe looking for a bolthole. 'Mrs Farmer, number twenty-six. A boy. Nine pound one.'

'Bit of a whopper like his father then!' said Hari.

She forced a smile. 'Yes.'

There was a pause as they regarded each other again for a few moments and then she spoke.

'I don't want you to think I've been avoiding you, Hari,' she said, tucking a stray lock of hair behind her ear.

'I didn't think you were,' he replied, knowing full well she was.

There was another pause and she fiddled with her hair again.

'And I want you to know that if I'd have known you were one of the GPs for Fry House I would never have applied for the job.'

He looked puzzled. 'Why ever not?'

'Because I wouldn't want to cause you any trouble.' She gave him a shy look. 'I mean, if people found out about . . . you know.'

'There's been a lot of water under the bridge since Hastings,' said Hari.

'There has, but—' Pain flitted across her face as tears sprang into her eyes.

'Oh, Grace.' He put his arm around her shoulders.

She buried her face in his chest and sobbed. He held her for a moment as her sadness washed over him.

After a moment she raised her head and stepped out of his embrace. 'I'm sorry.'

'It's all right. We're friends after all,' he said softly. Taking his handkerchief from his pocket and offering it to her, he said, 'Now, let me buy you a cuppa.'

Dabbing her eyes, Grace forced a brave little smile and nodded.

Taking her arm, Hari led her towards the brightly lit windows of Mosher cafe at the end of the street.

Connie sat with her chin resting on the heel of her hand, her foot tapping in time with the beat as she watched the dancers swirling and twirling around the festively decorated Hackney Town Hall. It was the first Friday in December and she and Malcolm were at the Friends of Fry House's Christmas dance again. As with last year, she'd managed to bag another bargain from Alma's stall but this time it was an apple-green dress with a snug boat-necked bodice, capped sleeves and a circular skirt held out by a frothy petticoat.

'Here we go,' said Millie's voice behind her. 'Two G&Ts.'

Connie turned to find her friend standing behind her with a happy smile on her face and holding two drinks. Millie was still living with her mum because Jim was refusing to pay her maintenance for Patricia. Millie had had to return to work as, what with chipping in for bills and having to pay to have Patricia minded during the day, Millie's purse strings were pulled pretty tight. She hadn't been able to run to a new dress for the dance but, even so, was getting more than a few second looks in her sophisticated mulberry satin cocktail dress.

Millie sat on the chair next to Connie and took a sip of her drink. 'It's a good turnout.'

'Yes,' agreed Connie. 'Mrs Broderick, the Friends secretary, said they were all out of tickets two weeks ago.'

'Well, everyone seems to be enjoying themselves, especially your superintendent,' said Millie, casting her eyes across the hall.

Miss O'Dwyer had commandeered a table close to the buffet and, if her flushed cheeks were anything to go by, she had been imbibing Jameson's steadily for the past two hours. Wearing a drop-waisted crêpe gown and a looped string of pearls, she was in deep conversation with Mrs Howard, who used to be the Nursing Association's chairwoman but was now president of the Friends of Fry House. Ranged behind her were some of Connie's colleagues while others tripped the light fantastic under the central mirror ball with their husbands, fiancés and boyfriends.

'Is your Dr MacLauchlan here?' asked Millie as she scanned the dancers.

'I don't think so,' Connie replied, in what she hoped was a casual tone.

She knew full well he wasn't because for the past two hours every time the heavily carved ballroom doors swung open, she'd been disappointed not to see him stroll in.

'Is that nurse who knew him before here?' asked Millie.

'No, she's visiting relatives and couldn't come.'

Millie raised an eyebrow, which Connie ignored as she smiled at her friend. 'So, are you enjoying yourself?'

'I certainly am,' said Millie, studying the couple on the floor.

'Thanks for inviting me, Connie, although do I feel a bit of a gooseberry with you and Malcolm.'

'Hardly,' Connie replied. 'He's spent most of the time at the bar with Mr Granger, the area Scout commissioner.'

Millie looked down the room towards the twinkling ten-foot Christmas tree to where Malcolm stood alongside the Scout commissioner, who appeared to have been inflated with a foot pump after he'd put his suit on.

Millie nudged Connie. 'Just like old times, eh? You and me.'

'Oh yes,' laughed Connie.

'Remember those two gunners in the Trocadero at Piccadilly?' asked Millie.

'How could I ever forget,' Connie replied. 'I didn't think we'd ever shake them off.'

'And then the three American sailors me, you and Eva got stuck with in the Lyceum,' continued Millie. 'And what about the two Polish airmen we got caught in an air raid with and we all had to shelter down Chancery Lane Station?'

'Happy days,' Connie replied with a wry smile. 'Half-starved and with bombs dropping on our heads day and night.'

'But we had some good times, too,' protested Millie.

'Yes, we did,' Connie agreed. 'Like when I danced with every man who asked me at the VJ dance in the Regency, do you remember?'

'Yes, I do,' said Millie bleakly. 'It was the same night I met Alex, and now look at me. Four years later, I'm back living with my mother and my daughter's a child from a broken home.'

'Have you seen him again?' Connie asked, palpably feeling her friend's heartbreak.

Millie nodded. 'I ran into him last week when I was shopping along the Waste. He had a blonde on his arm this time instead of a redhead.'

Connie put her hand on her friend's arm. 'Oh, Millie.'

'It's all right but I can't help thinking that this time last year I was a happy wife and I'd just found out I was expecting and now . . .' Millie forced a too-bright smile. 'But never mind, water under the bridge, and all that.'

The music stopped and the two girls clapped as the band turned over their music sheets ready for the next number.

'And what about you?' said Millie as the dancers took their places again. 'You've been engaged a whole year and this time next year you'll be swanning around the dance floor as Mrs Henstock.'

'That's very unlikely,' said Connie. 'I can barely get him on the dance floor this year, so I don't suppose I'll fare much better next.'

The bandleader tapped his baton as the string section led their fellow musicians into 'I Only Have Eyes for You'.

'Alex loved this song,' said Millie, a bleak expression on her face. 'He's such a lovely dancer.'

Although it was over a year ago, the memory of Dr MacLauchlan's perfect rhythm, skilful footwork and the feel of his arm around her waist came, unbidden, into Connie's mind.

Chapter Nineteen

The December daylight was disappearing fast and the temperature hovered somewhere just above freezing on the Tuesday after the dance as Connie reached the main gate of Brentwood Mental Hospital.

The train had been delayed outside Seven Kings and so, instead of pulling into the station at three twenty-two, it had arrived just after half past. This in itself wouldn't have been a disaster if it wasn't for the fact that the bus from the station only ran once an hour and she'd just missed it. So, telling herself a brisk walk would get the warmth back to her feet, Connie turned left up the hill and headed for the hospital.

That was twenty minutes ago and now, after trudging up Warley Hill carrying a bag with Paul's Christmas present, she had arrived.

The main block of the hospital was housed in a Victorian mock-Gothic building made of red brick. With its false buttresses at the corners, a central entrance that looked like a castle keep and a lofty bell tower to one side, it was an imposing sight. However, the grandeur the architect had hoped to achieve was totally undermined by the pair of shoddily painted main doors.

Crunching through the ice that had formed on the puddles in the gravel driveway, Connie tramped on. She walked up the sweeping baronial steps and was soon in the main reception area.

Well, it would have been the reception area if there had been anyone to receive her.

To her right there was a fireplace with an embossed Tudor rose at each end and a brass plaque commemorating the founding members of Essex County Lunatic Asylum, 1853. Above this the county crest was held upright by two winged angels sheltering in what looked like a barn.

On her other side was a half-glazed door with a heavy embossed surround through which muffled voices could be heard, so, rubbing her hands to restore the circulation, Connie walked in.

In contrast to the chill of the hall she'd just left, the room she entered was stifling and the smell of paraffin and cigarettes clogged the atmosphere.

There were two women in the office bashing away at typewriters. The woman nearest Connie was in her late twenties, with bleached hair piled up on her head, bright red lipstick and wearing a pair of impossibly high heels. Her fellow clerk looked to be ten or so years older and had her unnaturally red hair pinned into two tight rolls behind her ears. She had somehow squeezed her size 18 figure into a size 14 suit.

'Good afternoon,' Connie said when it was clear neither woman was going to acknowledge her. 'I'm trying to find Albert Ward.'

The older one of the clerks looked up.

'It's infested with cockroaches so it's closed until the fumigators come,' she said, flicking her cigarette over the already overloaded ashtray on her desk. 'Who you visiting?'

'Paul Gillespie,' said Connie.

'You got the admissions book, Rita?' the older one called across.

'Right here, Lil.' Rita pulled the ledger on the corner of the desk towards her. 'When did he come in?'

'Two weeks ago, on the eighth of November,' Connie replied. 'From Bancroft Hospital.'

'Newcomer, then.'

Seeing Connie's startled look, Lil chuckled. 'We've got some here who were put away when the old queen was on the throne. I think Fred the Prophet is our oldest nutter, isn't he?'

'Well, him or that old woman in Beatrice Ward with her bald doll,' Rita replied, as the painted nail of her right index finger ran down the page. 'Here he is. Gillespie. Male, seventeen years from Weaver Street, E1.'

'That's Paul,' said Connie.

'Leopold Ward.' She indicated the direction with a sweep of her hand. 'Through the door at the bottom, turn right and then left at the end and go straight down. Leopold is the last ward. You'll have to ring the bell and someone will unlock the door.'

Connie thanked them and left them to their work.

Pushing open the double doors, Connie found herself in the corridor that ran the length of the building. If the reception area was chilly, then the main passageway was positively glacial, complete with whistling winds. The smell that caught in Connie's throat was reminiscent of the antelope house in London Zoo. A handful of men and women shuffled back and forth along the corridor, while others leant against the walls staring blankly ahead. One woman had wedged herself up against a drainpipe and was twirling her hair, another lay silently crying on an abandoned hospital trolley.

Stepping around a suspicious pool of liquid on the floor, Connie headed for the last ward at the end of the corridor, the sound of her heels echoing on the tiles.

Pressing the bell button beside the door to one side, she waited. After what seemed like an eternity, the lock turned.

The door was opened by a stocky young woman in her early thirties; she had very short blonde hair and not a trace of make-up. She was wearing a nurse's uniform complete with frilly cap, starched collar and cuffs and apron.

'Yes?' she asked, her close-set eyes looking Connie over.

'I've come to visit Paul Gillespie.'

'Are you family?'

'No, I'm—'

'It's only supposed to be family on a Tuesday,' the nurse replied.

'I'm Sister Byrne. Paul's district nurse,' Connie continued, holding the other woman's gaze.

The nurse looked her over again, then stood aside. 'He's in the recreation room at the end.'

Connie stepped in and this time the odour of unwashed bodies and stale urine clogged her nose.

The nurse locked the door and, pocketing the enormous bunch of keys, disappeared back into the office, slamming the door behind her.

Passing the closed door of the observation room, Connie headed for the recreation room – a large rectangular room with a selection of armchairs in which unshaven men sat, staring out of the tall curtainless windows into the garden beyond. A couple of older men were propped up asleep on the aged sofa in front of the empty fire grate and next to the chimney alcove was a patient strapped into a wing-back chair.

'I'm looking for Paul Gillespie?' she called to the two orderlies dressed in grubby white jackets sitting at a table at the far end of the room. They were playing cards and paid no attention to the men around them.

'Behind you,' one shouted, briefly looking up from his hand.

Connie turned, looked again at the patient restrained in the chair and then walked over.

Stopping just in front of him, she stared down in horror at the contracted, wasted body, shaven head and food-stained clothes.

'Paul?' she whispered. 'Paul, it's me, Sister Byrne.'

Paul turned his head and stared at her for a moment, then tears welled up in his eyes.

Although she could see her breath in the chilled air of the so-called recreation room, Paul was wearing only a thin grubby shirt with no buttons and a pair of ragged grey trousers fastened with a safety pin, with a damp patch around his crotch. His bare feet were not only dirty but blue and there were crusty deposits on his chin.

Connie stood there aghast for a moment, then marched up to the two orderlies.

'Is sister in the office?' she asked.

The once facing her nodded. 'But I think she's busy,' he called after her.

Stopping outside the door marked Sister West, Connie knocked.

'Come.'

Connie went in.

The nurse responsible for Leopold Ward was sitting behind a desk, her feet resting on the upturned wastepaper bin and a cigarette in her mouth. Open in front of her was a copy of *Woman's Realm*.

'Sister West!' Connie said.

'Yes,' she replied.

'I've come to visit Paul Gillespie,' Connie replied, forcing a pleasant smile.

'Who?'

'The young man in the recreation room,' Connie replied. 'He seems to have had a little accident so I was wondering if I could give him a freshen-up?'

Sister West eyes narrowed. 'We don't allow relatives to do nursing tasks, Miss . . . ?'

'Sister,' said Connie. 'Sister Byrne. I'm Paul's district nurse.'

'*Were*.' Sister West gave her a smug smile. 'You *were* his district nurse but we're caring for him now.'

Biting back the obvious reply, Connie smiled. 'I know, but I thought as I was here, I could save your staff the trouble and get Paul ready for supper.'

Sister West regarded her cagily for a moment, then shrugged.

'The linen cupboard and the sluice are by the entrance to the ward,' she said, turning her attention back to her magazine.

The two orderlies were where Connie had left them and the older one who was facing her was shuffling the next hand.

'Would you take Paul back to his bed for me, please?' asked Connie in her best matron voice. 'If you're not too busy.'

The two orderlies exchanged a glance but didn't move.

'Or shall I call sister out?'

'All right, we 'eard yer,' said the older one, throwing his cards down.

The two orderlies dragged themselves to their feet and lumbered towards the recreation room.

Connie located Paul's room number on the blackboard on the wall then, after collecting fresh sheets, towels and a skip from the linen cupboard, made her way there.

Quickly stripping the top bedclothes and removing the suspiciously moist draw sheet, Connie deposited the dirty linen in the skip. She had just laid a towel across the bed when the orderlies pushed Paul into the room.

Standing either side of him, the orderlies hooked their arms under Paul's.

His face contorted with pain.

Connie tried to catch his legs to lift them but the older orderly was in the way.

'One, two, three,' he said.

Paul bellowed as the two men dragged him from his chair and heaved him on the bed, scraping his shins on the metal edge as they did.

Giving her a belligerent look and shoving the antiquated chair Paul had been sitting in to one side, they clumped out.

Closing the door behind them, Connie went over and sat on the bed beside Paul who was huddled, foetal-like.

Reaching out, Connie stroked Paul's forehead. His eyes opened, he looked up at her and a tear rolled down his cheek.

Buttoning his shirt and with his regimental tie dangling around his neck, Hari strode out of his bedroom and along the short passageway to the lounge.

Flipping his cuffs down as he reached the fireplace, Hari rummaged around amongst the letters, business cards and loose change on the mantelshelf until he found his cuff links.

Having secured his sleeves, Hari looked in the mirror and, with a well-practised move, slid the double Windsor knot of his tie into place.

Satisfied, he scooped up his spare change and keys and shoved them in his pocket. Then glanced at his watch. Half past five! For goodness sake, the meeting started in an hour and he still had to get there.

Soon after joining Dr Marshall's practice, Hari had volunteered to be part of a committee looking at the future development of surgery-based services in the area and tonight he and four other members of the East London GP Working Group were going to chat to the local health official about a few proposals.

Of course, he still had the splenetic and obtuse obstacle that was Dr Marshall to overcome before any improvements could be introduced to Christ Church surgery, but Hari had decided to cross that particular minefield when he had secured the funds, which was one of the reasons why he needed to make the meeting tonight. The other being that he didn't want to disappoint Dr Gingold, who had taken him firmly under her wing.

Still, if he was lucky with the buses he could make it in time – just.

Shrugging his jacket on, Hari unhooked his coat and hat from by the door and strode out, taking the stairs two at a time. He secured the front door, set his hat at its usual angle and then headed off.

Mentally running through the surgery items he needed to order the next day, Hari turned into Commercial Street and practically knocked Sister Byrne off her feet in the process.

As always she looked very fetching, this time in a moss-green fitted coat with a velvet collar and cuffs and a jaunty little hat.

'Dr MacLauchlan. I wasn't—'

'I'm sorry,' he said. 'I was miles away.'

'Don't worry,' she replied. 'No bones broken.'

A 135 bus trundled around the corner, which he still could catch if he sprinted.

Sister Byrne stooped to retrieve the shopping bag that had fallen on the pavement, but Hari beat her to it and scooped up the box wrapped in Christmas paper that had spilt out.

'Been shopping?' he asked, as the red bus to Cannon Street Road whizzed by them.

She gave him a brittle smile. 'No, I've been visiting a patient. Paul Gillespie.'

'How is he?'

Her eyes filled with tears. 'Doctor, it . . . it . . . was . . .' She covered her face with her hands.

Without thinking, Hari gathered her to him as she sobbed against his shoulder. Aware they were attracting some curious glances, Hari stepped back into a doorway, pulling her with him.

After a moment she straightened up. 'I'm sorry, doctor, I—'

'Please don't apologise,' he said, offering her his handkerchief. She blew her nose.

'I'm not usually like this but I've been bottling it up . . .' She started weeping again.

'Come with me,' he said, taking her by the elbow.

Guiding her through the inquisitive crowds waiting at the bus stop, Hari walked them across the road towards the Ten Bells at the corner of Fournier Street.

As Spitalfields market had shut up shop some hours before, the pub was fairly quiet so Hari ushered Sister Byrne, who was still struggling to compose herself, into an empty booth at the back.

'What can I get you?' he asked.

'Gin and tonic, please,' she replied, making use of his handkerchief again.

Hari went to the bar.

A crowd of roughly dressed market porters, with unshaven faces and pints in their hands, eyed him guardedly, as did the corpulent landlord with them. Taking out a pound note, Hari held it aloft.

The barman jumped into life and, flipping the tea towel over his shoulder, waddled over.

Hari ordered their drinks and, thinking he'd phone Dr Gingold to square things in the morning, he carried them back to the booth.

As he reached the table, Sister Byrne raised her head and smiled.

Hari smiled back. 'One G&T.'

Placing it on the Double Diamond coaster in front of her, he slid into the booth beside her.

He took a mouthful of his single malt. 'Now, tell me about Master Gillespie.'

She recounted her visit to the Brentwood Mental Hospital.

'And they obviously haven't been helping him eat as he's lost such a lot of weight.' With a shaky hand she lifted her drink. 'Paul looks like he's just come out of Belsen and it's clear as the nose on your face that he's not been washed for days or had his clothes changed.'

'That's appalling,' said Hari.

'That's what I think,' she said, a lock of her copper-coloured hair escaping from behind her ear. 'Added to which, all of his books and clothes have disappeared so I had to find him something to wear in the communal wardrobe. And if the fact he's reduced to wearing frayed cast-offs isn't bad enough, he's been shoved into a bedroom that would make a police cell look homely and then they strap him in a chair all day in a freezing room.' She paused. 'It's just not right. Paul's only seventeen and although he needs physical care, there's nothing wrong with his mind so I can't understand why the board couldn't send him to a home that specialises in caring for people with Paul's condition instead of locking him away on a geriatric ward in a mental

258

hospital.' Tears welled in Sister Byrne's eyes again so she gulped another mouthful of G&T. 'His poor mother believed that the National Health Service would care for him when she was gone, but—'

'Then we must make it,' said Hari.

She looked bewildered. 'How?'

'Fight their decision and get Paul moved to a place that's right for his age and condition.' Hari raised an eyebrow. '"Each According to Their Needs", as the saying goes.'

Her eyes opened wide. 'Do you think I could? Get him moved, I mean?'

'It won't be easy,' Hari replied, noting, not for the first time, that her eyes were very blue.

'I don't care,' she replied. 'I have to try.'

Hari put his hand on her arm. '*We* have to try.'

'Thank you, doctor,' she said gratefully.

'My pleasure,' Hari replied. 'And if you ever feel the need again, my shoulder will always be available for you to cry on.'

Sister Byrne gave a throaty laugh. 'I'll remember that, Dr MacLauchlan.'

Hari took a long sip of his Scotch and concentrated on getting his pulse back to its regular beat.

'So,' he said after a pause. 'Is it Constance or Cornelia?'

She looked surprised.

'Dr Gingold,' he explained. 'She called you Connie when she said you used to be one of the nurses attached to her practice.'

'I was during the war,' Connie said.

'So is it Constance or Cornelia?' persisted Hari, studying the shape of her mouth.

'Constance Marie,' she replied. 'After my great-aunt.'

'Well, I'm Jahindra Harish Chakravarthi, after my great-uncle. Hari to my friends.'

'And I'm Connie to mine.'

'Nice to meet you, Connie,' said Hari, offering his hand.

Connie took it.

'Nice to meet you too, Hari,' she replied, oblivious to the havoc the sound his name on her lips was having on his emotions. She regarded him thoughtfully for a moment, then spoke again. 'I hope you don't mind me asking, but what's India like?'

'It's difficult to say,' replied Hari. 'I mean, green and pleasant land pretty much sums up England but India is like a dozen different counties in one. You have the tropical south with its monsoons and impenetrable forests, the massive central plain criss-crossed by rivers, the Thar Desert in the west and the Ganges delta to the east and, of course, the cool slopes of the Himalayan foothills where my family comes from.'

'Whereabouts?'

'Northern Rajputana between Jaipur and the Punjab,' Hari replied.

'Rajputana,' she repeated softly. 'It sounds so exotic I can almost picture the snow-capped mountains.'

Hari smiled. 'Well, we're a fair bit south of them so think more meandering rivers, lush shores and massive rocky plains rather than purple-headed peaks, although we do have jungles, too, with tigers, not to mention ancient palaces and temples.'

Connie sighed. 'It sounds romantic.'

'It is. Perhaps your husband will take you. It's the perfect place for lovers,' he said, mesmerised by the shape of her mouth.

Connie laughed. 'Some chance. I'd have trouble getting Malcolm on the ferry to the Isle of Wight, let alone a ship to India.'

Hari smiled but didn't comment.

Connie glanced at her watch. 'Goodness, is that the time? I am sorry for holding you up when you're so obviously off somewhere.'

'It was just a meeting,' he replied. 'And in truth, you've probably saved me from hours of boredom.'

'Even so, thank you.' She glanced at the clock behind the bar and then finished the last of her G&T. 'I'm supposed to be meeting Malcolm at seven and, as always, I'm late.'

'I'm sure he won't mind.'

She gave a wry smile. 'You don't know him.'

She stood up and Hari rose to his feet. 'Thank you for your time and the drink, Dr MacLauchlan, and offering to help me get Paul moved.'

She proffered her hand again and Hari took it.

'My pleasure,' he replied, enjoying the smallness of it in his palm. 'And it's Hari.'

She gave him a little smile then, hooking her handbag over her arm and picking up the bag with Paul's present in it, she left the booth.

Hari watched her thread her way through the evening drinkers, then swallowed the last of his whisky. If he was waiting for Connie Byrne to arrive, the last thing he'd be thinking about was punctuality.

Balancing the tray holding three mugs of cocoa and three pieces of cake, Connie opened the door and walked from the chilly hallway into Mrs Henstock's warm parlour.

Malcolm was sitting on the sofa with his pipe in his mouth and his eyes closed, listening to the nightly nine o'clock concert.

His eyes opened as she walked in.

'Thank you, my dear. It's Rachmaninoff's piano concerto number two,' he told her, conducting with his pipe. 'Marvellous piece, isn't it?'

Connie forced a smile.

She'd have chosen something a bit jollier but she'd already ruined Malcolm's evening, so listening to what he preferred was the least she could do.

Connie placed the tray on the table, then took his mother's cup over to the occasional table beside her armchair.

'I really am sorry, Malcolm,' said Connie for the umpteenth time. 'I know how you enjoy a good western.'

'It doesn't matter,' he said in a voice that said otherwise. She'd been half an hour late and even though she'd apologised repeatedly, Malcolm was obviously not happy about missing his film.

'We could go on Thursday, if you like,' said Connie, tucking her skirt under her and sitting next to him.

'No, we can't,' he replied. 'Because, as you know, I've agreed to help Nigel set up his Great Western layout in his loft.'

'Can't you do that on Saturday?'

'No, as I told you on Friday, Connie,' said Malcolm, as if explaining to a five-year-old. 'I've got a planning meeting with the district Scout leaders all day Saturday, which is why we were going to see *Fort Apache* tonight.'

'Well, what about next week?'

'The Odeon changes the programme on Sunday,' said Malcolm.

Connie sighed. 'I am sorry. I didn't mean to be late, but—'

'Let's just enjoy the music, shall we?' he cut in as the next piece of music started.

Connie lapsed into silence.

The door opened and Mrs Henstock, who had been on the telephone, came back into the room.

'Everything all right with Aunt Beebee?' asked Malcolm, as his mother resumed her seat in the fireside armchair.

Hilda nodded.

'Mercifully, yes,' she replied, popping her feet up on the pouffe and draping the tartan blanket over her legs. 'Doctor said it was just a touch of blood pressure but she should be fine if she rests up for a few days.' A serene smile spread across her face. 'I do love Beethoven. Is it symphony number five or seven, dear?'

'I'm not sure,' muttered Malcolm.

Connie looked at him but, not meeting her gaze, he buried his nose in his mug of cocoa. She sipped her drink as Mrs Henstock hummed along tunelessly to whichever dead composer's dreary music was blasting out of the wireless.

Connie gazed up at the patterned lampshade above her before shifting her attention to the pastoral painting in the alcove. Having counted the cows, birds and people in the idyllic scene for a few moments she moved onto the dusty books on the shelves under the window.

She spotted Malcolm's old school atlas amongst his *Scouting for Boys* annuals and an image of Paul, as she'd found him that afternoon, flashed through her mind.

'I have to get him out,' she said as the last chord died away.

'Who?'

'Paul.'

Malcolm looked puzzled.

'The young man I went to see this afternoon,' Connie explained. 'The one I've been telling you about.'

'That's very commendable, dear,' said Mrs Henstock sweetly.

'I wouldn't get your hopes up,' added Malcolm flatly, taking his cake from the plate. 'You can't just march into the town hall and demand they do this, that and the other and I imagine the same goes for your health boards.'

'Malcolm's right,' chipped in his mother. 'Demanding this and that won't get you anywhere.'

'I'm not demanding, I'm appealing,' said Connie.

'Against what exactly?' asked Malcolm through a mouthful of crumbs.

'Putting an intelligent young man in a mental hospital instead of a specialist residential care home,' Connie snapped. 'Surely it's worth a try, otherwise we might as well forget all this Cradle to Grave stuff and just reopen the workhouses.'

'All right, Connie,' he said. 'Let's just suppose for the sake of argument that by some miracle you convince the board to reconsider this boy's case, what about the doctor who signed the order for him to go?'

'Dr Marshall,' said Connie in a small voice.

Malcolm gave her a patronising look. 'Well, from what you tell me about him he's not going to take kindly to you challenging his medical judgement. In fact, I wouldn't be surprised if he didn't make a formal complaint about you.'

'Yes, I know,' Connie said, trying shift the image of a furious Dr Marshall from her mind. 'But what can I do?'

'Well, if you ask me you'd be better off dropping the whole thing,' said Mrs Henstock. 'Or you might find yourself out of a job, Connie.'

'I don't care,' said Connie, 'I can't just leave Paul there to rot, and even if you don't think I'll get anywhere, Dr MacLauchlan does.'

Malcolm gave her a sharp look. 'Dr MacLauchlan?'

'Yes, he said he'll give me a supporting letter,' said Connie.

'When did you see him?'

'I ran into him on my way back to Fry House,' Connie replied lightly.

'You didn't mention it,' said Malcolm.

'Didn't I?' she said, knowing full well she hadn't.

Malcolm's eyes narrowed. 'You seem to have a lot to do with this doctor MacLauchlan.'

'That's hardly surprising given most of my patients belong to his surgery,' said Connie.

'So when did you see this Dr Macwhatsit?' asked Mrs Henstock, regarding Connie over the top of her spectacles.

'As I was walking back to Fry House,' Connie replied.

Malcolm's mouth pulled into an ugly line. 'So the real reason you were late wasn't because you were held up at the hospital but because you were chit-chatting with this blasted fellow.'

'I was very, very upset if you must know,' Connie replied. 'And we only had one . . .' She looked down at her cocoa.

'One what?' asked Malcolm, turning to look at her.

'Drink,' Connie replied.

A flush spread up Malcolm's cheeks. 'Oh, I understand now. My whole evening's been ruined because my fiancée was boozing in a pub with another man.'

'Disgraceful,' muttered his mother.

'We had one drink,' said Connie.

'One drink, was it?' he said, tapping his pipe into the ashtray beside him.

'For goodness sake, Malcolm,' snapped Connie.

'Don't you take that tone with Malcolm,' his mother said. 'He's been looking forward to seeing that film all week and he couldn't because you were knocking back liquor with another man.'

Malcolm jumped up and strode over to the fireplace. He pulled his tobacco pouch from his jumper pocket. 'I think I've made it quite plain on a number of occasions that I don't like you having anything to do with the fellow,' he said, refilling his pipe. 'But it seems my wishes are of no account.'

'I was upset,' Connie said, her hands clutched tightly together on her lap. 'Don't you understand? I was actually in tears when I met Dr MacLauchlan. And all he did is what anyone would do, which was to try to comfort me.'

Malcolm jammed his pipe between his teeth and didn't reply.

Giving him an approving look, Mrs Henstock turned her attention on Connie. 'For goodness sake, Connie, haven't you got any sense of propriety? You're engaged.'

'Thank you, Mum,' said Malcolm with a weary smile. 'I'm glad someone understands how I feel.'

Basking in her son's approval, a smug expression spread across

Mrs Henstock's face. She patted Malcolm's hand. 'I'm your mother.'

Staring at the members of the Henstock Mutual Admiration Society, Connie's forehead started to pound.

She stood up.

'You know what, Malcolm,' she said, picking up her handbag. 'I've got a bit of a headache coming on so I think I might just call it a night and go back to Fry House. And don't worry, I'll walk myself to the bus stop.'

'So here's to our Becky on her engagement,' said Connie, raising her glass to the young woman standing next to her.

'To our Becky!' shouted her fellow nurses from Fry House, saluting their colleague with their G&Ts.

It was just before seven and Connie and most of the Fry House nurses were in the main bar of the Artillery Arms.

The pub had the standard style of dark panelled walls, wooden floors and etched-glass mirrors behind the bar, in front of which were shelves stacked with neatly placed spirit glasses. Overhead was a brass candelabra and a ceiling stained brown with decades of nicotine-laden cigarette smoke. However, as it was now just ten days to Christmas, the hostelry's somewhat sombre decor had been given a festive look with the addition of paper chains slung between the rafters and a Christmas tree dressed with baubles and tinsel in the corner.

Situated on the corner of Gun Street and Artillery Row, it was crowded with both locals in baggy jackets and flat caps and City types with their briefcases and ties, all enjoying a well-earned pint or two at the end of a hard day's work.

'So,' said Hattie, leaning across Connie to speak to Becky. 'When's the wedding?'

Connie moved out the way so Becky could answer questions about her wedding plans.

'Isn't that your friend who's married to the politician?' Lydia tapped Connie's shoulder.

Turning, Connie saw Millie craning her neck in the doorway.

'Over here,' called Connie, beckoning to her.

Holding her coat close to avoid sweeping drinks off tables, Millie squeezed through the crowded bar to join them.

Millie took off her coat and hooked it on the stand. 'I'm sorry it was a bit last-minute but I thought you wouldn't mind.'

'Of course I don't.' Connie embraced her friend. 'I'm just glad you could make it at all. Who's got Patricia?'

'I took her down to Mum's,' said Millie. 'I'm working over the weekend so she was going tomorrow anyway and it'll give Mum an extra day to spoil her.'

'How are they?'

'Very happy,' said Millie. 'They send their love and say you must come down to see them soon.'

'I will,' said Connie. 'Are you spending Christmas with them?'

'Yes,' said Connie. 'It's Patricia's first and I've got a feeling they might go a bit overboard.'

Connie laughed. 'Isn't that what grandparents are supposed to do?'

'Here you go, girls, two G&Ts,' said Rose, handing them both a drink with ice and a piece of lemon floating in it. 'Just what the doctor ordered.'

Connie took a long mouthful and held her glass up.

'Ahhhh!' She gave an exaggerated sigh. 'If only G&Ts were on prescription.'

'If only,' agreed Millie.

Rose laughed, then made her way back to the alcove which the Fry House nurses had commandeered.

'So how are things?' asked Millie.

'Busy,' said Connie as she and her friend tucked themselves into a corner. 'Although now the new trainees have found their feet it's a little better and once Christmas is over things should ease up a bit. Although I still think we'll have to advertise for more nurses in the spring.'

'Good luck with that,' said Millie. 'There can't be a hospital or community not looking for more nurses. I think there's more pages of adverts in the *Nursing Mirror* than there are with articles.'

'I know,' agreed Connie. 'We're even thinking of advertising in the West Indies.'

'I suggested that to Miss Dutton, but she won't hear of it,' said Millie.

The door opened and a handful of Sally Army members

walked in. One of them was carrying an accordion. Tucking themselves in the corner at the other end of the pub, they started a lively rendition of 'God Rest ye Merry Gentlemen'. Some of the customers joined in, so Connie and Millie turned further into their corner.

'How's Malcolm?'

Connie shrugged.

'Same as ever,' she replied, burying her nose in her drink.

Millie gave her a querying look. 'Are you and Malcolm all right?'

'Of course we are,' Connie replied, forcing a smile.

They were. It was two weeks since their argument and it had all blown over.

Malcolm hadn't raised the issue when they'd met for their usual Friday night drink three days later and, not wanting to remind him of their tiff, Connie had been careful not to mention Dr MacLauchlan's name in conversation since.

Connie knocked back her drink in one. 'Drink up and I'll get you another.'

Millie grinned. 'Why not indeed.'

Taking her friend's empty glass, Connie jostled her way back to the bar.

As Ted the landlord and his wife Dolly were busy at the other end of the bar, Connie rested on the counter and waited to be served.

'Evening, sister,' said a gruff voice in her ear.

Connie turned and found herself staring up into Micky Murphy's hardbitten face.

He was, as always, dressed as if he were meeting royalty in a dapper striped suit, silk tie and with his gold accoutrements strung about him. A Churchill-size cigar was clamped tightly between his teeth.

'Hello, Mr Murphy. How are you?'

'Oh, you know, turning a penny here and there, sister,' he replied, the diamond ring on his left pinkie twinkling in the light. 'And yourself?'

'Overworked and underpaid,' Connie replied.

'Aren't we all,' he chuckled.

'And is Mrs Murphy well?'

'Too well,' he said, cigar smoke escaping from his nostrils as he spoke. 'I could do with her being laid up for a week or so to stop her spending my money.'

'And how's Pamela?'

A mushy expression spread across Micky's brutal features. 'As bright as a button and such a chatterbox!' He rolled his eyes. 'Between 'er and Tina I can't get a word in edgeways, but I tell you, when she calls me Dadda, I swear me heart's going to burst.' His eyes shone with moisture. 'I'd walk barefoot across the desert just to make my little princess smile. And you' – he nudged Connie playfully – 'were the lovely nurse who gave her to me.'

'Well, I think your wife did most of the work,' said Connie.

'So she keeps telling me.' He took a large mouthful of Scotch.

'What can I get you, miss?' asked Ted.

Connie gave her order and the publican ambled off.

'You lot getting in the Christmas spirit?' Micky asked, indicating the nurses laughing and joking in the alcove.

'Yes and someone's just got engaged,' said Connie.

'You?'

Connie shook her head. 'No, I'm already spoken for.'

'Anyone I know?' asked Micky.

'Yes, that chap I introduced you to last year in Petticoat Lane who works in the Highway Department at the council,' said Connie.

Micky looked visibly relieved.

'I'm glad to hear it,' he replied. 'Because when I saw you being all pally-pally with that darkie doctor in the Ten Bells a few weeks back, I thought perhaps you'd got yourself hitched up with him.'

Images of Hari's blunt chin, the liquid brown of his eyes and his bone-melting smile flashed through Connie's mind.

'Do you mean Dr MacLauchlan?' she asked in what she hoped was a light tone.

'That's him – the one you tried to get me to take my little Pamela along to.' Micky tapped his cigar ash on the floor. 'I don't mind telling you, I was surprised when I saw you together, sister, because you never struck me as being the sort of girl that would be seen with his type.'

Somehow Connie maintained her pleasant expression. 'As I said before, Dr MacLauchlan is an excellent doctor and a kind, compassionate and caring man.'

'Don't get me wrong,' said Micky in a conciliatory tone. 'I've heard a lot of people around here like him and I ain't saying he's like that bunch of spades down in Canning Town or the wops who hang around Cable Street, but it's common knowledge, all coloureds are after is getting their hands on a white woman.'

'Are they?'

He nodded. 'Gives them standing with their own kind, you know what I mean? So be warned.' He winked. 'Under all his posh ways, that Dr Whatshisname is the same as the rest of them and I wouldn't want to see a nice girl like you ruin yourself over him.'

Connie stared at him.

'There you go, two G&Ts,' said Ted, placing two glasses in front of Connie on the counter. 'That'll be—'

'I'll get them,' said Micky, swallowing the last of his drink.

'Maybe next time.' Pressing a half a crown in the publican's chubby hand, Connie picked up her drinks. 'Give my regards to Mrs Murphy.'

Fixing a pleasant smile on her face, Connie turned and hurried back to her friend.

'My goodness,' said Millie. 'Who's upset you?'

'Some stupid idiot at the bar,' Connie replied. 'He's lucky I didn't pour these' – she held up their drinks – 'over his head.'

'Well, I'm glad you resisted the urge to waste two perfectly good G&Ts,' said Millie, taking hers. 'What did he say anyway?'

'Something about one of the local doctors,' Connie replied.

Millie took a mouthful of drink. 'Talking about local doctors, who's the nurse who knows the dashing Dr MacLauchlan?'

Over the rim of her glass Connie scanned the bevy of nurses but couldn't see Grace.

'I thought Grace was coming tonight, Beryl,' Connie called across.

'She was,' her colleague called back. 'But an old friend invited her to the theatre.'

Chapter Twenty

The electric fire set in the ornamental Victorian fireplace buzzed as the three bars glowed red. Connie pulled her cardigan a little closer as she ran through the list of visits in the clinic diary which was open on the desk in front of her.

It was a quarter to eight on the Monday before Christmas and already there was ice forming on the nurses' office window.

Tonight she was first midwife on call, which was why she was sitting in the nurses' office, across from Moira Brett the Hackney Road sister, and taking handover.

'I updated the list of the mums who are either due now or are already a week over in the diary after yesterday's clinic,' said Moira, pushing her glasses back up the bridge of her nose again. 'The only one I need to tell you about is Mrs Cotton from Cleveland Street who's only eight months by dates but has been having pains and a bit of spotting all week.'

Connie made a note of it in her pocket book. 'Yes, I saw her last week and thought her bump had dropped.'

'Then there's Cath Gordon in the Peabody buildings,' continued Moira.

'Goodness, hasn't she delivered yet?'

Moira shook her head. 'I told her if she was still here on Boxing Day I'd have to send her to the hospital.'

'Well, let's hope that gets baby moving,' said Connie.

Moira grinned. 'It usually does.' She yawned and stretched. 'That's all of them, Connie.'

'Thanks.' She put the notebook in her bag on the chair beside her.

'Go on, you get changed and head off home,' said Connie. 'And I'll see you tomorrow.'

Moira stood up. 'Thanks. Have a . . .'

'Don't say it!'

Moira put her index finger to her lips. '. . . night.'

'Let's hope.'

Moira left.

Switching off the table light, Connie left the room and headed for the kitchen to make herself a hot drink.

The kettle was recently boiled, so within a few moments Connie was walking out of Mrs Rogerson's spotless kitchen with a steaming mug of cocoa.

As she walked back through the house to the office, the usual mid-week noise of a dozen nurses washing their hair and doing their laundry drifted down the stairwell from the floor above.

A door opened above and 'Moonlight Serenade' filled the space overhead.

Connie sighed.

Pushing aside the memory of over an hour of cajoling Malcolm for a single turn around the floor at the Christmas dance, she continued towards the office but as she passed the table in the hall the phone rang.

Being number one nurse on call meant you could be tucked up in bed all night or out until dawn delivering a baby. As she'd managed a full eight hours' sleep the last two nights she'd been on rota, Connie figured it was her turn for an all-nighter. Pity it had to be in sub-zero temperatures.

Putting her mug down, Connie took the pen from her top pocket and picked up the receiver.

'This is Fry House. Sister Byrne speaking. How can I help?'

'Praise God,' sobbed the man down the phone. 'Connie, it's Michael Weinstein. There's something wrong.'

Connie drew to a halt outside the back door of Weinstein's chemist ten minutes later. Finding the door on the latch, she went in and, with her bag in hand, hurried up to the living quarters above the shop.

Briskly walking past the front room and spotless kitchen, Connie continued up the narrow stairs that led to the room in the eaves where the servants had lived but was now the Weinsteins' bedroom. She found Esther lying on the bed staring at the ceiling with red-rimmed eyes. Michael was kneeling beside her, his hands covering his face as he sobbed silently.

271

He looked up as Connie walked in.

'In there.' He indicated the bowl on the washstand covered with a draped towel.

Connie closed the door quietly and placed her bag on the floor. She walked over. Lifting the cloth, she gazed down.

Curled up with its eyes closed was a small but perfectly formed baby boy. It looked to be somewhere between twenty and twenty-two weeks' in gestation, a few weeks earlier than Connie's notes stated but establishing Esther's exact due date had been difficult. Without the layer of fat it would have acquired during the last weeks in utero, all the newly formed veins criss-crossing his tiny body were visible. The baby's umbilical cord was still attached to the placenta and, mercifully, the whole of the membrane sac that formed the afterbirth was intact, which would reduce the risk of infection.

Closing her eyes, Connie said a silent prayer for Esther and Michael's son, then lowered the towel and went over to the bed.

Sitting beside Esther, she took her hand. 'I'm so sorry.'

Michael wiped his eyes with the back of his hands. 'It was so quick. Esther had pain as she was lighting the Shabbat candles. I got her upstairs to bed but by the time I got back from phoning you, it was over and . . .'

He covered his face with his hands again.

Esther touched her husband's arm and murmured something Connie didn't catch. He nodded but continued to sob.

Esther turned and looked at Connie. 'Why?'

'I don't know.'

'It's so unfair.'

'It is.'

'His will, I suppose,' said Esther, fingering the gold Star of David around her neck.

The lump in Connie's throat blocked off any reply.

Michael raised his head and looked at the bowl on the stand behind Connie. 'We were going to call him David after Esther's cousin who died in Auschwitz.'

'I'm afraid I'll have to take him,' said Connie. 'But I don't have to do it now if you want to get the rabbi—'

'Thank you, Connie,' said Michael, forcing a grateful smile. 'I'll ring him now.'

He stood up and left the room.

Esther squeezed her hand. 'Are you sure?'

'Of course,' said Connie. 'It's fine.'

And it would be as long as the local health authority didn't hear about it.

Esther placed her hands on her stomach. 'It's odd but I still feel as if he's inside me.'

'You will do for a few days until your body returns to normal,' Connie said.

Esther's gaze moved back to the ceiling as a fat tear rolled down her cheek.

Connie stood up and, going to the bowl, she removed the towel and lay it flat. Then, lifting David Weinstein out, she swaddled him and took him over to the bed.

'Would you like to hold him again?'

Esther nodded and Connie placed the tiny bundle in his mother's arms.

Michael came back into the room. 'He says he'll be here in an hour. I've rung Alma and Rosa too and they're also coming.'

He sat down next to his wife on the bed and hugged her.

Connie stood up and picked up her bag. 'Again, I'm so sorry for your loss. I'm on all night if you need me,' she said, as she walked to the door. 'I'll pop back in the morning.'

'Thank you,' whispered Michael without taking his eyes from his wife and son.

The lump in Connie's throat thickened. She turned away and, as it was wrong for a nurse to cry in front of a patient, hurried out of the room.

Pulling out a dog-eared record card from the treatment room filing cabinet, Connie scanned the front cover. Noting that Mrs Engels, whoever she was, had delivered a bouncing baby boy in 1944 and hadn't been seen since, Connie put it on the pile of redundant files balanced on the chair beside her.

The clock over the door was showing five to eleven o'clock and usually at this time on a Friday morning she would have been busy bandaging scalded arms, dabbing iodine on grazed knees and picking debris out of cut heads while wondering what was for lunch. Today, however, their only patient since ten o'clock was Gerald Moss, who'd caught his hand in a grinding machine. He was being ably looked after by Grace which gave Connie the opportunity to do something she'd been planning to do for months: weed out the patient records.

The reason for her lack of patients wasn't because the locals were suddenly being more safety conscious, but because it was the day before Christmas Eve and people had better things to do than get their dressings changed at Fry House.

For men, of course, today was the day they larked about on the factory floor or sat around drinking tea in offices until lunchtime when they adjourned to the pub, but for the women there was no slacking. While the menfolk propped up the bar in their favourite watering hole on Christmas Eve, the women of the area were out scouring the markets for last-minute bargains and collecting their meat from the butcher.

Her mother would be amongst those foraging for Brussels sprouts, tangerines and candied dates from the stalls along the Waste. Maud would also have to join the long queue at Harrisons the butcher, next to Whitechapel Station, where she was registered for meat. Like most women in the area, her mother paid six pence a week into the butcher's Christmas club as a way of saving for the expensive chicken, breaded joint of ham and jellied tongue they would enjoy during the Christmas festivities.

Maud did the same at the Home and Colonial a few doors further on, which covered the cost of the fruitcake, cheese, chocolate and other luxurious groceries required over the festive period.

It was because she didn't want the ignominy of having to trail after her mother like a five-year-old that Connie had put herself down to be the only on-call midwife tomorrow. Sadly for them, her sisters Mo and Bernie had no such excuse.

The door opened and Miss O'Dwyer walked in, bringing a whiff of fried fish from the kitchen with her. As ever, she had a baby balanced on her hip.

'Let's say hello to nice Sister Byrne, shall we?' she asked the infant in her arms who watched Connie with enormous eyes.

'Who's our young visitor?' Connie asked, as the superintendent strolled over.

'This is Timothy Beal,' said Miss O'Dwyer, holding the three-month-old upright so he could see Connie.

'What, Mrs Beal from Gladstone Mansions' little 'un?' asked Connie.

'Yes, isn't he getting a size?' said the superintendent, deftly stopping the child grabbing a handful of her hair.

'He is,' said Connie. 'But what's he doing here?'

'Well, I thought it would be a kindness to his mother, what with her having the twins, if I minded him while she popped down the market.' Miss O'Dwyer pressed a wet kiss on the infant's forehead. 'He's a darling boy, so he is.'

Something thumped on the floor above their heads, accompanied by hoots of laughter.

'Bejesus,' said the superintendent, looking up. 'Sounds like a herd of elephants up there, not a dozen Queen's Nurses.'

Connie laughed. 'They're just excited at going home.'

There was a squeal of wheels as Grace moved the partition screen aside and Mr Moss walked out holding his bandaged hand aloft. Nodding at Connie and Miss O'Dwyer, he trudged out of the treatment room.

The rusty wheels squeaked again and Grace stepped out from behind the curtains.

With her blonde hair swept back in a French knot and her nurse's belt buckled at least a notch or two tighter than Connie's, she smiled.

'Is that Mrs Beal's baby?' she asked, as she glided towards them.

'Yes it is,' said Miss O'Dwyer, twisting the child so he could see who the new voice belonged to.

Grace's expression softened as she gazed at Timothy. 'It looks as if his eye has cleared up,' she said, making a happy face at the infant.

Connie gave her a questioning look. 'His eye?'

'Yes, he had conjunctivitis and was being seen by Dr MacLauchlan when I popped in on Monday.'

'I didn't see a new Christ Church surgery patient in the diary,' said Connie.

'No . . . no . . . it wasn't about a patient, it was something else.' Grace smiled. 'Nothing really.'

Biting back the questions she wanted to ask Grace about the whys and wherefores of her visiting Dr MacLauchlan, Connie

275

turned her attention back to her task and rammed Hannah Petroski's maternity record back in the box file.

The phone on the desk sprang into life and Miss O'Dwyer
picked it up. 'Fry House and you'll be speaking to superintendent
O'Dwyer, so what can we be doing for you this fine afternoon?'

Miss O'Dwyer glanced at Connie. 'Yes she's here, doctor, and
of course you can speak to her.' She offered Connie the telephone. 'It's Christ Church surgery.'

Connie's heart leapt into her throat, then thundered off ten to
the dozen as she took the handset.

'Sister Byrne here,' she said, imagining Dr MacLauchlan in his
office at the other end.

Unfortunately, it was the surgery's other doctor who replied.

'I want you at the Weinsteins' in ten minutes,' barked Dr
Marshall.

'Yes, doctor,' said Connie, already on her feet. 'Right aw—'

He slammed the phone down.

Connie replaced the receiver.

'What's he all riled up about?' asked Miss O'Dwyer.

'I don't know,' Connie replied, unhooking her mac from the
back of the door and shrugging it on. 'But by the sound of it
you'd better get someone to ask Mrs Rogerson to put my lunch
in the oven.'

After deciding to go on foot rather than unchain her bike,
Connie arrived at the Weinsteins' fifteen minutes later. Setting
the Father Christmas advertising Epsom salts which hung on the
door wobbling, she went in.

Mercifully, there were only a couple of customers and they
were being dealt with by Mr Cohen, the retired pharmacist who
covered when Michael and Esther were on holiday. He was being
assisted by Sonia, who had left school and now worked for the
Weinsteins full time. They both gave her a sympathetic look as
she passed them.

Connie heard Dr Marshall's disgruntled tones as she entered
the passageway at the back of the shop. Taking a deep breath,
Connie hurried up the stairs.

By the time she reached the bedroom on the top floor, Dr Marshall's tone had moved from angry to furious.

Steeling herself, Connie entered the room and found Esther in bed with the covers held up to her chin. Michael sat beside his wife with his arm around her and a very worried look on his face.

Dr Marshall stood at the foot of the bed, his legs apart and his hands on his hips, glaring at both of them.

He turned as Connie walked in.

'Dr Marshall,' said Connie. 'What seems to be the problem?'

'Mrs Weinstein has septicaemia,' Dr Marshall pronounced.

Connie cast an experienced eye over her patient, looking for anything that might indicate a fever brewing or septic shock, but there was nothing.

She took the thermometer from her nurse's case and shook the mercury down.

'I'll take her temperature.'

Dr Marshall glared at her. 'There's no necessity as I've already made my diagno—'

'If you could pop this under your tongue, Mrs Weinstein,' Connie said.

Esther opened her mouth, then closed it over the glass thermometer. Dr Marshall looked as he was going to speak again, so Connie took her wrist.

Counting the second hand for half a minute, Connie took Esther's pulse, then removed the thermometer and read it.

'Both normal,' Connie said, popping the thermometer back in her bag. 'And she doesn't appear clammy or shivery which I would expect with septicaemia.'

Dr Marshall face went scarlet. 'Are you questioning my diagnosis?'

Connie heart thumped uncomfortably in her chest. 'I'm just saying—'

'Nothing of any consequence, I assure you, nurse,' he interrupted with a dismissive wave. 'It's clear to me that Mrs Weinstein has retained products of conception which has led to her developing a septic uterus.'

Connie looked puzzled. 'If that's so, I don't really understand why you called me.'

'I did toy with giving Mr Weinstein a dose or two of stilbestrol to see if we can shift things along,' he continued. 'But now it's too late for half measures so it's a D&C. I know it's Christmas Eve but there's not a moment to lose,' Dr Marshall blustered on.

'I'll have a word with Old Shottington, the medical director, and he'll sort things out at the London when I get—'

'No!' screamed Esther, clasping her stomach. 'I won't let you kill my baby.'

'Sister Byrne, tell her,' Dr Marshall barked. 'Tell she's miscarried and so she's not pregnant.'

Connie gave him a glacial look. 'I think Mrs Weinstein knows that, Dr Marshall.'

'It seems not as all she's been doing since I arrived is blather on about still being pregnant,' snapped Dr Marshall.

'Because I am, I am,' sobbed Esther.

'Peace, peace, Esther,' soothed Michael. 'Doctor is only trying to do what's best.'

Esther's frantic eyes fixed on Connie.

'I am. I am. I know I am, here.' She pressed her clenched fists to her chest.

She dissolved into a flood of tears and mournful wailing, interspersed with mumbled pleas to Jehovah.

Michael looked helplessly from Dr Marshall to Connie and back again.

Connie sat on the bed and put her arms around Esther.

'I know it's hard to come to terms with,' she said. 'But you saw David yourself.'

'I know, but . . . I can feel him still here.' Esther placed her hands protectively over her abdomen.

Connie studied the shape of her patient's stomach a little more closely.

'I've wasted enough time with this,' bellowed Dr Marshall. 'I'm afraid if your wife can't see reason, I will have to make other arrangements.'

'What sort of arrangements?' asked Michael.

'I'll have to talk to the psychiatrist at St Mungo's and have your wife committed,' said Dr Marshall.

'Committed!'

'Well, she's clearly not in her right mind,' Dr Marshall replied.

Michael gave Esther a worried look. 'Perhaps we could wait until after Boxing—'

'Goddamn it, man!'

'I'm just asking for . . .'

Ignoring the two men, Connie turned back to her patient. 'Have you had any bleeding?' she asked softly.

'I had a bit on the towel for a day or two but then nothing.'

'Tingling breasts or any milk oozing?'

Esther shook her head.

Connie stood up and spread her right hand across Esther's pubic bone. Then she placed the other a few inches above her navel. Gently she pressed her fingers, feeling a definite and firm curve.

Esther gripped her wrist. 'I know I sounds like a *meshugener*, but—'

'What are you doing, nurse?' barked Dr Marshall.

'I'm examining my patient,' said Connie, taking her stethoscope from her bag.

Ignoring the GP's belligerent expression, Connie placed the end on Esther's stomach.

Michael came over. 'What's the matter?'

'I'm not sure,' said Connie.

Michael held his wife's hand and Esther closed her eyes.

Connie listened, then shifted the percussion cup to her patient's right side.

Praying silently, Connie strained her ears again.

'Really, nurse, I don't see why you're doing that,' snarled Dr Marshall. 'I've told you my diagnosis and—'

'Shh,' hissed Connie as she heard a rapid pitter-patter through the noise of Esther's inner workings.

'What is it?' asked Michael.

Connie straightened up and smiled. 'I think you're right, Esther. You still have a baby in there.'

'Impossible,' said Dr Marshall.

'Very, very rare,' Connie replied. 'But not impossible.'

'It is true?' asked Michael.

'No, it's not.' Dr Marshall's jowls quivered for a moment, then he forced a laugh. 'Mr Weinstein, be sensible. You saw for yourself—'

'But if there's a chance,' said Michael, 'perhaps we should wait and check if Sister Byrne's is right.'

'I assure you she is not.' Dr Marshall shook his head. 'I'm sorry, but if we don't remove every scrap of the afterbirth, your wife's womb will become septic and that could prove fatal.'

Michael looked terrified.

Although arguing with a doctor's diagnosis could mean instant dismissal, Connie squared her shoulders.

'Dilating Mrs Weinstein's cervix and scraping her uterus with a curettage certainly would be fatal for the twin she might still be carrying,' she said, looking Dr Marshall straight in the eye. 'And if Mrs Weinstein was forced to undergo a D&C,' she continued, 'and she was pregnant, whoever performed the procedure would be aborting the baby, which is a criminal act.'

Dr Marshall's complexion went from red to puce and the vein on his right temple started throbbing.

'This has gone far enough,' he bellowed. 'You're as hysterical as she is, I'm phoning the psychiatrist and I'll get Mrs Weinstein taken in and—'

'I'm sorry, doctor,' said Connie. 'But if you do I'm going to telephone Fry House and get Miss O'Dwyer here. In fact, if necessary, I'll get every midwife in the clinic to examine Mrs Weinstein.'

Dr Marshall's eyes bulged and his jowls quivered as he glared at her. Connie glared back.

After what seemed like an eternity, Dr Marshall looked away and snapped his case shut.

'You haven't heard the last of this,' he snarled as he stormed from the room.

Connie and the Weinsteins stared after him while his heavy footsteps clumped down the stairs.

The back door slammed shut and Michael looked at Connie.

'Is it true?' he said incredulously.

'I've only come across this once before when I was a trainee midwife, and not as far along in a pregnancy as this. You'll have to see the consultant obstetrician.'

'But what made you suspect?' he asked.

'Well, as far as I can see, there's no sign of infection, the top of Esther's womb is still firm and I definitely heard a heartbeat,' Connie replied. 'But what made me suspect in the first place was Esther's insistence that she was still pregnant.' She smiled. 'A mother knows.'

*

After being alternately hugged and sobbed over by both Michael and Esther, Connie finally closed the door on the happy pair some twenty minutes later.

Turning her collar up against the chill air and with a grin as wide as a Cheshire cat's on her face, Connie headed back to Fry House.

Although it was only just after two, many of the shops were already putting up their shutters in readiness for the four-day break from trading.

The public houses were already spilling over with people from the nearby factories and offices having a Christmas drink before heading off home to their families.

Connie, too, would be heading off to her mother's after Lizzie Copland, one of the nurses who had started at the same time as Grace, took over at nine.

Stepping aside to let a mother pushing a pram pass, Connie turned into Grey Eagle Street. It wasn't the quickest way back to the clinic, but she had written a note about the Weinsteins, which she could pop through the surgery door and this way she'd avoid the market workers dismantling the stalls in Wentworth Street market.

The Christmas holiday stillness was beginning to settle as the lights from the houses glowed amber in the gathering midwinter dusk, and the street lamps dotted along the pavement lit her way. Almost of their own accord, Connie's eyes went to the two windows of the flat above the surgery. They were darkened and her smile lost a fraction of its sparkle.

Connie was just about to put her foot on the first step of the surgery when the door opened and Hari came out.

He was dressed against the cold in a long camel overcoat, his college scarf tucked in the front and a chocolate-coloured fedora at a jaunty angle on his head.

Transferring the suitcase he was carrying to his other hand, he locked the door. As he turned, he spotted Connie and smiled.

A warm glow spread through her and she smiled back.

'Connie,' he said, trotting down the steps to meet her. 'What are you doing here?'

'I might ask you the same thing, Hari,' Connie replied. 'From what you were saying last week, I thought you'd be on the train to your aunt's by now.'

'No, I'm meeting up with a friend for a quick drink in town before I catch the eight-thirty,' he explained. 'That's my excuse, but why aren't you at home with your nearest and dearest?'

'I volunteered to cover the late on call so the others could get away,' said Connie. Her grin returned. 'And I'm very pleased I did.'

She told him about Dr Marshall's phone call and the events at the Weinsteins.'

His expression became increasingly incredulous as Connie related the story.

'My goodness,' he said when she'd finished. 'I've read about the phenomenon in scientific papers, of course, but I can't ever recall an actual incidence.' He chuckled. 'I'm surprised, and delighted for them.'

'I know, me too. I've written you a note about it.' She offered it to him.

As Hari's took it, his fingers brushed hers, sending a quiver of excitement through her.

He read it, then slipped it into his pocket. 'I'll contact the Elizabeth Garret Anderson Maternity Hospital first thing on Tuesday. Professor Myerson is the head of Obstetrics there and I worked with him in Leeds. He'll be more than happy to look after Esther, I'm sure, and I'll oversee all her treatment at home personally.'

'Thank you,' said Connie. 'I knew you would.'

'My pleasure,' he said. 'I'll have to in any case as I doubt Michael will let my colleague within a mile of his wife now.' His eyes twinkled mischievously. 'I bet Dr Marshall wasn't at all pleased with you.'

Connie's happy expression vanished. 'No, he wasn't. I wouldn't be surprised if he made a formal complaint about me.'

'I don't see how he can,' said Hari. 'After all, you've saved him from making a terrible mistake and committing a crime.'

'If there is a baby,' said Connie.

'You're an experienced midwife, so my money's on you. If you say there's a baby, then there's a baby,' he replied. 'And a quick X-ray next week will prove you right.'

'Christmas is the time for miracles, is it not?' she laughed.

Hari laughed too, the deep, rich tone of it rolling right over her. 'It certainly is.'

'And babies,' Connie continued.

'Especially babies,' agreed Hari. He paused. 'I should go.'

Connie nodded. 'Me too.'

Suddenly the joyfulness, wonder and delight of discovering Esther's baby swept over Connie anew.

'And have a very Happy Christmas, Hari.'

Without thinking, Connie flung her arms around his neck, but as her lips brushed Hari's five o'clock shadow she stopped laughing.

Embarrassed, she sprang back.

'I . . . I'm s . . . so sorry,' Connie stuttered as an unreadable expression passed across Dr MacLauchlan's chiselled features. 'I don't know . . .'

Stepping forwards, he took hold of her upper arms and drew her to him. For one ridiculous moment Connie thought he was going to press his lips onto hers, but then his warm mouth brushed her cheek instead. For the briefest of moments she felt the hardness of his body against hers, then he released her.

The warm smile that she saw too often into her dreams lifted the corners of his mouth. 'And a very Happy Christmas to you, too, Connie.'

He touched the brim of his hat, turned and strolled away.

With her heart dancing a fandango in her chest, there was nothing for Connie to do but stare after him because, even if her shoes had been on fire, she was rooted to the ground.

Hari yanked the salon door of the Railway Arms open. Rosalind gave him a sweet smile. 'Thank you, kind sir,' she said, stepping through. It was just before six o'clock.

They entered the warmth of the public house, full of City revellers enjoying a quick drink like themselves before going off to their families to start the Christmas celebrations. Leaving Rosalind in one of the corner booths, Hari headed towards the bar, returning a few short minutes later with their drinks.

He and Rosalind had been seeing each other pretty regularly for the past nine months – well, as regularly as his on-call rota and her teaching preparation and marking allowed. Mostly they met up in town to see the latest release at the cinema or theatre.

'One vodka and lime with ice,' he said, placing her drink on the Mackeson beer mat in front of her.

She picked it up. 'Cheers!'

'Cheers!' he replied, taking the seat opposite her.

'So,' she said as he took the froth off his half of bitter. 'All set for a well-earned weekend off?'

'Yes, I am,' Hari replied. 'What time's your train again?'

'Seven forty-five,' she replied, taking a delicate sip of her drink. 'So I've plenty of time.'

As she was heading off to stay with George and his family from King's Cross and he was travelling to Waltham Abbey from Liverpool Street, it had seemed sensible for them to have a Christmas drink halfway between in Farringdon.

Hari smiled. 'Good.' He took another mouthful of beer. 'I meant to ask earlier; how did the christening go the other weekend?'

'It was wonderful,' said Rosalind. 'We were so lucky with the weather as it had been raining cats and dogs on the Saturday but as we got ready for church the clouds parted and although it was freezing cold, at least we didn't get soaked to the skin . . .'

As Rosalind ran through the escapades of her family both young and old, Hari smiled and added the odd comment as required.

'. . . and finally, at seven-thirty, we put a very tired special little boy to bed and we all collapsed in front of a roaring fire in the lounge.'

'Sounds like you had a great day,' said Hari politely.

'We did,' said Rosalind. 'It's a pity you couldn't have come.'

'I'd have loved to, but—'

'. . . you had a report to write.'

'It had to be done.' He shrugged apologetically.

Rosalind smiled. 'I know. I have to write up the end-of-year report for the Schools Department so I know what a headache it can be.'

Hari gave a short laugh. 'You're not kidding and I'm sorry, Rosalind, but maybe I'll get to meet your family sometime soon.'

Taking his pint to his lips, he took a long draught before placing it back on the cork coaster.

Rosalind looked at him for a moment, then she too picked up her drink.

'Actually, Hari,' she said, running the parrot-topped cocktail

284

stick around the edge of the glass with her finger. 'You know my Cousin Mildred I've told you about?'

'Who's engaged to the chap in the tank regiment?' said Hari.

'That's her.' Rosalind's eyes flickered over his face. 'I wasn't going to mention it for a few weeks, but she's getting married just after Easter and I wondered if perhaps you'd like to come with me.'

Hari forced a smile. 'April, I'm—'

'It's in the village in East Sussex where she grew up,' Rosalind cut in. 'It's so quaint with a Norman church and duck pond on the green.'

'Sounds idyllic,' Hari said.

'Her mother, Aunt Sissy, is my mother's younger sister and as there was only a year and a day between their birthdays they were naturally very close,' said Rosalind. 'Sissy was always my favourite aunt and I don't know what I would have done without her when Mother died. I'm going to be a bridesmaid, so my aunt has invited you, too.'

Hari's friendly smile widened. 'That's very kind of her but I wouldn't want to impose on her when she's already got a houseful—'

'Don't be silly,' laughed Rosalind. 'After the way I went on about you at the christening last week, she said she feels like she knows you already.'

Hari smiled. 'I'm not sure about just pitching up on such an important family event and—'

'I tell you what,' interrupted Rosalind. 'Why don't I organise for us to visit in the new year so you can meet her properly?'

Hari patted his breast pocket. 'I haven't got my diary with me so I'm not sure about my on-call and the thing is—'

'That's all right,' Rosalind replied, smiling happily across at him. 'Telephone me next week and let me know when you're free. Of course,' she continued, giving him a look, 'we don't have to stay with my aunt as I know a quiet little hotel by the river in Salisbury, we can catch the branch line to the village on Saturday.'

She regarded him expectantly.

He should say yes, of course. After all, they got on well, they were roughly the same age, both professionals, from the same social background, so to move their relationship into a more permanent one that was heading towards engagement and marriage was the obvious next step.

Hari swallowed hard and tried to scrape the right words together as a band of steel tightened around his chest, cutting off his breath.

'Rosalind, I . . . I . . .'

He gave up.

She stared at him for a moment, then grabbed her handbag.

'I'm sorry,' she said, fumbling to get it open.

'Rosalind,' he said.

She looked up.

'It's me that should be sorry,' he said sincerely.

She extracted a handkerchief. 'It's all right.' She blew her nose. 'I've known from the start you're in love with someone else.'

Hari looked puzzled. 'Honestly, Rosalind, I haven't been seeing anyone else behind your back.'

She gave him a plucky smile. 'I know, you're not that sort of man but you are in love with someone else.'

Hari didn't argue. How could he? After holding Connie in his arms, he knew she was right.

'I'm sorry, truly I am,' he repeated.

Shoving her handkerchief back, Rosalind pulled out a compact. 'I think I realised after our first couple of meetings but I thought that perhaps you were trying to put an unhappy affair or engagement behind you and we might make a go of it, but . . .' She snapped open the powder case and took out the puff.

'I'm sorry, Ros,' he repeated, as she dabbed the puff over her nose. 'I like you, I really do and if things—'

'Let's just leave it there, Hari,' she said, raising her hand. 'I really don't think I can take the "if things were different" speech.'

She stood up and so did Hari.

'I'll find you a taxi,' he said.

Rosalind gave him a brittle smile. 'It's all right, I'll find my own.' She offered him her hand. 'Goodbye, Hari.'

He took it. 'Goodbye, Ros.'

She forced another smile then, with tears gathering on her lower eyelids, she hurried out of the pub.

Chapter Twenty-One

'. . . and may that almighty hand guide and uphold us all,' said the lisping voice of George VI from the Murphy radio on her mother's sideboard.

It was five past three and now she and her two sisters had cleared away the remnants of the Christmas dinner, Connie was sitting on her mother's sofa beside Malcolm, surrounded by all her family. And she meant all, because this year their little brother Bobby was home.

In truth, scraping the door frame at six foot one and with a thirty-eight-inch chest, he could hardly be described as 'little' any more, but to Connie he would always be her kid brother.

Twenty-three with a mop of curly hair and blue eyes, he was the closest sibling to Connie by age and appearance. Wearing a rather smart Italian sports jacket and well-cut slacks, he'd evidently been using his army pay to kit himself out in style.

He'd been called up for National Service as the troops were returning after VJ day five years ago. He'd been allocated to the Sappers and was now a fully qualified mechanic. Much to his mother's dismay, he'd signed on for a further five years when his compulsory service had come to an end. He'd served in Germany, Aden and Egypt, and would be shipping out to Burma before Easter, which is why he'd been given extended leave over Christmas.

He had been down the pub with the rest of the menfolk and was now sprawled in the armchair in the corner. Sensing her gaze on him, he looked over and winked. Connie grinned and winked back.

The strains of 'God Save the King' blared out for a minute or so and, as it faded, the members of the Byrne family let out a collective sigh.

'He's such a lovely man,' said Maud, who was wedged in her

usual chair by the hearth. 'It brought a tear to my eye 'earing him talk about his grandson Charles like that.'

'Makes you realise the king and queen are just like us,' said Bernie, perched on the arm of her husband's chair.

'Yeah, just like us, they are,' said Mo's husband Eddy, sitting on a kitchen chair that had been brought through for the occasion. 'Except with big houses, flunkies and lots of money.'

Maud gave him a sharp look. 'I won't hear a word against them, not after they came down here during the Blitz.'

Eddy smiled. 'Just stating the facts, Mum, that's all.'

'My Eddy's right, though, ain't he, Mum?' said Mo. 'They've got at least half a dozen houses dotted all over the place and most folk round here live doubled up with some other family.'

'Well, it's not the king's fault,' said Connie's mother. 'It's your chum Attlee. He's the one who promised us this, that and the other and has he changed anything? Has he my eye,' she said, answering her own question.

'As the shop steward said at our union branch meeting last week, it's not easy dismantling a system that has kept the ordinary working man in chains for centuries,' continued Eddy. 'But once we—'

'Never mind the ordinary working man,' snapped Maud. 'What about the ordinary working woman? I spend half my life queuing and I still have to hand over a ration book even though the war's been over four years. And I'll tell you this for nothing . . .' She folded her arms emphatically. 'I won't be voting for them again.'

Eddy shifted around in his chair. 'But if you vote the Tories back in—'

'And I'll not have any more of your Bolshevik talk in this house, thank you very much, Eddy Page,' cut in Maud, giving her son-in-law a withering look. 'Not on Jesus' special day.'

There was an uneasy silence and then the door burst open as Mo's boys, all dressed in their best clothes and their hair brilliantined flat, dashed in.

'Can you help us set up the track, Uncle Malcolm?' asked the eldest, Arthur, who had his new Hornby train set tucked under his arm.

'Course I can,' said Malcolm, already out of his seat. 'Where shall we put it?'

Glancing around, Arthur pointed to the window alcove behind where Connie and Malcolm were sitting. 'What about there?'

'Perfect,' said Malcolm. 'If I shift the sofa forward, we should have plenty of room.'

Connie rose to her feet, as did her two sisters as their other halves came forward to help Malcolm move the furniture.

'It must be time to put the kettle on,' said Maud, picking up her knitting and looking expectantly at her daughters.

Mo and Bernie gave a collective sigh and headed for the door, followed by their sister-in-law Sheila. Connie picked up an empty plate from the coffee table and started after them.

'We'll make a cuppa,' said Mo, taking the crockery from her. 'If you make sure my Eddy and Mum don't come to blows.'

Connie laughed and her sisters left. With the sofa now in the middle of the floor, she looked around.

'Here you go, sis,' said Bobby, shifting over and patting the space beside him. 'Room for a little one.'

Tucking her skirt beneath her, Connie squeezed in next to him.

'Just like old times,' he said, sliding his arm around the back of the armchair to give her more room.

Connie smiled. 'Yes, it is.'

Bobby wriggled. 'Although I don't remember you having such a big bum.'

Connie elbowed him in the ribs. 'Oi, watch it or I'll tell Mum.'

'Tell Mum what?' asked Maud, looking up from her needles.

'I thought she said she was going deaf,' whispered Bobby.

'It comes and goes,' Connie whispered back. She raised her voice. 'Bobby's calling me names, Mum.'

'She started it,' Bobby replied.

Their mother rolled her eyes and, reaching over, turned the volume knob on the radio.

Connie grinned at her brother and he grinned back.

'It's good to see you,' Bobby said, giving her an affectionate hug.

'And you,' said Connie, as the sound of the BBC opera orchestra filled the room. 'Are you still enjoying army life?'

289

'I blooming well am, travelling the world and getting paid for it,' he replied. 'And especially now I'm up for my sergeant's stripes.'

'Oh, Bobby, that's wonderful.'

'I'm keeping schtum until its official,' he said. 'But I had to tell my favourite sister.'

'Well, you make sure you send me a letter as soon as it is so I can tell everyone,' said Connie.

Bobby glanced at their mother humming along to 'White Christmas'. 'Thanks for not mentioning to Mum I've got a new girlfriend.'

'That's all right,' said Connie. 'I thought I'd spare you the daily interrogation. Is it serious?'

A look of love softened her brother's eyes.

'I hope so,' he said, quietly. 'We've only been walking out properly for a few months but . . . I just know it's got to be Chrissie.'

Connie squeezed his thigh. 'I'm so happy for you.'

'You'll like her.'

'I'm sure I will,' said Connie. 'And you must bring her to the wedding.'

'I intend to, don't worry,' Bobby replied. 'Con? I hope you don't mind me asking, but you don't seem to be your usual jolly self, is everything all right?'

Connie forced a light laugh. 'Of course. I'm just a bit tired, that's all. You know, work and everything.'

'Everything?'

'The wedding,' said Connie, feeling the weight of her impending nuptials pressing down on her. 'The way Mum goes on about it you'd think it was her getting hitched, not me. I tell you, Bobby, if she mentions rainbow bridesmaids to me one more time I swear I'll scream.'

Bobby gave her a sympathetic look. 'What about Malcolm's mother?'

'Well, if it were down to her we wouldn't be getting married at all,' said Connie. 'But her main bone of contention is us getting married in St Martha's and St Mungo's. We're all meeting up in a few weeks to go through the guest list and I know she'll bring it up again.'

'I think perhaps you and Malcolm would have been better off eloping,' said Bobby.

'Very wise,' said Connie. 'I tell you what, with Mum going on at me in one ear and Malcolm's mother whinging in the other, I sometimes wish I'd never said yes.'

Connie's gaze drifted past her brother to where Malcolm scrambled about on the floor with her nephews fitting O gauge track into a circle.

'Well, there's nothing to stop you changing your mind,' said Bobby.

Something stirred in Connie but she damped it down and turned back to her brother. 'Don't be silly.'

'Don't get me wrong,' continued Bobby. 'Malcolm's a nice enough bloke and all that, but—'

'But?'

'I just thought you'd end up with someone who'd be a bit more, well . . . interesting, so you can have some fun.'

Connie's gaze returned to Malcolm, who was winding up the engine while the boys huddled around him. He lowered it onto the tracks and attached it to the carriages. He released it and the whole train shot off as the boys whooped with delight.

'I just want you to be happy, sis, that's all,' Bobby added softly in her ear.

Malcolm looked up and smiled.

Although the feeling of oppression pressed down on Connie again, she smiled back.

With an over-filled stomach and a good brandy just settling nicely on top, Hari sank still lower in the upholstery of the armchair and let his eyelids close. The strains of the BBC Opera orchestra drifted out from the ancient domed radio on the sideboard and Hari felt himself start to drift away.

'I'm sorry to disturb you, dear,' said a soft voice with just a trace of Highland brogue. 'But would you mind putting another coal or two on the fire?'

Blinking away his sleepiness, Hari smiled. 'Of course not, Aunt Janet.'

His father's older sister was three years off being an octogenarian, but she had nothing of the little old lady about her.

While she didn't have his or his father's six foot plus height, at five feet ten she towered over most women. With broad features and sturdy limbs, even now she could outwalk most men and still did as the countryside was her passion.

In her younger years it had been the Highland hills where her husband had been a steward on one of the large estates but now, since Uncle Sandy had gone to meet his maker, it was in the Essex countryside she hiked each day with her two Highland terriers, Scruff and Gamble, at her heels.

However, despite his aunt's outdoor life, when Hari had kissed her cheek when he'd arrived the day before, it was as soft as a child's and her embrace conjured up happy memories of long school holidays.

Gripping the knobbly arm of the chair, he pulled himself up.

The two dogs snoozing around her feet looked up but, realising his movement signalled neither a walk nor food, they lowered their heads again

'That was a lovely dinner as always,' he said, taking the shovel from the bucket and digging it into the nuggets of coal.

'Thank you, dear,' she replied. 'It's nice to have a man to cook for.'

Hari smiled and threw half a dozen coals on the fire.

In contrast to the rambling hillside house she'd lived in all her married life, his Aunt Janet had retired to a snug Victorian cottage in Sun Street behind Waltham Abbey, just down from the medieval church.

It only had two bedrooms but, as she pointed out, she only had one living relative – Hari – so to have three would be a waste.

'Thank you, dear,' she said as he returned the shovel to its stand next to the fire irons. 'An old body feels the cold.'

'Do you want me to fetch a shawl?' he asked.

'No, no,' his aunt replied. 'I'll be fine now, thank you kindly.'

Hari sank back in the armchair.

'So what have you been up to since we last met?' she asked.

'As I said over dinner, I'm living in something akin to a Dickensian garret and stuck with a so-called partner who treats me as a houseboy.'

'Yes, yes,' said Aunt Janet. 'I know all that, but what about *you?*'

'To be honest, I've been so busy at the surgery I haven't had much time for socialising although I did have a couple of beers with Eddy Rollingson a few weeks back.'

'You mean little Roly-poly, who came with you for the holidays at the end of your first year at Repton?'

'Yes, that's him, he sends his regards,' said Hari.

'How kind of him to remember,' his aunt replied.

Hari laughed. 'Although I don't think he'd thank you for remembering his nickname as he's head of Pathology at King's now. He and a few of the class of '33 are organising a hike in the Lakes next spring and asked if I'd like to tag along.'

'I hope you said yes,' said Aunt Janet.

'I certainly did,' Hari said. 'And I had a letter last month telling me that some of the chaps from Changi are having another get-together next year in Chichester,' Hari said.

'Splendid.' Aunt Janet's eyes twinkled. 'Anyone else?'

Hari toyed with mentioning Rosalind for a moment, then decided not. No point raising his aunt's hopes.

'I'm not sure what you're getting at, Aunt Janet.'

She tutted. 'You ken very well, Jahindra Harish Chakravarthi.'

'Oh, you mean hockey,' he replied innocently. 'Well, the Old Bartonians were fourth in the league this year and we're hoping for great things next season.'

'I'm sure that will be wonderful, my dear,' Aunt Janet replied. 'But then so would settling down with a . . .'

'Bonny wee lassie,' said Hari.

'Indeed.'

'And when I find one, I will,' Hari replied.

'Well, you will na find one tearing up and down the muddy pitch after a cork ball, will you?'

'Stranger things have happened,' he replied lightly.

'To be sure,' she agreed with a gracious incline of her head. 'But I'd venture to say you'd increase your chances considerably, Hari, if you ventured onto a dance floor.'

'And you're right, of course,' agreed Hari. 'And I would have done just that three weeks ago at the Fry House Christmas dance had I not been on call.'

His aunt's stern expression softened. 'Well, I suppose there's always next year.'

Hari smiled and the clock chimed the half-hour.

'There's time for me to make us both another cup of tea before the afternoon play starts,' he said.

'That would be lovely,' said Aunt Janet.

Hari reached out to take her empty cup, but as he did Aunt Janet laid her hand on his forearm. 'You know, when the army wrote and told me you were alive after VJ day, I . . .' Tears welled up in her soft grey eyes.

Hari placed his hand over hers.

'I know, Atjan,' he said, using his childhood name for her.

'I just want to see you happy with a family of your own before—'

'And you will.' Bending forwards, Hari pressed his lips onto her forehead. 'Promise.'

She smiled and they exchanged a fond look.

Picking up her cup, Hari placed it with his own on the tea tray, then carried it out to the minute scullery at the back of the house.

While he waited for the kettle to boil, Hari laid out a fresh tray with the necessary crockery then, leaning back on the table, he gazed out through the half-glazed back door.

As he studied his aunt's wintry cottage garden and the mossy brick wall beyond, the memory of Connie Byrne's lips on his cheek swept over him and his heart ached.

Aunt Janet would certainly consider Sister Byrne a 'bonny wee lassie'. He'd thought the same ever since he'd set eyes on her, but no matter how pretty her coppery curls, how beguiling her expressive blue eyes or how pleasing her curves, he'd be as well to remember she wasn't just a 'bonny wee lassie' but a 'bonny wee *engaged* lassie' with another man's ring on her finger.

Chapter Twenty-Two

Connie swerved in an attempt to avoid a pothole in the road but the front wheel of her bicycle ran straight through a puddle, splashing both her legs with icy rainwater. Connie barely noticed as she turned left into Buxton Street and headed for the clinic.

It was just after three p.m. and the first day back after Christmas and New Year. As expected, it had been bedlam. She'd had a morning list as long as your arm, full of patients who had returned from visiting relatives over the festive period and who now needed their dressings changed.

If that wasn't bad enough, one of the nurses had rung in first thing to say her back was in spasm after doing the hokey-cokey on New Year's Eve and she couldn't make it in to work. Added to which, both the first and second on-call midwives had still been out on deliveries when another anxious father had phoned at eight-thirty, meaning the next nurse on the list had to go immediately, leaving Connie and Jane to cover her early morning visits. So with four extra visits on top of her own, Connie hadn't needed a diversion along Cambridge Heath Road because of an unexploded bomb which meant she'd missed her midday meal and had to find someone to cover her afternoon dressing clinic so she could continue with her remaining visits.

But, despite all that had happened since her alarm had woken her that morning, Connie was happy. She was happy because today Hari was back from his week away. That said, although she was eager to find out if he'd had a good Christmas, there was the awkward issue of the impulsive hug and peck on the cheek she'd given him the last time they'd met.

She was sure he would regard it as just a friendly gesture, which it was, and he'd probably have forgotten about the whole incident by now but, unfortunately for Connie, the memory of his cheek against her lips and the feel of his arms around her was still fresh in her mind.

However, after turning the matter over, she'd decided that as he'd probably had a day much like hers, she would welcome him back with a treat, so instead of turning into Brick Lane she carried on into Bishopsgate and headed for Petite Bertrands, the upmarket cake shop and tea rooms opposite Liverpool Street Station.

Hari would no doubt be ploughing through his accumulated paperwork by now in an attempt to clear it before evening surgery. He could probably do with a macaroon to soak up his coffee.

Trying to decide between a fruit or custard tart for herself, Connie rolled to a halt just outside the double-fronted shop.

In its previous incarnation, the Petite Bertrands had been the Two Spoons cafe, a grubby working-men's eating house owned by Mosher and Zelda Levy, who had sold up the previous year. After they'd gone, the new owners set to work and a couple of months later the scaffolding and tarpaulin had come down to reveal a smart Parisian *patisserie* complete with matte-brown exterior, a coffee-coloured fluted canopy and art nouveau-style floral designs traced in gold on the windows.

Securing her front wheel to a lamp post, Connie studied the array of delicate pastries and cream cakes in the window and was just trying to decide between a puff slice and a raspberry torte, when she caught sight of Hari through the window.

Dressed in his everyday topcoat, he was sitting at one of the tables towards the back of the restaurant. Connie's mouth lifted in a smile but then she saw that sitting opposite him, looking beautiful in a red coat with a fur collar and cuffs, was Grace.

Hari was listening intently as Grace, her face full of emotion, talked rapidly, twisting a lace handkerchief between her fingers.

Grace paused and looked at Hari with red-rimmed eyes. Connie saw him shake his head and say something, and Grace burst into tears. Reaching forward, Hari took Grace's hand.

Something akin to ice water drained through Connie's veins. Feeling sick now rather than hungry, and with her vision blinded by tears, she grabbed her cycle. Jumping on, she scooted it across the pavement and off the kerb. A hooter blasted in her ear as a lorry swerved around her, its driver shaking his fist as he passed.

Standing up on the pedals, her thighs aching as she cycled hard, Connie picked up speed and, with tears streaming down her cheeks, headed to Fry House.

'Oh, Hari,' sniffed Grace, 'Do you think your friend will be able to sort this mess out?'

'If William Matterson can't, nobody can,' Hari replied. 'And here he is now.'

The bell above the cafe door tinkled and a slightly built man in his early thirties wearing a smart suit and horn-rimmed glasses walked in.

Hari stood up.

'Bill,' he said, standing up to greet the newcomer. 'You found it OK?'

'I just followed your instructions from the station,' Bill replied as the two men shook hands. 'You're looking well.'

'You too,' said Hari, gesturing to the empty seat at their table. 'Being called to the Bar obviously suits you. This is Grace Huxtable.'

Grace stood up.

'Nice to meet you, Mr Matterson, and it's good of you to give up your time,' she said, shaking the barrister's hand.

'My pleasure, Miss Huxtable,' he replied, taking the seat alongside her. 'And I'm only too happy to help out Hari, my old Goon Hut comrade.'

Hari signalled to the waitress behind the counter for another round of tea, then resumed his place opposite Grace.

Reaching down, William opened his briefcase and took out a file which he placed on the red-checked tablecloth. 'Hari has told me in general terms about your problem, Miss Huxtable,' said William, taking his pen from the top pocket. 'I must warn you from the outset that cases such as yours are rarely straightforward. Even if they are uncontested.'

'I thought that would be the case,' said Grace. 'But I—'

She looked at Hari and tears welled up in her eyes again. He reached over and took her hand.

'For Grace and Sarah's sake, the situation needs to be put on a proper legal footing,' Hari said.

'Very well.' Bill took the top off his pen. 'Now, if you can tell me the story as you see it, Miss Huxtable.'

'It started in Hastings, 1940, when I was at the Memorial Hospital . . .'

With the muscles in her thighs screaming with pain and a jagged gash through her heart, Connie all but collided with the gate of Fry House as she careered into the back yard. How she'd made it back was a mystery because instead of the traffic around her, all she'd been aware of was the sight of Hari holding Grace's hand.

Thankfully, there was no one in the back yard so, after stowing her bike in the rack, Connie grabbed her bag and ran upstairs to her bedroom. Closing the door behind her, she dashed to the sink and turned on the tap. Taking her flannel from the hook, she soaked it under the cold water for a moment, then held it to her eyes and breathed deeply as she banished the scene in the cafe from her mind.

After a long pause and with the ache in her chest receding a little, Connie smoothed down her dress and forced her head up.

Tucking a stray lock of hair back behind her ear and checking her face in the mirror over the sink, Connie left her room and started back downstairs. The afternoon dressing clinic was just finishing up and Connie could hear the other nurses tidying things away and preparing the room for the next day.

The door to the superintendent's office opened and Miss O'Dwyer stepped out, cradling a sleeping baby in her arms.

'Sure, I thought it was you flying through the back gate like a banshee with the furies on your tail,' she said, automatically rocking back and forth. 'Your young man rang and said he'd be a bit late picking you up.'

Connie was puzzled. 'My . . . ?'

'Your fiancé, Malcolm,' laughed the superintendent. 'He said he'd been sent down to Canning Town to look at a sewer, but as he'd got the van he'll collect you on his way back.'

Connie sighed. 'Oh all right.'

'Well, you could try sounding a bit more enthusiastic to see the poor fella,' said Miss O'Dwyer.

'I am, of course I am,' said Connie.

The superintendent gave her a querying look. 'Is everything all right, me dear?' she asked softly.

Connie forced her brightest smile. 'Yes, fine, really. I've just a bit of a headache coming on, that's all. Malcolm's mother is having tea at my mother's so they can discuss wedding plans.'

'Oh, you poor darling,' said Miss O'Dwyer with a concerned expression on her face. 'I tell you what. We've pretty much got things under control down here, so why don't you run yourself a nice hot bath and have forty winks before your man arrives.'

Giving Miss O'Dwyer a grateful look, Connie hurried back up to her room. Closing the door, she collapsed onto her dressing table stool. With tightness pinching the corners of her eyes, Connie sat there watching the scene in the cake shop play over and over in her mind's eye.

Gazing at her reflection in the mirror, her mouth pulled into a determined line. Yanking the pins out from the plaited bun at the back of her head and letting her hair unravel, Connie grabbed the brush. Malcolm, her fiancé, the man she loved and who she was going to marry in a few short months, would be collecting her later to take her to her mother's to talk about wedding plans with Mrs Henstock, so why should she care who Hari MacLauchlan was holding hands with over a chocolate eclair?

With his hair still damp from the bathroom, Hari trotted down the steps of the surgery at six-fifty, congratulating himself on being showered, shaved and changed just twenty minutes after closing the door on the last patient. Naturally, as it was the first day back after the Christmas break, he'd expected the morning surgery to be frantically busy and it had lived up to his expectations. However, he'd still found time to complete the letter about Paul's care while munching his way through his lunchtime fish paste sandwich, as he knew Connie wanted to send it to the appeal panel as soon as possible. After meeting with Grace and William, he'd been back at the surgery at four-fifteen, just as the first of his evening patients were gathering outside.

He'd cheerfully worked his way through the multitude of sore throats, swollen joints and phlegmy coughs that evening, knowing that at any moment Connie Byrne would be walking through the treatment room door and smiling at him. However, by the time it got to five-thirty, it was clear she wasn't coming. Uncharacteristically, he started to worry. What if she was unwell or had had an accident as she cycled around? By the time he'd thrown the latch after the last patient had departed, he was almost convinced she must be lying unconscious in a hospital bed.

He had to go to Fry House to make sure she was all right and, thankfully, Paul's letter gave him the perfect excuse to pitch up there. Having decided to go, he'd dithered over whether to just shower and change his shirt, then put his work clothes back on to make it look as if he was just popping in after surgery or change into a suit and tie to make it appear as if he'd just dropped in on his way out. In the end he'd opted for something in between and now wore a pair of cavalry twill buff-coloured slacks and his Donegal jacket with matching waistcoat.

Walking briskly down Commercial Street, Hari turned right at the Ten Bells pub into Duval Street and within a few moments he was taking the front steps at Fry House two at a time.

A number of nurses who were dressed up for an evening out were milling around in the hallway and they gave him welcoming smiles as he strolled in.

The office door opened and Miss O'Dwyer stepped out. 'Good evening to you, doctor, and what can I be doing for you?'

Hari smiled. 'I was just passing and wondered if I might have a quick word with Sister Byrne if she's in? It's about Paul Gillespie's appeal.'

A motherly expression spread across the superintendent's face. 'Ah, God bless and keep him, and sure you can.' She looked up at a young nurse descending the stairs. 'Will you be an angel, Winnie, and give Connie a quick knock?'

The nurse retraced her steps back up to the living quarters above.

'Thank you, superintendent,' said Hari, feeling overwhelmingly relieved that Connie was upstairs in her room and not on the critical list in the London Hospital.

'Have a good evening, won't you, doctor,' said Miss O'Dwyer.

Having finished checking their make-up and hair in the hall mirror, the gathering of nurses bustled out and Hari was left alone.

Clasping his hands behind his back, he wandered across to study a poster urging people not to turn their backs on the facts and to have a chest X-ray.

He had just read to the bottom when he heard footsteps. He turned to see Connie coming down the stairs wearing a Royal Stewart tartan pencil skirt, green ribbed jumper and black high-heeled ankle boots that showed her shapely figure and slender legs off to perfection. Her hair, usually pinned up under her felt nurse's hat, curled down over her shoulders.

A strange emotion flashed across her face as she spotted him, but then she gave him a dazzling smile.

'Hari, what are you doing here?' she asked, descending the stairs like a catwalk model.

'I was passing and thought I'd drop in my letter for Paul's appeal.' Hari retrieved the envelope containing Paul's letter from his inside pocket. 'I thought I might see you at some time today, but when you didn't call I thought I'd drop it round.'

'I intended to pop round all afternoon but you know how it is the first day back after Christmas.' She rolled her eyes. 'Honestly, it's been one blooming thing after the other today.'

'It's been much the same at the surgery,' Hari replied, offering her the letter.

She took it and popped it into the handbag hooked over her arm.

'Did you have a nice Christmas?' she asked, smiling sweetly up at him.

'Quiet,' he replied. 'What about you?'

She gave a light, happy laugh. 'Oh, just family as always, but we had great fun with the children. My sister Mo's eldest son was given a board game compendium so we organised a knock-out championship on Boxing Day.'

'Sounds very lively,' said Hari.

'It was,' laughed Connie.

Being just a few inches apart, he would only have to encircle her waist to draw her into his embrace. Hari pressed his arms firmly to his side.

They stared silently at each other for several heartbeats, then the front door swung open and Malcolm, in all his tweedy splendour, strolled in.

He looked somewhat taken aback to see her.

'Oh, Connie, you're ready,' he said as the door swung closed behind him.

Again, an emotion Hari couldn't interpret flashed across Connie's face, then she laughed again and threw herself into Malcolm's arms.

'Of course I am, darling,' she said planting a lingering kiss on his cheek. 'I've been counting the minutes.'

Malcolm gave her a brief peck on the forehead and his attention shifted to Hari. 'It's Dr MacPherson, isn't it?'

'MacLauchlan,' Hari said with a professional smile.

'Of course.' Malcolm offered his hand. 'Good to see you again.'

Steeling himself, Hari took it. 'And you. Although I almost didn't recognise you out of your Scout uniform.'

'So what are you doing here?' Malcolm asked, extricating his fingers from Hari's grip.

'Dr MacLauchlan was just dropping off a letter on his way out,' said Connie.

'Well, it's a bit of luck I was late then or he'd have had a wasted journey,' Malcolm said. 'I had to deputise for the head of department at the Cubbit town sewage works this afternoon.'

Hari smiled pleasantly. 'Sounds as if you've been up to your ears in it.'

Connie gave Hari a cool look. 'Well, thank you for dropping the letter in and I hope you don't think we're being rude but we really have to go.'

'Anywhere nice?' asked Hari.

'No, just dropping Connie to her mother's,' said Malcolm.

Connie slipped her arm through her fiancé's. 'Malcolm's mother's coming over so we can go through the guest list.'

'When is the happy day again?' Hari asked, although the date was seared into his brain.

'October the seventh,' said Connie.

'Time enough then to get things in place,' said Hari.

'It will be if Connie stops chopping and changing,' said Malcolm ruefully.

'Oh, Malcolm,' giggled Connie, nudging him playfully in the ribs. 'Every bride wants their big day to be perfect, don't they, Dr MacLauchlan?'

'So I've heard,' said Hari flatly.

Malcolm rolled his eyes. 'Women!' he laughed, inviting Hari to join in.

Hari didn't.

'Actually, I've just had a thought, sweetheart,' said Malcolm. 'While you and Mum are counting up the numbers, what say we try and squeeze Dr MacLauchlan in somewhere.'

'That's very kind of you,' said Hari. 'But I wouldn't want to put you to any trouble.'

'Nonsense,' said Malcolm. 'We'd love to have you join us for our happy day.' He slid his arm around Connie's waist. 'Wouldn't we, Con?'

Connie's lovely blue eyes ran over Hari's face and she smiled. 'Yes, that would be just perfect.'

'Thank you, I'll look forward to it,' said Hari, struggling to maintain his agreeable expression. 'Have a nice evening.'

Their gazes locked for a second, then she snuggled up to Malcolm.

'You too.'

Turning on his heels and with studied leisureliness, Hari ambled back to the main door, shoved it open and strode out.

Hari marched back to the surgery without seeing or hearing anything of the journey and almost broke the key in the lock in his haste to let himself back into the surgery. He slammed the front door shut behind him.

Letting himself into his flat, he threw his keys in the fruit bowl on the table and switched on the percolator that stood on the cabinet next to the draining board.

Resting his hands on the sink, Hari's shoulders sagged as he hung his head. The coffee pot bubbled into life but, suddenly changing his mind, Hari flicked the switch to red and marched into the lounge. Yanking the sideboard door open, he took out a bottle of single malt and a glass and poured himself a double. He knocked it back in one and poured another. Strolling over to the window, he took a sip of his drink as he gazed unseeingly at the scrubby backyard and the grey slate tile roofs of the houses opposite before turning away. Scooping up the current issue of the *British Medical Journal* from the coffee table as he passed, Hari threw himself into the fireside chair and turned to the Situation Vacant section at the back.

Chapter Twenty-Three

'Can Connie pour you another cuppa, Mrs Henstock?' said Connie's mother.

'That's very kind of you, Mrs Byrne,' replied Malcolm's mother. 'But I haven't yet finished this one.'

'What about another slice of Battenberg to soak it up?' suggested Maud.

'Not for me, thank you, Mrs Byrne,' Hilda replied. She smiled sweetly. 'I find shop-bought cakes a little rich for my digestion.'

The band of pain around Connie's forehead, that had started the moment she'd opened the door to Malcolm's mother, tightened further. But it could have been worse.

Although they'd been held up in Commercial Road by a fruit lorry shedding its load, thankfully Malcolm had dropped her at her mother's a full fifteen minutes before Mrs Henstock was due to make an appearance.

And what an appearance. Although it was no more than a twenty-minute walk from her house in Nelson Street, Malcolm's mother had arrived in a taxi and had swept in wearing a calf-length coat with an astrakhan collar, cuffs and matching hat under which she wore a pre-war-style fitted suit accessorised with a string of pearls.

Not to be outdone, Maud had put on the dress she'd bought from her Littlewoods catalogue for Christmas.

Connie's mother's gracious hostess expression chilled a little.

'I'll have another slice,' said Millie, who was sitting next to Connie and, as matron of honour, was helping with the planning. 'It's delicious.'

She took a piece and placed it on the plate beside her cup.

Connie gave her a grateful look.

Millie, who'd also had the afternoon off, had brought six-month-old Patricia along with her and the little girl was now sitting happily on a blanket in front of the fire playing with the collection of wooden spoons, saucepan lids and clothes pegs.

'So, if we've all had enough to eat and drink,' said Maud, opening the shoebox with the word's 'Connie Wedding' written on the side, 'shall we look at the arrangements we've got so far?'

Malcolm's mother inclined her head regally.

Maud lifted out a buff-coloured school exercise book along with a pencil and well-used eraser.

'Right,' said Maud, taking her reading glasses from her pocket and securing them on her nose. 'So far we have sixty-eight on the guest list; a dozen on your side and thirty-two on ours plus twenty-four friends.'

'Don't you think having so many Byrnes is a little one-sided?' asked Mrs Henstock.

'Well, we can't help having a big family,' said Maud. 'And, of course, Great Aunt Min, God love her, is almost ninety so St Peter might be calling her any time, plus Cousin Noreen's husband has just applied to emigrate to Canada so there's another four that might not make it.'

'But even so, you'll have double our side,' said Mrs Henstock. 'It will make the church look unbalanced.'

'Don't worry,' said Millie. 'If there's too many on the bride's side I'll get the girls from Fry House to shift over.'

Mrs Henstock gave a heavy sigh but said no more.

'As you know, the church and hall's been booked since last year but we ought to start thinking about the food,' said Maud. 'Now, I've had a word with Flo who waitresses for Globe Caterers and she says she can do us a sit-down for half a crown a head.'

'And what would that consist of?' asked Hilda.

'Vegetable or tomato soup, steak and kidney pie, followed by apricot upside-down cake and custard or baked apple for afters,' said Maud.

'No aperitif or canapés?' asked Hilda airily.

Maud looked confused.

'There's sherry included in the price and ice cream for the children,' said Connie quickly.

'The Globe lot put on a good spread, but if you've something else in mind, Mrs Henstock, I'll have a word with Flo and see what she says,' added Maud.

'I was thinking more of a wedding breakfast than a "spread". Something more like this.' Reaching down, Hilda withdrew a card from her handbag and handed it to Connie.

It was a menu from a wedding she must have attended at one time or another and the food options were printed in ornate lettering on stiff gold-embossed card.

'Malcolm's boss at the council and his wife are coming, along with the rector, the archdeacon and the president of the Conservative club, and I'm sure they would be expecting something a little more refined than soup and pie,' said Hilda, her sharp voice intensifying the throbbing in Connie forehead.

Forcing a smile, Connie looked up. 'It sounds lovely and I did look into having vol-au-vents to start and chicken as the main course, but it would have been six pence extra per head, adding one pound fourteen shillings to the total price and I can buy the bridesmaids' material down the Lane for that.'

'And don't forget,' chipped in her mother. 'There's money to be put behind the bar as well.'

'Surely a sherry for the women and a pint for the men is enough alcohol,' said Mrs Henstock.

'This is a wedding, not a wake, we're planning.' Maud folded her arms across her substantial bosom. 'And I'm not having anyone say we haven't given our Connie a proper day.'

Mrs Henstock pursed her lips. 'To my way of thinking, marriage is a solemn occasion, not a—'

'I'm sure they won't, Mrs B,' Millie cut in. 'I'm sure it will be a day to remember.'

Connie's mum smiled.

There was a scream. Startled, they looked around to see that Patricia had fallen sideways.

Millie got up and went over to her.

'Mummy's here, sweetie, all done,' she said in a sing-song voice as she picked her daughter up. She pulled a face. 'I think someone needs a new nappy. Can I use the kitchen, Mrs B?'

'Course you can, luv,' Maud replied, her gaze softening as it rested on the baby. 'The old newspapers are under the sink.'

Picking up her basket, Millie settled Patricia on her hip and left the room.

Maud turned a page in her notebook. 'Now, let's talk about

Connie's seven attendants. She's thinking of having them as rainbow bridesmaids.'

Hilda looked puzzled. 'What do you mean?'

'I've got a picture somewhere.' Maud rummaged around in the shoebox, lifting out a dog-eared copy of *Woman's Own* from under the clippings of headdresses, cakes and flowers. She gave it to Malcolm's mother. 'See. They each wear a different colour of the rainbow. Since the clothing rationing has finished, it's become all the rage,' added Maud. 'And it's what Connie wants, isn't it, luv?'

She looked at Connie.

'Once the summer fabrics come out down the Lane, I'll be deciding on—'

'Who to put in what colour,' cut in Maud.

Holding the magazine as if she'd just fished it out of the toilet, Hilda studied the picture for a moment, then looked up. 'It's a little common, isn't it?'

Maud's face flushed purple.

'No, it's modern,' she snapped. 'Of course, as matron of honour, Millie will wear something different.'

Mrs Henstock looked astounded. 'You can't have a woman who has left her husband as your matron of honour, Connie, it's an affront against all decency to—'

'You don't know all the circumstances, Mrs Henstock,' said Connie.

'I don't have to because walking out on your marriage is—'

'Listen, Mrs Henstock,' cut in Connie's mother, stabbing the exercise book with a chubby finger. 'It's my Connie's big day and if she wants her best friend Millie Smith as her matron of honour then, come hell or high water, she'll have Millie Smith as her matron of honour.'

'Well.' Mrs Henstock sniffed. 'I don't think it's right.'

Maud's mouth pulled into a hard line. 'Don't you?'

'No I don't,' Mrs Henstock shot back. 'And I'd have thought your pope would feel the same.'

'What's the pope got to do with anything?' said Maud. 'Millie's a proddy like—'

'I'll think I'll see how she's getting on,' said Connie.

With her temples hammering and before either of them could

reply, she hurried out of the room into the cool of the hallway. Resting her head against the closed door, she took a couple of deep breaths to clear her head, then headed for the kitchen at the back of the house.

Millie was just pinning Patricia's nappy in place when Connie walked in. She looked up.

'What are they talking about now?' she asked, slipping her daughter's rubber pants on.

'Nothing much,' said Connie, tickling Patricia under the chin. 'But I think our Bobby was right when he said I should have eloped.'

Dr Atwell twisted the handle, pushed the door open and stood back. 'As you can see, Dr MacLauchlan, everything in the clinic is purpose-built.'

Squeezing past the rotund senior partner of the Ingrebourne practice, Hari strolled into the pristine treatment room.

'Very impressive,' he said, casting his eye over the brand-new examination couch, electric steriliser and sparkling stainless-steel dressing trolley.

Having finished morning surgery promptly at twelve, Hari had handed over to his new locum, Dr Amanda Scott, who was covering his afternoon calls and evening surgery. After grabbing a quick bite in Liverpool Street Station's buffet, he had caught the twelve-forty Colchester train, which had deposited him at Romford Station just after half past one.

Taking a taxi from the station, he'd suffered a twenty-minute monologue about what Atlee and his chums were doing wrong from the disgruntled taxi driver. Trying to politely ignore him, Hari looked out of the window as his cab inched its way between pens of sheep and cattle in the cobbled marketplace. Hari could have imagined he was in any small town in the Home Counties but as the Georgian buildings gave way to Victorian townhouses and then grander art deco semis, it was clear the population looked to the capital just twenty miles away for its main employment. However, it was only after the taxi swung around the ominously named Gallows Corner and headed north that the town's post-war role become evident.

Standing in neat red-brick blocks on either side of the road were the terraced council houses with small front gardens and red-tile roofs that were being built to provide housing for those needing to move out of the East End. Many of them already had curtains up at the windows and flowerbeds planted up, while further along the street the bricklayers and roofers were working to complete similar dwellings.

Now it was somewhere close to three o'clock in the afternoon and Hari had almost concluded his tour of Duckwood Drive Clinic, the two-year-old health centre that served the community health needs of the LCC's new council estate at Harold Hill.

The clinic itself was a double-storey yellow-brick affair with an entrance with two glazed doors. There was a covered pram shed to the right which had its own entrance at the far end. The building sat in its own grounds with the greenery of Dagenham Recreation Park fanning out on both sides behind it.

In addition to the usual community services such as district nurses, chiropodists and speech therapist, the clinic had two GP practices: the Hilldene and Ingrebourne, the latter of which Hari was visiting this afternoon.

'This is the smaller of the two treatment rooms,' said Dr Atwell as he followed Hari into the room. 'And, like the larger one I showed you earlier, there is a sluice attached.' He indicated the doorway at the far corner. 'We use this one for minor procedures such as the removal of foreign objects from orifices, silver nitrate application and any gastric, faecal or urinal interventions that need to be undertaken.'

Hari gave his prospective colleague an appreciative look, then followed him back into the corridor.

'As you no doubt saw on your way here,' continued Dr Atwell, 'the estate, which will comprise of just over seven and a half thousand homes when it's completed, is expected to have a population or around twenty-five thousand people, mostly young families rehoused as part of slum clearance programmes in east London.' He grinned. 'Given where your present surgery is located, I wouldn't be surprised if you see a few familiar faces hereabouts.'

Hari smiled politely.

'As you can see,' said Dr Atwell as they strolled into the atrium at the front of the building, 'although we share our facilities with the Hilldene practice, we each have our own receptions and office space.'

Hari glanced around at the two separate hatches with each practice name clearly printed on a sign above, while neatly dressed practice clerks behind the counter were filing notes and dealing with patient enquiries.

In the late January light streaming through the tall Crittall windows, the crisp lines of the fixtures and fittings screamed modernity – Hari couldn't help comparing the light, airy space with the run-down waiting room and dark hallways of Christ Church surgery. The building he now stood in bore no reference to the past, only the future.

Dr Atwell ushered Hari back into the corridor and then through the double doors leading to his office.

After letting Hari walk past him into the room, Dr Atwell closed the door and took his place behind the desk.

Hari sat in the comfortable chair on the other side.

'Well, that's the tour of Duckwood Drive Clinic in its entirety,' said Dr Atwell.

Hari crossed his legs. 'And very interesting it was, too.'

'I'm glad you found it so,' said Dr Atwell. He leant back, making the chair creak in the process. 'Because of the number of young families who are rehoused here, the Romford Urban District Council and the LCC have designated this clinic as one of those to be at the forefront of child and maternal health, the care of chronic disease and the promotion of health in schools and factories.'

'It's the sort of thing we on the East London GP committee are already engaged in,' said Hari.

'I guessed as much,' said Dr Atwell approvingly, 'which is why doctors Driscoll and Penne, the other partners in our Ingrebourne Practice, were excited to receive your application.'

Hari smiled again. 'That's very kind of you to say.'

'Speaking frankly, Dr MacLauchlan, when Dr Worsley announced he had decided to hang up his stethoscope as senior partner, the rest of us saw it as a golden opportunity to move forward into new ways of doing things.'

'I see.'

Dr Atwell frowned. 'Don't get me wrong, Worsley is a sound chap and a good doctor, but I'm afraid he is less than enamoured with the new health system and you'll know that for such programmes to be effective, the general practitioner, who knows his patients intimately, must be fully behind any new initiative or treatment.'

'I certainly do,' said Hari, as an image of Dr Marshall shouldering his golf clubs flitted through his mind.

Dr Atwell rested his elbows on the blotter. 'We didn't detail this in the advertisement but in addition to the seven hundred pounds per annum salary and a car allowance, we have negotiated with the LCC for you to be given accommodation in one of the houses in the Noak Hill area, to the north, which boarders onto the Neave county estate.'

'That's very generous,' said Hari. 'And certainly something worth considering.'

'Good.' Dr Atwell stood up. 'I'm sure you'll understand that as it's now three forty-five—'

'You have to get ready for evening surgery,' said Hari, rising to his feet.

Dr Atwell smiled. 'Indeed.'

He walked to the door and Hari followed.

'It's been good to meet you, Dr MacLaculan,' said Dr Atwell, offering his hand.

'You too,' Hari replied, shaking it. 'You don't have to come down, I can see my way out.'

'Thank you,' said Dr Atwell. 'Just to add, although I don't know your circumstances, there is a nursery and junior school within walking distance of the accommodation on offer.'

Hari smiled, and leaving the amiable Dr Atwell to prepare for his patients, he made his way back to the reception area. After the obliging receptionist telephoned for a taxi, Hari strolled outside into the chilly afternoon.

Crossing the road, he sat on the bench outside the police station to wait for his ride back to catch his train.

Everything about the practice was up to date and working there would offer Hari the chance to be at the cutting-edge of the new NHS. If he was offered the job, it would require lots of time and energy to make it a success but Hari was excited by the idea of a new start.

Of course, he knew that even the challenge of building a thriving practice in a different place and with new people wouldn't be enough to erase the thoughts of the woman who dominated his every waking moment, but it might go some way to fill the void.

An eastbound goods train heading out of Liverpool Street rattled over the railway arches at the end of Seabright Street as Connie closed Mrs Parnell's front door.

It was twenty to four on a bright but chilly Valentine's Day. Breakfast had been a noisy affair as the morning post was pounced upon by the nurses. Naturally, there were squeals of delight as they opened cards from their boyfriends and fiancés. As usual, there was nothing for her. She tried not to mind too much as that was just Malcolm.

Hopping on her bike, Connie slotted in behind a number 8 bus laden with school children on their way home.

Shooting past the blackened bombsite by Turin Street, Connie was soon turning left into the top end of Brick Lane. She pulled up outside Christ Church surgery as the clock church was striking the hour.

She hadn't been to the surgery for a couple of days and although she wasn't exactly avoiding Hari since finding out the truth about him and Grace, the pleasure of sharing a coffee with him had gone. However, today a letter had arrived amongst all the Valentine's cards and she had to tell him about it.

Ignoring the conflicting emotions of anticipation mingled with despondency, Connie secured her bike to the railing and trotted up the few steps to the front door.

The house was quiet, but just as she was about to knock the door opened and Grace walked out.

She was wearing a very fetching woollen suit and a smart crocodile-skin handbag hung from her arm. Surprise flashed across Grace's face and her cheeks flushed for an instant, then she smiled. 'Connie, I didn't expect to see you here.'

'I could say the same,' Connie replied tartly. 'Isn't it your day off?'

'Y . . . yes . . . yes, it is,' stammered Grace. 'I just needed to ask Ha— Dr MacLauchlan about something. Something personal—'

The door opened and Hari appeared.

He was jacketless with his collar open and his sleeves rolled up. Connie's heart swelled with the sight of him until she remembered who was standing between them.

'Sister Byrne,' he said with his usual friendly expression on his face.

'Good afternoon, Dr MacLauchlan,' Connie replied, giving him a professional smile.

Hari's dark eyes ran over her face and Connie's heart lurched.

'Thank you, doctor, I'll leave you and Sister Byrne to get on,' said Grace, stepping round Connie.

'All right,' Hari called after her. 'And let me know as soon as you hear anything.'

The front door slammed and the house fell silent again.

'I hope I'm not intruding,' said Connie when they were alone.

Hari's smiled widened.

'Not at all, Connie. Grace just needed my advice about something.' He stepped back. 'Come in, come in. Take a seat while I finish off.'

Connie walked in to the consulting room, catching a faint hint of Hari's aftershave as she passed him.

Swallowing the lump in her throat, Connie made herself comfortable on the seat next to the desk while Hari strolled into the sluice. After a few moments of clattering around, he emerged drying his hands on a towel.

'Now,' he said, perching on the edge of the desk nearest to her. 'First things first. How are you this fine morning?'

'Very well,' said Connie. 'Mrs Purdy has finally delivered her baby and the Feldman twins' conjunctivitis has cleared up.'

'I'm talking about you,' laughed Hari. 'I hope that fiancé of yours sent you a dozen red roses.'

'I'm afraid flowers set off Malcolm's hay fever,' Connie replied lightly.

'Well, what about a card?' Hari asked.

She shook her head. 'He probably only realised it was Valentine's Day when he got to work, so I expect there'll be a hand-delivered card waiting from me when I get back.'

Hari frowned.

'However,' continued Connie. 'I did get something in the post that cheered me up.' She pulled a manila envelope from

313

her blazer pocket. 'It's from the Welfare Board. They've allowed Paul's appeal.'

'And so they should after all the effort you put into your letter,' said Hari, beaming at her.

'And yours,' Connie replied, the pain of Malcolm's thoughtlessness fading a little under Hari's warm gaze.

He reached across the desk and picked up his diary. 'When is it?'

'March the ninth,' said Connie.

'What time?' Hari flipped through the pages to the appropriate one.

'One-thirty at Claybury Hospital.'

'I'll mark it in,' he said. He took his pen from his top pocket and, removing the top with his teeth, scribbled an entry.

'You're going to come with me?'

'Of course,' he replied, discarding the notebook on his desk. 'Unless you don't want me to.'

Connie gazed at him in amazement. 'No. Yes,' she stammered. 'I'd be grateful if you would as I'm sure they'll take the matter much more seriously if you're there. Thank you.'

'Good,' said Hari, slipping his pen back where it belonged. 'It's a date. If you—'

The door flew open and Lenny Moony, one of Micky Murphy's henchmen, burst into the room.

'Where's the doc?' he bellowed as his piggy eyes fixed on them.

Hari rose from the desk. 'I'm here.'

Lenny dismissed him with a wave. 'Not you. Marshall.'

'Dr Marshall's not here yet,' said Connie.

'What time's he coming?'

Hari glanced at his watch. 'Not for an hour or more. What's the problem?'

'It's Micky's little 'un,' said Lenny.

'What's the matter with Pamela?' asked Connie, also standing up.

'I dunno,' Lenny replied, running his stubby finger through his cropped hair. 'She's sort of gone all floppy like, and she's breathing funny.'

Hari grabbed his bag.

'Where do they live?' he asked, already halfway towards the door.

'White Row,' Connie replied.

Lenny blocked their path. 'Mrs Murphy told me to fetch Marshall, urgent, not—'

'I'd step aside, if I were you, old chap,' said Hari, looking coolly at Micky's bully boy.

Indecision and panic flashed back and forth across Lenny's bovine features for a second, then he moved aside.

'Wise decision,' said Hari grimly, striding out of the room with Connie hard on his heels. 'And call an ambulance.'

With her heart banging in her chest, Connie ran into the Micky Murphy's house just ten minutes later and by the time she'd reached the bottom of the carpeted stairs, Hari was already halfway up.

There was no need to wonder where Pamela was as her mother's cries rang down from above. Leaving the door on the latch for the ambulance men, Connie ran up after Hari, her shoulders brushing the flock wallpaper as she did.

Pamela's bedroom was a fairy castle confection of pink satin bows and white lace and there were more china dolls on display than could be found in Hamleys shop windows, but what seized Connie's attention wasn't the myriad of expensive toys, but Micky Murphy's three-year-old daughter lying lifeless in her mother's arms.

'What happened?' asked Hari, taking the child and gently placing her on the bed amongst her teddies and golliwogs.

'I don't know,' sobbed Tina, her impeccably made-up face streaked with tears. 'She's been a bit off colour for the past few days, but—'

'In what way unwell?' asked Connie as Hari searched for the pulse on Pamela's neck. 'Has she been sick or had earache?'

Tina shook her head. 'Just a few sniffles, that's all.'

'Any spots or rashes?' asked Hari, dragging his stethoscope from his bag.

'No, nothing,' wailed Tina, hovering beside her daughter's inert body. 'Nothing. She was running around and playing an hour ago.'

Placing the ends of the stethoscope in his ears, Hari slid the percussion cup under the bodice of Pamela's blue candy-striped dress. He shifted it around a bit, then breathed out hard.

He raised his head and looked at Connie.

'Fifty-two and thready,' he said softly and they exchanged a worried look.

He lowered his face and sniffed. 'Has she had some sweets?'

'No, just tea and a bun with me half an hour ago.' She started crying. 'What's wrong with my baby?' Her gaze darted wildly around the room. 'And where's Micky? He should be here. Where is he?'

Connie put her arm around the woman's shoulders to calm her. 'Lenny's gone for him. He won't be long and the ambulance will soon be here.'

Flipping the stethoscope around his neck, Hari leant forward and lifted the child's eyelids. 'The pupils are dilated.'

Taking Pamela's right hand, he dug his thumb into the nailbed of her index finger.

'What are you doing?' screamed Tina.

'Trying to get a reaction.' Hari straightened up and, chewing the inside of his mouth, studied his patient.

'Has she had anything else this afternoon?' he asked.

Tina considered the question for a moment and then she started. 'I gave her a junior aspirin because she was a bit hot and a spoonful of tonic.'

Hari mouth pulled into a hard line. 'What tonic?'

'Dr Marshall's,' Tina explained. 'Swears by it, does my Micky.'

'Where is it?' asked Connie.

'In the bathroom,' said Tina.

Leaving Hari trying to wake Pamela, Connie dashed from the room and into the black and yellow fitted bathroom at the back of the house.

Knocking the pastel-coloured bottles of bubble bath and beribboned tubs of talcum powder into the tub as she rushed past, Connie yanked open the mirrored door of the medicine cabinet. Rummaging around amongst the hair trimmers, tooth-brushes and half a dozen nail vanishes, Connie grabbed a brown glass bottle with Vitality Restorative Preparation printed on the label.

Connie sped back to the bedroom and handed it to Hari, who scanned the label then looked at Tina.

'One teaspoon?'

Tina shook her head.

'Tablespoon,' she squeaked, covering her mouth with her painted fingertips and weeping.

Hari threw the bottle aside and grabbed Pamela's shoulder.

'Connie, we have to wake her,' he said, shaking the child. 'And we need to get this stuff out of her.'

Rushing to the window to let in some cold air, Connie threw it open and was just about to dash down to the kitchen to mix up a salt and water emetic to make Pamela vomit, when Micky burst into the room followed by Lenny.

With his eyes bulging and his face an unhealthy shade of purple, Micky took in the scene for a second or two, then lunged at Hari.

'Get your dirty hands off my Pammy,' he bellowed, the veins on his forehead standing out in ugly relief.

Grabbing Hari by the lapels, he hauled him upright, ripping his jacket in the process.

'Let go of me,' Hari shouted, twisting out of his grasp. 'I'm trying to—'

Connie's heart lurched as Micky aimed a punch at Hari's head, but Hari jerked back just in time.

'For God's sake, man,' shouted Hari. 'Can't you see I'm here to help—'

'Why didn't you get Marshall?' bawled Micky, glaring at his wife. 'We don't need no fucking help from no half-caste.'

Connie ran over, but Micky shoved her aside.

She stumbled back and collided with the bedside table, knocking the Snow White bedside lamp to the floor.

Micky sprang at Hari again and grabbed him around the throat. Hari tried to break free as Micky clenched his fist and aimed another blow at Hari's face.

'For the love of God, Micky,' Connie shouted, regaining her balance and grabbing the man's beefy arm. 'Hari's trying to save Pamela's life!'

The colour drained from Micky's bulldog-like features. 'What?'

'Your wife gave Pamela some of your tonic and it's got a powerful opiate in it,' said Hari, hurrying back to his patient and raising the child up.

'So,' said Micky. 'It's just a pick-me-up. It ain't never done me no harm.'

'But you're a fifteen-stone man,' said Hari. 'So I doubt you'd even feel the effect of the drug, but for a two-and-half-stone child the amount of morphine in a teaspoon, let alone a table-spoonful, could be fatal.'

Micky turned to his wife. 'You stupid cow, what have you done?'

'I didn't know, Micky! Honest!' she screamed. 'You know I wouldn't do nuffink to hurt her. It's not my fault.'

'Don't blame your wife, Mr Murphy,' said Hari. 'It's not her fault, she wasn't to know that this so-called pick-me-up has a potentially lethal drug in it.'

Tina started sobbing. 'Please don't let her die, doctor.'

Hari felt the pulse in Pamela's throat. 'It's up a bit but still less than it should be.' He rubbed the child's breastbone and she moaned.

He looked at Connie. 'Salt water, quick.'

Racing past the child's dumbstruck parents, Connie hurried down to the kitchen. Filling a cup with water, she added a gen-erous dollop of salt and then carried it back up to the bedroom.

When she re-entered the room, Hari had turned Pamela to face towards the stiff breeze coming through the open window.

He looked gratefully across at Connie as she came in.

'Don't just stand there, Murphy,' he barked. 'Lend a hand.'

As Micky held his daughter upright, Connie steadied the girl's head while Hari poured the salt mixture down Pamela's throat.

'Come on, sweetheart,' coaxed Connie in a low voice as Hari checked the child's eyes again.

'She is going to be all right, isn't she?' asked Tina, clutching onto her husband's expensive jacket.

'Talk to her,' Hari said to Micky.

'Pammy baby,' he croaked, a sob audible in his gruff voice. 'Open your eyes for Daddy.'

The child didn't move.

Connie and Hari exchanged another worried glance then

Pamela jerked, gagged and vomited all over Hari's trousers.

Her eyelids flickered.

'That's it, Pamela,' said Connie, rubbing the girl's hand vigorously. 'Wake up.'

Pamela's eyes opened a little and she coughed.

As Connie held her upright and supported her head, Hari pressed her abdomen and Pamela vomited again, this time over her fluffy rug with a picture of a kitten on it.

A bell sounded outside in the street.

Connie turned and looked at Micky's sidekick. 'Fetch the ambulance men up.'

Lenny rushed off and reappeared in a few moments with two ambulance men carrying a stretcher. Micky gently lowered his daughter onto the stretcher and Pamela's mother tucked the red blanket around her.

Hari took Connie aside. 'I know she's brought a lot up, but . . .'

'I know,' she said in a low voice. 'Morphine is quickly absorbed in the gut.'

'Indeed, so she's not out of the woods yet.' He gave her a wry smile. 'I don't want to impose, but will you go with—'

'Of course,' Connie replied. 'I'll stay with the family until we know what's going on.'

'Good and take the bottle of tonic with you.' He gave her a little smile, then turned back into the room. 'Sister's going to the hospital in the ambulance with Pamela and you can meet her there.'

Tina held Pamela's hand as the girl was carried out and she and her husband watched anxiously as the stretcher was loaded into the waiting ambulance. Lenny was sitting behind the wheel of the Daimler ready to take Micky and Tina to the hospital. A crowd had gathered across the street, curious to know what had happened.

'Have you got a phone?' Hari asked Micky.

'On the hall table,' Micky replied, holding the car door open as his wife climbed into the back of the vehicle.

'I'll phone the hospital and speak to the doctor in Casualty so they have everything ready,' said Hari.

He turned away but Micky grabbed his arm. 'Tell me who's responsible, doc, and I'll make 'em sorry they were born.'

Hari's mouth pulled into a hard line. 'That won't be necessary, Mr Murphy. I'll make sure they are brought to book.'

Micky gave a sharp nod and clambered into the car next to his wife. He slammed the car door shut and the Daimler sped off.

Hari placed his hand on Connie's arm.

Connie turned and found herself sinking in to Hari's chocolate-brown eyes.

'And thank you, Connie,' he said, softly squeezing her arm.

Their eyes locked and Connie's heart did a little double step then Hari strode back into the house.

Connie grabbed the handrail at the back of the ambulance and was just about to climb in when she looked back.

Hari was standing in the hallway with the phone to his ear. His jacket was ripped, his tie had come loose and there was vomit down his trousers. Connie's heart ached at the sight of him and, in all honestly, she didn't think she'd ever seen him look better.

After he'd finished talking to the consultant in A&E, Hari hastened upstairs to retrieve his bag, then he headed back to the surgery. He arrived some ten minutes later and found a handful of patients sitting in the waiting room.

'Has Dr Marshall got anyone with him?' he asked a red-faced man sitting just inside the door as he marched past.

'No, he ain't started—'

'Thank you,' Hari called over his shoulder.

Without bothering to knock, he walked into the consulting room.

Dr Marshall was on the phone with his back to the door. 'Yes, Cheeky Boo, I miss you, too—'

Hari cleared his throat.

Dr Marshall looked around. 'I'll call you back.' He slammed the receiver down and jumped to his feet. 'What's the goddamn meaning of all this . . .' He looked Hari up and down. 'And what in the blue blazes has happened to your trousers? You look like one of the dossers in Itchy Par—'

'I've just come from Mr Murphy's house in White Row,' Hari cut in. 'Do you know him?'

Dr Marshall flicked a speck of dust off his sleeve. 'He drops in from time to time, what's the matter with him?'

'Nothing, it was his daughter Pamela I was called to,' said Hari.

Dr Marshall snorted. 'I suppose she sneezed and her mother thinks she's at death's door.'

'Actually, Marshall, three-year-old Pamela Murphy may well be at death's door, thanks to you,' said Hari, jabbing his index finger at his colleague.

A deep flush coloured Dr Marshall's quivering jowls. 'How dare you—'

'She's at death's door because she was given the so-called tonic you sold to her father,' interrupted Hari. 'The tonic containing morphine, not to mention nine micrograms of Cannabis Indica and five micrograms of chloroform in every ounce. It's a miracle she was still breathing when I arrived.'

Alarm flashed across Dr Marshall's heavy features, then his sneer returned.

'Her mother's to blame, stupid woman,' he said. 'The ingredients are written on the side.'

'I doubt Mrs Murphy can read Latin,' said Hari. 'And besides, it was written in illegible lettering so small that even I had trouble reading it. And, contrary to the Ministry of Health directive number 46, there was no warning on the label that it should not be given to a child.'

'Well then, Crowther at the chemist is culpable,' said Dr Marshall, taking a crumpled handkerchief from his top pocket and mopping the sweat from his brow.

Hari regarded him coolly. 'Had it been a NHS prescription, you'd be right, Marshall, but as it was a private prescription issued by you for payment then I'm afraid the responsibility for the safe administration of the medicine lies with you as you are the prescribing doctor.'

Dr Marshall's piggy eyes narrowed. 'Is the child all right?'

'I don't know,' Hari replied. 'Once I've changed, I'm going to the hospital to find out. But you'd better pray she is because otherwise I'll be going from the hospital straight to Leman Street police station to make sure you'll be up on a charge of manslaughter.'

'But . . . but h . . . how was I to know?' stammered Marshall. 'It . . . it's not m . . . my fault.'

Hari strode over to Marshall and, placing his hands on the desk, loomed over him.

'And even if by some miracle Pamela does survive, don't think you're off the hook, Marshall, because I will be reporting you to the BMA for negligence and professional misconduct.' He jabbed his finger again at the man behind the desk. 'You're finished this time, Marshall, and if you want my advice I'd make myself scare because I think Micky Murphy will be wanting to have a word with you very soon indeed.'

It was just after six when Hari pushed open the doors to the London Hospital's canteen. The smell of boiled cabbage and the chatter of nurses and auxiliary staff on their evening break washed over him.

Like every other hospital cafeteria he'd ever been in, the walls were tiled to shoulder height and painted a nondescript sage green above. The wooden tables, scrubbed white over the decades, were evenly spaced along the side walls, very like the beds in the wards. At the far end of the room a pot-stove pumped heat into the ancient cast-iron radiators while a brown wireless on a purpose-built shelf high on the wall blasted out 'Music While You Work', a hangover from wartime when the evening shifts in the factory would have been in full swing.

Stepping aside to let a couple of hospital porters out, Hari scanned the room. The refectory was a sea of lilac-stripped uniforms and frilly hats; Connie, in her plain navy dress and felt hat, was easy to spot sitting at one end of a long table.

Taking his place at the back of the small queue at the counter, Hari gazed at her through the knot of people waiting to pay at the till.

She looked tired and forlorn as she stirred her cup of tea.

Fancy not sending her flowers! Malcolm really didn't deserve her and Hari knew his heart wouldn't be able to stand the pain of seeing her day in and day out once she became Sister Henstock.

With a sigh, he looked away.

He ordered his coffee and, after handing over a ha' penny, he carried it carefully down the line of tables towards her.

As he put his cup down next to hers, she looked up and smiled. 'Oh, I wasn't expecting to see you,' she said.

'I thought it would be easier than trying to phone,' said Hari. He pulled out the chair to stop himself taking her in his arms there and then.

'Have you been to the ward?' she asked.

'I have and Pamela's stable,' he replied.

Connie crossed herself and looked heavenward. 'Thank God!'

'Indeed,' said Hari. 'I spoke to Dr Carmichael, the consultant, and he says the next few hours are crucial but had we not reached her when we did, she certainly wouldn't have had a chance.'

With her mug clasped between her hands and her elbows resting on the table, Connie gazed across at him. 'You were marvellous.'

'It's what I'm trained to do,' Hari replied, basking in her admiration. 'You were pretty outstanding yourself, jumping in front of Micky Murphy's fist like that.'

'Well, I thought he was going to pan you.'

'So did I, but I could have taken him,' he said.

She looked incredulous. 'Could you?'

Hari held his blasé expression for a moment, then grinned. 'Not a chance,' he laughed. 'He'd have made mincemeat of me.'

Connie giggled and they collapsed into a fit of laughter, earning them curious glances from people close by.

As their merriment subsided, Connie's blue eyes locked with his for several self-conscious heartbeats, then Hari pulled himself to order.

'So,' he said, swallowing the lump in his throat. 'How are the plans for the wedding coming along?'

'Oh, you know,' she joked, rolling her eyes. 'My mum wants this and his mother wants that. I had a fight with my mum about the flowers.'

'Surely the bride should have the final say?' said Hari.

Connie raised an eyebrow. 'You've never meet my mother.'

Hari laughed.

'Anyway, battles aside, we've just got to decide on the last-minute things like the seating plan and hymns,' she continued. 'There's so much to think about and I'm constantly having to make a choice.'

'Well, whatever you choose I'm sure it will be your lovely day, Connie.' Hari placed his cup carefully back in the saucer.

'I know exactly what you mean about making the right choices because I've been trying to come to a decision over the past few weeks, too.'

'Sounds serious,' she said, taking a sip of her tea.

'Connie, I went to look at a GP practice in a new health centre in Harold Hill outside Romford a few weeks back,' he continued. 'I was very impressed with the set-up and they are keen to expand into areas I already have an interest in. I got on well with the senior doctor and a week ago I received a letter offering me a partnership. I have been mulling the matter over in my mind and I have decided to accept.'

Connie stared at him in disbelief. 'But you can't. I mean, you actually diagnose what's wrong with patients and give them the correct treatment.'

'I know—'

'You don't shout at them,' she continued.

'And that's why I'm certain an up-to-date and enthusiastic doctor will step into my shoes,' Hari explained, feeling his heart sink with every word he spoke. 'I'm sorry if it's a bit of a shock but as we've worked so closely together this past year, I wanted to tell you first.'

Connie stared bleakly at him for a second or two before finding her voice. 'Well, I can't pretend I'm not surprised, Hari, but if that's what you want then I wish you well. Anyway, by this time next year I'm likely to have someone swaddled in pink or blue to worry about, so Christ Church surgery's new GP will probably have a new district nurse, too,' she said, with a dazzling smile that sliced him through to the marrow.

A gruff voice cut between them. 'Oi, oi, doc!'

Hari looked around to see Micky Murphy bounding towards them, his waistcoat unbuttoned and his tie hanging loose around his neck.

Hari rose to his feet.

Connie did too and stepped closer to Hari, her shoulder just touching his upper arm.

'Any news?' she asked as they faced Micky together.

He nodded.

'Pammy opened her eyes about half an hour ago,' the guvnor of Spitalfields replied, tears swimming in his eyes.

'I'm so pleased to hear that,' said Connie.

'You and me both, sister,' Micky replied. 'Course they'll have to keep an eye on her for a few days, but the consultant chap said there was no reason why she wouldn't make a full recovery.'

'That's very good news,' added Hari.

Micky's bloodshot eyes shifted from Connie to Hari and an oddly chastened expression settled on his heavy features.

He adjusted his stance with a shrug and cleared his throat.

'Now, here's the thing, doc, you ask anyone and they'll tell you that Micky Murphy's a straight-up geezer. You play fair by me and I'll play fair by you. Now there ain't no pretty way to say this so I'm just going to say it right out. Cause you've got a touch of the tar brush, I may have said the odd thing or two that ain't right and proper, but I tell you straight' – Micky placed his beringed right hand on his chest – 'as God is my witness, after what you did for my Pammy today, you and me, doc, are muckers of the first order.'

He offered his hand and Hari took it.

'Thank you, Mr Murphy,' he said.

'I mean it, doc,' continued Micky, doing his best to shake Hari's arm from his shoulder. 'Someone messes with you and they'll find themselves messing with me. We're like them Musketeer fellas, all for one and all in it togever.'

'I count it an honour,' said Hari as Micky finally released his hand.

Micky pulled his lapels down smartly. 'Right, now that's done I ought to get back to Tina.'

'Give her my best wishes,' said Connie.

'I will, luv, and thank you, too,' said Micky.

'And tell her I'll pop in when Pamela's out of hospital,' said Connie.

Micky nodded, then his gaze moved between them.

'She's a diamond girl, is our Sister Byrne,' he said with a soft glint in his eye.

'I know,' Hari replied.

They exchanged a meaningful look and then Micky smiled.

'And don't forget, I'm a man of my word so from naw on, doc,' he tapped the side of his nose, 'I'll see you right.'

Chapter Twenty-Four

It was just before midday on the first Friday in March and patients had been queuing along the street when Hari had opened the door at 8.30 and he'd been working flat out since then. After the incident with Pamela Murphy two weeks before, Dr Marshall had taken his advice and promptly put himself on sick leave the following day. After his colleague's abrupt departure, the surgery had been almost unmanageable. Once word got out that Marshall was no longer at the practice, patients who were registered with the surgery but had no current records came out of the woodwork.

Unfortunately, many of these patients had long-standing conditions such as undiagnosed diabetes, chronic ulcers and, in one sad case, advanced cancer of the jaw which the patient had been treating with cloves and whisky, thinking it was toothache.

Faced with such a backlog of patients needing detailed assessment, Hari had put on special Wednesday and Thursday afternoon surgeries to deal with those who hadn't been seen for six months or more. Having done the last of those yesterday, the workload had returned to busy rather than frantic.

Having finished writing up his last patient's notes, Hari picked up his empty mug and went to the dresser to get a refill.

He'd just taken the pot from the hotplate when there was a knock on the door.

'Come!' called Hari, continuing to pour his drink.

The door opened but instead of a patient Mr Shottington, the senior consultant at the London Hospital, stepped into the room.

Somewhere in his late forties, Algernon Shottington's well-fed frame was stuffed into a double-breasted frock coat and matching waistcoat, his pinstriped trousers strained at the seams and a Trinity College silk tie was secured in a knot at his throat. A thick gold chain stretched across his ample middle and his masonic cuff links were clearly visible, poking out from beneath his jacket sleeves.

As far as Hari could make out, Shottington had been part of the fixtures and fittings at the hospital since before the war and although the consultant despised the new NHS he had nonetheless wormed his way onto many of the organisation's influential committees and working parties. If asked to describe Old Algie in two words, pompous and arse were the ones that sprang most readily to mind.

'Mr Shottington, this is an unexpected surprise,' said Hari with a charming smile. 'We don't see you in this neck of the woods very often.'

'Perhaps not, but I like to keep an eye on things,' said the surgeon.

'Any things in particular?' asked Hari, stirring milk into his drink.

Shottington waved a manicured hand airily. 'Oh, you know, this and that. Mind if I sit?'

'Of course.' Hari raised the pot he was holding. 'Coffee?'

'Not for me, thank you,' he replied. 'Plays havoc with the ulcer. One of the troubles with getting on a bit. Nothing works as it used to.'

Hari smiled politely.

The chair on the other side of the desk creaked as Shottington settled his considerable bulk into it and Hari sat back down.

Resting his elbows on the arms of the chair and lacing his hands across on his paunch, Mr Shottington placed his bowler on the pile of patients' notes awaiting filing and surveyed the surgery.

'You seem to have shifted things about a bit,' he said, eyeing the line of new grey metal filing cabinets along the wall.

'Oh, you mean getting rid of the woodwormed cupboards and putting the patient notes into alphabetical order?' said Hari. 'Getting an improvement grant from Area and replacing the old steriliser and electric fire in the waiting room? Yes, I suppose you could say I've shifted things around a bit.'

A benevolent smile lifted the surgeon's heavy features. 'Ah, you young men and all your new ways of doing things.'

'I believe the Greeks were the first to devise an alphabetical system for keeping records, so I'd hardly call that a modern innovation,' Hari replied.

Mr Shottington's jovial expression wavered a little. 'Perhaps, but all these miracle antibiotic drugs and new surgical procedures make it hard for someone like me, who trained when the king's father was on the throne, to keep up.' Shottington chuckled. 'I tell you, it's not easy for us old dogs to learn new tricks.'

'Us?'

'Yes, old chaps like me and Bert Marshall,' said Shottington.

'Ah,' said Hari. 'So this is about Pamela Murphy.'

'Yes, yes,' said Shottington a little impatiently. 'A regrettable incident, no doubt, but without any lasting consequences, and is it any wonder he got in a muddle with demands from the Ministry arriving in every post?'

Resting his elbows on the blotter and linking his hands together, Hari regarded the consultant coolly. 'I would say a child almost dying is a little more than just a regrettable incident, don't you think? And Marshall wasn't muddled, he was negligent. If I had been out on a call instead of in the surgery, Marshall would be up on manslaughter charges by now.'

Mr Shottington's jowls quivered a little. 'Look, old man. I'll admit Marshall's let things slide, but he's having a bit of trouble with the little woman at home just now and he's got his other practice to consider too, so I'm hoping you're not going to add to poor old Bert's woes by reporting this nonsense to the BMA.'

'Well, I'm sorry to disappoint you, but that is exactly what I am going to do,' Hari replied. 'In fact, the letter went off last week.'

'That's unfortunate,' growled Shottington, all pretence at civility vanishing in an instant.

'And why would that be?'

Shottington's eyes narrowed as they ran over Hari's face. 'You may have the letters after your name, Dr MacLauchlan, but as far as the medical establishment is concerned you are a jumped-up punkah wallah doctor from the colonies and if you have any hope of progressing in your career you are going to have to cooperate. Show whose side you're on.'

'Are you threatening me, Mr Shottington?' asked Hari pleasantly.

Mr Shottington gave him a patronising smile by way of a reply.

'Well, let me tell you, old man,' Hari continued. 'I've refused to "cooperate" with a Japanese sword at my throat, so I'm hardly going to be moved by your threats. Marshall and that crook Crowther at the chemist have been selling a so-called tonic containing alcohol, chloroform, cannabis extract and morphine which very nearly killed a small child.' He scowled at the man opposite. 'However, I may be able to offer Marshall a way out. I'm sure his golf and drinking partners in the BMA would be quite happy to sweep the matter under the carpet but the Ministry will take a more critical view. I'm putting my report in regardless of anything you might say, but if Marshall is claiming that personal problems combined with chronic fatigue caused by running two practices resulted in the near-fatal poisoning of a child, then perhaps the men from the Ministry would be more sympathetic to Dr Marshall's case if he's already relinquished the Christ Church practice by the time they start investigating.'

'And I suppose you want to take over the practice,' said Shottington.

Hari smiled. 'As a punkah wallah, I'd fit right in, wouldn't I? Amongst my Jewish, Turkish, Polish and West Indian neighbours and I'm sure Mr Merriweather, the minister in charge of the north-east London area, will agree.'

An unhealthy flush crept up Mr Shottington's throat and a tic started beneath his right eye. Hari regarded him unyieldingly as the surgeon chewed on his lips.

'Very well,' he barked, rising to his feet. 'I'll put your proposal to Marshall.'

Hari stood up and offered his hand.

Ignoring it, Shottington snatched his bowler from the desk.

'You might have won this time, MacLauchlan,' he said, jabbing his hat at Hari, 'but we'll be taking a keen interest in you from now on.'

Hari smiled. 'Thanks for the warning.'

Shottington gave him another bellicose look, then stomped towards the door.

'And if you want to know whose side I'm on,' Hari called after him, 'it's my patients'.'

*

It was the 9th March and the day of Paul Gillespie's appeal hearing. Connie studied her reflection in the long mirror on the back of her bedroom door.

She pulled a face and after deciding that the close-fitting maroon hat made her look too old, she took it off and put it back in the hat box on the bed. Pressing the lid firmly in place, Connie shoved it on top of the wardrobe. She then scooped up the dozen or so dresses she'd tried on before settling on her current outfit and quickly put them back on their hangers.

After much deliberation, she'd decided on a long-sleeved sky-blue dress with a full skirt and Peter Pan collar. She teamed it with a wide red patent belt, her red ankle boots and a matching handbag.

It was just after twelve-thirty on the afternoon of Paul's appeal hearing.

A cat or something must have woken her at about four in the morning and Connie had lain awake, staring at the tassels of the ceiling lamp, until the pale dawn light crept around the edge of her curtains. She must have drifted off to sleep at some point, though, because her alarm had woken her three hours later and she'd only just made it to the refectory as Mrs Rogerson was finishing off.

Having the whole morning to herself before meeting Hari, Connie had intended to catch up on a few little jobs, like taking her shoes to the cobbler and then mending the unravelled hem of her best suit, but somehow she couldn't settle to anything.

She'd finished lunch about half an hour ago although, in truth, she'd just picked at Mrs Rogerson's fish and chips as she didn't seem to be hungry.

Connie studied herself for a moment in the mirror then, grabbing the hairbrush, she battled her unruly locks into a ponytail, securing it with a bow made from a scrap of the dress material.

Placing the brush alongside her comb on the dressing table and now worrying she looked too young, Connie slipped on her three-quarter-length jacket, picked up her handbag and left her room.

Skipping down the front steps of Fry House a few moments later, and with the sun warming her face, she headed for Christ

Church surgery. As she turned into Grey Eagle Street she stopped dead.

The outside of the surgery was covered with scaffolding from pavement to roof and on the top level stood three men in buff overalls and flat caps. Two were scraping away at the dilapidated masonry paint while the third was fixing new guttering into place. If this wasn't surprise enough, even at this distance Connie could see the front door had been painted with a very sophisticated black gloss.

Picking her way carefully through the various planks and poles lying on the pavement, Connie mounted the freshly whitewashed steps to the front door.

But if she was amazed by the surgery's external renovation, her jaw was positively on the floor when she stepped over the threshold. Gone was the faded brown wallpaper in the hall and in its place were replastered walls painted to waist level in a practical cocoa-coloured paint with pale green emulsion above. To brighten the entrance further, at evenly spaced intervals along both walls were framed posters of rural scenes depicting farmyard animals, bare-footed children playing in front of thatched cottages and horses pulling heavy ploughs.

As she stood amazed at the transformation, the door to the consulting room opened and Hari stepped out.

He grinned. 'Surprised?'

Connie laughed. 'Speechless more like.'

He strode towards her and grabbed the waiting room door.

'Wait till you see this.' He threw the door open and Connie peered in.

The room was decorated in the same colours as the hallway, and the ramshackle chairs had been replaced by metal ones with moulded plywood seats and backs. There were pictures fixed on the wall here too but this time they were colourful health posters reminding patients what measures they could take to promote their own wellbeing.

'My goodness,' said Connie as she gazed around. 'How . . . ?'

'Micky Murphy.' Hari winked. 'Didn't I tell yer, doc, I'd see yer right,' he said, mimicking the local guvnor's gruff tones.

Connie laughed. 'It looks so different.'

He strode across the surgery and out the door. 'And I bet you've never seen this looking so bare?'

He flung open the door of what had been the storeroom.

Connie followed him out and peered in.

The room, which the last time she looked had been full of rusty ironwork and dusty medical equipment, was bare and painted in the same decor as the main surgery. The old lino had been replaced and in the window the glass pane that had been cracked for as long as Connie could remember had not only been replaced, but there was a venetian blind hanging from it.

'My goodness,' she said, staring in disbelief at the transformed room. 'Where's it all gone?'

'To the scrap dealer, although some could have very well gone to a museum it was so ancient. I've got a desk coming in a week and a couple of filing cabinets. But you should see the consulting room,' said Hari, ushering Connie along the corridor.

Opening the door for her, Hari stepped back so she could enter. Connie stepped into the room, the smell of fresh paint making her nose tingle. Apart from the walls being a warm cream colour she didn't see anything different until she spotted a sparkling stainless-steel sink through the sluice door.

The century-old chipped tiles had vanished and in their place were bright white ones. The Victorian plumbing had also been stripped out and replaced with pipework that wouldn't have looked out of place in the London. There was even the latest electronic Little Matron autoclave model with a myriad of coloured gauges and dials running down one side.

'Oh my goodness,' she said as she gazed around the small space. She frowned and looked at Hari. 'But—'

Hari held up his hand. 'I know what you're going to say: "Where did he get it all?"'

'Well, yes,' said Connie. 'You don't want the police dropping by to ask you about a theft from a hospital or decorators' yard.'

'Micky's given me a receipt for everything and he's written to the Area Health Committee outlining his contribution as a local businessman to the "welfare and health of the people of Spitalfields and Shoreditch". I was hoping to show you sooner, but—'

'Yes, sorry,' said Connie, turning and, in the confined space of the sluice, finding herself just inches from Hari.

Painfully aware of his nearness, she looked up. 'Our newest crop of students are still finding their feet so I've been up to my ears sorting them out.'

Hari's dark eyes ran slowly over her face and then he smiled. 'As long as you're not avoiding me,' he said in a low voice.

Stifling the urge to fling her arms around his neck and kiss him, Connie forced a smile. 'What a shame you won't be here to enjoy it.'

She caught sight of the clock on the wall. 'Goodness, is that the time? The trains only run every half an hour so we'd better get a move on if we want to arrive before one-fifteen.'

'Ha ha,' said Hari, stepping back into the consulting room. 'I've something else to show you before we head off. Follow me.'

Grabbing his jacket from the back of his chair, he guided her back into the passageway but instead of heading for the front entrance he turned towards the rear of the building.

'Ta-dah!' Hari flung wide the door to reveal a car practically filling the handkerchief-sized backyard. 'It's an Austin 8,' he said as Connie descended the two steps and walked towards the gleaming car.

He followed her out and stood beside her.

'It's not a Daimler but it's got a four-speed gearbox and can do up to fifty-six miles an hour,' he said, polishing the already spotless bonnet with his sleeve. 'It's not new but only has eighteen thousand miles on the clock.'

Although she didn't have a clue what that signified, she looked impressed.

'So you see,' he said, grinning and taking her basket from her as he opened the passenger door, 'we don't have to worry about the trains.'

Tucking her skirt under her, Connie lowered herself into the seat, then swung her legs in.

'Comfy?' asked Hari, casually leaning his arm on the top of the door.

'Yes, very,' said Connie, smiling happily at him.

'Then let us away.' He straightened up and started to close the door, but then paused and leant in. 'Oh, and by the way, you look very nice.'

*

333

Connie shifted on her chair in an attempt to get some feeling back into her rear. She and Hari were sitting in front of the Health Authority's Appeal Board in a third-floor committee room in the old Victorian asylum, which had been recently renamed Claybury Mental Hospital.

Although there were a half-dozen Victorian radiators fixed along the wall, the expanse of the committee chamber was clearly too much for them and, as the watery late winter sun was already behind the buildings opposite, the air in the room was so cold that Connie could see her breath.

Despite arriving at 1.30, she and Hari had only been called in ten minutes ago and, according to the clock above the head of the four members, it was already fifteen minutes past two.

She stole a furtive look at Hari, who was sitting on her right, only to find him gazing at her. He gave her an encouraging little smile which, despite the frigid atmosphere of the room, caused a warm glow to spread through her.

Unlike Malcolm, who was a somewhat hesitant driver, Hari's strong hands had spun the wheel and changed gear with confidence as they'd sped through Stratford and on to the leafy suburbs of Woodford. But it wasn't just the relaxed way he negotiated the traffic that had made the three-quarters-of-an-hour drive to the hospital in Woodford so enjoyable, but the sheer pleasure of being alone with him. It was wrong, of course, given that she was engaged to Malcolm and he was involved with Grace, but although her head kept telling her she shouldn't yearn for him so, her heart wasn't listening.

Pushing the unsettling thoughts aside, Connie tucked her hands into the folds of her winter coat to keep them warm.

Mr Humphrey, the chairman of the board, muttered something to the red-faced, portly matron sitting to his right, then turned to his left to whisper something to Miss Frobisher, the hospital's ancient sparrow-like almoner, and Dr Cummings, a youthful-looking houseman.

Getting a curt nod by way of reply from the uninterested doctor, the panel's chairman pulled his papers together.

'Miss . . . Miss,' he said, scrutinising Connie through the thick lenses of his spectacles.

'Byrne,' said Connie with a willing smile. 'It's Sister Byrne, actually.'

Mr Humphrey sniffed and glanced over the paper in his hand again. 'It says in your letter of appeal that you and Dr MacLauchlan are here to speak on behalf of Paul Gillespie.'

The matron regarded her suspiciously. 'We usually only allow relatives to address the panel—'

'I know,' said Connie. 'And that's why I'm very grateful to you all for giving me the chance to speak as I was Paul's district nurse and I cared for both him and his mother.'

She gave the panel members a warm smile which none of them returned.

Hari shifted in the chair beside her and recrossed his legs.

'Well, in truth, Sister Byrne, Dr MacLauchlan,' continued the chairman, 'although we're grateful for your interest I don't really understand the point of you coming. It's obvious to anyone that the patient can't take care of himself so he will have to remain in an institution.'

'Yes, I understand,' said Connie in as even a tone as she could manage. 'But despite his outward disabilities, Paul is an intelligent young man so I'm asking that he be moved to a home rather than remain in a large institution, which would be more suitable and where his mother's friends can visit him and he will be able to carry on with his hobbies.'

Miss Frobisher's almost invisible eyebrows rose. 'What sort of hobbies?'

'He's been studying African mammals recently as well as the history of China.' She laughed. 'And, like all seventeen-year-old boys, he's mad about motor cars.'

Hari sat forwards. 'As you can see from my supporting statement, I corroborate Sister Byrne's assessment and strongly recommend that Paul Gillespie would benefit greatly from being moved to a stimulating environment with access to education and a home environment suited to his physical and mental wellbeing.'

Connie gave him a grateful look, but the panel was less impressed and Mr Humphrey turned to speak to the fresh-faced Dr Cummings.

'If you could give us your opinion, Dr Cummings?' said Mr Humphrey.

Dr Cummings glanced sideways at the file open on the table and stubbed out his cigarette.

'Gillespie,' he ruminated, taking a crumpled pack of Rothmans from his jacket pocket. 'Can't say I can place him.'

Although Hari's pleasant expression didn't waver, his right foot flicked up and down rapidly.

'He's seventeen with light brown hair, hazel eyes and has cerebral palsy of all four limbs,' said Connie.

'Ah, yes,' said the doctor, lighting another cigarette. 'I know him in passing but all I've seen him do is stare out of the window.'

'That's probably because he's just lost his mother,' Connie replied.

'I'm sure we can all sympathise with that,' said Hari, with a touch of annoyance in his tone.

The panel shuffled their papers again and didn't seem to share the sentiment.

'His mother looked after him tirelessly all her life, taking him on trips to the zoo and to the seaside,' continued Connie. 'He can read and tap out words and his teacher—'

'He has a teacher?' asked the almoner, as if she'd been told there was a talking horse outside the room.

'Yes, a Miss Fergusson,' Connie replied, tucking a stray tendril of hair behind her ear. 'She came in three times a week and even in the few short months she was with him, Paul made marvellous progress.'

Mr Humphrey sifted through his file and held up a sheet. 'But the original medical report states quite clearly that Paul Gillespie is, and I quote, "mentally retarded and showed no evidence of any understanding".'

'But that's not true,' said Connie heatedly. 'Paul is able to do long multiplication and fractions. Miss Fergusson, Paul's teacher, assesses him as being of above-average intelligence and . . . ' She looked down.

Dr Cummings blew a ring of smoke upwards. 'That's all very well, nurse, but—'

'It's sister,' Hari's voice cut in icily. 'Sister Byrne is a fully

336

qualified Queen's Nurse. And perhaps it would be wise to disregard Dr Marshall's opinion on this matter as he is about to face an investigation by the British Medical Association for malpractice and fraud and will be lucky to avoid being struck off.'

Dr Cummings shot him an irritated look and then returned his attention to Connie. 'And, sister, even if we accept that somehow the boy isn't simple, we can't just move people around willy-nilly.'

'No, we can't,' chipped in the matron. 'People used to care for their retarded children at home but now with this new NHS system, we have three applications for every bed.'

'I'm sure you do,' said Connie. 'Which is why I'm asking you to consider moving Paul to Buntingford House in Chigwell.' She opened her handbag and fished out the glossy brochure. 'It's a home that specialises in caring for young people with disabilities like his.'

'Is it run by the health authority?' asked Miss Frobisher.

Connie shook her head. 'It's a charity and has staff who organise day trips and activities.' She stood up and placed the leaflet on the table. 'It would be ideal for Paul and only a half-hour train journey from Liverpool Street.'

Mr Humphry pursed his lips. 'I can't see how we could justify paying for a private bed when we have places of our own.'

An image of Paul soaked in his own urine and strapped to a chair flashed through Connie's mind and tears pinched the corners of her eyes. 'But surely—'

'No, we can't,' Dr Cummings interrupted, closing the file in front of him.

'After all, the boy has a roof over his head,' added the matron, 'which is more than can be said of some.'

'Indeed,' said Miss Frobisher, adjusting the fox fur drape around her bony shoulders.

'Thank you both for taking the time and trouble to put your points of view forward.' Mr Humphrey smiled condescendingly at them. 'We will consider the merits of this case and let you know the result of your appeal in—'

'But can't you see?' Connie burst out. 'If you leave Paul in Brentwood Mental Hospital, you'll be condemning him to a living death.'

337

Mr Humphrey gave them a bland smile. 'Thank you, Miss Byrne, Dr Mac—'

'They're the Irish Infantry colours you're wearing, aren't they, Dr Cummings?' said Hari.

Connie turned and looked at him incredulously.

Although he'd worn the same inscrutable expression throughout the proceedings, now his dark eyes were like chips of flint and his mouth was pulled into an uncompromising line.

Dr Cummings looked taken aback. 'Yes. Yes they are,' he replied, smoothing the green red and blue striped tie that Hari referred to.

'So you saw action in North Africa,' said Hari.

'And Italy,' said Cummings, his chest visibly swelling. 'I see you were RAMC,' he said, indicating Hari's tie.

Hari nodded. 'In the Far East and in a Jap POW camp for three years.'

The panel looked at him with admiration, as well they might.

'Damn inhuman the way the Goons treated you chaps,' said Mr Humphrey.

Miss Frobisher nodded. 'Hanging was too good for them.'

'Yes, they should have been put in camps and treated the same,' said the matron.

Hari's right eyebrow rose. 'Well, at least we had a roof over our heads,' he said smoothly.

The matron's cheeks flamed red.

'But of course,' continued Hari in the same light tone, 'we could save ourselves a lot of bother and expense if we adopted Herr Hitler's solution to disabilities. What was the phrase the Nazis used to describe people like Paul?' He looked up as if trying to remember, then clicked his fingers. 'Ah yes, "lives unworthy of living".'

'Really, Dr MacLauchlan,' snapped Mr Humphrey, his complexion turning an unhealthy puce and his eyes bulging. 'I don't think I like your tone.'

'And I am *certain* I don't like the attitude of this so-called appeal panel. Tell me, if you can, how does "each according to his need" fit into your deliberations? Surely Paul Gillespie is exactly the sort of person Professor Beveridge had in mind when he wrote his report.'

The chair scraped across the bare boards as Hari stood up.

'Let's go, Connie,' he said softly, taking her elbow.

Looking at him through unshed tears, love surged up in her.

Feeling his strength surrounding her, Connie rose to her feet and turned towards the four people who held Paul's fate in their indifferent hands.

'Thank you for your time,' she forced out over the lump clogging her throat.

Hari took a folded handkerchief from his pocket and handed it to her. She dabbed her eyes as he led her gently towards the door but, as he opened it for them to leave, Hari turned and addressed the panel again.

'I'd like you to ask yourself this question while you're deliberating. Why did thousands of men and women sacrifice their lives to defeat Hitler if a cold, impersonal Victorian institution is the best we can offer Paul Gillespie?'

Waiting for the lights to change at Gardeners' Corner, Hari stole a quick look at Connie, sitting beside him in the passenger seat.

When they'd got back in the car after leaving the appeal panel, she'd valiantly rallied to his attempts to cheer her, but by the time they'd passed the Green Man at Leytonstone they had lapsed into silence. That was forty minutes ago and now she just sat staring miserably out of the window. He didn't blame her, he didn't feel too cheery himself.

The amber light flashed on so Hari put the car into gear and they moved off. They turned right into Commercial Street and, a few moments later, Hari rolled to a halt outside Fry House.

Hari pulled on the handbrake.

'Here we are, home safe and sound,' he said, turning in his seat to face her.

'Thank you, Hari, for coming with me to the panel,' she said, giving him a brave little smile.

'My pleasure,' he said.

'And I thought what you said was marvellous,' Connie replied, her blue eyes full of admiration.

Hari stretched his arm and rested his hand lightly on the back of her seat. 'Thank you but I do wonder if my little outburst didn't do more harm than good.'

339

She shook her head and the thick curl of her ponytail brushed across the back of his hand. Hari's fingers tightened on the leather seat to stop himself from catching it.

'It doesn't matter,' she said, oblivious to how close she was to being kissed. 'You were right and I was glad you were there with me whatever happens.'

'This isn't the end, Connie,' he said seriously. 'If that bunch of pompous idiots turn down our appeal we'll take it further.'

She looked puzzled. 'Can we?'

'One of the small advantages of being a POW is that you get to meet people from all walks of life.' He gave her a wry smile. 'I've shared half a bowl of rice with chaps who are now MPs, barristers, partners in accountancy firms, journalists and belted earls, so we'll take it to the Houses of Parliament if necessary.'

'Oh, Hari,' she whispered, tears brimming again. She pulled his handkerchief from her sleeve and dabbed her eyes again, then laughed. 'Look at the mess I've made of your hanky,' she said, holding it out to show him the dots of mascara. 'I'll wash it and let you have it back.'

'Don't worry, I've got dozens.' He smiled.

Connie smiled back, then she caught sight of his watch.

'Goodness, I should let you go,' she said. 'You'll have people queuing outside the surgery soon. See you tomorrow.'

'Yes, see you tomorrow,' he replied.

Grabbing her handbag from the footwell, Connie opened the door. She hesitated and then before he realised what she was doing, she leant across, kissed him on the cheek and jumped out.

Hari sat frozen to the spot as she hurried up the nurses' home stairs and disappeared through the door.

When he'd told her that she looked nice, he was lying. With the wintry sunlight burnishing her copper hair, her warm smile, blue eyes and the slimness of her belted waist, she didn't look nice, she looked absolutely gorgeous.

Of course, it wasn't just her outward desirability that captivated him, it was her inner loveliness, too. He'd seen it in everything she'd done since the day they'd met but today, seeing her determined to fight the world for Paul, made the beauty of Connie complete. Sadly, as he stared dumbly after her, he resolved to do what he'd been putting off doing and write to Dr

Atwell to accept the offer of a partnership at Duckwood Drive Clinic.

Somehow Connie's legs carried her into Fry House but as soon as she was through the door, she staggered into the nearest chair. Resting back, she closed her eyes and relished the fading sensation of the roughness of Hari's cheek on her lips.

She took several deep breaths, trying to calm the thoughts whirling round in her head.

Opening her eyes, Connie stood up and went over to the telephone on the hall table and picked up the receiver. She dialled and it rang three times before it was picked up.

'Good afternoon, Bethnal Green Town Hall, how can I help you?' said the telephonist in a posh cockney voice.

'Extension 102, please,' said Connie.

'Trying to connect you now, caller,' said the girl at the other end of the line.

There was a click and the line buzzed. After a couple of seconds, the phone was picked up. 'Roads and Highways.'

'Malcolm, it's me.'

'Connie, you know receiving personal calls in council time is frowned upon,' he said in a hushed tone.

'I know and I'm sorry,' said Connie, clutching Hari's handkerchief tightly in her hand. 'But I need to talk to you.'

It was just before eight in the evening by the time Connie turned into Malcolm's street and people were already closing their curtains and putting out the milk bottles ready for the morning. Reaching his mother's front door, Connie paused and took a deep breath to steady her pounding heart then, pressing her lips firmly together, she reached for the knocker.

She banged it twice and a dog a few doors along started barking.

Thankfully for Connie's fluttering stomach, Malcolm opened the door within a few moments. He was dressed in his old clothes with his shirt collar open and his sleeves rolled up.

'Hello, Malcolm.'

'Hello, Connie.'

He stood back and she walked in.

341

He turned his cheek towards her as she passed but she didn't take him up on the offer.

'I thought I might at least get a kiss for ducking out of the troop's committee meeting,' he said, closing the door behind her.

Connie turned and forced a smile. 'Is your mother in?'

He shook his head.

'I think she's at the church arranging flowers, she was already out when I got in,' Malcolm said. 'Do you want a cup of tea?'

Connie let out a long breath and shook her head. 'No, thank you.'

'Do you mind if I make myself a—'

'Could we go into the lounge?' asked Connie.

Malcolm looked puzzled but pushed open the parlour door. 'Of course.'

Clutching her handbag tightly, Connie walked in.

'Aren't you going to take off your coat?' he asked as he followed her in.

She shook her head again.

He laughed. 'This is all a bit dramatic, isn't it?'

'I'm sorry, Malcolm, but would you sit down, please?' Connie cut in, her heart starting to pound again.

Malcolm shrugged and lowered himself onto the sofa.

He slapped both hands on his thighs. 'So, Connie, what is it you have to talk to me about that couldn't wait until tom—'

'I can't marry you, Malcolm,' Connie blurted out.

'Don't be silly,' he laughed. 'We've got it all planned.'

'I'm sorry. I thought once we married, things would be all right but I now—'

'I know what this is all about,' said Malcolm.

'Do you?'

'Of course, it's wedding jitters.' He laughed. 'I'm told everyone has them—'

'Will you listen to me for once, Malcolm,' snapped Connie. 'It's not wedding nerves; it's me. *Me.* Do you understand? *Me.* I don't want to marry you.'

'But—'

The front door banged.

'Malcolm, are you home?' his mother's shrill voice demanded from the hallway.

'In here, Mum,' he shouted, standing up.

The door opened and she strode in.

'Why aren't you at Sco—' She spotted Connie. 'Oh, you're here.'

'I needed to speak to Malcolm,' said Connie.

'But it's his Scouts night, you know that,' Mrs Henstock replied.

'Yes, but—'

'Well then, you know how much the boys depend on him—'

'Connie says she's calling off the wedding,' Malcolm said, as if announcing the arm had come off his favourite teddy.

His mother's mouth pulled into a tight bud.

'That's why I had to speak to Malcolm urgently,' said Connie, feeling the burn of Mrs Henstock's stare. 'I'm sorry but I thought it best to say something before—'

'She doesn't mean it, do you, Connie?' said Malcolm. 'It's just the wedding jitters.'

'The jitters, my eye. Playing fast and loose behind my poor Malcolm's back more like.' Hilda gave her a distasteful look. 'I always said you were a flighty piece.'

Malcolm glanced nervously at his mother. 'Now, Mum, there's no need for—'

'Go on, Malcolm, ask her if you don't believe me,' spat Hilda, her eyes still fixed on Connie.

With a sigh, Malcolm turned to Connie. 'Is there anyone else, Connie?'

Images of Hari flashed through Connie's mind, but she held Malcolm's gaze.

'I promise you, Malcolm,' she said in as calm a voice as she could muster. 'I am not seeing anyone else.'

He raked his fingers through his hair. 'Then why, Connie, why?'

'Because I don't love you, Malcolm,' Connie said quietly.

All three of them stared in silence for a few seconds, then Malcolm collapsed onto the sofa and, resting his elbows on his knees, held his head in his hands.

Going over to him, Hilda slipped her arm around her son's slumped shoulders and turned her glare on Connie.

'I'm sorry,' said Connie. 'I really am but—'

'Don't apologise to me,' cut in Hilda. 'I didn't want Malcolm to marry you in the first place. Don't think I didn't know that you saw my Malcolm as a cushy meal ticket, what with him having a steady job in the council and all.' Her mouth pulled into an ugly shape. 'Now sling your hook, and don't come back.'

Connie twisted off her engagement ring and placed it on the coffee table.

She took a step back. 'I'll cancel everything and if there's any money to come back from the deposits I'll get someone to drop it around.'

'Make sure you do,' snapped Hilda, hugging Malcolm in her bony arms. 'And we'll have all my family's engagement presents back while you're at it. And I warn you. We have a list in case any of your family takes a shine to any of the expensive items.'

Connie regarded her coolly for a second, then shifted her attention to her ex-fiancé.

'Goodbye, Malcolm,' she said quietly.

He didn't reply but his features crumpled and he covered his face with his hands.

With a sigh, Connie turned and headed for the door but as she closed it behind her she heard Hilda speak again. 'Good riddance, that's what I say, because we don't need her, do we, sweetness?' she cooed in a little sing-songy voice. 'And just you wait and see. In a couple of days things will be back as they always have been; just you and me happy together.'

Chapter Twenty-Five

Connie squeezed her eyes tight for a second and then, opening them again, she looked back to the top of the nurses' rota and started working her way down the column of figures.

She was sitting at the spare desk in Miss O'Dwyer's office trying to make sense of the March timesheets so she could make sure they reached the local health authority by the payroll cut-off the following week.

It was just after three in the afternoon and it was a whole thirteen days since she'd broken off her engagement with Malcolm. She hadn't heard from him at all, but given his mother's venom towards her that night, perhaps it wasn't surprising. Now the tug of war between his mother and Connie was over, he was probably content to slip back into his old life of Scouting, model railways and train-spotting.

Although the scene with his mother had left her shaken and upset, it wasn't half as bad as when she'd broken the news to her mother. Predictably, Maud had ranted and raged and had refused to speak to her for a week. Having been practically thrown out of her mother's house, she'd tracked her dad down on the allotment. He'd made a typical dad joke about being glad he didn't have to be trussed up like a prize turkey all day but then he'd hugged her and told her he didn't mind who she did or didn't marry as long as she was happy. He'd also told her to take no notice of her mother because 'you know what a two and eight she gets into when she's got the hump'.

Thankfully, despite her mother threatening Mo and Bernie with the wrath of the Almighty and all his saints if they spoke to Connie, they totally ignored her and had been touchingly supportive. Her friends too, had rallied around, especially Millie, who said she felt sure Connie had made the right decision.

However, the thing that had preyed on her mind even more

than her eventful break with Malcolm was the fact that it was also thirteen days since she and Hari had attended Paul's appeal panel.

Allowing for some hours of intermittent sleep each night, this meant she'd spent approximately two hundred and twenty-one hours reliving every moment of being with Hari that day. It was pointless, of course, but what could she do?

Rubbing her temples in an attempt to loosen the tight band that seemed to have become a permanent fixture of late, Connie picked up her pen and checked down the column of figures again.

As she reached the bottom of the page, the door opened and Miss O'Dwyer strode in carrying two cups.

Connie gave the superintendent a wry smile. 'I thought you were just popping out.'

'Ah, well, now you know how it is,' Miss O'Dwyer replied. 'And wasn't I just on me way back from the kitchen when Mrs Jessup strolled in with her triplets, so I had to have a cuddle or two but I'm back now with some tea to keep us going.'

She offered Connie a cup.

'Thanks,' said Connie, taking it from her.

'Have you made any rhyme or reason out of the thing yet?' the superintendent replied, taking her seat behind her desk.

'I have,' said Connie. 'You took off the four hours when Mavis and Evelyn worked their half day instead of adding it on and you'd recorded half of Wendy's duties under Carole's name. Now I've made the corrections, the sums tally.'

Miss O'Dwyer looked heavenward and crossed herself. 'Praise Mary.' She winked. 'Didn't I know the first time I clapped eyes on you you'd be the best of women?'

Connie smiled. 'I'd save your bacon, don't you mean?'

She laughed and Miss O'Dwyer joined in.

'We ought to get them in the post to the payroll department or none of us will be getting paid,' Connie said. 'I'll pop them around to the main sorting office later.'

There was a knock on the door.

'Come!' bellowed Miss O'Dwyer.

The door opened and Beryl's head appeared around the edge of it.

'Sorry to disturb you both,' she said, looking anxiously at them. 'But by the sound of it, World War Three is about to break out in the baby clinic. Grace is supposed to be in charge but one of the mums said she ran out in tears about five minutes ago and hasn't come back. I think she's locked herself in the linen cupboard. I'd take over myself but I've just been called to a delivery and everyone else is still out. Sorry.'

Connie and Miss O'Dwyer rose to their feet.

'Thank you, me darling,' said Miss O'Dwyer to Beryl. 'I'll take charge of the clinic, Connie, if you find out what the fiddle and fight is with Grace.'

Leaving Miss O'Dwyer to restore order in the treatment room, Connie headed for the linen cupboard at the far end of the hallway. Before she reached it, she could hear muffled sobbing from behind the door.

Stopping outside, Connie hesitated for a second then knocked lightly. 'Grace.'

There was no answer.

'Grace, it's Connie. Could you open the door, please?'

There was a pause and the lock snapped back.

Connie walked in.

The narrow storeroom smelt of carbolic soap and starch. The walls were lined with pine shelves on which freshly laundered sheets, blankets and towels were stacked. There was a dress rail with pressed nurses' uniforms hanging on it and a round skip with a laundry bag hooked in place. Under the window at the far end, sitting on the wicker laundry basket and looking red-eyed and weepy, was Grace. She glanced up as Connie came in.

'I'm sorry, but Mrs King's little girl just—' Tears welled up and she covered her face.

Closing the door, Connie went over and sat beside her.

'What about Mrs King's little girl?' she asked.

'She . . . she looked so like Sarah.'

'Your sister's child?' asked Connie, remembering the photo she'd seen in Grace's room.

Grace looked up. 'She not my sister's, she mine. Sarah's my daughter and . . .' More tears rolled down her cheeks. 'It was her second birthday last week.'

347

She covered her face with her hands.

'I . . . I . . . just m . . . m . . . miss her so much,' she sobbed.

Connie pulled a towel off the shelf beside her and handed it to her fellow nurse.

'Thank you,' said Grace, taking it from her.

'Just don't tell Mrs Rogerson,' said Connie. 'Or she'll be after both of us.'

Grace forced a wet-faced smile.

'Where is Sarah now?'

'With foster parents,' Grace replied. 'But now this new Maintenance Order Act has come in, I'm hoping to get some financial support from her father so I can have her back with me. Hari said—'

'Is he the father?' asked Connie, the sound of blood pounding through her ears almost drowning out her own voice.

Grace looked puzzled. 'No. Why would you think—'

'But I saw you in the teashop together.'

'He was just trying to help me—'

'But he's not Sarah's father?' Connie repeated.

'No, Connie.' Grace gave a wry smile. 'I wouldn't be in this position if he was. Hari and I are just friends.'

The floor tilted for a second or two as Grace's words sank in.

A weight she didn't realise was pressing down on her suddenly lifted leaving her light-headed and with an overwhelming urge to laugh. Thankfully, given the circumstances, she managed to hold it back.

'But I don't know what I would have done without him these last few months,' continued Grace, her voice seeming to come from a long way away. 'When you saw us in the teashop we were meeting Hari's barrister friend from Chang prison, who specialises in such cases. Everyone said I should put her up for adoption and get on with my life but I just love her too much.'

'Didn't Sarah's father offer marriage when he found out?' asked Connie.

'He's already married,' Grace replied. 'We met in Hastings in 1940. He and Hari were in the same field unit . . .'

Grace told Connie the all-too familiar story of a wartime romance.

'I'm sorry, Connie,' Grace concluded, giving her a sheepish

smile. 'Hari wanted to tell you but I asked him not to until it was all sorted out.'

Feeling a sudden rush of affection for Grace, Connie put her arms around the young woman's slight shoulders.

'You poor thing,' she said, giving her a hug. 'But you should have told me. Perhaps I could have helped.'

'Hari said you would try, but I was afraid you'd think badly of me.' Taking a handkerchief from her uniform pocket, Grace blew her nose. 'Even with the way things have turned out, I don't regret a thing because I loved Giles so much nothing else in the world mattered except being with him. Can you understand that, Connie?'

Images of Hari suddenly flashed through Connie's mind making her heart swell and her pulse race.

'I certainly do, Grace,' said Connie. 'I most certainly do.'

'Are you, Connie?'

Connie stopped shuffling the carrots around on her plate with the knife and looked up. 'Am I what?'

'Going to eat that sausage?' repeated Harriet, who was sitting opposite her at the supper table.

It was now seven-thirty, three hours later, and Connie was in the refectory surrounded by her fellow nurses who, at the end of a long, hard day, were having their well-earned suppers.

'No,' said Connie, trying to gather her wayward thoughts together. 'You can have it if you want.'

'Ta very much,' said Harriet, spearing it with her fork. 'Can't let one of Mrs Rogerson's bangers go to waste.'

Connie gave her a weak smile.

'Are you all right, Connie?' her friend asked, slicing into her windfall.

She wasn't, not by a long chalk, but Connie forced a smile.

'Yes, I'm fine,' she said. 'Just not very hungry, that's all.' She stood up. 'Actually, I think I'll head off to my room.'

Leaving the bustle of the dining room behind her, Connie dashed up the two flights of stairs.

With her head spinning, she closed her door and leant with her back on it while the conversation with Grace replayed in her mind for the umpteenth time.

As her pounding heart settled, Connie opened her eyes and stared blindly through the window at the roof opposite.

Connie turned the wireless on and music filled the small room. She hummed along for a bit but, after the second song, she flipped it off again. She put the plug in the sink and turned on the tap so she could rinse her stockings through, but when it was full she changed her mind and let the water out.

She sat on the bed and gazed at her reflection in the mirror again for a long moment, then jumped up, stripped off the jumper and skirt she'd put on earlier and opened her wardrobe.

She pulled out her navy dress with the white collar and her fern-green gown with box pleats, both of which she then discarded. She tried on three more dresses before settling on her new half-circle black skirt and lilac blouse with a patent belt to complete the outfit.

She put on her shoes and jacket, then picked up her handbag, but as she reached for the door handle she paused.

Spinning around, she threw her coat over the back of the chair, dropped her handbag on the floor and then, kicking off her shoes, threw herself on the bed.

With her hands clasped across her middle, Connie stared blindly up at the ceiling as wild emotions raced through her. Wide-eyed, she studied the fringe of the lampshade until she could stand it no longer. Jumping off the bed, she shoved her feet back in her shoes, scooped up her handbag and jacket and ran out of her bedroom.

Hari pulled on his tie knot to loosen it and get some air to his neck. Although it was damp and chilly outside, thanks to the new boiler provided by Micky, the consultation room was somewhat stuffy. Still, he shouldn't complain as not only did he now have constant hot water throughout the property, but the ancient radiators in the waiting room and his accommodation above actually worked.

Surgery had run on a bit that evening so although it was now quarter past eight, a time when he would normally have been getting ready to tune in to *Twenty Questions* before listening to the evening news, he was still doing his paperwork.

Well, that wasn't strictly true. In truth, he'd filed the last set of patient notes ten minutes ago and since then he'd been trying to compose the two most difficult letters he'd ever written: his acceptance of the partnership at Duckwood Drive Clinic and his resignation from Christ Church surgery. But what choice did he have? Although it broke his professional heart not to see the innovations and improvements he'd planned for the surgery come to fruition, he had to write those letters. The thought of working with Connie once she was a married woman strengthened his resolve.

Hari poured himself a strong coffee, then took another sheet of headed notepaper from the stationery rack, but as he reached for his pen the front door banged shut.

Cursing himself for not locking it after the last patient, Hari was just about to rise from his chair when the consulting room door burst open and Connie strode in.

She was red-cheeked and her copper curls fell wildly around her shoulders. Her blue eyes sparkled brightly.

'Thank goodness,' she said, putting her hand to her chest as if to steady her rapid breathing. 'I thought I might have missed you.'

'What—'

She put her hand up. 'I need to tell you something but I don't want you to say anything or make any comment until I've said my piece.'

Hari settled back in the chair.

Looking at the ceiling for a moment or two, Connie took a deep breath. 'It's like this, Hari. My friend Millie, you know the one I told you about with the baby – well, she was in love with Alex. They were made for each other but he went away and she married Jim and it all went wrong. We were talking a while ago and she said . . .' Connie paused and frowned. 'Actually, come to think of it, she's said it a couple of times . . . She said I should be sure, completely sure, that I'm marrying the right man and if I had any doubts, any at all, then I should . . . should . . .' A damp curl of hair fell across Connie's face and she stopped to tuck it behind her ear. She began again. 'And I have had doubts . . . I have for a long time, months in fact, but after we went to Paul's appeal I realised I couldn't marry Malcolm, so I broke off our engagement.'

Hari was aghast. 'You called off the wedding two weeks ago!'

She nodded.

'Why didn't you tell me?'

'Because of Grace,' Connie replied.

'What's Grace got to do with this?'

'Please, Hari. I did ask you not to say anything.'

He sighed and sat back in the chair.

'I saw you holding hands in Petite Bertrands and I thought you were involved, so I held everything inside. I just thought you were being nice to me because you *are* nice, and that there couldn't be anything more . . . but today, in the linen cupboard, Grace explained about Sarah and told me that you were helping her get custody of her daughter.' Connie took a deep breath to steady herself. 'Then I couldn't stop wondering if maybe, just maybe, I wasn't imagining things and that the way you were when we were together, was more . . . more than just . . .'

A shiver of anticipation ran up Hari's spine.

'And once I let that thought run, I realised that perhaps . . .' Connie shifted her weight from one foot to the other. 'And I don't want to embarrass you . . . but I can't marry Malcolm or anyone . . . ' Connie's expression crumpled. 'Oh dear, I'm sorry, Hari, I'm making a real pig's ear of this and—'

'Connie,' Hari said, in as even a tone as his crashing heart would allow, 'what exactly are you trying to tell me?'

Clasping her hands together in front of her, she gave him a sheepish smile.

'I love you,' she told him in a tiny voice. 'I love you, Hari.'

Now, not only did Connie feel hot and sweaty, but utterly foolish too.

The sensible bit of her head had tried to stop her setting out on the half-mile sprint from Fry House to the surgery, but her heart wouldn't listen. Even her aching calf muscles and the blister had seemed worth the pain but, now, with Hari staring silently at her from behind the desk, she was beginning to wonder if she'd actually taken leave of her senses.

'I'm sorry, bu . . .' she blurted out when she could stand the silence no longer.

Hari slowly rose to his feet and Connie held her breath.

'And . . . and you don't have to say anything,' she burbled.

Stepping out from behind his desk, he came towards her.
'In fact, I'm not really expecting . . .'
He stopped in front of her and Connie raised her head.
'I just had to tell you,' she said in a strangled voice.
Hari's dark eyes ran slowly over her face and Connie's heart started beating in double time.

He looked down at her for what seemed like an eternity, then he smiled, cupping her face gently in his hands as he lowered his lips onto hers.

Connie stood motionless for a couple of seconds as her emotions caught up with her senses.

Then he lifted his head. 'I don't just love you, Connie. I absolutely adore you and—'

Her mouth stopped his words and she flung her arms around his neck.

He responded by gathering her into his embrace as his mouth pressed onto hers in a demanding kiss. His arms tightened around her as he lifted her off her feet. Connie wrapped her legs around his hips and he walked her to the wall, pressing her against it. His mouth left hers to plant feathery kisses across her cheek and down her neck, which sent excited shivers through her. With her heart beating wildly and her stomach fluttering uncontrollably, Connie clung to him, enjoying the thrill of her breasts being pressed against the hard muscles of his chest. Her hand raked through his hair, then across his back while his ran up and down her leg, rustling her skirt in the process.

Grabbing his hair, Connie raised his head. 'Let's go upstairs.'
Hari laughed and loosened his embrace.

Holding hands and between kisses, they careered down the hallway. Hari threw the bolt across the surgery entrance but as he opened the door to his flat, Connie broke free.

'Where do you think you're going?' he laughed, reaching to catch her.

Connie blew him an exaggerated kiss. 'Where do you think?'

Hari caught her around the waist but Connie twisted out of his embrace and raced up the stairs.

'Come back here, you cheeky wench,' Hari shouted after her as he took the stairs two at a time behind her.

Laughing, Connie paused long enough on the first floor to blow him another teasing kiss before tearing up the next flight of stairs. Hari galloped after her and caught her as they reached the top. Gathering her into his arms, he lowered his mouth on hers in a nerve-tingling kiss as they swung into the main bedroom.

Connie kicked her shoes off and, with their lips touching, Hari hopped on one leg and then the other as he plucked at the laces of his brogues.

Setting the springs protesting, they collapsed on the bed in a tangled embrace. Connie tore Hari's tie off and started on his shirt buttons while Hari did the same to her blouse. His hand cupped her breast as his lips traced a line along her collarbone. Not to be outdone, Connie's fingers ran through his chest hair while she kissed every part of him that came within range.

He pressed his mouth on hers again as his hand slid down her leg and under her skirt. Connie shivered as his fingers caressed up her stocking and reached the warm flesh of her thigh. The fluttering in Connie's stomach intensified and, with a sigh, she wound her legs around his hips and pulled him onto her.

His kiss deepened for a moment, then he raised his head. 'We shouldn't. Not like this.'

Connie frowned. 'Don't you want to?'

He raised an eyebrow.

'I certainly do,' he replied, pressing his erection against her. 'But me and you, we're for ever, aren't we, Connie?'

Connie slipped her arms around his neck and smiled. 'Yes, we are, Hari.'

'Then I want to do this right,' he said. 'I need to meet your family, then speak to your father, then we can sort out churches, wedding lists and receptions.'

Connie laughed. 'I suppose I can take that as a proposal of marriage, shall I?'

'You most certainly can, my darling,' he replied.

Connie pulled him down and kissed him.

'Then I accept,' she said softly, staring up into the face she'd loved for ever.

Connie stared up into his dark eyes and just as she was about to sink into them again, Hari raised himself up and got off the bed.

'What are you doing?' she asked.

He took her hand. 'I'm getting you off that bed before I change my mind.'

'I'll be all right from here,' said Connie as they reached the corner of Christian Street.

'Are you sure?' said Hari, stepping into a doorway and taking her with him.

'I'm certain,' said Connie.

Although the Kiwi polish clock hanging in the boot-mender's window showed it to be almost a quarter past three in the morning, across the road the lights were already being switched on in Spitalfields market.

Having removed themselves from the temptation of the bedroom, she and Hari had spent the best part of the night on the sofa wrapped in each other's arms. They had drunk coffee and talked about everything from the elastic in her navy knickers going in the middle of a netball match in the third year to him being hauled up in front of the dean of Medicine while at university for dressing the medical school skeleton as a ballet dancer, and everything in between.

When the national anthem played on the wireless, Connie had said she really should be going and Hari had agreed but another four hours flew by before she actually put on her coat. She would be at morning report in four hours but it didn't matter. Nothing mattered now that Hari loved her.

Smiling down, he slipped his arms around her and held her close. 'So when will I see you again?'

Connie gave him a wry smile. 'In about eight hours when I pop in at the end of my morning visits as usual.'

He lowered his lips on to hers briefly. 'How will I survive until then?'

'I'm sure your morning patients will help you pass the time,' Connie replied and kissed him back.

'I'll get some lunch in.' He kissed her briefly. 'Will you be able to speak to your family?'

Connie nodded. 'I'll go around to Mum's after work but I should be back by the time you've finished evening surgery.'

'Excellent,' he replied. 'I'll make us supper.'

355

Stretching up, she gave him a peck, enjoying the roughness of his unshaven cheek. 'I love you.'

'And I adore you.'

They kissed again and then Connie hurried off towards Fry House, waving briefly as she got to the back gates.

She located the back door key in its hiding place behind the rubbish bins and slipped through the door. The house was deathly quiet, so taking off her shoes Connie tiptoed along the corridor and into Miss O'Dwyer's office. Feeling her way around the furniture to the desk, she switched on the desk lamp and picked up the telephone. She quickly dialled the familiar number.

It rang three times, then it connected. 'East End Maternity Hospital, Sister Evans speaking, how can I help you?'

'Good morning, it's Sister Byrne from Fry House here, I'm sorry to disturb you but I believe Sister Smith is doing a bank shift with you tonight?' asked Connie.

'Yes, she's on B ward,' said the voice. 'I'll just put you through.'

The phone went quiet for a minute or two, then someone picked it up.

'Sister Smith speak—'

'Millie, it's me,' she said, cupping the mouthpiece with her hand. 'You'll never guess.'

Hari eased up on the accelerator and drew the car to a halt beside the door Connie had indicated. He pulled on the brake and looked across at her.

'Here we are then,' he said, giving her a wide smile.

'So we are,' she replied, returning a nervous one.

It was now three days since she'd burst into his surgery and made his life complete. Although he was glad he'd held back from making love to Connie, he wasn't made of stone, so he was thankful they'd decided to set a date for 1 July, a little over three months away. Of course, they couldn't make this official until he'd spoken to her father and he couldn't very well do that until he'd presented himself to the family, which is why he was dressed formally in a charcoal-grey suit with regimental tie.

'Do you think they are ready for us?' he asked.

'I should think they've been ready for an hour,' said Connie.

'Don't worry, sweetheart. I'll be on my very best behaviour,' he said, moving his finger across his chest. 'Cross my heart.'

She gave him a wry smile. 'It's not you I'm worried about, Hari, it's my mother.'

Grinning, Hari got out of the car and, strolling around to the passenger side, he opened the door.

'Come on then, the-future-Mrs MacLauchlan,' he said, taking her hand. 'Introduce me to my in-laws.'

Connie got out.

'Looks like word has got around,' he said as she straightened her skirt.

Connie glanced at the knots of neighbours chatting on doorsteps and pretending to be polishing their door knockers in the middle of a Sunday afternoon.

'Well then,' she said, slipping her arm around his neck, 'let's give them something to talk about.'

She kissed him and he hugged her close.

'You're a wicked woman, Constance Byrne,' he said as she released him.

'I certainly will be, Hari MacLauchlan,' she replied, giving him a sideways look that tightened his stomach.

She reached for the knocker but before she got to it, the door opened.

Standing in the doorway was a motherly looking woman in her late forties who he guessed was one of Connie's sisters.

'Hello!' she trilled, giving Hari a quick look-over.

'Hello, Mo,' said Connie, stepping in and hugging her sister briefly.

'And you must be Hari,' said Mo, offering him her work-worn hand.

'And you're Connie's big sister, Maureen,' he said, taking it. 'I've heard a lot about you.'

'Likewise, I'm sure. And it's Mo,' she said, herding them into the narrow passageway. 'Come in. Mum and Dad are in the front room with the rest of them.'

'I can't wait to meet them,' Hari said as Connie led him in.

The front room was packed wall to wall with members of the Byrne family who were either standing behind or squashed onto all available seats. The older children of the family were sitting cross-legged in their best clothes while a couple of toddlers scrabbled about amongst them. Hari guessed that one of the younger women standing by the dining table, which was laden with food and crockery, must be Connie's other sister, Bernie.

Connie's father, a kindly looking man in his mid-sixties uncomfortably buttoned up in his Sunday best, was sitting in one of the fireside chairs while Connie's mother, a rounded pint-sized woman, with scraped-back grey hair and wearing a dress and jacket with a diamanté broach on the collar, sat in the other. Although every pair of eyes in the room were fixed on Hari, only Mrs Byrne's were boring into him.

As they stopped in the middle of the tufted rug, Connie slipped her hand into his.

'Hello, everyone, I'd like you to meet Hari,' she said.

He and Connie stood hand in hand as the family said their collective 'hellos' and 'how dos' while Hari acknowledged them with a smile.

She squeezed his hand. 'Hari, this is my mum and dad.'

'It's lovely to meet you, Mrs Byrne,' he said, giving Connie's mother his warmest smile. 'Connie has told me so much about you I feel as if I know you already.'

Her lips pulled tightly together. 'Hairy, is it?'

'Hari. It's pronounced Hari,' he replied, with a polite smile.

'That's an odd sort of name, if you ask me,' she replied.

Hari felt Connie tense beside him but he maintained his polite expression.

'It's short for Harish,' he said, matching the older woman's implacable stare. 'But my full name is Jahindra Harish Chakravarthi MacLauchlan.'

Mrs Byrne's eyes narrowed and Hari turned his attention to her husband.

'It's a pleasure to meet you, too, Mr Byrne,' he said, offering his hand.

Connie's father stood up.

'Good to meet you, son,' he replied, shaking it.

Connie guided him towards the two women guarding the refreshments. 'And this is my sister Bernie and my sister-in-law . . .'

Twenty minutes later, after he'd been introduced to all the family individually, including her affable brother Jim, the formalities were complete. Much to their collective relief, the children were sent out to play 'nicely' in the backyard until tea was ready.

While the women set out the food and organised the making of the tea, Hari chatted to Connie's father and the other male members of the Byrne family about football, cricket and the running specification of his car. He also told them a little about his family and disappointed them all by admitting that although he'd ridden on several elephants in his time, he'd never shot a tiger. Finally, after Connie and her sister returned, carrying a teapot each, Mo announced the food was 'open'.

'Mind your manners,' said Bernie, giving the two older boys a hard look as they surged forward to fill their plates. 'You and Connie go first, Hari.'

Lightly placing his hand around Connie's waist, he guided her forward.

'Are you all right?' asked Connie in a low voice as they selected their sandwiches.

'Never better,' he replied. 'Although please don't ask me to recite everyone's name just yet.'

Connie smiled. 'I know, there are a lot of us, aren't there?'

Hari popped a sausage roll on his plate. 'I've counted eighteen if you include the babies.'

'Wait until you meet all my cousins,' said Connie.

Hari pulled a horror-struck face. Connie laughed as they stepped aside to let the others take their turn at the table.

Holding their plates in their hands, Connie and Hari milled around chatting to various members of the family as everyone munched their way through the spread. Once most of the sandwiches and cakes had disappeared, Jim and Sheila made their excuses and left with their children. As Mo and Bernie cleared the teacups away, their husbands wandered out to see what the children were up to. Connie led Hari to the sofa. As they took their seats, Hari nudged his thigh against hers. She nudged hers back and they exchanged a private look.

'Connie tells me you have an allotment, Mr Byrne,' said Hari as his prospective father-in-law settled himself back in his chair.

'That I have, down by the gas works,' Arthur replied. 'I grow mostly veg but now we don't have to dig for victory, I've planted the odd flower or two. Was your father much into his garden?'

Hari smiled. 'I'm afraid not.'

'And is it right your mother's a princess?' asked Connie's mother.

Hari smiled warmly at her. 'She is, Mrs Byrne, but then all female members of a Raj family are addressed as such, so there are hundreds of them in my family.'

'So what does that make you, a sir or something?' asked Arthur.

'In India it might.' Hari laughed. 'But the only designation I ever use is doctor.'

'Huh,' said Maud, adjusting her bosom with her folded arms. 'Your mate Millie married a nob, didn't she, Connie? Not that it did her much good.' She turned her caustic gaze on Hari. 'Left to bring up a kid by herself cos her posh old man skipped off with a bit of skirt.'

Connie gave her mother an exasperated look, but Hari continued to smile politely.

'Have you got any family in England, Hari?' asked her father.

'Yes, I have my Aunt Janet who lives in Waltham Abbey,' said Hari.

'We're having lunch with her next Saturday,' said Connie.

'She can't wait to meet Connie,' added Hari.

He cast a fond look her way and was rewarded with a dazzling smile.

'So what are you, then?' asked Mrs Byrne, her tart voice slicing between them.

Fashioning his face into a pleasant expression, Hari looked at her. 'I assume you're referring to my religion, Mrs Byrne, in which case I can tell you that although my mother and her family are Sikhs, I was baptised in the Anglican church in Rarpinde and confirmed into the Church of England during my fifth year at Repton, but I have to tell you honestly after three years as a Japanese POW, I'm not sure I can subscribe to any formal religion.'

'Well, my Connie's been brought up a good Catholic like all my children,' said Mrs Byrne belligerently.

'I know that,' said Hari. 'And I will do everything and anything I can to support her practising her faith.'

Connie's mother studied him suspiciously for a moment, then resumed chewing her lips.

There was a long pause and then Mr Byrne cleared his throat. 'Connie tells me now you've decided to stay put in Spitalfields you've got great plans for your surgery?'

Hari briefly outlined his plan to expand the surgery and offer more services.

'I can then contract another doctor on a sessional basis and provide a wider range of services, including child immunisation and family planning clinics,' Hari concluded.

Mr Byrne looked impressed. 'Sounds as if you've got it all mapped out, young man. Doesn't he, Mother?'

Connie's mother regarded him thoughtfully. 'I hope you don't mind me saying so, Hari, but you don't look as dark as I thought you would.'

Connie gave her mother a look that would have made a hospital consultant quiver like a jelly, but which bounced harmlessly off the elderly woman.

'Really?' Hari said lightly.

'Yes, you look more like an Eyetie than a darkie,' Maud continued cheerfully. 'I suppose that's down to the white side of your family.'

'It could very well be.' Hari took hold of Connie's hand. 'And I'm glad I meet with your approval, Mrs Byrne, especially as I would like to have the opportunity to speak with your husband.'

Shock flashed across Connie's mother's face. 'But you hardly know each other—'

'We know each other well enough, Mrs Byrne,' cut in Hari. He lifted Connie's hand to his lips and kissed her fingers. 'Don't we, darling?'

Connie gave him another dazzling smile that swelled his chest. 'Yes, we do.'

They exchanged another private look and her mother sniffed loudly.

Tearing his gaze from the woman he loved, Hari looked at her father. 'So if I might buy you a pint sometime soon, Mr Byrne?'

'I'll be in the Northern Star Monday lunchtime, if that's convenient, son,' said Mr Byrne.

'Then I'll be seeing you there,' said Hari.

Hari squeezed Connie's hand. 'I've had a lovely afternoon, but I'm afraid we have to make a move, don't we, sweetheart?'

'Yes we do,' Connie replied.

Hari stood up and so did Connie. She gave her father a hug and kiss before giving her mother a quick peck on her averted cheek.

Her father took his hand. 'Good to meet you, Hari, and it's Arthur.'

Hari turned to Connie's mother. 'Goodbye, Mrs Byrne.'

Flashing her new NHS dentures at him, Maud Byrne forced a smile. 'Goodbye, Hairy.'

Hari slipped his arm around Connie's waist and they left the house. He opened the car door for Connie and she climbed in. Scooting around to his side of the car, Hari jumped in.

Connie was slumped in the passenger seat with her eyes closed and a drained expression on her face. As he put the key in the ignition, she rolled her head towards him and looked at him bleakly.

'Well,' he said, turning on the engine and grasping the steering wheel. 'I think that went very well, don't you, darling?'

Chapter Twenty-Six

'And as you're going to Old Ford Road, Rose, would you mind adding Mrs Grundy to your list and then perhaps Beryl will take Mr Dalloway off your visits,' said Connie, looking across the heads of the two dozen or so nurses crammed into the treatment room for morning report.

'Sure,' said Rose, making a note.

It was just before eight o'clock on the first Monday in April and as Miss O'Dwyer was on a week's holiday, Connie was in charge of Fry House; hence her giving the daily report.

A whole week had passed since she'd taken Hari to meet the family. Connie had purposely not dropped in for her usual mid-week visit to her mother. She was still simmering with fury at her mother's unforgivable rudeness towards the man she loved. Not that Hari seemed to be put out by her mother's bare-faced animosity, he'd even found it mildly amusing and had pointed out that the rest of her family had welcomed him warmly. He'd also told her that if he'd taken notice of every racial slur or insult thrown his way, he'd never have survived school, university, the army and Japanese captivity. He was right, of course, but it didn't stop Connie feeling the pain for him.

In contrast with their dreadful visit to her mother's, the trip into the country to see Hari's Aunt Janet was a complete delight and by the time she'd got halfway through her first cup of tea, she'd already heard the story of how ten-year-old Hari had escaped by the skin of his teeth when he'd tried to take a short cut across the field where his Uncle Sandy kept his prizewinning Angus bull and, much to Hari's consternation, by the time the kettle went on for the second time, his aunt was talking Connie through the family photo album.

'I think that's it,' said Connie, scanning down the diary. 'Except to say that a letter from the Area Health Board arrived in Saturday's post informing us that from the first of January next year, domiciliary midwifery services for Spitalfield and Shoreditch, which we currently provide, will be moved into the Maternity Department of the London Hospital.'

There was a collective groan from around the table.

'And at the same time,' continued Connie, 'the Area's district nurses – that's us – will be moved to the first floor of Valence Road Clinic.'

'So those of us who are Queen's Nurses and midwives will have to decide where to go,' said Moira.

'Yes, I suppose we will,' said Connie. 'As from the first of January, the two roles will be separate.'

'That's such a shame,' said Fran.

'I know,' said Connie. 'But it's been on the cards since the NHS started and we're one of the last to have our services split, but it seems the London Hospital got the short straw and will be in charge of our community midwifery services from the new year.'

'What are you going to do, Connie?' asked Wendy.

'I'm not sure. I haven't decided . . . ' From nowhere, a yawn escaped her.

'What's the matter, Connie?' asked Fran. 'Not getting enough sleep?'

'It's all that dancing she's been doing with you know who,' added Rose, grinning at her.

'It's not the dancing making her so tired,' laughed Beryl, nudging the nurse next to her. 'If you know what I mean.'

'I certainly do,' agreed Wendy. 'But then who can blame her?' She gave an exaggerated wink and the nurses laughed.

The on-call phone rang in the hall and someone picked up.

There was a pause and then the door opened and Jane, who was on a day off and not in uniform, poked her head around the door.

'It's a Mr Daly in Lolesworth House,' she said. 'Says he thinks his wife is miscarrying—'

'I didn't know Mary Daly was pregnant again,' cut in Connie.

'Yes, she booked in a few weeks back and is about four months',' Rebecca replied. 'She didn't look well then, poor woman, although it's hardly surprising seeing she's got a house-ful and her youngest isn't a year old yet.'

'Well, her husband would like a midwife to come,' said Jane. 'So who's on call?'

'Mary is,' said Connie, rising to her feet. 'But I know her well so I'll go.'

With her thighs screaming with pain, Connie swung into Thrawl Street some ten minutes later and nearly ran Patrick Daly over as he dashed out from Lolesworth House.

'Praise be! It's yourself, sister. Mary's bleeding bad,' he said, crossing himself.

Stepping off her bike and leaving it with Mr Daly, Connie grabbed her bag and raced up the stairs two at a time until she reached the third floor. Half a dozen or so women dressed in their wraparound aprons with cigarettes dangling from their mouths turned to look at Connie as she hurried along the land-ing to the Dalys' flat. Without pausing, Connie pulled on the string dangling through the letter box and, releasing the latch, pushed the door open.

Passing the younger children huddled wide-eyed and silent on the sofa in the lounge, Connie dashed along to the bedroom. Mary, whose pallor was as white as the pillow beneath her head, lay curled up on the bed with her eyes closed and a grey army blanket draped over her. The cot wedged between the Dalys' double bed and the wall contained the twins while Peter lay kicking his legs on the bed next to his mother.

As Connie entered the room, Mary turned and opened her eyes. 'Sister, I . . . the baby's come away and . . .'

Connie snapped open her bag. 'When?'

'This morning,' Mary forced out between clenched teeth.

She clutched her stomach and curled forward. 'Sweet Mother of God!'

Connie pulled back the blanket and gasped.

The thin skirt of Mary's dress was blood-soaked from the waist down and the bedclothes beneath her were stained an om-inous shade of dark red.

With her heart thundering in her chest, Connie ran to the door.

'Call an ambulance,' she shouted at Mary's neighbours, shocking them into action. 'Tell them it's urgent.'

Connie dashed back to her patient and found Mary even whiter with her lips now a distinct shade of blue.

'Mary!' Connie shouted. 'Wake up, Mary!'

The two toddlers in the cot started to wail.

'Come on, Mary, your children need you,' yelled Connie. 'Open your eyes.'

Mary's eyes flickered open.

Relief flooded over Connie.

'That's it, Mary. The ambulance is coming, but you must stay awake,' she said, snatching the two untouched pillows beside Mary's head. 'Roll over for me, Mary, and lift your bottom.'

Grimacing with pain, Mary struggled onto her back, then lifted her hips a fraction and Connie shoved the pillows under her.

'Breda!' she called, taking the towel from her bag and wiping the fresh blood from her forearms.

The Dalys' eleven-year-old daughter appeared at the door. 'Ma?'

Mary's eyes flickered open again and softened as she gazed fondly on her firstborn.

'Could you be a good girl and get me a large mug of water, please, sweetheart?' said Connie in as steady a voice as she could manage. 'And I need an old towel, too.'

Breda nodded and left.

Taking Mary's limp hand, Connie felt for her pulse. She didn't need to count the beats to know it was not only weak and thready, but dangerously fast.

Breda Daly returned with a couple of grey rags over her arm and handed Connie a chipped mug.

'Is it the baby making Ma sick?' Breda asked, looking fearfully at her mother.

'Yes, it happens sometimes,' Connie replied, giving the child a reassuring smile. 'But once she gets to hospital they should be able to help her. Now, you go and make sure your brothers and sisters are all right while I look after Mum.'

Breda nodded and went back in the lounge where Connie could hear her getting a game of I-spy going.

The appearance of their elder sister had quietened the twins in the cot and they now sat sucking their thumbs and watching Connie tend their mother. Peter lay contentedly on the bed. The front door banged and Mr Daly stormed back into the flat. Connie pulled the blanket back over his wife just as he rounded the bedroom door.

'How is she?' he said, squatting down beside the bed and taking his wife's hand.

'Stable,' said Connie, wishing it were so. 'But we have to get her to hospital. Is there anyone who can have the children?'

'Mrs Cohen below has said to send them down,' Mr Daly replied.

'Well, take them down, then go and wait for the ambulance,' said Connie.

Mr Daly nodded, then kissed his wife's clammy forehead. He went to the door. 'Will you come and kiss your mother?'

A lump formed in Connie's throat as Mary's children trooped in one by one. Breda scooped up the sleeping Peter and placed him over her shoulder, the other two girls took hold of the twins' hands and the family left.

The flat fell silent. Pulling back the bedclothes, Connie cast her eyes over her patient.

The towel between Mary's legs was already saturated as the bright red stain under her spread further. By her reckoning, Mary had lost at least two pints of blood, possibly three, which was a great deal more than she would have expected from a spontaneous miscarriage.

'Mary,' said Connie, shaking her patient gently. 'Can you tell me what exactly happened?'

Mary opened her eyes and tears welled in them again. 'You should have seen him. Such little hands and feet, but so small he would have fitted into the palm of . . .'

Her face crumpled.

'You what, Mary?'

'I poked him out with a knitting needle,' she whispered.

A cold hand closed around Connie's heart.

'I know I'm wicked and shall go to hell,' continued Mary. 'But we can barely feed and clothe the ones we have without adding to their number—'

The front door banged open.

'In the end room!' Patrick Daly shouted from the other end of the passageway.

Two burly ambulance men appeared carrying a rolled-up stretcher. Connie replaced the sodden towel between Mary's legs and then stood back to let the ambulance men do their job. When they'd tucked his wife under the red blanket, Patrick took her hand.

'There you go, me darling,' he said with a crack in his voice. 'The docs at the London will soon have you fixed up and fit again.' He kissed her hands, making them wet with his tears. 'And remember what Father Flaherty says about bowing to God's will in all things.'

Mary gave him a heart-wrenching smile by way of an answer and then her gaze rested on Connie.

'Will you say a prayer for me?' she asked as the ambulance men carried her from the room.

Tears pinched the corner of Connie's eyes and she nodded, fervently hoping God was listening.

Reaching down into the pram, Michael Weinstein gently lifted his new daughter out from amongst the pink blankets and frilly lace covers.

'Hello, Hannah, welcome home,' said Connie, smiling at the infant.

Hannah Weinstein gave a windy smile and then, oblivious of her besotted parents' gaze, went back to sleep.

Although it was now some two and half hours since the ambulance carrying Mary had departed, with its bell ringing and its tyres squealing, Connie was still shaking from the incident. She'd done three or four visits before popping back to Fry House and ringing the hospital. She was informed that Mary had been given three pints of blood on arrival, then taken down to the operating theatre and had not yet returned.

The sister in charge of Casualty added that they'd had trouble bringing Mary's blood pressure up from its critical level and even when they had, the doctor hadn't been able to rouse her from her unconsciousness, nor had Mary responded to pain stimuli, which was even more worrying.

With nothing more to do but wait, Connie set out on her remaining calls. By eleven o'clock, however, with thoughts of poor Mary and her aborted baby still troubling her, Connie felt a cuddle from the newest member of the Weinstein household would help.

Hannah had been born by caesarean section eight weeks ago, at two months earlier than her due date. As Hari promised on hearing Esther's condition, Professor Myerson at the Elizabeth Garret Anderson had taken over Esther's care. This had been pretty straightforward until the five-month mark, when Esther started showing traces of sugar in her urine and was taken into hospital.

Having languished there on bed-rest for five worrying weeks while baby Weinstein grew, Esther was finally taken in to theatre the week after Easter. Weighing less than a bag of sugar, Hannah had nonetheless taken her eight weeks in an incubator in her stride. Finally, having doubled her weight, she'd been allowed home to get on with the rest of her life.

As ever when Connie visited the Weinsteins, there was tea and a hefty slice of cake, which Esther placed on the packing case next to her.

'She is the most perfect baby ever born,' said Michael. 'And so clever! I swear she turned her head when I called her name yesterday.'

Esther rolled her eyes.

'Listen to him,' she said. 'She'll have her name down for Oxford next time you call.'

'Cambridge,' corrected Michael, tickling his new daughter's hand to make her fingers curl around his enormous one. 'And why shouldn't I? Anyone with half an eye can see my girl's a genius.'

'See!' said Esther to Connie. 'What did I say? Wrapped around her little finger.'

Connie laughed. 'And just as it should be.'

Esther grasped Connie's hand firmly.

'Thank you, Connie,' she said, a tear shimmering in her eye. 'If it wasn't for you standing up to Dr Marshall she wouldn't be here.'

'No, she wouldn't,' said Michael firmly. 'When I think of what might have happened, I—'

He pressed his lips onto his daughter's downy head and closed his eyes.

'To be honest,' Connie said over the thickness in her throat, 'losing a twin past four months and having the other survive is very, very, rare.'

'Rare, shrare,' said Esther. 'The fact of the matter is he's a doctor and so should know about such things.'

'I'm just thankful for everyone's sake he's gone,' said Michael. 'But it's a pity he had to nearly kill a child before the authorities stepped in.'

'Him and that shyster Crowther,' added Esther. 'How is Mr Murphy's little angel?'

'Fully recovered,' said Connie. 'In fact, I saw Pamela only last week when I attended the Shoreditch Junior School's assembly.'

'So I hear things are changing at Christ Church surgery,' said Michael, 'and not just the paint on the walls.'

'Yes, they are,' said Connie. 'Now Hari's set up a second consulting room, he's persuaded Dr Gingold, who specialises in treating children who fail to thrive, to do a monthly surgery. He's also got the Area Health people to agree to fund a part-time GP to work Monday and Wednesday and she started two weeks ago.'

'She?' said Esther.

'Yes, Dr Amanda Scott,' said Connie. 'She's been covering as locum for the past three months but is really looking for something more permanent. Her husband was killed in the push across Germany, leaving her with a two-year-old son. She was a GP in Bermondsey before the war, so the Spitalfields and Shoreditch area holds no surprises for her.'

'It all sounds very up to date and modern,' said Michael.

'Now he's decided not to take the post in Harold Hill, Dr MacLauchlan is determined to make Christ Church surgery one of the best in the area.'

'I'm sure his patients are very pleased,' said Esther.

'I know we are,' chipped in Michael. 'No more illegible prescriptions.'

'Or complaining phone calls,' added Esther.

'Oiya,' said both Weinsteins, rolling their eyes.

'Now,' said Connie, swallowing the last of her tea, 'I've been here a full fifteen minutes and haven't yet had my promised cuddle from Miss Weinstein.'

'One cuddle coming up,' said Michael. Manoeuvring his daughter into position, he handed her to Connie.

Tucking Hannah into the crook of her arm, Connie adjusted the baby's blanket and gazed down at the sleeping infant.

Hannah gave a little sigh that squeezed Connie's heart with longing.

'So beautiful,' she said softly, noting the hairline purple veins on Hannah's closed eyelids and the minute eyelashes.

'I agree,' said a deep voice.

Connie looked up.

Hari was standing in the doorway of the chemist's back room dressed in his cavalry twill trousers, Harris tweed jacket and matching waistcoat with his regimental tie at his throat.

'Which one of them?' laughed Michael.

'Both,' said Hari. He shook the pharmacist's hand. 'I'm so pleased your daughter's home at last.'

The new father's eyes grew misty again as he shook Hari's hand.

'I'd say having a baby in her arms suits our Connie, wouldn't you?' said Esther with a twinkle in her eyes.

Hari's eyes softened a little as they gazed on Connie. 'I certainly would.'

Crossing the space between them, he slipped his arm around Connie's waist and kissed her on the cheek. 'Hello, darling. I spotted your bike chained up outside so thought I'd pop in.'

'I'm glad you did,' she said, drawing strength from his closeness.

'Bad morning?'

She forced a smile. 'I've had better.'

He hugged her affectionately. 'Well, perhaps this will cheer you up, my love. I just had a phone call from Mr Humphreys, the chairman of Paul Gillespie's appeal tribunal.'

'And?' asked Connie.

Hari grinned. 'They granted the appeal and have agreed that he be moved to Buntington House. We'll both be getting an official letter this week sometime, but they wanted to let me know.'

'Oh, that's wonderful,' Connie cried. 'Did they say when?'

'Probably in about six weeks,' Hari replied. 'And I thought once he's had a few days to settle in, we might take a Sunday afternoon drive out to see him, what do you say?'

'Sounds just perfect,' Connie replied.

Standing up, she planted a light kiss on his cheek and Hannah gave a little cry of protest.

'I know I haven't got the same claim on the lovely Hannah as Connie, but may I have a cuddle, too?' he asked.

'Of course you can,' said Michael.

Hari held out his arms and Connie gave Hannah to him, catching the scent of his aftershave as she did.

'Hello, young lady,' said Hari as he settled the baby in his arms. 'You don't know me but you're going to see me a great deal over the next few years. Mainly, I'm afraid, for things you won't like but I hope, despite the fact I'll be sticking a needle in your leg at regular intervals, we can still be friends.'

Esther laughed. 'I'm sure you will.'

'And you'll be seeing Sister Byrne, too, but only so she can make sure you're growing properly,' Hari continued. 'Although she'll be Sister MacLauchlan by the time you get to know her.'

'Well, she will be if Dr MacLauchlan meets her father in the Northern Star in a bit,' said Connie, giving Hari a wry smile.

Esther laughed. 'So that's why you're all spruced up on a Monday lunchtime, Hari, to impress your prospective father-in-law.'

'Indeed,' said Hari. 'And much as I'm enjoying holding this lovely young lady, I ought to head off.'

He handed Hannah, who was still sound asleep, back to her father.

'So should I,' said Connie, taking up her nurse's bag from the floor. 'I'll walk out with you.'

Having said their goodbyes to Esther and Michael, Connie and Hari wove their way through the customers in the shop and out into the street.

'Well, wish me luck,' said Hari as Connie plonked her bag into her cycle basket.

'Good luck,' said Connie.

Slipping his arm around Connie, Hari kissed her briefly, then jumped into his car which he'd parked in front of the chemist and drove off.

Connie watched him speed away for a second, then turned to unlock her bicycle. As she did, two women walked past.

'Did you see that?' said one, tutting loudly.

'I certainly did,' her friend replied. 'Disgraceful! And her a nurse, too.'

Just thirty minutes after leaving Connie, Hari drew up outside the Northern Star public house. A modest Victorian beer house with a painted sign over the door and tinted windows with the breweries' names painted in gold across them, it sat on the corner of White Horse Road and Matlock Street and had probably been serving the local population of dockers and craftsmen for nigh on a hundred years.

Getting out and locking the car, Hari slipped the keys in his pocket and pushed open the squeaky door to the public bar.

The interior of the pub had the same comfortable time-worn feeling as the exterior, with half of the U-shaped polished counter to one side with a frosted-glass panel screen off the salon bar.

It was just after twelve-thirty on the first day of the working week and, as Hari had suspected, the handful of customers frequenting the watering hole were pensioners. Tucked in the corner were two old men in flat caps both with a roll-up dangling from their lips, crouched over a game of cribbage while another couple of senior citizens were setting up a game of dominos. The publican, polishing a short glass behind the bar, was a jovial-looking chap with a bald head and bushy moustache.

As the double-hinged door swung back and forth behind him, the whole bar turned and looked at Hari.

'Over here, son!'

Hari looked around and saw Connie's father sitting at the far end of the room alongside a long rubber mat and pitted dartboard.

'Get yourself a drink and come over.' Mr Byrne held up his empty glass. 'Mine's a pint of brown.'

The publican flipped his tea towel over his shoulder and put down the glass as Hari strolled across to the bar.

'Pint of brown and half of bitter shandy, please,' said Hari.

The landlord took a pint glass from the rack above. 'You must be Connie's doctor chap.'

'Yes, I am,' said Hari.

'Lovely girl is Connie, lovely girl,' said the publican, placing Mr Byrne's frothy pint on a towelling runner.

'I agree,' said Hari.

'She's always been my favourite, she has.' The landlord placed Hari's drink next to the other. 'That's a bob and three.'

Hari gave him one and six, then popped his thru'penny bit change in the Sally Army collection tin. He picked up the two drinks and went over to join Connie's father.

'Ta, son,' said Mr Byrne as Hari placed his drink in front of him.

Hari took the chair opposite him and took a mouthful of shandy.

'You're not a drinker then,' said Mr Byrne.

'Not really and certainly not at lunchtime when I've a full surgery later, although I am partial to a single malt on a special occasion. Have you got anything running?' Hari asked, indicating the ancient wireless sitting on a shelf with the racing commentary playing.

Mr Byrne shook his head. 'I ain't never seen a poor bookie, so I keep my money in me pocket. You?'

'I might have a couple of bob on the Grand National and a shilling each way on the Gold Cup but that's about it,' said Hari.

Connie's father nodded approvingly. 'Me old father was one for the horses. Used to pawn his best suit on Monday and put a couple of coppers on something running in the three o'clock then get himself down to the dock gates to wait in line for the chance of a day's work. Sometimes he'd be lucky but more often than not he'd back something with three legs so he'd have to break his back all week to earn enough for me mother's housekeeping and to get his suit out of hock ready for Friday night mass.'

'Your father was religious then,' said Hari, pleased to find Connie's father was a lot chattier when his wife wasn't around.

'Not so much religious as scared witless of me mother. If he wasn't turned out proper to take us to confession on a Friday night and mass on Sunday, then he might as well leave the country.' Arthur chuckled. 'My father was as tall as you with flaming red hair and a temper to match, but when my mother had her dander up he'd hide in the coal hole rather than face her.'

Hari laughed.

Arthur scrutinised his face. 'I don't suppose your father had to pawn his jacket at any time?'

Hari gave a wry smile. 'I shouldn't think so.'

'And his father?'

'Was a doctor in Edinburgh,' said Hari. 'As was my great-grandfather.'

Arthur took a mouthful of beer. 'And am I right in thinking you played down your mother's family a bit?'

'Just a little,' said Hari. 'But after spending three years as a starving POW, I regard many things, such as rank and status, quite differently.'

Arthur nodded. 'I can see why you might. I'm also guessing you're not short of a bob or two either.'

'Not now the Indian government has lifted the restrictions on banks,' Hari replied.

Arthur nodded approvingly. 'I was in the trenches alongside a Sikh regiment at Neuve Chapelle.'

'Were you?'

'Yes. They always looked smart with their turbans and polished boots, they did, even when the rest of us looked like Thames rats. Blood-fierce fighters they were, I can tell you. Used to frighten the willies out of the Germans, especially with their curved knives.'

'Well, Sikh warriors are known for their ferocity in battle,' said Hari.

'They had bloody good officers too,' Arthur added. 'Not like our stupid lot. But you know what Tommies are like for complaining.'

Hari smiled. 'They'd be complaining to St Peter that there was nothing in Heaven to complain about.'

'Exactly,' said Arthur. 'But those Sikh boys never carped. Not once. They were . . . what's the word?'

'Stoic,' said Hari.

'That's it – stoic.'

They both swallowed another mouthful of their drinks, then Arthur spoke again.

'Did you see that little worn statue of the Virgin on our mantelshelf when you were around our house?'

'I did,' said Hari.

'That were my mother's. Her mother gave it to her and she was holding it when she died. Marie O'Riley was her name.'

'Connie's middle name,' said Hari.

'Yes, she was named for her,' said Arthur. 'My dear mother raised thirteen of us in two rooms and on pennies and halfpennies, but she never laid a hand to us, not once. She worked from morning till night scrubbing other people's floors and still kept our home spotless. Sometimes we had nothing but potatoes for days and yet she'd always have enough in the pot for a poorly neighbour.' A misty look crept into his eyes. 'I loved my mother and I tell you, my darling Connie's just like her.'

Hari put down his drink and looked the other man in the eye. 'I love Connie more than I can say, Mr Byrne. I have asked her to be my wife. She has made me the happiest man alive by saying yes, but we both very much want your blessing before we make our engagement official and start planning a wedding.'

Arthur smiled. 'I could tell from the way you two looked at each other that you were meant for each other, so if she's happy to have you as a husband then I'm happy to welcome you to the family.'

'Thank you, Mr Byrne.' Hari offered his hand. 'I can also promise you that I will care for her and do everything in my power to make her happy.'

'I know you will, son,' said Arthur, taking Hari's hand.

They shook, then Connie's father stood up. 'I think this might warrant something a little stronger, don't you think?'

'Well, perhaps half a measure and well watered,' said Hari, rising to his feet.

They went to the bar.

'Right, Bill,' said Arthur, addressing the landlord. 'This is Dr Hari MacLauchlan, who will soon be my new son-in-law, so I'm after buying us both a Scotch.'

'Right you are.' The landlord looked expectantly at Hari. 'We've got Black and White or Haig. What's your poison?'

Ignoring his protesting taste buds, Hari smiled. 'A Haig will do nicely.'

Although it was mid-April, the rain lashed against the window of the City of London crematorium as if it were a mid-November.

Connie sat on a hard wooden pew at the back of the mock-Victorian chapel wearing her newest uniform and freshly steamed felt hat. Her attention, like everyone else's, was focused on Mary Daly's wooden coffin.

In the pews in front of her were many familiar faces from Lolesworth House, plus others she didn't recognise. In the front row sat Patrick Daly in a well-worn suit and next to him was a man who could have only been his brother. In front of them, and standing beside Mary's coffin, was Father Flaherty.

He had conducted Mary's funeral mass in St Anne's before the main funeral party had travelled in procession to the crematorium.

Because of her duties, Connie hadn't been present at Mary's service, but Miss O'Dwyer had given her the time off to attend her patient's final committal.

As Father Flaherty prayed over Mary's body, Connie cast her gaze over him. Dressed in his full regalia of lacy surplice, black stole and belt along with his pinched-top cap, he dominated the gloomy sanctuary, his gimlet eye ensuring his flock maintained proper order and reverence. As he raised his arms in exhortation to Mother Mary, his eyes rested on Connie. He regarded her impassively for a second or two, then his gaze swept onto another.

'. . . life is short and the hour of death unknown,' he continued as two ushers from the local undertakers Tadman and Sons stepped forward. They took hold of the edge of the red velvet curtain and Father Flaherty raised his right hand theatrically.

'As we take leave of our sister, Mary Catherine Daly, give our hearts peace . . . '

Blocking off her ears to the priest's booming voice, Connie bowed her head and crossed herself as she said her own prayers. There was a squeak as the usher closed the red velvet curtain around the coffin and then the sound of weeping as the other usher turned the wheel behind.

The rumble of the coffin travelling into the furnaces sounded and Mr Daly covered his face with his hands, his brother placed a consoling hand on his shoulder.

The congregation sat quietly for a moment then, mindful of the mourners from the next funeral congregating outside, they stood and made their way through the open door to the surrounding gardens. Connie followed them out.

She waited until those offering Mr Daly their consolation had drifted away, then she walked over.

'It's good of you to come, sister,' he said, looking at her through red-rimmed eyes.

'I'm so sorry, Mr Daly.'

He forced a smile. 'Thank you for all you did.'

'I wish I could have done more,' said Connie.

'No one could have. Even the docs at the hospital couldn't save her,' Mr Daly replied. 'Internal hem-something they called it.'

'Haemorrhage,' said Connie.

'That's the thing,' said Mr Daly. 'They said she'd punctured a main blood vessel when she . . .' He covered his eyes with his hands. 'We would have managed somehow. Why did she do it?'

Connie didn't reply.

After a moment, he recovered himself. 'Sorry, sister, it's just . . .'

'I know,' said Connie. 'How are the children?'

'The younger ones don't really understand but our oldest four have taken it right bad,' said Mr Daly.

'What will you do about them?' asked Connie.

'Well, Breda's almost twelve so she can sort out the boys and her two sisters for school and look after them until I get home, but it's the three young'uns that are the trouble. I'm all right for a few weeks as me brother Pat and his missus are over but I can't afford to have someone mind the twins and Peter when they go back. I was tearing my hair out with the worry of it until I spoke to Father Flaherty.'

'And he knew exactly what to do, no doubt?' said Connie.

'He did so.' A smile lifted Mr Daly's thin face. 'God love him, he said he knew of an orphanage who would take them. It's a bit of a way from here, but it's in a big house in the country so there'll be plenty of room and fresh air to help them grow.'

'But Peter's not a year yet,' said Connie as an image of Mary's baby happily kicking his legs on the Dalys' marital bed came into her mind.

'I know and it fair breaks me heart to send them from me, but it's run by the Poor Sisters of Nazareth and Father Flaherty assures me they'll be well cared for.' Something behind Connie caught Mr Daly's eye. 'Will you accept my apologies, sister, but the funeral director fella looks as if he wants a word. Thank you again for all your help.'

He walked away.

Connie walked over to Mary's handful of floral tributes, she was just reading the dedications when someone appeared next to her.

Connie turned and found herself looking up at Father Flaherty's sour face.

'Good afternoon, sister,' he said.

'Father,' Connie replied.

His eyes shifted to the posies and floral arrangements at their feet. 'A sad business.'

'Heart-breaking.'

'And when I heard what Mary had done, I almost refused to give her God's blessing for her eternal rest,' he continued.

'I'm sure you did,' Connie replied.

He gave her a fierce look. 'No sin can go unpunished.'

'I pray not,' Connie replied, feeling her anger rise.

'But as Mr Daly has paid for a mass in his wife's memory to be said every month for a year, I agreed,' he said.

'That was very magnanimous of you,' said Connie, through tight lips.

Father Flaherty's sanctimonious expression returned. 'I just pray that God, in his infinite wisdom and compassion, will pardon Mary for what she did and let her into his eternal kingdom.'

Holding the priest's pompous gaze, Connie raised an eyebrow. 'I'm certain, Father Flaherty, that the Almighty will forgive Mary all her trespasses but I wouldn't be so confident about yours.'

Father Flaherty's eyes bulged and his face flushed purple. 'How dare—'

'She was a loving mother who was worn to the bone trying to care for the eight children she already had,' Connie said, not caring who might hear her. 'She could barely afford to put food

379

on the table, but you didn't care about that, did you? In fact, you don't care about people like Mary and Patrick and their poor children, all you care about is having people bow and scrape to you as a way of inflating your self-importance. You refer to yourself as Christ's representative on earth but rather than showing Jesus' compassion to Mary and her family, you browbeat and bullied her with the fear of eternal damnation into becoming pregnant again.'

'Be careful, Sister Byrne,' the priest said menacingly.

Supressing a lifetime of learnt subservience, Connie matched the priest's pitiless gaze.

'As far as I'm concerned, it wasn't God's great plan, but you.' She poked her finger at him. 'You, Father Flaherty, with your arrogance and pride, that put Mary in her grave as surely as if you'd severed her uterine artery yourself, and let me tell you this. After seeing what your out-of-date religious teachings did to Mary, I am going to go out of my way to promote modern family planning methods to every mother in my care.'

Chapter Twenty-Seven

'Are you warm enough, Mum?' asked Connie.

'I'll do,' her mother replied. 'As long as Father Connor gets a move on.'

Mo, who was standing on the other side of their mother, looked at her watch. 'It's only ten to six, Mum.'

'And it's Father McGonagall who's in charge this year,' added Bernie, who was standing next to Connie.

Connie and the other female members of the Byrne family had gathered at St Martha's and St Mungo's church on the first Sunday in May. The male members of the Byrne clan were having a swift half before the pageant kicked off.

As usual, the route was packed with the family and friends of those taking part in the parade, all from the congregations of the half-dozen or so Catholic churches in the area. Set out along the route, outside houses and shops, were small white-draped altars adorned with statues of the Blessed Lady, rosaries and images of saints for the priests to bless as they passed. Her mother had spent the week ironing the lacy linen, unpacking the plaster statue of the Virgin Mary, washing it gently in soapy water, then setting up her window sill display as usual. Sadly, although before the war every house in the street would have their improvised altars ready for the priest to pass, this year only her mother and Mrs Murphy at number 12 had bothered. It seemed that the Luftwaffe had not only destroyed the old streets but old traditions too.

In the distance the sound of the various brass bands could be heard. Although the procession was primarily to mark the crowning of the Virgin Mary, there was always a festival atmosphere to the proceedings as, along with crucifixes and banners, one lucky local girl was chosen to be the May Queen while a young lad carried the Virgin Mary's crown.

Like all of those who were born and brought up in one of the many Catholic churches in the area, Connie had been coming to the annual parade for as long as she could remember, but this year there was an added excitement in the family as Bernie's eldest daughter, Marlene, was one of the May Queen's attendants.

'It shouldn't be long now,' said Bernie, stretching her neck to see what was going on. From a distance it was hard to make out what was happening as all they could see was a flurry of black and white as the priests and altar boys lined up in the appropriate order.

She and Mo exchanged a look.

'It's a pity Hari couldn't come,' said Connie's eldest sister.

'Yes, but he presenting a paper tomorrow at the Annual General Practitioners' Conference so he's driving up to Birmingham today.'

'A paper what?' asked her mother.

'It what they call it when someone does a piece of research and presents it to a conference,' explained Connie. 'Hari did a survey of his patients, looking at their illnesses and their living conditions, to assess how things like housing, income and number of children might affect a person's health.'

'My goodness,' said Bernie. 'That sounds like a lot of hard work.'

'It was,' Connie replied. 'He spent hours analysing the results, but it was worth it because it's being published in *The Lancet* next month.'

'Well, if you ask me a doctor's job is to fix you up when you're queer,' said her mother with a sniff. 'Not to poke and pry into things that don't concern them.'

'Well, I for one would rather have a GP like Hari who takes the time and trouble looking after me and mine than that old quack I've got,' said Mo.

'So would I,' added Bernie. 'Perhaps when him and Connie are married, he'll put us on his books.'

'Sorry,' said Connie with a regretful smile. 'A doctor's not allowed to treat his relatives.'

'Well, the way things are going we won't be his relatives, will we?' said her mother with a nonchalant expression. 'It's been a month since he asked your father but I still don't see an engagement ring on your finger.'

'As I've explained at least three times before, Mum,' Connie replied, 'Hari has asked his mother to send his grandmother's ring as my engagement ring and it takes at least two months to come from India by secure courier.'

'Do you know what it looks like?' asked Mo.

Connie shook her head. 'Hari says it's a surprise.'

Bernie sighed. 'How romantic. Don't you think, Mum?'

'If you like that sort of thing,' Maud replied. 'But I'm sure you could have found something just as good here. Have we got a date yet for this wedding?'

'We're thinking the first of July,' said Connie.

'Two months!' cried her mother. 'How am I supposed to get a wedding organised in two months?'

Connie and her sisters exchanged a look. 'Well, the thing is, Mum—'

'The church will be all right but it's a pity you cancelled all your arrangements with Malcolm or we could have just changed the date on the Memorial Hall in Ben Johnson Road,' Maud cut in, counting the weeks off on her fingers. 'You'll have to have summer flowers as the spring ones will be gone by then but at least Winnie around the corner has almost finished your wedding dress.'

'Don't be daft, Mum,' laughed Bernie. 'Connie's not going to wear the dress she was going to wear to marry Malcolm.'

'Why not?'

'Because she's marrying Hari,' Bernie said, looking incredulously at their mother.

Maud looked perplexed. 'He won't know.'

Mo and Bernie both rolled their eyes.

'The thing is, Mum,' said Connie. 'We've decided we want a quiet wedding with just close family and a few friends.'

Her mother's mouth pulled into a tight line. 'Have you now?'

'Yes, we have,' said Connie firmly.

Maud folded her arms. 'Well, perhaps that's wise under the circumstances.'

'What do you mean, Mum?' asked Connie.

'You know, with Hairy being . . . different.'

'His name is Hari, Mother,' snapped Connie. 'And we're not having a quiet wedding because I'm ashamed of him, we're having a quiet wedding because we want to be married as soon as possible.'

'You don't have to get sharp with me, Connie,' said her mother with wide-eyed innocence. 'No one can accuse me of being colour prejudiced, not after the way I helped that West Indian family around the corner when they moved in, but not everyone's as fair-minded as I am, and you know how people like to talk.'

Connie and her mother eyeballed each other for a moment, then her mother looked at her watch. 'It's ten past six. What does that blooming priest think he's playing at keeping us all hanging around like this? I'm going to go and give him a piece of my mind.'

She turned and elbowed her way towards the church gates.

Tears sprang into Connie's eyes so she turned and stared at the shutters of the sweet shop opposite as she fought to hold them back.

Bernie rubbed Connie's upper arm affectionately.

'Don't take no notice of her,' her sister said quietly.

'It's hard not to,' said Connie.

'Well, we think Hari's an absolutely lovely fella and just right for you, don't we, Mo?'

Connie's gaze shifted from one sister to the other.

'I blooming well do,' agreed Mo, standing next to Bernie. 'And it seems to me you've had more fun in a month with Hari than you had in a year with Malcolm.'

A blissful smile spread across Connie's face. 'I certainly have.'

'Whoo-hoo,' laughed her sisters in unison.

Although memories of long evenings wrapped in Hari's arms flitted through Connie's mind, she raised a cool eyebrow.

'Yes, we've been dancing and to the theatre and even visited the Tower of London for the day,' she said innocently.

Her sisters laughed and Connie joined in.

There was a blast from a trombone and the crowds around them cheered. Connie looked around to see Father McGonagall, crucifix held high and flanked by altar boys, start moving through the church gates, followed by a group holding aloft colourful saints' banners.

As the procession advanced towards them, Mo slipped her arm through Connie's. 'You do know, little sis, that when you and Hari are married some people will say some very unkind things, but I won't be able to sort them out in the playground for you this time.'

Connie nodded.

'Yes I do, big sis. They've already started, but,' she said, closing her hand over Mo's work-worn one, 'I didn't think my mother would be one of them.'

'Will this be all right, Paul?' asked Connie, stopping beside the bench under a cherry tree.

Paul gave a wobbly nod of his head and Hari put the brakes on the wheelchair.

It was two weeks after the May parade. Hari had collected her from Fry House just after two and they had driven in through the front gates of Buntingford House some fifty minutes later.

The house was around two hundred years old, set in acres of parkland and within walking distance of picturesque Chigwell village. However, despite its historic appearance, when you walked through the front door of the old house it was a different story as the residential home was full of the most up-to-date equipment, like hoists, lifts and individually moulded armchairs. As his mother had always dreamed of, Paul had his own room on the first floor, which looked out over the vegetable garden. There was a shelf onto which Connie put the books she'd brought with her, alongside the small radio tuned in to the Home Service so he could hear the daily schools programmes. He was spotlessly clean, his youthful stubble had been freshly shaved and he was wearing his own clothing. However, by far the best thing about Buntingford House was the kind and friendly staff.

Connie sat down next to Paul and, taking his beaker from the bag hanging from the handles, offered him a drink. Hari strolled a few yards to the low wall that marked the end of the terrace.

'It's just breathtaking,' he said, gazing across the vista of rolling Essex countryside.

As the temperature was somewhere close to seventy-five

degrees Fahrenheit, Hari had left his jacket in the car and loosened his tie. He now stood a few yards from Connie with his sleeves rolled up, revealing his well-defined forearms.

'I agree,' said Connie, noticing, not for the first time, how his trousers fitted snugly around his rear. 'And a whole world of difference from the Brentwood Mental Hospital, isn't it, Paul?'

Paul gave a moan and nodded emphatically. He grabbed Connie's hand and shook it, looking at her with gratitude in his eyes.

'My pleasure,' she said softly. 'And you've Dr MacLauchlan to thank too. He was the one that swung the panel in your favour.'

Paul groaned his agreement.

Hari turned and smiled. 'That's all right, old man. You'd have done the same for me.'

Paul gave a guttural hoot and rocked back and forth in his seat.

Connie and Hari laughed too.

Strolling back under the shade, Hari sat down beside Connie and took her hand. 'I was saying to the matron that Buntingford House should be a model for all long-term facilities.'

'Did I hear her ask you to consider becoming a member of the trust board?' asked Connie.

He nodded, dislodging a quiff of hair. 'She did and I said I'd think about it.'

They sat back and enjoyed the scene for a few more moments, then a round-faced nurse in a white uniform and a traditional cap came hurrying across the lawn.

'I'm sorry to break up the party,' she said. 'But Paul is booked in for a little physio before supper to loosen up those legs of his, so if you don't mind.'

'Not at all, sister,' said Connie, popping Paul's cup back in the bag. She stood up and, leaning forward, kissed Paul on the forehead. 'I'll be back next month and I know Mrs Morris said she'll be visiting very soon, too.'

Paul gave her a crooked smile.

'Goodbye, Paul,' said Hari, shaking the young man's unbending right hand. 'And I'm glad everything worked out.'

Paul groaned again by way of reply and the nurse kicked the brakes off the wheelchair and started for the house.

As she watched Paul being wheeled back to his new home, tears suddenly welled in Connie's eyes.

'Well done, Connie,' said Hari softly. 'If it hadn't been for you, Paul would have spent the rest of his days in something akin to a Victorian workhouse.'

Raising her head to look up at him, and surrounded by the stillness and fragrance of the garden, Connie found herself falling into Hari's fathomless dark eyes. 'You know when I first realised I loved you, Hari?'

'When you saw me lance the boil on the back of Mr Jessup's neck?'

'No, you great loon,' said Connie, pretending to hit his arm. 'When I saw you at the tribunal arguing Paul's case. You were just brilliant.'

Hari caught her around the waist and hugged her to him. 'And do you know when I fell in love with you, my darling Connie?'

'I have no idea, but don't say "the first time you walked into my surgery" because that's just too corny,' laughed Connie.

'Well I won't because it's not true,' he replied. 'I fell in love with you before that. I was eating my supper in Alf's Cafe in Commercial Street and you swept in, wearing the dress you're wearing now.'

Connie's eyes opened wide. 'I don't remember.'

'Of course you don't, you just breezed in, paid Alf what you owed him and breezed out again,' he said. 'I didn't know who you were but I'd say you caught my heart straight away.'

Connie raised an eyebrow. 'Your heart?'

'Well, my interest, let's say.' He grinned down at her. 'After all, you have got gorgeous legs.'

Connie laughed.

Hari lifted her off her feet and kissed her as the warm summer breeze swirled around them, enveloping them in the scent of the summer garden.

Hari's lips pressed onto hers and as his arm tightened around her, Connie's pulse raced with excitement. After a long, exhilarating kiss, Hari released her. His eyes were dark with desire, but with a sigh he returned her feet to the ground and slackened his embrace while still keeping his arms around her.

'I love you,' he said.

'And I love you,' Connie replied.

Hari stared down at her for another long moment, then he kissed her briefly. 'And now, my darling, I think we should conclude our lovely afternoon in the country in the time-honoured British way – with a nice cup of tea.'

May and Rose's teashop was a short walk from Buntingford House's front gate and opposite the mock medieval-style Victorian church.

The bell above his head tinkled as Hari pushed open the door and Connie entered, her full skirt brushing his legs as she passed.

The teashop, with its pastel wallpaper and tables covered with lacy white cloths, was typical of its kind. There was a photo of the king behind the counter, which stood at the end of the shop, and there was a selection of ornamental and novelty plates fixed to the wall. There was also a corkboard on the wall advertising the WI summer sale and the Children's Fun and Frolics Day in the vicarage garden. With half the available tables occupied, the shop was busy but not overwhelmingly so.

'You find a seat and I'll order our tea,' Hari said as he closed the door.

Connie nodded and, threading her way between the matrons of the parish, headed for a table for two in the window.

Hari ambled over to the counter.

A jolly motherly looking woman in a frilly apron and with fluffy greying hair appeared from the door behind the counter carrying a loaded tray. She gave him a second look and then a warm smile.

'Just give me a moment, young man,' she said, 'and I'll be with you.'

'No rush,' said Hari, looking across at Connie. 'No rush at all.'

Sitting now with the mellow sunlight burnishing her copper hair and highlighting the new crop of freckles the stroll in the garden with Paul had created, she looked absolutely gorgeous. His gaze ran up the smooth slimness of her bare arms and then onto the swell of her breasts as he remembered the sensation of them pressed against his chest. It had taken all his powers to hold back when they'd found themselves in bed on the night she'd dashed into his surgery two months ago. And he was pleased they'd done so, but he was equally glad they weren't planning on a long engagement.

'Thank you for waiting, my dear,' said the cafe owner as she slipped back behind the counter. 'What can I get you?'

'Tea for two and a selection of cakes, please,' Hari replied.

'Any sandwiches?'

'No thank you, just cakes.'

The old woman's eyes twinkled. 'Right you are, although I would have thought your young lady is sweet enough.'

Hari smiled.

'One and nine, please, sir,' she continued. 'And I'll bring your order over in two shakes of a lamb's tail.'

He handed over the money and made his way to the table where Connie sat gazing out of the window.

'Penny for your thoughts,' he asked.

She raised her head. 'I was just thinking, what a pretty village.'

'Yes, it is,' he said, taking the chair opposite. 'With the church in the middle and the old squire's hall up on the hill, it's so typically English. It's hard to believe it's just three-quarters of an hour's drive from the surgery.'

'Wouldn't it be lovely to live somewhere like this?' asked Connie, gazing out of the window at the handful of village shops.

'Tea for two and a selection of cakes,' said the teashop owner as she placed a loaded tray on the table between them.

'Thank you, they look scrummy,' said Connie. 'We were just saying what a pretty village you have.'

'Why, thank you, my dear,' said the shop owner. 'Have you been out for a Sunday afternoon drive?'

'No, we've been visiting a friend in Buntingford House,' Connie replied.

'Lovely place, me and May puts on a special tea for those poor luvs every month,' said the woman. 'Enjoy your tea.'

She bustled off to serve another customer.

Connie poured milk into their cups and stirred the teapot.

'What would you like?' Connie asked, pointing at the cake stand.

'A scone, please.'

Connie manoeuvred a fat fruit scone onto his plate and a

cream slice onto her own. She poured the tea and they chatted as they worked their way through the delicious refreshments.

'Mmm, that was just perfect,' Connie said as she laid the pastry fork on her empty plate.

Swallowing the last mouthful of tea, Hari reached into his inside breast pocket and extracted a small pouch.

'Talking of perfect,' he said, pulling open the drawstring and dropping the contents into his palm. 'I know you've had a bit of a wait . . .' He took her hand. 'But I hope this makes up for it.'

Connie stared down as Hari slipped the ring onto the third finger of her left hand and her eyes opened wide with astonishment. 'Hari, is it . . . it can't be a—' She splayed her fingers and stared incredulously at the ring.

'Yes, it's a ruby,' said Hari. 'It was my grandmother's. Her father had four stones cut from a polished ruby in his insignia and mounted in a ring for each of his four daughters. The stones on either side are half-carat diamonds.'

'When you said a family ring, I thought—' Connie twisted her hand and the gems sparkled in the light from the window.

'I can have it adjusted, if necessary—'

'No, it fits perfectly.' She stretched across and kissed him. 'Thank you, Hari. It's beautiful.'

'Just like you,' he said, inordinately pleased to see her wearing his ring at last.

'Now,' he said, still holding her hand. 'I know we've mentioned it once or twice, but now you have a proper engagement ring and the church and the restaurant are booked, I was wondering if perhaps I could put in an order for some little MacLauchlans.'

'Do you have a quantity in mind?'

'I was thinking perhaps four,' he said, rubbing his thumb lightly across her knuckles. 'With the option of another if one should arrive unexpectedly.'

'I think that can be arranged,' she replied. 'And when would you like the first delivered?'

'I was thinking as soon as possible,' said Hari.

'Well, there is a nine-month waiting time, but I'll see what I can do.' She squeezed his hand. 'I didn't think I could love you more and suddenly I do.'

As the love emanating from Connie's amazing blue eyes

washed over him, all the divergent elements of his life fell into perfect alignment. Lost for words, Hari just smiled.

'Everything all right over here?' a woman's voice asked.

'Yes, thank you,' said Hari, tearing his eyes from Connie.

'Yes,' said Connie. 'It was just perfect.'

She and Hari exchanged a private look as the proprietor cleared their crockery.

'I hope you don't mind me saying,' she said as she stacked the cups, 'but you look like a couple getting ready for their wedding.'

Hari laughed. 'Is it that obvious?'

'Well, it is a bit. I only mention it in case you and your intended were looking for somewhere to live.'

'That's very kind of you,' said Connie. 'But my fiancé's a doctor and we'll be living in the flat above the surgery,'

'A doctor.' The elderly lady gave Hari a respectful look. 'That's a pity as there're half a dozen new four-bedroom houses being built at the other end of the village, near to the station and shops, and we on the parish council are keen to see young families move into the village.'

'They sound ideal,' said Connie. 'And who wouldn't want to bring their children up in such a place, but perhaps in a few years when we've got something behind us.'

The proprietor looked disappointed.

Hari squeezed Connie's hand. 'It wouldn't hurt to take a look while we're here, would it, Connie?' said Hari.

'I suppose not,' said Connie unenthusiastically.

'The first two are almost finished and you'll see the plots of the others are already marked out,' said the woman, putting the last items on the tray. 'Straight down the high street, past the church and they're on your left.'

Picking up the loaded tray, she went back to the kitchen.

Hari stood up and held out his hand.

'Shall we walk?' he asked as they stepped back into the street.

'If you like,' said Connie, taking his arm. 'But you've just taken over the practice and we have the wedding and everything to pay for, so I'm wondering if looking at houses we can't afford is a good idea?'

Hari smiled and patted her hand. 'Perhaps, but I'm just

391

thinking ahead to where we might like to raise our little tribe of MacLauchlans.'

It was somewhere close to seven-thirty by the time Hari brought the car to a stop outside Fry House. Pulling on the handbrake, he leant across and pressed his lips onto Connie's.

'Happy?'

'Very,' she replied, catching the last remnants of his aftershave.

'Me too,' he said, gathering her to him and kissing her deeply.

Connie closed her eyes and, as the thrill of his lips set her senses tingling, found herself regretting it was still several weeks before they were man and wife.

With a sigh, Hari released her lips. 'This isn't getting my shirt ironed.'

'Or my stockings rinsed.' She kissed him again. 'I'll see you tomorrow.'

He kissed her back. 'Sleep well, darling, and I'm glad we went to see the houses.'

He tooted and she waved as he sped off back to the surgery.

Connie sighed. Actually, she wasn't glad they'd seen the houses because the one at the back of the small development, with a garden overlooking the surrounding farmland, would have been absolutely perfect for a growing family, but at two thousand seven hundred pounds, it was far beyond what they could afford.

Putting the only small disappointment of the day out of her mind, Connie trotted up the steps and into the nurses' home.

The clinic downstairs was quiet and in darkness but above her head the familiar sounds of hairdryers humming and water running drifted down as the nurses prepared for the start of the new working week. As Connie put her foot on the first step, someone called her name from above.

Looking up, Connie saw Jane, in a fetching frilly pink dressing gown and with a head full of curlers, peering over the balcony.

'Oh, I'm glad you're back,' she called down. 'A Father O'Connor rang to speak to you after lunch and he called again about an hour ago. He said could you ring him back?'

'Did he say what it was about?' asked Connie.

Jane shook her head. 'But he said it was urgent,' she added, disappearing back from whence she'd come.

Connie went into the nurses' office and, picking up the telephone receiver, dialled one hundred.

'Operator,' said a woman's voice almost immediately.

'Could you put me through to Stepney seven four three one, please?'

There was a click and the phone started ringing at the other end.

Perching on the edge of the desk, Connie raised her left hand. The evening light glanced off the facets of the stones making them sparkle anew. When Hari said he'd asked his mother to send the ring, she had expected something of sentimental value and modest, and if this ring was one of four, how blooming big was the original ruby?

Someone picked up the phone. 'St Martha's and St Mungo's rectory,' said the soft Irish lilt down the phone. 'And it's Father O'Connor speaking.'

'Father, it's Connie Byrne here, you phoned me earlier.'

'Ah, yes, Connie, my love, thank you for phoning back,' the priest said. 'I'm so sorry to have to tell you, but there's a little setback with your wedding.'

'Why, in the name of the saints above, can't Father O'Connor marry you?' Maud asked, staring at Connie in disbelief.

'Because I've been placed outside the church's sanction,' Connie replied.

She and Hari were standing in her mother's kitchen with the opening bars of *ITMA* playing on the wireless. Her mother was sitting on one side of the drop-leaf pine table and her father was sitting on the other, their used supper plates and half-drunk cups of tea in front of them.

'You mean you can't go to mass?' asked her mother, the colour draining from her face.

'Or go to confession and be absolved of my sins, receive the last rites or any other holy sacrament, including being married by the church,' said Connie.

Her mother crossed herself twice. 'When did you find this out?'

'Father O'Connor rang and told me on Sunday,' said Connie.

'Sunday!' screeched her mother. 'And I suppose you didn't think it was important enough to tell me straight away?'

'Of course it's important, Mother,' snapped Connie. 'I've thought of nothing else since I spoke to him, but we didn't come sooner because we've spent the past three days trying to sort the problem out. We even went to see the bishop him—'

'Sweet Mary Mother of God,' Maud whispered, clutching the crucifix at her throat. 'The bishop knows?'

'It was him who sanctioned the order,' said Connie quietly, the weight of her banishment pressing down on her.

Hari put his arm around her and gently rubbed her upper arm. Connie looked up and smiled, then squared her shoulders.

Maud stared dumbly at her for a moment, then her eyes shifted to Hari standing beside her and back to Connie.

'I suppose the bishop got to hear you're set on marrying a heathen and he's—'

'Now, now, Maud,' interrupted her father. 'Don't take on at Hari—'

'Take on!' screamed her mother, turning her spite on her husband. 'The bishop has stopped our Connie getting married in church and you tell me not to—'

'Hari has nothing to do with it,' Connie cut in. 'It's me. I'm the one who's caused the trouble. One of my patients already had eight children and . . .' Without naming her, Connie told them about Mary.

'Well, God rest her soul,' said her mother when she'd finished. 'But you know it's not for us to question God's divine wisdom and I don't see why—'

'At the graveside I gave Father Flaherty, from St Anne's, a piece of my mind. I told him . . . '

As Connie repeated what she'd said to Father Flaherty, her mother's face took on an expression of utter horror. 'I can't believe a daughter of mine would say such a thing to a priest.'

'Well, I did and he complained to the bishop,' said Connie.

'What will people say?' Maud wrung her hands. 'There must be something you can do.'

'There is,' said Connie. 'The bishop has graciously agreed that if I make a full confession of my sins to Father Flaherty and accept any penance he might impose, plus swear on the Holy Scriptures that I'll not contradict the church's teaching on the procreation of children in future, then I will once again be sanctified by the church.'

'Well, there you are then,' said her mother, looking visibly relieved. 'If that's all—'

'But I'm not going to,' said Connie. 'And I tell you, Mother, if Father Flaherty was standing here now, I'd say the same again. I've seen too many women old before their time because they spend most of their adult life either pregnant or with a baby on the breast. Before the war there was no way to avoid it, but now we can and surely all women should have a choice. It's better for women and their children, even if diehards like Father Flaherty can't see it.'

Her mother shifted her gaze onto Hari. 'And I suppose you think Connie's right?'

'I certainly do,' said Hari, resting his hand lightly on Connie's waist.

Her mother shrugged. 'Well, Connie, it's up to you and you always were the headstrong one of the bunch, but unless you swallow your pride then you'll have to call off the wedding, won't you?' she said, sounding quite jolly about it.

'I'm bitterly disappointed that we can't get married in St Martha's and St Mungo's . . .' Connie took Hari's free hand. 'But we've discussed the situation and have decided to get married in Shoreditch Town Hall instead.'

Her mother's mouth pulled into a tight line. 'Have you now?'

Hari's embrace became a little firmer. 'Yes, we have, Mrs Byrne.'

Maud's eyes became flint-like. 'I suppose you're happy now, aren't you?'

'Not at all,' said Hari.

'Don't give me that,' sneered her mother. 'You talked my poor Connie out of the big white wedding she's always dreamt of and now she can't even get married in church. My Connie was brought up a good Catholic and she'd never have spoken to a priest like that before she met you. Bloody darkie.'

'Mother!'

'Don't you shout at me, my girl,' bellowed her mother. 'I speak as I find. And he—' She jabbed her finger at Hari. 'He might wear fancy suits and speak like a toff, but scratch the surface and he's just like the rest; likes to have a white woman on his arm to show off.'

Connie clenched her fists. 'Don't you dare speak about Hari like that.'

'It's all right, Connie,' Hari said softly.

'No, it's not, Hari, not by a long chalk,' she replied. 'And I won't put up with having my own mother talking to you like that. Not now, not ever.'

Her mother crossed her arms 'Won't you now?' she said, looking at a point just above Connie's head.

'No, I will not,' Connie replied icily. 'You're the one set on this stupid big white wedding, not me, I really don't care. And as much as I wish we could marry in my church, I want to be Hari's wife more so we will be getting wed, as planned, on the first of July but in Shoreditch Town Hall instead of St Martha's and St Mungo's.'

'Well, I won't be there,' said her mother.

Connie's jaw dropped. 'But you've got to be.'

Maud turned her face away and stared at the wall.

'Don't take no notice of her, luv,' said Connie's father, giving his wife a furious look which she totally ignored. 'We'll be there to see you and Hari tie the knot. Don't you worry.'

'You can go if you like, Arthur,' said her mother, folding her arms tightly. 'But I won't.' She looked at Connie and her eyes narrowed. 'And I'll tell you this, my girl, unless you're married by a Catholic priest in a Catholic church then as far as I'm concerned, you'll be no better than—'

'That's enough, Maud,' cut in her father.

'Don't you—'

'I said *enough*!' bellowed her father in a voice Connie hadn't heard him use for years.

Maud pressed her lips together but kept her eyes fixed on Connie.

She held her mother's furious glare for a moment, then picked up her handbag.

With tears stinging the corner of her eyes, Connie hugged her father, then looked back at her mother's averted face.

'There'll be a seat reserved for you in the registry office and a place set on the top table at the reception so it's up to you, but whether you're there or not, Mum, Hari and I are getting married on the first of July.' She hooked her arm in Hari's. 'Come on, Hari, we're leaving.'

'So I hope you can see, Miss Byrne, that our premier function suite has adequate space for your guests while maintaining an intimate atmosphere,' said Mr Pugh, the well-fed but immaculately turned-out manager of the Bishopsgate Hotel.

Connie glanced around at the twinkling chandelier, tall mirrors, plush velvet curtain and beech sprung dance floor of the Royal Mint Room.

'What do you say, darling,' said Hari, standing beside her. 'Are you happy with the arrangements for the reception?'

Connie squeezed his arm. 'Oh, I certainly am.'

It was just after three-thirty on a Thursday afternoon and a week after telling her parents their change of plan and having spent the past hour going through menus, floor plans and a variety of table layout options, they had just about crossed the Ts and dotted the Is for their big day.

They had booked the wedding at the town hall the day after their abrupt departure from her mother's house. As Connie had the day off, Hari had taken a few hours off before evening surgery so they could sort out their wedding lunch, which was after all only five weeks away.

'Very good, sir, madam,' said the manager, smiling happily at them. 'We will need the final numbers and any special instructions two weeks before the date but, other than that, all I need from you now, Dr MacLauchlan, if it's not too much trouble, is a deposit.'

'Not at all,' said Hari. 'Will you take a cheque?'

'Naturally, sir,' said the manager, ushering them towards the door. 'If you'd like to follow me to the office.'

With her arm in Hari's, Connie strolled out of the spacious reception room and back into the hotel lobby, with its fitted pile carpet and yielding sofa.

As it was the middle of the afternoon, the clerk behind the long teak counter was filing the afternoon post into the cubby holes behind him and young porters, in their maroon and gold uniform, were loitering about by the cloakroom sharing a surreptitious cigarette.

As the manager led them towards his office tucked under the stairs, Connie spotted a sign for the ladies.

'Hari, would you mind if I powdered my nose?' she asked.

'Of course not,' he replied. 'I'll meet you here when I'm done.'

Having availed herself of the poshest lavatory she'd ever been in, Connie reapplied her lipstick and returned to the foyer. Thinking she might have a quick look at the sample menus while she waited, she headed for the chair beside the window but, as she got halfway across, a familiar voice cut across her musing.

'Connie?'

She turned to see Malcolm, standing just an arm's length away.

In his workaday grey suit and navy and red tie, Malcolm looked very much the same as the last time she'd seen him almost three months ago.

'Malcolm,' she said. 'What are you doing here?'

'Mr Riley is addressing a meeting of the Chamber of Commerce upstairs and forgot his notes so rang through to the office for me to fetch them. What about you?'

Connie replied. 'I'm here booking my wedding reception.'

'Oh.'

'You did get my letter, didn't you?'

He nodded.

'I just thought it would be better if I told you about me and Hari,' said Connie.

He gave her a tight smile. 'It was good of you to take the trouble. When's the big day?'

'The first of July.'

Pain flitted across his face but he glanced up and around at the sweeping staircase, gilt-framed oil paintings and crystal splendour of the late Victorian hotel.

'This is a bit of a step up from the Memorial Hall in Ben Johnson Road, isn't it,' he said, as his eyes returned to her face.

There was a pause and Malcolm shifted his weight onto the other foot.

'How are you, Malcolm?' asked Connie.

'Very well,' he replied instantly.

398

'I'm pleased to hear it.'

'Yes, I'm very well in fact,' he continued. 'I've been promoted at work to be deputy clerk of works for drains and sewers under Mr Gower.'

'Not before time after all the hard work you do,' said Connie.

Malcolm acknowledged her response with a self-satisfied smile.

'And I've taken on organising the Model Railway Club's regional event next year and there's even talk of us at the Great Eastern Railway Society hosting the 1952 national conference,' he continued.

'That sounds marvellous,' said Connie.

The hotel manager's door opened and Hari strolled out.

'All done, darl—' He spotted who she was talking with as he crossed the foyer. 'Oh, hello, Malcolm,' he said as he joined them.

Malcolm gave a cursory nod. 'Hari.'

All three of them regarded each other politely for a long moment but no one spoke.

'Malcolm's just delivering a file to his boss who's in a meeting upstairs,' Connie said, when the silence became unbearable.

'Is he?' said Hari.

There was another awkward pause.

Malcolm shifted his weight again. 'Connie tells me you're getting married in a few weeks.'

'Yes, we're just finalising the details,' said Hari.

Malcolm forced a jolly laugh. 'Running her down the aisle then, are you, Hari, before someone steals her away?'

Connie felt a blush rising, but Hari just smiled.

'So how are you, Malcolm?' he asked.

'Me?' Malcolm puffed out his cheeks. 'Never been better. I was just saying to Connie how, since we split, things have been on the up and up.'

'Good,' said Hari.

'Yes,' continued Malcolm. 'As well as a step-up at work and being seconded onto the railway club committee, I'm courting.'

'Are you?' said Connie.

'You don't have to sound so surprised,' said Malcolm, giving her a sharp look.

'Did you meet her at work?' asked Hari.

'No,' Malcolm replied. 'Miriam's the vicar's niece and is lodging with the family. She was also a Cub leader at her last church and jumped at the chance to join the 7th Stepney when I asked.'

'I'm very pleased for you,' said Connie, slipping her arm into Hari's.

Malcolm's eyes flicked onto her hand in the crook of Hari's arm.

'And who knows?' He gave a hearty laugh. 'It might be me and Miriam finalising our wedding details soon.'

Connie didn't reply and Hari looked at his watch.

'Darling, we ought to go if we want to finalise the invitations with the printer today,' he said.

'Me, too,' said Malcolm.

There was another long pause and then Hari offered Malcolm his hand.

'Goodbye.'

After a moment's hesitation, Malcolm took it. 'Bye.'

Letting go of Hari's arm, Connie stepped forward and, catching a faint hint of Old Holborn and linseed embrocation, kissed Malcolm swiftly. 'Bye, Malcolm.'

She retook Hari's arm and walked out of the hotel with the man she loved.

Chapter Twenty-Eight

'So, we have booked the Royal Mint function room at the Bishopsgate Hotel,' said Connie. 'It can seat up to sixty, so can easily accommodate our party.'

'How many have you got coming now?' asked Mo.

'Forty-eight,' Hari replied. 'Including the children.'

'And it's going to be three courses,' added Connie.

'Oh, that sounds wonderful,' said Bernie. 'Doesn't it, Mum?'

Their mother, who was sitting in her usual parlour chair, continued her intense study of the empty fire grate and didn't reply.

It was just after three on the Whitsun weekend and two days since they'd run into Malcolm. As West Ham had a home fixture, her father and her brothers-in-law had taken the boys along to see their team, the girls had stayed at home and were playing mothers and babies in the backyard with their dollies. Mo had made Connie and Hari a welcoming cuppa, which they were just finishing now.

Her sisters gave her a sympathetic look.

'It's cream of chicken soup to start,' said Connie, damping down her disappointment, 'followed by spring lamb and vegetables, then sherry trifle for the adults and ice cream for the children.'

'There'll also be wine on the table and an open bar,' added Hari.

'We'd better keep an eye on our other halves then, Mo,' said Bernie, winking at her older sister.

'We certainly will.' Mo laughed. 'Did you hear that, Mum? Lamb's your favourite, isn't it?'

There was no response and the three sisters exchanged frustrated glances.

There was an uncomfortable silence, then Bernie spoke, 'Who have you got coming on your side, Hari?'

'Just my Aunt Janet from the family,' he replied. 'Plus a few friends from my medical school days and their wives. I've also invited Dr Gingold, who has been a very good friend to me since I arrived at Christ Church surgery; Connie used to work with her, too. William Matterson, my chum from Chang, is my best man.'

'So you've got it all under control then,' said Mo.

'More or less,' said Hari, taking Connie's hand. 'Wedding at twelve and lunch at one. Connie's ordered the cake and the flowers. We've booked the photographer and sent out the invitations. I've got the cars to organise, so the only thing to do is for Connie to find something to wear.'

Bernie looked at her in dismay. 'You haven't bought your outfit yet?'

Connie shook her head.

'Well, you'd better get a move on,' said Mo. 'You've only got a month.'

'I know, but the bride's mother is meant to go with her to choose her dress, so I was hoping you would come with me up the West End next Saturday, Mum,' Connie said to her mother's averted face.

Everyone waited expectantly, but their mother didn't speak.

The wound across Connie heart cut a little deeper.

Hari squeezed her hand and she forced a brave smile.

Picking up her handbag, Connie stood up.

'Well, we ought to get back,' she said as Hari rose to his feet.

While her mother pointedly ignored them, Mo and Bernie hugged her and said their goodbyes to Hari.

Tucking her arm in his, they walked over to her mother.

Connie unfastened her handbag and took out a cream envelope with a pair of embossed wedding bells on the corner.

'This is your invitation to my and Hari's wedding, Mum,' said Connie, placing it on the small table beside her mother. 'I know we've said a few things and been at odds over this, but you are my mum and I really want you to be with me on my wedding day.'

Her mother picked up the envelope and, pulling out the card inside, she held it at arm's length to read.

'Please say you'll come,' Connie whispered as her mother scanned down the invitation.

There was a pause and then her mother tossed it into the blackened fire grate.

Hari put his arm around Connie's shoulders. 'Come on, sweetheart, let's go home.'

Opening the flat's front door, Hari switched the light on and walked in.

'Tea or coffee?' Connie asked, hooking her coat up behind the door.

'A nice cuppa would be lovely,' he replied.

'You sort out the wireless and I'll make it.'

Flashing him a too-happy smile, she started towards the kitchen but, as she passed, Hari caught her hand.

'Sweetheart, are you sure you're all right?'

She looked puzzled. 'About Mum, you mean?'

'I'm sure she'll come round,' Hari replied.

Connie shrugged. 'That's up to her. If she doesn't want to be at my wedding, then I can't make her, can I?'

'No, but—'

'And after the way she spoke to you, Hari, perhaps I don't want her there anyway,' said Connie.

Hari didn't comment.

'And why should I worry?' Connie continued. 'It's our wedding, not hers, and now we haven't got her sticking her two pennies' worth in we'll be able to have what we want.' She gave him a dazzling smile. 'Now, let's not talk about my mum. Do you want some cake?'

'Just a sliver.' He slapped his stomach. 'Got to keep in shape for the new hockey season.'

Connie threw her arms around him and kissed him noisily. 'You look in pretty good shape to me already.'

Laughing, she twisted out of his embrace and practically skipped into the kitchenette.

Giving her a worried look, Hari went over to the sideboard and flicked the switch on the wireless.

'Hari?' she called from the kitchenette.

'Yes, sweetheart,' he replied, turning back his cuffs while he waited for the valves to warm up.

There was a clatter of cups from the kitchen.

'I was wondering if I could learn to drive after we're married.'

'Of course you can,' he replied, twiddling the knob to tune in to the Light programme. 'In fact, I was going to suggest it myself.'

The strains of 'Buttons and Bows' sounded out from the radio and Connie started singing along.

'Have you organised a room for your Aunt Janet at the hotel yet?' she asked.

'I'll do it when we drop in to finalise the reception numbers in a couple of weeks,' Hari replied, sitting on the sofa and picking up the newspaper. 'I'm driving her down on the Thursday before the wedding and William's kindly offered to drive her back on Sunday afternoon.'

The kettle whistled, but she didn't reply.

'I've also booked a long-distance call to speak to my mother when she arrives in Lahore next week,' added Hari.

Still no answer from Connie, but the kettle shrieked for attention.

Hari hurried into the kitchen. Connie was standing by the table with her hands covering her face, sobbing.

Switching the gas off as he passed, he gathered her to him and she buried her face in his chest.

Feeling powerless to take away her pain, Hari held her as she cried, hoping somehow to diminish her grief.

'How could she, Hari?' she wept. 'How could my own mother not come to my wedding?'

He couldn't answer her so just held her tighter while her emotions unravelled.

After a few moments, as her crying started to subside, Hari spoke.

'Look, Connie,' he said, 'if it's us not getting married in church that's upset your mother, we could postpone the wedding for a month or so to see if there's some way around this—'

'No, Hari,' said Connie, looking up at him with tears shimmering in her blue eyes. 'I don't give a jot what my mother, Father Flaherty, the bishop or even the pope himself says because in four weeks and two days, I'm going to become Mrs Jahindra Harish Chakravarthi MacLauchlan come hell or high water.'

Hari smiled.

'Yes, you will, my love,' he said, smoothing a damp lock of coppery hair from her forehead, 'but, Connie, if you want me to do anything, anything, to make things better, just say.'

Running her hands up his chest, Connie wound her arms around his neck. Pushing herself against him, she stood on tip-toes and pressed her lips on his, sending his senses spiralling almost out of control.

'There is something you can do, Hari,' Connie said in a throaty voice that set his body pounding with need.

'What?' he forced out.

'Make love to me,' she whispered.

Hari closed his mouth over hers and this time he didn't argue.

Connie gave a deep sigh and snuggled in a little closer to Hari's warm body. His arm, resting idly along her back, hugged her in response. She opened her eyes and looked at her hand resting on the dark hairs curling on his chest. Without moving her head, which was resting on his shoulder, she gazed down the length of their bodies.

The pale, freckled skin of her leg, which was hooked over Hari, was in stark contrast to the toned, tanned lines of his body. Connie studied the jagged scar outlined on his hip for a few seconds, then moved her gaze over his flat stomach, his chest and onto his face.

He was lying with his eyes closed, his right arm tucked behind his head and a small smile playing on his lips.

Later, when Millie asked her what happened after Hari kissed her, Connie could honestly say she couldn't remember as the last hour was a blur of fingers, lips and tongues, which had culminated in a stunning experience that gave her a whole new understanding of womankind in general and herself in particular.

Stretching up, and because she could, Connie pressed her lips onto Hari's stubbly chin.

'I love you,' she said.

'And I love you, too.' He kissed her forehead, then shifted over so they were facing each other.

'Did I hurt you?' he asked.

'Hardly at all.' She kissed him. 'I didn't realise it would be so . . .' She smiled.

They stared wordlessly at each other for a moment, then Hari rolled over and got up.

Mesmerised, Connie watched him walk naked across the room to his chest of drawers, the legacy of his captivity clearly marked across his broad shoulders. Pulling open the top drawer he took something out then, turning, he walked back to her, allowing her to appreciate him further. He took her hand.

'Come.'

Surprisingly unconcerned by her own lack of clothing, Connie threw back the covers and stood up.

Walking her across the room, he positioned her in front of his long dressing mirror, then stood behind her. Enjoying the contrast of her pale curvy body against his darker muscular one, Connie smiled at him in the reflection.

He smiled back.

Something tinkled behind her and, raising his hands, Hari draped a necklace of white and blue around her neck.

'I was going to save these for the morning after our wedding, but I think I'd rather give them to you now,' he said.

He secured the clasp, then clipped a pair of matching earrings in place and rested his hands lightly on her shoulders.

'They aren't real sapphires, are they?' she said, playing her fingers across the sparkling stones.

'Yes, my love.' His smile widened. 'And they match your eyes perfectly.'

'They are beautiful.'

Their eyes locked in the reflection and Hari's arm slid across the smooth whiteness of her stomach.

'But not as beautiful as you,' he said softly, and then pressed his lips on the little shivery spot just under her ear.

Connie's skin tingled and, letting her head fall back onto his chest, she closed her eyes.

'Yes, operator, I'm holding,' said Hari. He placed his hand over the receiver. 'They are still trying to get the connection.'

Connie yawned. 'What time is it there?'

It was just after seven-thirty on a Saturday morning and a week after the first blissful night in Hari's arms. Connie was sitting in Hari's dressing gown with her toes curled under her on Hari's sofa drinking a welcome coffee with a slice of toast along-side. She'd been on call the night before so having handed over to the early midwife, had arrived at Hari's flat as the milkman was leaving his two pints. Hari was already up and dressed in his casual trousers and blue gingham shirt, a pot of coffee bubbling in the percolator. Connie had been called out to deliveries twice and was looking forward to snuggling down in bed, but only after they had spoken to Hari's mother on the other side of the world. The call had been booked for seven-thirty and they'd been trying since then to be put through.

Hari glanced at his watch for a second. 'Just about lunchtime.' He gave her an encouraging smile. 'Don't worry, it shouldn't be too long now.'

Connie nodded and took a bite of toast.

Leaning on the back of the chair, Hari gazed out of the window. He suddenly sprang into life. 'Mother, is that you?'

There was a pause. 'Yes, yes it is me . . . And yes, I'm well. And you?' Another pause. 'I'm pleased to hear it and how's Uncle Chat and Auntie Boo?'

His mother replied and Hari nodded. 'That's good to hear.' He rolled his eyes. 'No, of course I've not been working too hard.'

Connie mouthed 'liar' and Hari grinned.

'Yes, I'm eating enough,' Hari replied. 'Did you get the photograph?' His eyes grew soft as he gazed at Connie. 'Yes, you're right, Mother, she is very beautiful.'

His mother said something. 'Light copper,' he answered. 'Very fair with lots of freckles . . .'

Connie shook her fist at him and pretended to scowl.

'. . . which she hates.' He laughed. 'Yes, we might well have some unusual-looking children.'

His mother said something else.

'Yes, just two weeks today, I know,' said Hari. 'I wish you could be here, too, Mother, but we can have a big party when we come next spring.' He looked at Connie and beckoned her over. 'Yes, of course she'd love to talk to you.'

Uncurling herself, Connie stood up and took the receiver from Hari. 'Hello, Mrs MacLauchlan.'

'Hello, Connie, my dear,' a tinny-sounding woman's voice replied. 'Aren't these modern devices marvellous that we can speak to each other?'

'Yes, they are,' said Connie. 'I'm so pleased we can as Hari's told me so much about you.'

'That I nag him to eat, no doubt,' his mother replied. 'But now, as his wife, you can make sure he does.'

'I certainly will.' Connie looked at Hari. 'Three square meals a day, I promise, Mrs MacLauchlan.'

Hari threw his hands up and looked to the heavens.

'And make sure he doesn't work too hard,' added his mother.

Connie laughed. 'That might be more difficult, but I'll try.'

Hari mouthed 'what?' and she mouthed back 'work'.

'You're right,' his mother replied. 'Harish is like his father.' She sighed. 'I wish I could be there. I'm so proud of him and what he did for all those poor men in the camp, but when I heard he was alive all I wanted was for him to meet a girl who would love him and give him a family and now he is getting married and I can't be there.'

'I'm sorry,' said Connie, taking Hari's hand and snuggling into him. She changed the earpiece to the other side so he could hear his mother, too. 'We wish you could be with us on the first, but when we get back from honeymoon Hari is going to book our passage for next April. And we'll send you a photo album.'

'By airmail, Mother,' Hari said.

Connie looked startled, but Hari just grinned.

'Yes, so you'll only have a few weeks not months to wait,' she said, and tried not to think about the dent it would make in their household budget.

'I'm sure your mother is busy, busy, busy with this and that,' Mrs MacLauchlan said.

Connie hadn't seen her mother since they'd delivered the wedding invitation two weeks before.

'Not really,' said Connie as Hari hugged her a little closer. 'It's only a small wedding so Hari and I have done most of it.'

'Ah, well,' said Hari's mother. 'At least she can see you as a bride and enjoy the day with her family.'

'I'm sorry, caller, but you have two minutes left,' cut in the operator.

'It's so lovely to speak to you, Connie,' said her soon-to-be mother-in-law. 'I know my son and if he chose you then I know I'm going to love you like my own daughter.'

Tears sprang into Connie's eyes.

'Thank you,' she whispered and handed the receiver to Hari.

Untangling herself from his embrace, she went to the window and stared blindly out at the rooftops beyond.

'There's a letter and more photos from both of us on its way to you, Mother,' Hari said. 'And I'll send you more news with the photo album. Love you as always, MattaMatta.'

He put the phone down and came over to Connie.

Standing behind her, Hari gathered her into his embrace and kissed her on the head.

'Mother says you sound just lovely and she can't wait to meet you.'

'Me neither.' Connie turned to face him. 'But it seems unfair somehow that your mother, who would sail halfway around the world to see us get married if she could get here in time, can't be at our wedding, but my mother who lives half an hour's drive away refuses to come.'

Hari's mouth pulled into a hard line. 'She's still adamant, then?'

Connie nodded. 'Mo and Bernie have tried to talk sense into her but she won't budge. Even my brother Jim, who generally keeps out of arguments between us girls and Mum, went to see her but she sent him off with a flea in his ear. But I'm not surprised. If Bobby flying in from Frankfurt to be at the wedding won't make Mum change her mind, then I tell you, nothing on God's good earth will make her come.'

As Hari turned into Maroon Street, the small gang of boys playing cricket moved their wickets aside to let him drive through their cobbled pitch.

He'd finished surgery three-quarters of an hour ago and had told Connie he was going to a meeting and would collect her from Fry House on his way back.

Getting out of the car, he locked the door and then, stepping across a chalked-out hopscotch grid, marched to the Byrnes' front door. He knocked three times, attracting the attention of the dozen or so neighbours who had dragged chairs out into the street to enjoy the balmy June evening.

Shoving his hands in his pockets, Hari waited for what seemed like an eternity then, wearing her wraparound apron and a cantankerous expression, Mrs Byrne opened the door.

'Good evening, Mrs Byrne. May I come—?'

She slammed the door.

'Very well, I shall have to shout and hope you can hear what I have to say inside as clearly as the people out here can,' he bellowed, bringing at least a dozen more neighbours from their houses. 'I'm marrying your daughter Connie on Saturday, Mrs Byrne, and—'

The door opened again and Hari stepped in.

Giving him a withering look, Connie's mother turned her back on him and marched down the hall.

Taking off his hat, Hari shut the door and then followed her. By the time he'd reached the kitchen, she'd wedged her considerable hips into the chair by the fireplace.

'I suppose Connie sent you, did she?' she snapped as soon as he stepped into the room.

'No, she didn't,' Hari replied. 'In fact, she doesn't know I've come.'

'Well, you're wasting your time, anyway,' she said, folding her arms. 'I've got nothing to say to you.'

'Good,' said Hari. 'Then you won't interrupt.'

She gave him a look that would have sent him to his grave, then clamped her lips together.

'I'm a "speak as I find" sort of person, too, Mrs Byrne,' said Hari pleasantly. 'And I'd like to make something clear. I don't give a jot if you turn up at our wedding or not, but Connie does. And it's because I love her that I've come today.'

Connie's mother didn't move a muscle.

'Mrs Byrne,' continued Hari, 'you may not know this but there are babies alive and well today because of your daughter's skill as a midwife. There are also people whose pain and suffering have been relieved because of her competence as a nurse. No matter how busy or hard-pressed she might be, she has patience and a cheery word for all. Nothing is too much for her if someone is in need. Her fellow nurses value her as a loyal colleague and the younger nurses look up to her as someone they aspire to be. She fought tooth and nail to get a young man with disabilities into a proper home. It was her compassion and desire to provide practical help for the hard-pressed mother who died that led her to cross swords with this Father Flaherty who, in my opinion, has misused his power to punish Connie for wounding his overbearing pride. In three days' time, whether you like it or not, this wonderful and loving woman, who is your daughter, will do me the extraordinary honour of becoming my wife and I come this evening to explain to you why, if you really care about Connie, you should stop being so pig-headed.'

An angry flush spread up Mrs Byrne's fleshy throat and her mouth pulled even tighter.

'At the moment, Mrs Byrne, Connie is very angry with you, and after the way you've behaved towards her, I can't say I blame her. However, I know Connie still harbours a small hope that you will change your mind. Because of that flicker of faith in you, her mum, she'll forgive you in a blink of an eye and welcome you with open arms. But I warn you, if you don't get down off your high horse and be with her on her wedding day, your special mother–daughter bond with her will be broken for ever.'

Maud's eyes bulged and the flush spread to her cheeks.

'So,' he continued, 'if Mo telephones me on Saturday and tells me you've not gone to Bernie's house to help Connie get ready, for her sake I'm going to arrive here at eleven-fifteen to collect you. I will sit outside until eleven-thirty and then, not a minute later, I will drive off whether you're in the car or not, but that will be your very last chance to set things right between you and Connie.'

Although Mrs Byrne's face remained flushed, as his words sank in, some of the anger left her eyes.

'That's all I have to say.' He put his hat back on. 'Goodnight, Mrs Byrne.'

He was just about to retrace his steps to the street when the back door opened and Arthur, dressed in his scruffy allotment clothes, walked in.

'Hello, Hari,' he said, more than a little bewildered. 'I didn't think I'd see you again until Saturday, so what are you doing here?'

'Good to see you, too, Arthur,' said Hari. 'And I'm here to stop your wife making the biggest mistake of her life.'

411

Chapter Twenty-Nine

Her sister Bernie tilted her head. 'Doesn't she look a picture?'

'Absolutely beautiful,' agreed Mo, who was standing on her left.

Millie, standing on her right, nodded. 'Very stylish.'

It was five to eleven on the first Saturday in July, there wasn't a cloud in the sky and sun was streaming through the window, heralding the start of a perfect summer's day. However, Connie wouldn't have minded if lightning streaked across the sky and hailstones bounced off the window because, in just over an hour, she would become Mrs MacLauchlan.

Traditionally, a bride should go to her wedding from her parents' house but as that option was closed to Connie, she'd decided to spend her last few nights as a single woman with her big sister. After Hari got back from his meeting on Wednesday, they'd taken the last of her bits and pieces from Fry House, including her going-away case, to his flat, after which Hari had driven her to her sister Mo's house, where she'd left her weekend case and her wedding outfit the week before.

The whole household had been up since seven and after Mo had washed and dressed herself and the children, Connie had treated herself to a long soak in the bath until eight, when Bernie and her crew arrived. Leaving the men to mind the children, Connie and her sisters had gone to the hairdresser's where Mo and Bernie had their hair washed and set. Knowing Hari liked her hair down, Connie resisted her sisters' coaxing to have her curls pinned up, instead leaving it to curl and bounce naturally around her shoulders.

Millie, wearing a pretty summer dress, jacket and straw hat, had been there when they'd got back at ten-fifteen. Mo had kept a ready supply of tea going for the neighbours who dropped by to wish Connie well. Then, at ten-thirty, they'd packed Eddy,

Cliff and the children off on the three-bus journey to Shoreditch Town Hall, where her brother Jim and his family were meeting them.

'Thank you,' said Connie, smiling at the three women standing in Mo's front room.

Connie turned and gazed at herself in her sister's wall mirror that had been taken down from its place over the mantelshelf and stood upended on a dining-room chair.

A smile of satisfaction lifted the corners of her lips. Everything she was wearing, including her lacy silk underwear, was brand spanking new. The outfit she'd finally chosen after hours in Selfridges, John Lewis and Marshall & Snelgrove was a full-skirted white silk dress with large blue daisies printed on it. It was sleeveless with a scoop neckline and fitted bodice while the wide blue belt emphasised Connie's narrow waist. She'd bought an edge-to-edge bolero with three-quarter-length sleeves from the same collection. The ensemble was completed by navy court shoes and a matching handbag from Bourne & Hollingsworth. On her head she wore a tight-fitting velvet hat, also in navy, with a slight veil hanging from the brim. The hat alone had cost her the best part of a week's wages, but then it was for a once in a lifetime occasion.

'What time are the cars arriving?' Bernie asked for the third time in thirty minutes.

'Quarter past eleven,' said Millie. 'So we've got twenty minutes, is everybody ready?'

Mo and Bernie certainly were, dressed in their new crimplene dresses and jackets bought specially for the day.

'I think so,' said Mo. 'But where are Dad and Bobby?'

As if they knew they were required, the front room door opened and Connie's father and younger brother walked in.

Her father was dressed in a new navy suit, with his hair freshly trimmed, while Bobby wore a wide-shouldered American-style silver-grey suit and his regimental tie.

Although she'd promised herself she wouldn't, Connie glanced past them and the last little hope she'd harboured, even now, that her mother would come to her wedding was snuffed out. Although the corners of her eyes pinched, Connie smiled and hurried to her father.

He hugged her close as he always had and then stood back.

'You look absolute lovely, Connie,' he said in a voice heavy with emotion. 'I hope that Hari knows what a lucky chap he is.'

'I'm sure our Connie has told him,' said Bobby.

Everyone laughed as Connie stretched her eyes to disperse the tears gathering.

A horn sounded.

'The cars are here,' said Mo, peering through her net curtains. 'Quick, get the flowers.'

Everyone sprang into action as Bernie, Mo and Millie pinned corsages onto each other and Bobby and her father attached their buttonholes to their lapels.

'All set?' asked Millie as she handed Connie her small posy of summer flowers.

Connie smiled at her best friend. 'Yes, I am.'

'Then off we go.'

Bobby gave her a hug while Millie and her sisters kissed the air next to her cheek to avoid leaving lipstick marks, then all four of them hurried out to the first car, leaving Connie and her father alone.

'I'm sorry, Con,' her dad said with sadness in his eyes. 'I know you—'

'It's all right, Dad,' said Connie, giving him a bright smile. 'In an hour's time I'll be marrying Hari and nothing else matters.'

Her father offered her his arm. 'Well then, luv, let's not keep him waiting.'

Hari glanced at his watch and then again at the firmly shut front door.

He'd been up since seven and after a shower had presented himself to Louie's barber shop when it opened at eight for a hair-cut and close shave. William, who was his best man, had pulled up outside the surgery at nine-fifteen, just as Hari had arrived back, and they'd both been for a hearty breakfast at Alf and Marie's cafe to set them up for the day. Aunt Janet had arrived in a taxi from the hotel. Satisfied that everything was going to plan, Hari got himself ready. Mo had telephoned him just after eleven to assure him everything was running smoothly at their end but also to inform him that, despite the whole family's best efforts, Mrs Byrne hadn't arrived.

Although outraged, Hari hadn't been surprised, so at ten-fifty, after he had entrusted the ring to William and his best man and aunt had headed off to Shoreditch Town Hall to meet up with the other guests, Hari climbed into his car and drove the mile and half to his soon-to-be-mother-in-law's house and parked outside.

That was thirty-seven minutes ago. Now Mrs Byrne had precisely three minutes to swallow her pride and make an appearance or he would drive away and the die would be cast.

His gaze moved from the stubbornly closed front door to the netted front window behind which Mrs Byrne was certainly watching him.

Resting his left hand on the top of the steering wheel, Hari watched the second hand of his Rolex tick around once and then twice but, as it started on its third circuit, Hari turned on the engine and put the car into first gear.

Taking Connie's hand, her father helped her out of the Daimler, then thanked the driver by slipping him half a crown.

Millie came over. 'How are you feeling?'

'I admit I've got a few butterflies,' said Connie.

'That's only natural, but we're all here to support you,' her friend replied.

She was right, too. Apart from her family, there was a large group of familiar faces by the main entrance. Connie spotted the Weinsteins, with baby Hannah in a pram, chatting happily to Dr Gingold. Hari's Aunt Janet was on the arm of William Matterson and, in addition, nearly every nurse not on duty – including Miss O'Dwyer – was there to see her get married. However, although her wedding party was practically blocking the entrance to the town hall, there was someone quite important missing.

'Hari's not here?' said Connie as the unsettled feeling in her stomach intensified.

'I know, I know,' said Millie. 'But William said he's on his way.'

'On his way!' Connie looked at her watch. 'It's ten to twelve, he should be here by now.'

'I'm sure he'll be here any moment,' Millie said. 'William's just been in to see the registrar and everything is in order, so we can go in straight away.'

Going to the top of the town hall steps, Connie peered down the road towards Shoreditch High Street.

'Perhaps he's had a puncture!'

'Then he'll catch a taxi,' Millie replied.

'What if he's had an accident somewhere,' continued Connie as her heart started to race.

'Connie, try to stay calm,' said Millie in her I'm-a-nurse-and-it-will-all-be-fine voice.

Connie scanned the oncoming traffic 'But what if he's lying injured somewhere or even . . . There's he is!' she cried as she spotted the car.

'Right, I'll get everyone ready to go in,' said Millie, speeding off.

The car drew to a stop.

Hari got out of the car and Connie's heart did a little double step at the sight of him.

He was wearing a very well-fitted double-breasted navy suit with his RAMC tie smartly knotted at his throat while a new fedora, sitting at jaunty angle on his head, topped off his outfit perfectly. He was very handsome, very male and very late.

Connie hurried down the steps.

'For goodness sake, Hari, it's almost five to,' she said, once he was within earshot. 'I was getting worried about you.'

'I'm sorry, darling,' he said, going round to the passenger side of the car. 'I had an errand to run.'

'An errand!' snapped Connie. 'What, on your wedding day?'

He grinned. 'I know, but I'm sure you'll forgive me when you realise what it was.'

He opened the door and, after a bit of huffing and puffing, her mother clambered out.

She was dressed in the suit she'd worn for Bernie's wedding a decade ago and with her newest hat perched on her head. As always for a special occasion, she wore the marcasite brooch Mo had bought her for her birthday pinned on her collar.

'Mum, you're here,' said Connie, hardly daring to believe her own eyes.

'Of course I'm here,' her mother snapped back. 'Where else would I be when my daughter's getting married?'

'Oh, Connie, it's been such a lovely day,' said Millie, hugging her for the umpteenth time. 'I'm so happy for you.'

They hugged again.

'And he's so handsome,' added Millie, glancing over to the bar where Hari was chatting to Connie's father and younger brother.

Connie was standing by the wedding cake that she and Hari had cut about twenty minutes before and which the waitress was now distributing to the guests.

Connie's eyes glided over him. 'Yes, he is, isn't he?' she replied as a feeling of overwhelming love flowed through her.

After his last-minute appearance at the registry office, they had gone straight through to the airy function room and emerged fifteen minutes later as Dr and Mrs Jahindra Harish Chakravarthi MacLauchlan. Outside, between hugs of congratulation for Connie and slaps on the back for Hari, the photographer had managed to gather the various groups around them for their photos on the town hall steps. That done, hand in hand and showered in rice and confetti, she and Hari headed for their car to drive the ten-minute journey to the Bishopsgate Hotel.

That was three and a half hours ago and now the beautifully laid out food had been eaten, the toasts raised and speeches given. It was now just after three-thirty and it was time for her and Hari to say their goodbyes and head off for their hotel in Cambridge.

'Of course, what I want to know is how on earth he got your mother to change her mind,' said Millie.

'Me too,' said Connie.

'It must have been something pretty blooming spectacular, I'd say,' added Millie.

Connie looked over to the sofa where her mother was sitting with Mo and Bernie, smiling and laughing with her grandchildren and wishing people well.

'Yes, it must have been,' said Connie. 'I really wasn't expecting her.'

'What did she say about it?' asked Millie.

'I didn't ask her,' Connie replied. 'In fact, I haven't really said more than a few words to her. After the way she's behaved to-wards Hari, it's going to take more than her just turning up at the last minute to get us back on our old footing.'

'Well, you can sort all that out later when you get back from honeymoon.' Millie winked.

'Did someone say something about a honeymoon?' Hari said, slipping his arm around Connie and kissing her.

'Yes,' said Millie. 'I was saying it was time you love birds went off on yours.'

'I totally agree,' said Connie.

Millie went off to organise the wedding guests so Connie and Hari could say their goodbyes.

Hari drew Connie into his embrace. 'Happy?'

'Yes,' said Connie, enjoying the feel of her husband's arms around her.

'Have I mentioned you look stunning?' said Hari.

'A couple of times.'

He kissed her briefly. 'Well, let me say it again: you look stunning.'

'Thank you.' Connie gave him a wry smile. 'You don't look so bad yourself.'

He kissed her again. 'I love you.'

'And I love you.'

He lowered his head and Connie's mouth opened in anticipa-tion, but then a series of wolf-whistles cut between them.

Laughing, Hari took Connie's hand and they made their way down the line of family and friends towards the door. Having hugged and kissed everyone, they finally reached the end of the line where her parents were standing.

Connie stopped in front of her mother and they exchanged a look.

'You're a very pretty bride,' said her mother, giving her a ca-joling smile. 'And the dress is just what I would have picked for you.'

'Thank you,' said Connie.

'And, well now, perhaps I was a bit too quick to judge,' said Maud, a rare softness creeping into her eyes. 'And when all's said and done, I am your mother and you're still my daughter.'

They stared at each other for a moment, then her mother

stepped forward and hugged her. Connie stood stiffly for a moment, then hugged her back.

'I am,' said Connie, feeling the hurt and anger melt a little as she was enveloped in the softness of her mother's embrace. 'And I'm glad you're here to see me become Hari's wife.'

Maud released her and her gaze flickered onto Hari, standing beside Connie, and a bit of her old spark returned.

'Well, I very nearly wasn't as this 'usband of yours had his watch five minutes fast and he nearly drove off without me.'

'That's the last of them,' said Hari, discarding the assorted tin cans into a dustbin.

They'd driven off with the traditional collection of old tin cans trailing behind them but, once out of sight, they'd turned off into a side street so Hari could stop and cut them off.

Hari returned to the car. Resting his hands on the steering wheel, he looked at her.

'Right, next stop Cambridge but, before we go, I have two presents for you, one is in the car for you to open later but the other is for you to open now.'

He pulled an official-looking envelope with Dalglish, Dalglish, Holt and Wells stamped across the outside from his pocket and handed it to her.

Connie took out the letter and read it.

When she got to the bottom, she looked up at him with incredulity. 'You've bought the house in Chigwell village?'

He grinned. 'I have.'

'But how?' she said. 'I mean, how will we afford it?'

'I'll tell you all the details later, but be assured we can,' he replied.

'Oh, Hari!' She flung her arms around him.

'Of course, it won't be completed until January so we'll have to stay in the flat until then,' he said into her hair.

Connie let him go and sat back. She placed her hand over his. 'And I have two presents for you, too. One's sheer and lacy and I'll have to wear it for you to enjoy, and possibly there's another, but we'll have to wait a couple of weeks to be sure.'

Hari's dark eyes softened as he raised her hand and pressed his lips on it. 'I love you so much.'

She smiled. 'And I love you.'

He smiled then, kissing her fingers again, he released her hand.

'Right, Mrs MacLauchlan,' he said, turning on the ignition. 'We have a hotel booked in Cambridge and a long drive to—'

'Scotland,' said Connie.

He gave her a pretend scowl. 'How did you guess?'

Connie laughed as they pulled away. 'We're honeymooning in July and you told me to pack some jumpers and a rain mac. So let's be on our way – to Scotland and then the rest of our lives.'

Acknowledgements

I've really enjoyed bringing Connie's story to a happy conclusion. I've also had a great deal of fun exploring other areas of east London: Spitalfields, Shoreditch and Bethnal Green.

As in the previous books, I've tried to keep true to the standards of Connie's profession and mine as both a Queen's Nurse and district nurse, in Connie's case prior to the NHS and during the tough years of austerity immediately after the Second World War.

As always, I would like to mention a few books, authors and people to whom I am particularly indebted.

Again, to ensure that the treatment and care Connie gives her patients is authentic to the period, I have returned to nurses' biographies, including Lucilla Andrews's *No Time for Romance*, Edith Cotterill's *Nurse on Call* and *Yes Sister, No Sister* by Jennifer Craig, which, although set in Leeds, gives much of the flavour of post-war nurse training and culture, as does *Of Sluices and Sisters* by Alison Collin. I garnered a couple of self-published gems in my travels, including *My Life and Nursing Memories (from 1914 to 2008)* by Nurse Corbishley, and *Nurse! Yes, Sister?* by Dorothy Gill. I read Jennifer Worth's accounts, of course, of 1950s east London in her popular books *Call the Midwife* and *Shadows of the Workhouse*, although the most detailed account of a pre-NHS British Nursing Association came from Irene Sankey's biography, *Thank you, Miss Hunter* (unpublished manuscript). Ms Sankey became the superintendent of the East London Nursing Society in 1946, and it is her detailed account of that time that most helped me bring the Fry House nurses to life.

For Connie's professional life I have delved back into the textbooks of the period, including the *Handbook for Queen's Nurses* (1943); a 1940 edition of Faber's *Nurse's Pocket Encyclopaedia*

Diary and Guide; *Parenthood: Design or Accident?* by Michael Fielding, fourth edition (1943); *Psychiatry and Mental Health* by John Rathbone Oliver (1950); *Nursing and Diseases of Sick Children*, edited by. Alan Moncrieff, fourth edition (1943) and *A Short Textbook of Midwifery* by George F. Gibberd (1951), which has a number of medical illustrations that are not for the faint-hearted.

For Hari's background, I used the biography of Pat Cross, my good friend and fellow author Fenella Miller's Anglo-Indian mother. For his army service I drew on several prisoner-of-war biographies, most notably *Surviving the Sword* by Brian Mac-Arthur and *Quartered Safe Out Here* by George MacDonald Fraser for general background. I based his actual experiences as a medic on Ken Adams's biography *Healing in Hell*, an account of Adams's POW experiences as a field medic in Changi and Kanchanaburi hospitals. Many of the anecdotes Hari recounts are taken directly from Adams's experiences, which bear testament to the unbowed spirit and ingenuity of the medical staff. Colonel Dunlop, whom Hari refers to at his interview, was an Australian medic and war hero who was multiply decorated after the war for his bravery and leadership. He wrote extensively about his wartime experiences, with particular regard to improvised surgery and medicines in the Japanese prisoner-of-war camps.

I'm also grateful to my friend Chris Rundle for sharing with me her father Ron French's memories and mementos from his time as a Japanese prisoner of war. It helped me greatly to understand that the histories and biographies I'd used for research aren't just academic writings, but accounts of men like Ron who lived through the horror.

For Hari's dealings with the newly founded NHS, the first chapter of Geoffrey Rivett's *From Cradle to Grave: Fifty Years of the NHS* helped me set the scene, while Dr John Marks's autobiography *The NHS: Beginning, Middle and End?* gave me the details of how a general practice was set up and funded in the early days.

For background of the period, again I used *Our Hidden Lives* by Simon Garfield (2005), *Nella Last's Peace* edited by Patricia and Robert Malcolmson (2008) and *Austerity Britain 1945–51* by David Kynaston (2007). Although I can vividly remember the warmth and neighbourliness of the old streets around where I grew up, I added *The Only Way is Essex*'s very own Nanny Pat's account of her East End childhood *Penny Sweets and Cobbled Streets* to my collection of East End memoirs this year, along with Shire Library's *British Family Cars of the 1950s and 60s* and *Make Do and Mend*, which is a reproduction of the official Second World War leaflets. I've also added two issues of *Nursing Mirror* from 1948 and 1951 and three 1948 issues of *Woman's Own*, plus several late 1940s and early 1950s issues of *Housewife*.

I used several post-war photographic books, including *'Couldn't afford the Eels': Memories of Wapping 1900–1960* by Martha Leigh (2010), *The Wartime Scrapbook* by Robert Opie (2010), *The Forties: Good Times Just Around the Corner* by Alison Maloney (2005) and, although it is slightly later than the period Connie's story is set in, *London's East End: A 1960s Album* by Steve Lewis (2010), as this documented wonderfully the sights and sounds I remember as a child.

You can read more about my East End childhood on my website www.jeanfullerton.com.

I would like to thank a few more people. First, my very own hero at home Kelvin, for his unwavering support, and my three daughters, Janet, Fiona and Amy, for not minding too much that they are literary orphans at times. Second, my fellow authors in the Romantic Novelists' Association, and the London and South East and Chelmsford chapters in particular. I'd also like to thank the Facebook group 'Stepney and Wapping living in 60s and early 70s', who this time helped me get the details of the annual Catholic parades correct, and filled in other 1940s and 1950s local details I'd forgotten.

I'd like to thank my lovely agent Laura Longrigg, whose encouragement and incisive editorial mind helped me to see the wood for the trees. Last, but by no means least, a big thank you once again to the editorial team at Orion, especially Laura Gerrard, for turning my four-hundred-page manuscript into a beautiful book.